'I'd never met the right man. Until last Wednesday, that is.'

A spasm crossed his face. 'Don't, Joss—please don't!'

'It's true, every word.' She suddenly clasped his sleeves. 'Niall, you can tell me I'm crazy if you like—but I'm convinced you and I could fall in love very easily. And I don't mean just for a week or a month or even a year. I mean for a lifetime.'

His laugh grated on her nerves. 'People don't fall in love for a lifetime any more, Joss.'

'Yes, they do. People like me. And people like you.'

Her eyes searched his face for the slightest sign of relenting and found none.

Books you will enjoy
by SANDRA FIELD

LOVE IN A MIST

A disastrous early marriage had brought Sally a small daughter she adored, but had left her wary about the whole idea of love and commitment. Her friend urged her to go on holiday to St Pierre and try to come out of her shell. And there she met Luke Sheridan, who felt exactly the same way as she did . . .

CHASE A RAINBOW

Tascha was determined to trace the man who might be her father, even if it meant trekking off to the wilds of the Yukon and facing opposition from Seth Curtis every step of the way . . .

THE RIGHT MAN

BY

SANDRA FIELD

MILLS & BOON LIMITED
ETON HOUSE   18-24 PARADISE ROAD
RICHMOND   SURREY   TW9 1SR

*First published in Great Britain 1988
by Mills & Boon Limited*

© Sandra Field 1988

*Australian copyright 1988
Philippine copyright 1988
This edition 1988*

ISBN 0 263 76109 6

*Set in English Times 10 on 10½ pt.
01 – 8810 – 63616*

Typeset in Great Britain by JCL Graphics, Bristol

Made and printed in Great Britain

PROLOGUE

'ONE day you'll meet the right man,' Ellie MacDougal had repeatedly told her youngest daughter Joss, ever since the time when Joss had become interested in the opposite sex as something other than rowdy members of the baseball team. 'You'll know him right away. And that will be that.'

Joss had always had great faith in her mother's predictions, for Ellie combined sound Scottish common sense with a wild streak of romanticism, inherited from a Moravian gypsy who had very briefly, but entirely legally, been married to Ellie's grandfather. Besides, Ellie's own marriage gave credence to her predictions. Ellie had met George MacDougall at a church social forty years ago, had altered the place settings so he would sit beside her, and had married him six months later. 'The minute I saw him I knew he was the man for me,' she had told Joss on more than one occasion. 'It took him a little while to come round. But I convinced him in the end.' And she would toss her greying curls, and her eyes, dark as any gypsy's, would laugh at Joss. 'You'll see, the same thing will happen to you. You'll walk into a room some day and this man will look over at you, and bingo—you'll be lost!'

Secretly Joss pictured the scenario quite differently. She would meet her unknown lover on her father's farm in the springtime. She would be wandering through the orchard wearing a filmy white dress and a floppy hat bordered with flowers, and the sky would be blue and the air fragrant with the scent of apple blossoms; in her daydream she always managed to ignore the presence of the dandelions that bloomed at the same time as the apple trees, for dandelions did not seem the flowers of romance. But the grass would swish around her ankles and the bees would hum drowsily on the pale pink petals and then she would see him, standing further up the slope, waiting for her, her handsome, blue-eyed lover . . .

And here the daydream would end, for Joss could never quite picture the man's features. The blue eyes she was sure of, for they would complement her own eyes, which were hazel, flecked with gold. But was he blond, a lighter blond than her own tawny, sun-streaked curls? Or dark, hair black as the wings of the crows that nested in the elm trees west of the orchard? But crows, like dandelions, were not very romantic, and with a sigh Joss would return to the real world and abandon her imaginary lover, the man who was the right man for her, the only man in the whole wide world.

At the age of seventeen she left the village of Alderney in western Nova Scotia where she had lived on the farm with her four brothers and two sisters, and went to university in Halifax. She had grown up knowing what hard work was all about, so she obtained an honours degree in biology and chemistry without a great deal of difficulty; she sang a leading role each year in the musical put on by the drama club, and she dated a lot, for she was pretty and outgoing. Although she met several blue-eyed young men, none of them struck her to the heart; however, she was having enough fun that the omission did not trouble her. And every spring when the orchard burst into bloom she would remember, with an inward smile, her adolescent, romantic dream. At the advanced age of twenty-one she was still convinced that somehow she would meet the man who was her destiny in the way that she had always imagined.

CHAPTER ONE

JOSS was late for work. Again. She scurried along the pavement, from long practice dodging the tourists, the punk kids bedecked with chains, and the street vendors. Rock music blared from a shop front. A car horn blasted in her ear. Yonge Street in Toronto on a hot Wednesday in August . . . would Dante's Inferno be very much different? she wondered grimly, feeling her blouse stick to her back as she waited for the traffic light to change. She had been working at the bookshop all day, and in theory got off at four. But Cathy, her replacement, had been twenty minutes late for the second time in the past week, which meant that Joss now had exactly twenty-five minutes to get back from the bookshop to the hotel where she sang in the bar every evening from five until nine. She hated being late. She hated rushing. She hated Toronto in August.

Joss blinked rapidly, trying to blame the sudden stinging in her eyes on exhaust fumes. At that precise moment she would have given every cent she had saved all summer to be back in the orchard at home, where the grass was green, the fruit was ripening, and the tang of the distant ocean tantalised the nostrils. The Guernseys would be grazing in the meadow. Her mother's chickens would be clucking in their pen. The cats would be sleeping in the sun and Bert, the old collie, would be watching them from the corner of his eye; from long experience the cats knew Bert was too lazy to do anything other than watch.

The light changed. The crowd surged across the street, carrying Joss with them. She edged between a very fat lady and a tall young man in flowered shorts, and began to run. Mr Jodrey, who was the manager of the Red Lion Pub in the Swansea Hotel, was a stickler for punctuality.

By the time she arrived at the side entrance of the Swansea it was five to five. In the staff room she splashed cold water on her face, peeled off her cotton trousers and shirt, daubed herself with perfume and struggled into the embroidered peasant blouse and frilly green skirt that Mr Jodrey had provided for her; at the very beginning of the summer Joss had decided that her gypsy grandmother would have scorned so cute an outfit. She ran a brush through her hair, tried to disguise the shininess of her nose with powder, and outlined her lips in a soft apricot lipstick. Then, taking her time, she removed her guitar from its case and replaced the case in her locker. The guitar had belonged to her great-aunt on her mother's side. Great-Aunt Lucy, who had had lustrous dark hair and snapping black eyes, had run off with a travelling salesman and had died in a train crash under circumstances that had never been fully explained. Joss loved the guitar for its burnished wood and clarity of tone, and for its tie to an ancestry that sometimes, unexpectedly, would sing in her blood.

She took a quick glance at herself in the mirror, hitched up the waistband of her skirt, and left the room. Various corridors led from the staff room to the kitchen, the lifts and the basements; the one that Joss took underwent a sudden transformation past a pair of swing doors from linoleum and dull beige paint to rose carpeting and wallpaper. She hurried past the cloakrooms intended for the use of visitors to the bar, turned the corner, and saw the man a fraction of a second before he collided with her. Her action was instinctive: she thrust the guitar away from her to protect it from the impact and ran full into his chest

'Oh! Do be careful!' she gasped, two seconds too late. Then she looked up.

The man had blue eyes.

As though she was fitting together the pieces of a jigsaw puzzle, Joss saw that his hair was so dark a brown as to be almost black, that his cheekbones were prominent and his nose very slightly hooked, giving strength and character to a face that, beneath an intense masculinity, looked exhausted. The body against hers was bone-hard. His head topped hers by six inches. She thought foolishly, he can't be the right man. This is Toronto in August and my nose is shiny and I'm late for work. He can't be.

The man straightened, pushing her away from him by resting his hands on her shoulders. He said formally, 'I'm terribly sorry. Did I hurt you?'

One small part of her brain decided immediately that he would be a good singer, for his voice had depth and resonance. The other major part seemed to be paralysed. She stammered, 'I-I was more worried about my guitar.'

'I didn't touch it, I assure you.'

She was gazing upwards, mesmerised. Although his manners were excellent and his voice without inflection, his hands were still clasping her shoulders, and she would have sworn that behind the guarded blue eyes he was battling with a strong emotion. She could not have guessed the nature of that emotion. But she was certain it was there. The surety of her knowledge rather frightened her; she had never thought she had inherited any of the prescience of her gypsy ancestress. Struggling to collect her wits, she managed to say, 'You didn't hurt me, no.' And because she was almost sure that he was the right man, that her quest was ended, she gave him a brillant smile.

The light in the corridor shone down on her hair so that the tumbled curls were shot through with gold; her

her eyes reflected the leaf-brown of a woodland pool.
Her cheekswere flushed and her lips a warm, soft curve.
The man's fingers tightened their hold; the emotion she
had been so sure of flared to life in the deep blue eyes.

From behind them the clipped voice of Mr Jodrey
said, 'Miss Gayle, you're late.'

Along with the peasant outfit, Mr Jodrey had
conferred upon Joss a working name, for he had
disapproved of Joss MacDougall as too countrified. So
she had become Jocelyn Gayle for the duration of the
summer, and on the rare occasions when male
customers overimbibed or gave her undue attention she
was glad enough of a pseudonym. Now, however, it
took her a moment to realise she was being spoken to.

The blue-eyed man dropped his hands and turned. Mr
Jodrey surveyed them both with impartial coldness,
then said to Joss, 'This is the second time in a week that
you have been late. As I am sure you are aware.'

It was confusing enough to meet the man of her
dreams in a hotel corridor. To have to deal with Mr
Jodrey on top of that seemed quite unfair. But the job
at the pub paid well and Joss needed the money. Trying
to inject the words with some sincerity, which was
difficult because she was simultaneously deciding that
she disliked Mr Jodrey's prissy little mouth, Joss said,
'I'm sorry, Mr Jodrey.'

Mr Jodrey drew himself up to his full five-feet nine,
which made him exactly Joss's height. 'Your contract is
to sing from five p.m. until nine p.m., Miss Gayle. *Five*
p.m. Not,' he consulted his wristwatch ostentatiously,
'five-ten.'

The blue-eyed man said calmly, 'I'm afraid I must
accept some of the blame. Miss Gayle and I bumped
into each other—quite literally—and we were concerned
about possible damage to her guitar.'

At the time when Mr Jodrey had spoken, Joss's guitar
had been dangling from her left hand, and she and the

tall stranger had been staring into each other's eyes.
But Mr Jodrey did not argue, for something about the
blue-eyed man bespoke authority. His beautifully
tailored grey pinstripe suit? His unconscious air of
arrogance that announced he was accustomed to the
wielding of power? Whatever it was, Mr Jodrey gave
him an obsequious bow.

Trying very hard not to laugh, Joss said with false
humility, 'I promise I won't be late again.'

'Very well,' said Mr Jodrey, not looking quite as
obsequious as he transferred his attention to Joss. 'But
kindly proceed to the bar immediately, Miss Gayle.'

Joss's jaw dropped. How could she leave? She did not
know the blue-eyed man's name or where he was from
or whether he was a guest at the hotel. She might never
see him again. Disconcerting enough that she had met
him in Toronto and not in the orchard. Quite impossible
that she should lose him as soon as she had found him.
She looked up at him, blurted, 'Are you coming to hear
me sing?' and heard Mr Jodrey's hiss of indrawn
breath; Mr Jodrey did not approve of staff associating
with guests.

The stranger—although Joss had difficulty thinking
of him as a stranger—must have heard this hiss as well.
He inclined his head and said urbanely, 'That will give
me great pleasure.'

She bestowed upon him a generous smile in which
relief was predominant, then with a hunted look at Mr
Jodrey raised her guitar in salute and scurried down the
hall towards the Red Lion. It took every ounce of her
will-power not to look back over her shoulder. Her
heart was thumping in her breast in a way that she knew
had nothing to do with her race to get from one job to
the next, and certainly nothing to do with pre-
performance nerves. Her brain was whirling. Her knees
were weak and her hands, oddly, ice-cold. It seemed a
peculiar combination of physical symptoms to have

resulted from a chance meeting. Nor did it even resemble the state of mind Joss had always imagined for herself in the orchard. There she had smiled dreamily at the faceless man and had made a number of witty and provocative remarks before being enfolded in his embrace. Now, as she entered the dimly lit bar, she remembered the lean, hard body with which she had collided and shivered inwardly.

Because the Swansea billed itself as a family hotel, the Red Lion featured Jocelyn Gayle singing folk songs early in the evening, followed by either a pianist or a small band for dancing. The bar itself was modelled on an old English pub, with deep, comfortable leather chairs and rather a lot of highly polished brass. The walls were panelled in oak and decorated with reproductions of old inn signs. Joss's stool was on a little raised dias. She perched herself on the stool, arranged her skirts, and began to tune her guitar. The blue-eyed man had not yet arrived.

When she began to play, her fingers felt slow and awkward and her throat was tight. She sang 'Jeanie with the Light Brown Hair' and a couple of leisurely Irish ballads to warm up her voice, acknowledged the discreet rattle of applause, then launched into a medley of Beatles' songs. Her audience consisted of men in business suits, a group of women much more interested in the contents of their shopping bags than in her, a honeymoon couple holding hands and paying her no attention whatsoever, and a sprinkling of tourists who had supplied the applause. She had sung to far less attentive audiences; indeed sometimes sang for her own benefit alone. She settled in, feeling her voice begin to fill out and relax. She loved to sing, deriving considerable amusement from being paid to do something that she so enjoyed.

She was half-way through 'Streets of London', a song that always made her wish she was Cleo Laine, when a tall man in a grey suit walked into the bar, looked around with a self-possession she could not have matched and sat down at the table nearest to her. By the time he had adjusted the chair so that he was facing her, the waitress was at his side; he was that kind of man, thought Joss, wishing even more strongly than usual that she was Cleo Laine. After he had ordered a drink he sat back, resting his elbows on the arms of the chair, his hands making a steeple. His eyes were fastened on her.

Miraculously she did not forget the words of the song, her fingers automatically plucking the strings on her guitar. He's here, her brain whispered. He's here, sitting twenty feet away from you. Sing, Joss. Sing your heart out.

So she did sing, and it seemed as though all the words were vested with a special magic, the pathos of the old man with yesterday's newspapers and the old woman whose clothes were in rags. The chattering women with the shopping bags glanced her way; the noisier group of tourists, in the far corner, were swaying to the music. But Joss was not singing to them. With gathering confidence she was singing to the man who was watching her so intently. When the waitress had brought his drink he had kept an open bill. He's going to be here for a while, Joss thought exultantly. He's not going to leave after just one drink.

But then she came to the part of the song about loneliness and with her heightened sensitivity saw how his eyes dropped and his hand encircled the glass so tightly that his knuckles were white. So, despite his air of arrogance, all was not right with his world, she thought slowly. He must be lonely sometimes, this handsome stranger; for him the sun did not always shine. It was a strange conclusion to reach in a crowded city bar.

He did not look up again until she had come to the

end of the song and the genuine burst of applause had died down. Something more cheerful, she decided quickly, and chose an old Welsh ballad about a beautiful young girl whose eyes tended to wander from her dutiful fiancé to the village ne'er-do-well. The chorus was catchy and easily learned. The tourists joined in, and even the honeymoon couple clapped in rhythm to the music. The ending had a surprise twist. The blue-eyed man smiled, and Joss's heart fluttered in her breast.

She did not allow the momentum to die down. In half an hour, when Mr Jodrey made one of his seemingly casual perambulations of the bar, she had the entire place in the palm of her hand. She knew it. He knew it, too. She gave him a wide-eyed, innocent smile, and saw that the man in the grey suit was laughing at her. She grinned at him impudently. He likes me, she thought dizzily. And he's got a sense of humour. The man in the orchard had been too ethereal to have had anything as earthy as a sense of humour.

At seven o'clock she announced to her audience that after the next song she would be taking a short break; this was a requirement in her contract. In the middle of the song the group of tourists in the far corner got up to leave. The two women were grey-haired and plump, and could have come from any of the farms around Alderney; one of the men had drunk more than was good for him, although he was a cheerful drunk rather than a morose one, singing to himself as he lurched between the seats, leaning over the honeymoon couple to whisper something, then roaring with laughter. His wife, in the green cotton dress, was plainly mortified by his behaviour. Joss added another verse to the song, hoping to distract attention from them to herself.

'Come along, Tom,' she heard the wife say. 'Do come along. You're making a fool of yourself.'

'Gotta tip the singer,' Tom boomed. 'Let go now,

Millie. I'll leave when I'm good and ready.'

Millie, unhappily, let go. Tom bumped against the blue-eyed man's chair, said with a *bonhomie* impervious to the chill in those eyes, 'Sorry, friend. Great little singer, eh? Always been partial to blondes, I have.' Without waiting for a reply he pulled out a wad of bank notes from the back pocket of his trousers, peeled off a ten-dollar bill and shoved the rest of the money into his pocket.

Hoping to ward off an embarrassing scene, Joss finished the song, acknowledged the applause and said into the microphone, 'Thank you, ladies and gentlemen. I'll be back in ten minutes.' However, just as she stood up, shaking out her skirts, Tom negotiated the step on to the dias. Narrowly missing the microphone stand, he pushed the ten-dollar bill into the neckline of her blouse, his watch strap scraping her skin, and said thickly, 'Give us a kiss. Great little singer.'

The microphone was turned on; the whole room must have heard Tom's request. Her eyes glittering, Joss twisted away from him. But Tom, however drunk, was a customer, and the customer, according to Mr Jodrey, was always right. Therefore she must not tell Tom what he could do with his ten-dollar bill. Nor must she poke him in the nose. What she must do was get out of the pub without causing a ruckus.

The blue-eyed man stepped neatly between her and Tom. He took her by the elbow and said calmly, 'Please allow me to escort you.'

His grip was like a steel clamp; she would have had difficulty refusing. Already he was propelling her across the little stage, leaving poor Tom, no doubt open-mouthed, with only the microphone for company. Holding her head high, Joss walked swiftly between the tables and past the bar. Millie and her two companions were standing by the door. Joss forcibly slowed her steps, smiled directly into Mille's humiliated grey eyes and said, 'Thank you for clapping. I'm glad you enjoyed the singing.' Then she was being hustled through the door, down the corridor, and around the corner where she had first met her escort.

He brought her round to face him; his hold was not overly gentle. 'Does that kind of thing happen often?' he demanded.

Joss would not have had to be very observant to see that he was furious. 'Not often, no,' she said, both puzzled and flattered by his anger.

'So where was Mr Jodrey when you needed him?'

'If there's a real problem, either the bartender or one of the bellboys comes to my rescue . . . I don't understand why you're so angry—and you're hurting my elbow.'

Her words seemed to bring him back to himself. He dropped her elbow, wiping all expression from his face. 'I'm sorry,' he said.

'Oh, please,' Joss said in laughing dismay. 'Now I've made you angrier.' He did not smile back. He reminded her very strongly of the image she had had of Heathcliff when she was fifteen: brooding, enigmatic and disturbingly masculine. Trying to slow her heart-rate, which seemed to react to him quite indiscriminately, Joss leaned her guitar against the wall, then flicked the ten-dollar bill out of the neckline of her blouse, holding the money away from her rather as if it were a particularly loathsome spider. Then she glanced up at her companion; he did not look quite as grim. Encouraged, she said with great sincerity, 'Thank you for rescuing me. You got me out of a very awkward situation.'

'I couldn't have you hitting a customer,' he replied imperturbably.

She gave a delighted little chuckle. 'You could tell that I was tempted, could you?'

'The light of battle was in your eyes. But I'm quite

sure your boss would rank assault as a far more heinous crime than unpunctuality.'

'All crimes are heinous to Mr Jodrey. But assault would be a little more heinous,' Joss admitted, then heard herself add, 'I grew up with four brothers who often considered a good fight the easiest way to solve a problem.'

'In my experience it usually adds to the problem.'

'Certainly Tom might not have taken kindly to a clout on the nose,' she said gravely.

'And what will you do with the ten dollars?'

She wrinkled her nose. 'If I were rich I'd probably burn it, or tear it into shreds and throw them to the four winds. As I'm not, I'll put it in my bank account.' She looked at him through her lashes, her eyes alive with mischief. 'Another grand gesture down the drain.'

She had finally made him smile. But he smiled stiffly, as if he were not quite used to doing it, Joss thought, and remembered her intuitive sense that at some level he was quite dreadfully lonely. Close up his face was gaunt, his eyes of so burning a blue that they seemed to have drawn all the colour from the surrounding features. He looked like an over-trained racehorse, she decided thoughtfully, driven beyond his capabilities.

Under her scrutiny his eyes had veiled themselves. He said, 'And where did you grow up with your four brothers, Jocelyn Gayle?'

'Joss,' she said quickly. 'Please call me Joss. I grew up in Nova Scotia—and you haven't told me your name.'

'Niall.' He spelled it. 'I have a great objection to being called Neil with an e.'

He had not volunteered his last name. She had about five minutes of her break left in which to discover it. 'Your name sounds Irish,' she ventured. He gave such a non-committal nod that she abandoned subtlety. 'You haven't told me your last name.'

He raised one eyebrow. 'Diamond?'

'I'm sure you can sing, but I'm equally sure you're not Neil Diamond. Besides, he had an e in his name.'

'Let's use it anyway.'

Joss frowned. 'If you don't want to tell me your last name, just say so.'

'I don't.'

She had not expected such an unequivocal reply. 'Why are you being so mysterious?'

'Would you prefer me to be stuffing ten-dollar bills down your blouse?'

She flushed. 'I'd hate that. As you know.'

'So what's a nice girl like you doing singing in a Toronto bar?'

'Trying to keep body and soul together,' Joss said as lightly as she could, not liking the turn of the conversation, but quite unable to alter it to anything approaching her imaginary conversations in the orchard. '*I* could ask why a man as uptight as you is talking to a woman who sings in a bar. Couldn't I?'

'I'm asking myself exactly the same question.'

'Oh, are you?' Joss raised her chin and wondered if she would ever be able to enjoy the sight of apple blossoms again. 'Please don't let me keep you!'

'Are you by chance accusing me of being a snob?'

'You certainly sound like one.'

He ran his fingers through his hair in exasperation. 'Well, I'm not. You could be a garbage collector or a lady-in-waiting to the Queen—I couldn't care less.'

Oddly enough, she believed him. 'I'm neither one. I grew up on a farm, this is my first time in a big city, and I hate it,' she announced. She added astutely, 'So it's not my occupation that bothers you—it's your own behaviour.'

Again Joss saw that brief smile that seemed to hurt something deep within him. 'Very clever. You certainly say what's on your mind.'

'Something else my brothers taught me.' She decided to live up to her reputation. 'Are you going back to the bar after my break?'

During the long moment Niall regarded her unsmilingly, Joss had time to think that by now the man in the orchard would have clasped her to his bosom and rained kisses on her lips. She was sure the mysterious Niall was not going to clasp her to his bosom. Nor did he. He said flatly, 'Yes.'

She had not realised how frightened she was of his reply until after he had made it. She let out her breath in a tiny sigh. 'I have the feeling that everything you say means at least five other things besides.'

'You're not far wrong.'

She had known she was not. She said, 'I have go to back—my break's just about over.'

'Tom marked your skin.'

Surprised, Joss glanced down. Just above the embroidered ruffle of her blouse was a shallow graze left by Tom's watch strap. 'It's nothing,' she mumbled, and like someone under a spell watched Niall's finger trace the blemish on her flesh. His touch was like a lick of fire. It's just as well he hasn't put his arms around me, she thought wildly. I'd have melted on the spot. 'I have to go,' she stammered. 'I mustn't be late again.'

'Look at me, Joss.'

Knowing her cheeks were scarlet and her eyes no doubt as wild as her thoughts, she obeyed. Niall said harshly, 'Are you as you seem, Jocelyn Gayle?'

'I-I don't understand.'

'You seem so real—I feel as thought I know a great deal about you just by having watched you. You don't put up with any nonsense from men like Tom, yet you were kind enough to take a minute to talk to his wife. You sing with a deep feeling for the music. And you're so very beautiful.'

The faceless man in the orchard vanished for ever. Joss was left with a tall stanger whose burning blue eyes seemed to see right through her. 'I'm nothing out of the ordinary,' she said with faint desperation. 'I grew up on a farm. I've always loved to sing. I'm trying to make my way in the world. That's all.'

'You have no idea how rare a virtue kindness is,' Niall responded shortly. 'Disinterested kindness. Don't ever lose it.'

She should be back in the Red Lion, perched on her stool, singing for the guests. But she could not leave. Not yet. 'The reverse of your statement isn't true—I feel as though I know nothing about you,' she said. 'Not even your name.'

'You know I couldn't stand by and watch Tom maul you—you know that much.'

'Why not?'

He stirred restlessly under her scrutiny. 'Let's skip that question.'

'You couldn't have been jealous . . .'

'If you say not.'

'You're playing with me!' she burst out. 'Like a cat with a mouse. I hate games, Mr Niall Whatever-your-name-is.'

'Then stay away from me,' he answered with deadly calm. 'Because that's the only way I can play it.'

She hesitated. 'Is that why you brought me out here?' she asked painfully. 'To tell me that?'

'Yes,' he said sombrely. 'Yes, I suppose you could say that's why.'

Her fantasy collapsed like a punctured balloon; the man who should have been her soulmate would not even tell her his last name. Joss seized her guitar with less than her usual care, whirled, and fled down the corridor. She felt sick at heart. She had always envisaged the attraction between herself and her imaginary love as mutual. They would come face to

face and in a single perfect moment they would
recognise each other once and for all. No
misunderstandings. No conflict. Just the warm glow of
the noonday sun that casts no shadows . . .

There was no sign of Mr Jodrey in the pub. Joss said
a rather breathless good evening into the microphone,
tuned her guitar and began to sing some Broadway hits
that she knew from experience would be popular. 'The
Surrey with the Fringe on Top' brought Niall back into
the bar. Her voice wavered on a high note, for after his
words in the corridor she had been afraid he would not
reappear. The knot in her breast loosened; so he was a
man who kept his promises. With more gusto she sang
about corn as high as an elephant's eye and about the
perils and delights of Kansas City. The audience was
more mellow now, the waitresses busier, the smoke
thicker. She announced she was open for requests and,
her voice warm and true, sang 'Don't Cry for Me,
Argentina'. Niall was staring down at the tabletop, his
face inscrutable. But at least he was there, Joss thought,
her fingers caressing the strings.

The requests trickled in. Joss had learned ballads and
folk songs from her mother, war tunes and big band
songs from her father, and more recent hits on her own;
her versatility had been partly responsible for getting
her the job. She enjoyed the challenge of trying to grant
people's wishes, and was only rarely stumped. But at a
quarter to nine a little white-haired lady in an old-
fashioned taffeta dres, who had been tossing back
Martinis as if they were water, marched firmly up to the
dais and requested a Celtic song that Joss had never
heard of. She listened intently as the old lady went
through the first verse in a cracked voice, her diamond-
encrusted fingers tapping out the melody. Joss had
always been quick to pick up new tunes and within five
minutes had produced a reasonable facsimile of the
song. She glanced over at Niall's table to see if he had

been amused by her improvisations.

He was not there. His glass was drained. A tidy pile of notes lay on top of his bill.

Her fingers struck a discord. Frantically her eyes searched the room, but he was nowhere to be seen.

Said the little old lady, 'That was sweet of you, dear. Do you know "The Mountains of Moran"?'

Joss did. She got through it somehow, then sang 'The Whistling Gypsy' with less than her usual verve. Niall msut be waiting for her outside, she thought numbly as she smiled and sang and played. He did not want to get her into trouble with Mr Jodrey. So he had left a little early and would be waiting for her in the lobby or on the pavement in front of the hotel.

At nine sharp she swept the last resounding chord from her guitar, smiled, bowed, said her thanks into the microphone and threaded her way between the tables. Niall was not in the hall outside the Red Lion, nor was he in the corridor. Of course not, she told herself. That was still Mr Jodrey's territory. Niall was too discreet to wait for her there.

She stripped off her peasant outfit in the staff room, hung it up, and replaced her guitar in the locker. Anxious though she was, she took a moment to repair her make-up and run a brush through her hair. There was a hectic patch of colour on each cheek; her eyes were very bright. Aware that at some deep level she was breathing a frenzied prayer over and over again, Joss snapped the padlock on her locker and left the room.

The lobby with its gilt chandeliers and peach and green carpets was almost deserted. Six staff members. Twelve guests. No Niall. The doorman, red-faced and jolly in his brass-buttoned uniform, winked at her and said jovially, 'All through, Joss? Must be nice.'

She gave him a distracted smile. 'Russell, you haven't seen a tall man in a grey suit in the last few minutes, have you?'

'That's kind of like going to the library and asking for the book with the red cover,' Russell replied; he liked to tease the pretty young women on staff.

'Very tall, very good-looking, dark hair, blue eyes,' she said rapidly.

'About quarter to nine a man answering to that description got me to hail a cab. Tipped me two dollars, he did.'

Her face fell. 'Did you hear where he was going?'

Russell shook his head, regarding her inquisitively. 'Friend of yours?'

Her shoulders were drooping. Not looking at him, she muttered, 'I don't know.'

'Never seen you go after a man before.'

That was because she never had. She said urgently, 'Russell, if you see him again, will you try and find out his name for me? His first name's Niall. That's all I know.'

'Looked like kind of a tough customer to me. Things on his mind, I'd say. More important things than women.'

'Don't be a chauvinist,' she said absently, peering down the length of the street. Between the tall office buildings of downtown Toronto the sky was shrouded in darkness; the cars had their headlights on, and the traffic lights at the corner flashed their repetitive message of 'Stop, Caution, Go'. Too late for caution, she thought unhappily. Four hours too late. And she had nowhere to go but to the apartment.

Joss shared an apartment with an old schoolfriend, Magda Trevanian, who was also a singer and who had found Joss the job at the Red Lion. Magda, who had flamboyant red hair and a gorgeous body, sang with a band in a nightclub and never got home before two in the morning; consequently she was usually asleep when Joss left for the bookshop in the mornings, and sometimes a week would pass without them seeing each other. Now, as Joss trudged towards the subway station, she was glad the apartment would be empty. She did not want to have to describe an encounter that had ended so inconclusively, whose emotional overtones had been so intense. Instense for herself, she added as she tramped down the stone steps. Had she been wrong to sense that Niall had, in his own way, been as affected by the encounter as she? Wishful thinking? An extension of her romantic daydream? After all, if he had been affected, why had he disappeared? The normal response would have been to ask her for a date.

She showed her subway pass to the ticket agent and pushed through the turnstile. The platform was crowded, and almost immediately one of the blunt-nosed trains racketed out of the tunnel and hissed to a halt along the platform. Joss stepped aboard and stood near the sliding doors. Niall hadn't asked her for a date because he was married.

Come off it, she told herself firmly. Lots of married men pick up girls in bars. Certainly they don't make any secret of their last names. Anyway, he didn't look married.

Nor had he. He had looked, instead, very much a loner. Joss braced herself as the brakes squealed and the train juddered to a halt at the next station. Maybe he was unhappily married, she thought, and rather than deceive her he had simply left.

By the time she had travelled for two more station stops and had climbed the steps to the street again, night had fallen. She walked fast and purposely along the two blocks to the apartment, located on a narrow side street in an old Victorian house that in five years would no doubt be knocked down to make way for another of the box-like condominiums that dotted the neighbourhood; in the meantime the rent was affordable.

Magda was by nature untidy. Three shopping bags had been dumped on the faded old chesterfield,

Magda's jogging outfit lay in an exhausted heap on the floor and a pile of books had been thrown on the bamboo table that served as desk, eating place and sewing bench. Magda's cat, a fat, self-centred tortoiseshell named Nasturtium, took up the only other chair in the room. Joss had learned to live with Magda's untidiness for the sake of her cooking; Magda could take the most unpromising leftovers and transform them into dishes that would not have disgraced a five-star restaurant. But although Joss now drank some cream and spinach soup that had been left on the stove and consumed two fluffy braided rolls, she could scarcely have said what she was eating. Aimlessly she pushed her spoon around the bottom of the bowl. She had too much pride to phone her mother and explain that the right man had been the wrong man; and she was too tired, physically and mentally, to analyse why she had responded with such instinctive force to a complete stranger. Very carefully trying not to think at all, she washed the dishes, swept the kitchen floor, had a shower and went to bed. Nasturtium jumped up on the bed with her; her purr, the most energetic part of her personality, was obscurely comforting. Joss closed her eyes tightly and whisked herself from the stuffy apartment in Toronto to the beach that lay five miles from the farm, where the waves cavorted on the sand and the gulls, drenched in sunlight, wheeled in slow circles overhead. She was home, home where she belonged . . . and where the right man was still an unrealised dream in the orchard.

CHAPTER TWO

JOSS only worked for four hours at the bookshop on Thurdays, from ten until two; this was an arrangement that suited her well, enabling her to do household chores, banking and grocery shopping. She had woken that morning in a militantly rational mood, determined to put the mysterious blue-eyed Niall in his proper place. Because she was homesick she was vulnerable. Because she was vulnerable she had chosen to interpret a chance meeting with a stranger as a fulfilment of a youthful fantasy. The sooner she forgot him, the better. She was crazy to believe he was of lasting significance in her life.

Because she did not have to leave the the apartment until nine-thirty, she was still home when the mail was delivered. There was a business letter addressed to her from the research laboratory where she had worked for the past two summers and would have been working this summer had not government cutbacks obliterated half of the junior positions. She opened the letter. The director had received a grant and was offering Joss a full-time job starting in October as a research assistant level II.

She put the letter on the table, pouring herself another cup of tea. When she had graduated last spring with an honours degree she had applied to three medical schools and had been accepted at Dalhousie in Halifax and the University of Western Ontario, which was a couple of hours from Toronto. Two acceptances had been good for her ego. But she had also been pulled in another direction. Her parents were no longer young

26

and had never been rich, and Joss had very much wanted to get a job and be in the position to give them some of the things they had had to do without to raise their seven children. Even though Joss had always had summer jobs and had been largely self-supporting throughout university, her mother had been apt to slip twenty dollars into each of her letters, or to send generous packages including everything from home-made cookies to toothpaste. Joss would now like to be able to return those favours. If she went to medical school she faced another six years of scrimping for every penny.

She folded up the letter and put it in her purse, her hazel eyes reflective. She would have to make a decision soon, for the deadline for the final despoit for medical school was in ten days' time. If she accepted the job offer she would be home in Nova Scotia. She could visit the farm at weekends. With a sharp pang of longing she realised just how badly she missed her family. Maybe she would take the job, forget about medical school.

She left the apartment, spent a productive four hours organising the remaindered books on the long tables on the second floor of the bookshop, ran several errands and arrived at the Swansea with half an hour to spare. It took all her self-control to keep a steady pace as she rounded the corner where she had met Niall, but managed to do so. When she passed Mr Jodrey just outside the staff room she gave him a rather smug smile; they both knew she was almost never this early.

Joss took her time getting changed, tuned her guitar in the staff room, and determinedly kept her thoughts on the job offer and the very satisfactory state of her bank account. At seven minutes to five she walked sedately down the corridor to the Red Lion. Her father would be proud of her; her father was the rational member of the family.

The bar in the Red Lion, with its racks of shining

glasses and array of bottles, was on the right, just inside
the entrance to the pub. The counter was oval-shaped
with a brass rail and tall oak stools; a blue-eyed man
was seated on the stool nearest the entrance.

Joss stopped dead, nearly dropping her guitar. She
said flatly, 'What are *you* doing here?'

Today Niall was wearing casual white cotten trousers
and a short-sleeved red shirt. Lounging against the bar,
he gave her an unpleasant smile and indicated the two
glasses at his elbow, the nearer one almost empty, the
other full. 'Getting drunk,' he said.

She was suddenly furious, far angrier than she had
been with Tom the day before, angrier than she could
ever remember being. The gold flecks in her eyes like
tiny sparks, she said with dangerous quietness, 'Still
playing your little games, aren't you?'

He tipped back his head and drained the contents of
the nearer glass. His thoat was strongly muscled and
deeply tanned; she could see the dark tangle of body
hair in the open neckline of his shirt, and somehow that
stoked her rage. Taking his time, Niall replaced the
empty glass on the counter and picked up the full one.
'That's right,' he said. 'Cheers.'

'Why don't you just leave?' she seethed. 'Right now.'

'Tch, tch, Jocelyn Gayle,' he said mockingly.
'Remember Mr Jodrey—the customer's always right.
Particularly a customer who's spending as much money
as I am today.'

'Why are you *doing* this?'

'It's a free country.' Niall took a long pull at the new
drink.

He was not slurring his words and his movements
were perfectly controlled; yet she sensed in him an anger
that more than matched her own. She did not care. She
wanted to scream at him at the top of her lungs and
drum her heels on the floor. Keeping the bartender and
Mr Jodrey in mind, she muttered ferociously, 'I want

you to go away and leave me alone.'

'I didn't start this conversation. You did.' He added with great interest, 'You look like a jungle cat when you're angry. Those tawny eyes and that mane of hair. Am I allowed to buy you a drink? To congratulate you on being early for work?'

'No!'

He raised one brow. 'No, thank you?' he murmured.

She felt as frustrated as she had years ago on the rare occasions when her four brothers had ganged up on her, taunting her for being only a girl. No matter how loudly she had yelled at them or how hard she had beaten her pudgy fists against their chests, she had never been able to make any impression on them. Matters were not helped now when Niall said silkily, 'Don't try and bash me with your guitar, Jocelyn Gayle. I'm not Tom.'

Very much aware of the lean, powerful body under the casual summer clothes, a body which in no way resembled Tom's, Joss said with great venom, if no particular originality, 'I wouldn't think of it—I value my guitar.'

He had the audacity to laugh. 'Oh, dear. That does put me in my place. By the way, hadn't you better start singing? It's five o'clock.'

Despite her fondness for the memory of Great-Aunt Lucy, it would have given Joss tremendous satisfaction to have brought the guitar down on Niall's head. 'Just don't bother me between now and nine o'clock,' she said tautly. 'Do you hear me?'

'I've never been accused of deafness,' Niall said blandly. 'But if I might make a suggestion, I'd avoid "Streets of London" if I were you. Cleo Laine is the only woman who should sing that song.'

Unfortunately Joss agreed with him. 'I don't have the time to stand here trading insults with you,' she choked.

'No, you don't. Two minutes after five.'

Not trusting herself to say another word, Joss pivoted

and stalked past the bar to the dais. Someone had
shifted her stool and the microphone nearer to the
tables. Not bothering to move them, she sat down in a
swirl of skirts, adjusted the angle of the microphone and
said into it with a vivacity fuelled by anger, 'Good
afternoon, ladies and gentlemen. My name is Jocelyn
Gayle and I'm here to sing for your pleasure from now
until nine o'clock this evening. Please feel free
to request any songs you would like . . . and please
enjoy.'

With a wild clash of chords she threw herself into
'The Whistling Gypsy', a song she usually saved for
later in her show when the audience had warmed up.
She followed it by several extremely energetic Israeli
folk songs. In the final verse of the last song a tall man
in a red shirt sauntered between the tables and stretched
out in a chair just to her right. His foot was within six
inches of her green ruffled skirt.

Joss was in good voice and the adrenalin was still
coursing through her veins. She gave the man a vivid
smile, running her fingers through her hair in a
deliberately seductive gesture, and said into the
microphone, 'I've had a request from the gentleman to
my right. Cleo Laine's version of "Cavatina",
which you may also know as "He Was So Beautiful".'

With exquisite sensibility she played the first slow
arpeggio. She sang, looking directly into Niall's eyes.
She could tell she had taken him by surprise. More than
surprise: he looked stunned. Her voice caressed
the notes, giving each its due, as she held his gaze.

But then with a pang at her heart Joss remembered
the orchard and the beautiful man who had been
waiting for her there in the springtime, and in spite of
herself the poignancy of the song overcame her anger.
When she sang of shared moments and lingering
feelings she had to look away, and her audience was
absolutely silent as she ended the song.

In rare tribute there was an instant of quiet before the people in the pub began to clap. Joss bowed her head, fighting back tears, knowing her trick had backfired on her. She should have rehearsed the words in her head before she began to sing; had she done so, she would never have chosen that song.

' "Danny Boy"!' someone shouted from the back of the room.

Another surefire tearjerker, she thought wryly, and as the first chord rippled from her guitar she sneaked a glance through her lashes at Niall. He was staring full at her, his face a grim, frozen mask. Hastily she looked away, her blood pounding in her veins. Niall had been no more indifferent to that song than she had been.

From 'Danny Boy' she moved to the safer terrain of 'An English Country Garden'; enough emotion for one night. Perhaps because it was Thursday and near the end of the week her audience was very receptive, so that for minutes at a time Joss was able to ignore the man on her right, who was still steadily drinking, still seemingly unaffected by what he was drinking. She did not even look at him when she left the pub for her break; he was sitting at the same table when she returned and, as she sat down, winked at her sardonically.

She looked haughtily down her nose and then turned away, presenting him with her profile. She had a straight, decided nose and a firm chin. For her ears alone Niall drawled, 'I like a woman with spirit.'

Joss raised her chin perceptibly, sang a Caribbean fisherman's ballad and then a rather bawdy sea shanty that Great-Aunt Lucy would have enjoyed. The second half of the evening seemed to pass very quickly, and at nine o'clock when she announced into the microphone that her time was up Niall was still sitting at the chair nearest her. Had she consumed the amount of

alcohol that he had, she would have been flat under the
table; he, however, looked exactly as he had at five
o'clock. Furthermore, he looked as though he had
settled in for the night. Because one of Mr Jodrey's
strictest rules was that she not fraternise with the guests,
Joss could not do what she wanted to, which was sit
down at his table and talk to him. They wouldn't even
have to talk, she thought helplessly. Just to be with him
would be enough. So much for rationality.

Her face showing none of the turmoil of her
thoughts, she gathered up her guitar and left the dais
without a backwards look. A middle-aged couple sitting
near the entranceway signalled her over; they were from
Ireland, and, after telling her how much they had
enjoyed her singing, began discussing the words to 'The
Maid With the Nut-Brown Hair'. At any other time Joss
would have been delighted to learn a new verse to a song
that she loved; now, however, all she wanted to do was
escape from the Red Lion.

She did finally make her escape, and changed into her
street clothes in the staff room. She decided to leave the
hotel via the lobby again, on the off-chance that Niall
might be there. He was not. Gripping the strap of her
shoulderbag she turned on her heel, marched in the door
of the Red Lion, and walked past the bar. The seat
beside the dais was empty.

She blinked and looked again. Niall had quite
definitely gone.

The bartender was a young man called Claude
Montaigne who had only been working at the Red Lion
for a couple of weeks. Joss said hurriedly, 'Claude, did
the man in the red shirt leave?'

'He paid 'is bill and left right after you.' Claude
rolled his eyes. 'A big bill, a big tip. 'E can come back
any time.'

'Thanks.' Forgetting decorum, Joss ran across the
lobby and pushed against the swing door. Then she

stopped in dismay. It was pouring with rain. She had a
vague recollection that the weather report that morning
had mentioned rain, but she had been too busy
considering her job offer to pay much attention. She
had not bothered with a raincoat or an umbrella.

Russell was on duty outside, holding a huge umbrella
over some newly arrived guests. He grinned at Joss and
indicated the street running west. 'He went thataway,'
he called.

She knew Russell was referring to Niall. She drew a
deep breath and plunged out into the rain; fortunately
her cotton skirt and knit top were washable. As was the
rest of her, she thought ruefully as the cool drops pelted
her face and trickled down her neck.

The hotel took up the rest of the block. Joss ran to the
corner, her sandals slapping against the wet pavement,
and looked to her left and then to her right. A man in a
red shirt was stationed beyond the next set of traffic
lights, trying to flag down a taxi.

Clutching her bag she ran after him, and had her
father appeared in front of her and asked what she was
doing she could not have produced a sensible answer.
She reached the lights; she was perhaps forty feet from
Niall. A yellow cab had pulled up on the opposite side
of the street from him.

The walk signal flashed. Joss stepped off the
pavement.

To her right a car horn blared. Instinctively she
retreated, pushing her wet hair out of her eyes. A
souped-up jalopy with only one headlight was racing
towards her. The traffic light was red; instead of
stopping, the jalopy took the corner in a squeal of tyres.
Niall had already checked to see if there was anything
coming. As if everything was happening in slow motion,
Joss saw him step off the kerb into the path of the
the oncoming car

She screamed his name. *'Niall!* Niall, stop!' Then

she began to run, faster than she had ever run in her life.

His head had swivelled at the sound of her voice. He saw the car immediately and leaped backwards on to the pavement. The jalopy blasted its horn again and careened past him; the driver had not even touched the brakes.

Joss stumbled to a halt, grabbing at a newspaper stand for support, gasping for breath. The cab driver, who belonged to a group of people normally unshockable, had rolled down his window and was watching the retreating jalopy, shaking his head. Niall said sharply, 'Joss! Are you all right?'

Slowly she straightened. As a fifteen-year-old she had been a devotee of gothic novels; the hearts of their delicate white-clad heroines had been wont to skip beats with distressing frequency. But Joss had never known it could actually happen. She took a couple of steps towards Niall, amazed that all her joints seemed to be functioning and that she could put one foot in front of the other. 'I'm fine,' she said more or less truthfully. 'What about yourself?'

His hair was stuck to his skull and his shirt plastered to his body; he looked lean and dangerous, and somehow his next question came as no surprise. 'What the hell are you doing here?' he demanded.

The cabbie yelled, 'Hey! You two wanna go someplace?'

Over his shoulder Niall called, 'Pull over and start your meter. I'll be with you in a second.' Then he looked back at Joss. 'I asked you a question.'

Now that she had stopped running, her wet clothes were sticking to her body, making her shiver. 'I was following you,' she said.

'How flattering,' Niall sneered. 'You should have saved yourself the trouble.' But as he spoke he swayed a little on his feet, and for the first time Joss remembered the amount of alcohol he had consumed. She closed the gap between them, reached out one hand and rested it on his wrist. The contact shuddered through her body. 'Niall, why don't we go somewhere where we can get out of the rain and have a cup of coffee? Maybe even something to eat.'

He pulled his arm free. 'No.'

'Mister,' the cab driver shouted, 'I can earn more on a fare than sittin' here all night. You comin'?'

'No, he's not,' Joss yelled back.

'Yes, I am,' Niall snapped.

'You can't just leave me here!'

'I didn't ask you to follow me.'

'Then why did you come to the bar tonight?' she blazed.

The cabbie said in a loud voice, spacing each word, 'This is your last chance, you guys.'

'Because I'm a fool,' Niall said savagely. 'A goddamned fool.' Turning his back on her, he crossed the street in a few long strides, opened the back door of the cab and climbed in, then slammed the door shut; the cab's registration number was painted on the side.

'Ain't she comin', too?' the driver demanded. From her stance on the pavement Joss could see that he was young, with curly black hair and a broken nose. Presumably Niall answered in the negative, because the young man said, more loudly, 'She saved your life, fella! That car wasn't stoppin' for nobody.'

The scene had all the elements of farce; chivalry was found in strange guises. But through the driving rain Joss saw Niall lean forward, mouthing words she could not hear. The cabbie gave a philosophical shrug and called out to Joss, 'Sorry, honey. But a fare's a fare. There'll be another cab along in a couple of minutes.' In a swish of water he drove away.

Hugging her bag, Joss stood still by the news-stand. In the movies she would now hail another taxi, cry,

'Follow that car!' and trace Niall to his destination. They would have a dramatic shouting match in the foyer of his apartment building and then he would take her in his arms and kiss her passionately. Her hair, of course, would not be clinging to her face like wet seaweed.

She scowled into the rain. Had ten taxis appeared she would not have asked one of them to follow Niall, for although outwardly she was shivering, inwardly she was boiling with rage. The cabbie was right. She *had* saved Niall's life. But he had not seen fit to thank her. Oh, no! He had preferred to insult her and reject her and leave her standing in the rain. On a poorly lit side street, she noticed with a further upsurge of rage. Anyone more removed from her lover in the orchard could not be imagined. *He* would not have left her standing in the rain.

Right, she thought ironically, beginning to trudge back the way she had come; there was no point in hurrying, for she was as wet as she could possibly get. The man in the orchard would have thrown a velvet cloak around her shoulders, lifted her on the back of his milk-white steed and carried her off into the sunset. The cloak would have been trimmed with ermine.

She walked a little slower, hunching her shoulders, staring down at her sandals, whose straps were leaving ugly brown stains on her bare feet. I don't want a velvet cloak, she thought with painful honesty. Or a white stallion. All I want is a little common courtesy, and an explanation why Niall had turned up at the Red Lion for the second night in a row. The cloak and the steed were the trappings of romance. What she wanted was the real person. Niall, the man.

But Niall had chosen not to give her that. He had spoken to her in riddles, he had stared at her as if he hungered for her with all his soul, and then, twice, he had vanished.

She reached the traffic lights, carefully looked in all four directions, then crossed the street, heading for the subway station. She must forget about him, she adjured herself. He was no good for her. He was rude and full of anger. Secretive. Arrogant. Overbearing. Her steps quickened. The cab driver had shown her more consideration than Niall had. For reasons she could not begin to understand, Niall was a bitter, twisted man, and for her to believe even for a moment that he was the right man for her was lunacy. The right man existed, she was still convinced of that; but she had yet to meet him.

To Joss's surprise, when she was sitting at the bamboo table the next morning sipping a cup of coffee and reading the headlines, Magda opened her bedroom door and propped herself in the doorway. Magda had a mop of glorious red hair, a sexy body and come-hither green eyes, all of which concealed a practical, no-nonsense personality and a kindness strongly tempered by common sense.

Said Joss blankly, 'What are you doing up so early?'

Magda glided into the room, looked at the heap of her own clothes on the chair as if wondering whose they were, dumped them on the floor and sat down. The tortoiseshell cat jumped into her lap, kneading the folds of Magda's fashionable striped nightshirt. 'Is that all you're having for breakfast?' Magda said severely.

'I had a piece of toast.'

'You'd starve to death if it wasn't for my cooking.'

'No, I wouldn't—I'd be five pounds lighter.' Joss grinned at her roommate. 'You didn't get out of bed at eight-thirty to ask me what I had for breakfast.'

'Charlie proposed to me yesterday afternoon.' Reflectively Magda stroked the cat, her green eyes shrewd. 'I think I'll accept.'

Charlie was five-feet-ten, as thin as a rail, and quite frighteningly intelligent. He called himself an inventor, supporting this so far unlucrative vocation by working as a night-watchman at a construction site, a job that he said gave him lots of time to think. Although his features were instantly forgettable and his pysique nothing remarkable, he seemed quite unsurprised that a creature as gorgeous as Madga should spend all her free time with him.

Joss said drily, 'So would I be premature to congratulate you?'

Madga's full lips smiled provocatively. 'I believe you'd be quite safe.'

Joss got up, hugged her friend, a move not appreciated by Nasturtium, and said sincerely, 'I wish you both all the happiness in the world.'

'We'll probably get married in the autumn and move into Charlie's apartment.'

Charlie lived in the kind of apartment that landlords described as 'having possibilities'. Joss said dubiously, 'You won't have much money.'

'Not at first. But we will have,' Madga said calmly. 'I have faith in Charlie.'

Joss said impulsively, 'Magda, are you sure he's the right man for you?'

'Absolutely.'

'Did you know that right away?'

Magda tickled the cat's ears. 'He was different. So many of the men I meet at the club want to undress me within five minutes of meeting me. Whereas Charlie wanted to talk about the book I was reading. He didn't even kiss me until the fourth date, and then it was on the cheek.'

'So you didn't fall madly in love with him at first sight,' Joss said slowly.

'That only happens in books.' Magda tipped the cat on the floor. 'I'm going to brew some proper Colombian coffee—not that slop you're drinking. Want some?'

'Sure,' Joss said absently, wondering if Magda was right. Somethig had happened between herself and Niall, to that she would swear. But Niall had made it clear he did not want her, and she was dismayed that of all the men in the world her emotions had been touched by someone so unapproachable, so difficult, so angry. If she could only understand why he had such an effect on her, she might be better able to obliterate that effect. Because she was quite sure that after last night she would not see him again.

However, when Joss arrived at the side door of the Swansea Hotel at four-thirty that afternoon, a tall, blue-eyed man was waiting for her in the alleyway. He was wearing a trench coat over light grey trousers. Her footsteps slowed and she heard the bumpity-bump of her heart over the patter of rain on her umbrella. Happiness and anger warred within her; she remembered being left at the kerbside in the rain in the dark, put her nose in the air and reached for the door-handle.

Niall grabbed the sleeve of her raincoat. 'Don't go in—I've got to talk to you.'

Ineffectively she tried to pull her arm free. '*I* don't want to talk to *you.*'

'Please, Joss. I have to apologise. I behaved very badly last night.'

'You're so right. Let go of my arm.'

He dropped it instantly. She seized the door-handle and turned it, but Niall's foot was now wedged against the door. She said with icy calm, 'Move your foot. Get out of my life. And don't come back.'

He did not move his foot. 'I'll be leaving the city on Suday and I won't be back. But in the meantime I'd very much like to spend some time with you.'

'You should buy yourself a self-help book on dating,' Joss said nastily. 'None of them will recommend leaving a woman alone at night on a city street in the pouring rain as a way of favourably impressing her. Or if it does, you should ask for your money back.'

He suddenly moved forward and took her by the shoulders, his face so close to hers that it was reduced to a harsh, unsparing geometry of planes and hollows. He said urgently, 'I had some bad news a couple of days ago and I've been in a foul mood ever since, Joss. I drank too much last night—which is not a habit of mine, believe me. I shouldn't have left you, I know I shouldn't. But I didn't know what else to do.' His smile was wry. 'The cabbie gave me hell, too.'

'You didn't even thank me for warning you about that car.' She remembered how it had appeared out of nowhere, its brakes screaming, its headlight like a single eye. 'It could have killed you,' she said, and in spite of herself her voice shook.

His jaw tightened. 'I suppose it could have,' he said with an intonation that puzzled her. 'If you saved my life, Joss, you could at least have a meal with me after work tonight.'

He was still standing near enough that she could have reached up and smoothed the lines from his forehead. She said stiltedly, 'That's illogical.'

His smile this time was disarming. 'You're no creature of logic, Joss—I know that from the way you sing.'

She realised with a flash of insight that what Niall had just said struck at the roots of her dilemma about her future. The research job represented the logical side of her character, the detached, scientific side that Great-Aunt Lucy would have despised; but when Joss thought of a medical career she thought of family medicine, which, practised well, took into account the whole person. 'I'm both,' she said stubbornly.

'You're a woman of deep emotion—I'd swear to it. If I'm waiting for you at nine o'clock, will you have a meal with me?'

In a thin voice Joss said, 'Are you married?'

Her question did not seem to surprise him. 'No. Nor have I ever been.'

'How do I know that by nine o'clock you won't have disappeared again?'

'I swear I won't.'

'Why, Niall?' she burst out. 'Why do you want to spend time with me?'

Through the seams of her coat she felt his fingers tighten. 'Because I can't help myself,' he said.

She believed him instantly and unequivocally. 'So you feel it, too.'

'Oh, yes . . . you knew that, didn't you? I tried running away, but that didn't work. So for two days I'd like us to spend as much time together as we can.'

'Then you'll be leaving,' she said neutrally.

'And I won't be back. I want you to know that.' He must have seen the doubt and frustration in her face, because he added forcefully, 'Joss, I've never felt like this with a woman before—never knew I could feel this way. And believe me, that's no line. I almost wish it were.' He gave a humourless laugh. 'For reasons of my own, I couldn't have met you at a worse time.'

Joss hesitated, quite sure he would not share those reasons. 'I've never felt this way, either,' she said.

'Maybe we'll find out we can't stand each other if we spend more time together. That you love Italian food and I love Chinese. That you're a morning person and I'm a night person. That we're totally unsuited. It's worth a try, isn't it?'

'You might sing off-key.'

'You might grind your teeth.'

'Or I might have false teeth,' Joss said primly.

Niall laughed outright. 'Just as long as your eyelashes are real.'

She batted them demurely. 'A dollar forty-nine at the

cosmetics counter. Niall, that's only the second time I've heard you laugh.'

His smile faded. 'We might find we have nothing in common if we spend more time together. Or that we even dislike each other.'

He had spoken without conviction. Joss said, 'And what if we don't? What if we discover we both love fettucini and hate egg rolls? And that I can make you laugh? What then, Niall?' Her eyes searched his face. 'Will you still leave on Sunday?'

'I have to.'

In a spurt of anger she said, 'So where do you live, Outer Mongolia? No postal service? No telephone?'

'When I leave on Sunday I won't be in touch with you again,' Niall said inflexibly. 'So we can take the risk of seeing each other for a couple of days, or else I'll leave right now and I won't bother you again.'

'You're leaving the choice up to me? That's hardly fair, when I have no idea why you have to leave?'

'All I can assure you is that you won't be hurting a third person, Joss—there's no one else in my life.'

If she told him to leave he would do so, and she would never know if the strange attraction between them was real or unreal. But if she saw more of him and discovered that the attraction was indeed real, what then? Was he for some reason afraid of a close relationship, and consequently playing his cards close to his chest? Could she by Sunday make him change his mind? She had no way of knowing.

With a feeling that she was stepping off a very high cliff into thin air, Joss said quietly, 'I'll meet you here at ten past nine.'

Briefly he rested his cheek on her hair. 'Thank you,' he said equally quietly. 'Do you mind if I come into the bar around eight?'

Not wanting to reveal how much his gesture had affected her, she murmured, 'You must be getting bored with my repertoire.'

'Well . . .' she said inadequately. 'I'm going to be late again.'

'Off you go.' He reached round her for the door-handle.

The words were wrenched from her. 'Niall, I'm frightened.'

He made no attempt to touch her. 'If you want to back out, now's your chance.'

'Two days seem such a short time!'

'You can build up a lot of memories in two days,' he said harshly. 'Enough to last for a very long time. Or else you can play it safe and do nothing.'

'No. No, I don't want that.'

Niall's features gentled. 'It will be all right, Joss, you'll see.' He opened the door. 'I'll see you later.'

She slipped through the door, heard him close it behind her, and ran down the corridor. She had dreamed more than once of being balanced on the very edge of a perpendicular, pure white cliff. Sometimes she would glide through the air, lifted by invisible currents, bathed in sunlight. But other times she would fall, plummeting downwards with a scream tearing at her throat, knowing she would be dashed to pieces on the rocks below.

She was perched on the cliff-edge now; she could not have said which would be her fate.

CHAPTER THREE

PROMPTLY at eight o'clock Niall walked into the Red Lion. The pub was full, loud with conversation, thick with smoke. Joss had moved her stool by the piano, where she was surrounded by the usual Friday night group of singers, some of whom were in tune and some not. She saw Niall immediately, gave him a small, distracted smile and kept on playing. To her surprise he joined the group, adding his rich baritone to all the varied voices. He was very definitely in tune. They sang about the hole in Billy's bucket, the long way to Tipperary and the squid-jigging grounds; they waltzed around the billabong and deplored the houses made of ticky-tacky. Joss plucked her guitar and sang lustily and coached her group in the choruses; and in the small, still centre of her being was afraid. Nine o'clock, for once, came sooner than she would have wished. Without meeting Niall's eyes she said her goodbyes and fled to the staff room.

At exactly ten past nine she left the hotel by the side door, wearing a blue cotton jumpsuit and gold costume jewellery under her raincoat. Her eyes were very wide; her lips felt stiff. Niall was waiting for her, his collar turned up against the mist, his hair already damp. She had not been totally convinced he would be there. He said, 'You must be hungry, Joss.'

'Yes.'

'*Do* you like Italian food?'

She managed a smile. 'Yes.'

'Come on, then. I ate at this place on Monday; I think you'll like it.'

She scurried after him down the alley. The pavement was crowded. Niall took her arm, threaded it through his and kept on walking. His legs were much longer than hers. She trotted along at his side and said finally, 'Is the restaurant on fire?'

He slackened his pace. 'Sorry. I guess I'm in a hurry to have you sitting across from me at a table. No Mr Jodrey. No Tom. Just you and me. I made a reservation for nine-thirty.'

Joss could think of no reply to this. In a few minutes Niall led her down a flight of brick steps to a tiny restaurant in the cellar of an office building. Their table was tucked into a corner behind a white-washed pillar; Joss did not think this was coincidence. Scarlet geraniums bloomed in the deep window recesses, the tablecloth were red, and the seats very comfortable. Furthermore, no one was singing.

Niall said abruptly, 'Do you like to dance?'

'I love to.'

'Good, we'll go dancing after we eat. Tomorrow I thought we'd head out to the country.'

'I have to work.'

'Not until five.'

'I work at a bookshop in the day. From ten until four tomorrow.'

His eyes narrowed. 'Can't you get someone else to take your shift?'

'A couple of people owe me shifts. But——'

'Joss, we haven't got much time—let's not waste any of it. Phone someone now.'

Again she was afraid. Trying to disguise her feelings, she raised her eyebrows and said. 'Please, Joss?'

He laughed, took her hand and coaxed, 'Please, Joss.'

She'd climb a thrity-foot pole if he smild at her like that. Or a tall white cliff. She went to the telephone, and on her second try got a replacement. When she went back to the table the waiter was there, and it took several minutes to choose what they would eat and drink. Then, finally, she and Niall were alone at the table. He raised his wineglass. 'To our time together, Joss.' Obediently she drank. He added softly, 'Relax. I'm not going to eat you.'

Joss put down her glass. But before she could say anything, Niall took her hands in his and spread them on the tablecloth. 'No rings,' he observed. 'Pretty fingernails—indisputably your own. What colour is the polish?'

'Almond Blush.'

'Nice. What's this scar?' He ran one finger along her left knuckle.

'I fell off the tractor when I was four. Jake got spanked for it, because he's the one who dared me to get up there.'

'Which brother is Jake?'

'The second youngest. My favourite, actually. Niall, what is this, an inquisition?'

He looked up. 'I have a lot to learn about you in a very short time.'

She had the sense of being on a roller-coaster that was travelling faster and faster. 'Communication's a two-way street,' she observed.

'As long as you don't ask why I have to leave on Sunday,' he said with suppressed violence. 'I know you don't understand. I can't make you understand. But we're together right now—and surely the present is what counts?'

With seeming irrelevance Joss said, 'You have the bluest eyes of anyone I've ever met,' and could see his instant relief that she was nor pursuing the subject of Sunday.

He said with a boyish grin, 'And my lashes are my own—all part of the package.'

'You've got a scar on your thumb.'

He stretched out his right hand. Her brothers had all inherited their father's blunt fingers, but Niall's hand was long-fingered, beautiful to her in a way she had not thought a man's hand could be beautiful. His wrist was encircled by an elegant Swiss watch on a leather strap. He rubbed the sickle-shaped scar on his thumb and said, 'I got that playing hockey as a kid. Collided with the goal-post.'

Joss rested her chin on her hands, studying his features with secret pleasure. 'You have half a dozen grey hairs over each ear, a dent in your chin, and you're twenty-nine years old.'

He winced theatrically. 'Twenty-eight,' he said, adding with a wink, 'and eleven months. You're not a day over twenty-one.'

'I'm approximately one hundred and fifty days over twenty-one.'

'The youngest of a family of five.'

'Seven. I have two sisters as well.' She reeled off the names. 'Ross, Harvey, Glenis, Blanche, Jake, Gilbert, and me. Four of them married, three with children. I'm an aunt five times over. What about you?'

'You can't be an uncle if you have no brothers or sisters,' he said wryly.

It seemed a terrible fate to Joss to have grown up as an only child. 'Are your parents living?' she asked.

'My father is,' Niall said repressively. 'What are you doing in Toronto, Joss, when you're so homesick?'

She knew him well enough to realise that the subject of his parents was closed. Filing that fact for future reference, she explained about her research job and the funding cuts; this led to her decision about medical school versus a job in Halifax.

'If money were not a problem, which would you do?' Niall asked.

'Medical school,' she said promptly.

'Then do that. You'd make a very good doctor—that

disinterested kindness of yours. Besides, life's too short to find yourself caught in a job you don't want to do.'

'The voice of experience?' she ventured.

'I let myself get trapped in the fast lane. Executive in a big company, climbing to the top, working most nights and every weekend. Burn-out might be a fashionable term, but it's also a very real one.'

'The first time I met you I thought you looked exhausted.'

Niall did not elaborate, perhaps because their salads had arrived, tomatoes and basil in a garlic-flavoured dressing; Once the waiter had gone he said, 'Tell me more about your family.'

So Joss prattled on, bringing in her gypsy ancestress and Great-Aunt Lucy, the collie dog who never chased the cats and her mother's determined pursuit of her father forty years ago. As the man sitting across from her watched the play of emotion on her face, his blue eyes softened. Their salad plates were removed and replaced by bowls of linguini and Joss described some of the scrapes she had got into as a child. Niall remarked, 'Sounds like your brother Jake was the one who was always getting you into trouble—is that why he's your favourite?'

She twisted her wineglass. 'There was always an affinity between us, despite the eight-year age-difference. We even look alike. He's a widower now, with two little children. His wife died of cancer a year ago. He was so good to her . . . he took a leave of absence from his job so he could look after her at home, because she didn't want to go into hospital and be separated from the children. He was devastated when she died. But at least he had the satisfaction of knowing he'd gone everything he could for her.'

'She demanded a lot of him,' Niall said harshly.

Joss looked up, surprised; somewhere she had touched a nerve. 'She did, yes. But he had a lot to give.

And they both knew that had he been the one who was ill, she would have done the same for him.'

Niall shifted in his chair. 'It must have been hard on the children,' he said, still with that harshness in his voice.

'Of course it was. But at least they were involved in a very real way. Death wasn't made into some unmentionable act that happens in hospitals.'

'I can't imagine that it was good for them having her home,' he retorted.

'Then we'll have to disagree on that,' Joss rejoined hotly. 'Because *I* think a very sad situation was handled in the best possible way.' She took a gulp of Chianti. 'I'd much rather we disagreed over Chinese food than over something as basic as death.'

'We knew this sort of thing might happen when we agreed to spend the time together,' Niall answered curtly.

Joss looked down at her plate. She considered herself privileged to have witnessed the love between her brother and his dying wife, and for Niall to view the situation so differently upset her. She heard herself say, 'How did your mother die?'

'That's irrelevant.'

She sighed, pushing a clam around her plate, suddenly finding the cellar room claustrophobic. 'Let's go dancing,' she said. 'I don't want dessert.'

Niall made an obvious effort to speak more naturally. 'There's a Polish dance festival at the Harbourfront. Dancing for the general public after ten o'clock. Want to see what that's all about?'

'Sure,' Joss said agreeably, knowing they had retreated from the cliff-edge on to safe ground again. 'Sounds like fun.'

The big hall was crowded with tables and chairs, a colourful band on the stage playing the Polish equivalent to a polka, the dance-floor crowded with gyrating couples. Then costumed dancers circulated on the floor, helping to set up country dance sets. Joss and Niall joined three other couples. The steps were fairly simply, and in no time they were bobbing and hopping to the music, weaving in and out in increasingly intricate patterns. More couples joined in, so that for moments at a time Joss would lose sight of Niall. They danced a fast-moving polonaise that left her breathless, then the band struck up an old-fasioned waltz. She looked around the milling dancers for Niall's tall figure, not finding him, aware of a sudden anxiety. He couldn't have disappeared. He wouldn't do that. Edging off the dance-floor, she searched for him among the tables.

He was sitting on a chair against the wall, hunched over. She pushed between the tables, almost ran the last few feet, and knelt beside him. 'Niall! What's wrong?'

His face was deathly pale, his features contorted. 'Stitch,' he gasped. 'Happens sometimes.'

There was sweat on his forehead. She pulled a tissue from her pocket and wiped his brows; his hands were pressed to his ribs. 'Should I get a doctor?'

'No. I'll be fine.' Her face was very close to his; he muttered, 'Don't look so worried, Joss. I've let myself get out of shape the last year or so, that's all.'

He straightened slowly. His breathing seemed easier, and she let out her own breath in a sigh of relief. 'You frightened me.'

'Sorry. My own fault—should have been jogging every noon hour instead of chaining myself to a desk.'

'You're too thin. I bet you don't eat properly.'

'Yes, Mother,' he said with the ghost of a smile.

Joss blushed and spoke the literal truth. 'I don't want to be your mother!'

'Any Freudian worth his salt would be glad to hear

you say that.'

She giggled. 'I think you've recovered.'

'So much so that we should dance this waltz together.'
Niall stood up. 'It seems suitably lethargic.'

She loved it when he assumed that deadpan expression.
As they reached the edge of the dance-floor, Niall took
her in his arms. He had left his sweater and trench coat at
the coat check; his shirt-sleeves were rolled up. Joss
rested one hand on his shoulder, felt him take her hand,
and began to dance.

Within ten seconds she knew she was in trouble.
Beneath her palm she could feel the shift of his shoulder
muscles; he was holding her closely because the floor was
crowded, and the contact made her tingle from head to
toe. Although she had pictured an embrace in the
orchard, it had somewho never involved the actuality of a
man's body: bone and muscles, movement, flexibility
and strength. Someone bumped into her from behind,
thrusting her against Niall's chest; his arm tightened
around her waist. She closed her eyes and knew she had
never understood the meaning of desire before.

The waltz ended with flourish on the accordion. Into
her ear Nial muttered, 'You're dynamite, Jocelyn Gayle.
I think we'd better go for a good brisk walk.'

'Or a swim in Lake Ontario.'

'So it was mutual? I wasn't the only one consumed by
lust?' Joss had been staring at his shirt-front. He lifted
her chin, saw the shyness and confusion in her hazel eyes
and added, 'You don't need to answer—I can read your
mind.'

'I hope not!'

He chuckled. 'Apart from the fact that you make me
feel like Tristan, Antony and Romeo all rolled up in one,
do you know what's the nicest thing about you? You
make me laugh.'

She was still standing in the circle of his arms. 'I don't
think you've done much laughing recently.'

'No, I haven't.'

'You haven't told me what the bad news was,' she said, and felt the tensing of his muscles.

'Another closed area, Joss.'

'There are a lot of them,' she said, carefully keeping her voice light.

'Yes.'

'I've talked more about myself than you have about you.'

'I hope you'll continue to do so. You're like a breath of fresh air for me.'

Her brain was buzzing with questions, none of which she asked. 'So what's it to be next—the walk or the swim?'

'The lake's polluted, they say. So we could settle on a walk, couldn't we? Unless you're tired?'

'No, I'm fine.'

In a very real way Joss was telling the truth. Despite all the closed areas, she felt that she and Niall had made enormous strides that evening, for Niall, the most secretive of men, had acknowledged that she was good for him and that he desired her. Sunday began to seem like less of a barrier. Of her own volition she tucked her arm in his when they went outside; he smiled down at her, resting his own hand over hers.

Along the waterfront crowds of people surged and eddied like flotsam caught in invisible currents. Joss, used to a rural environment, found the constant movement, the raucous voices and loud music, the unavoidable body contact, fascinating for a while but ultimately wearying. After half an hour or so she said to Niall, 'If you like we could go to my apartment for coffee. My roommate's out right now, but she'll be home a little later.'

Niall stopped, looking down at her. The mist had turned her hair into a tangle of curls. 'Despite what happened on the dance-floor, I'm not going to jump on you, Joss.'

She knew she had been transparent: country girl in the big city. 'And what if I jump on you?' she said with attempted airiness.

'I might call for help. But then again, I might not.' He reached down and smoothed her cheek. 'You're blushing.'

'Your hands are cold.' She held his fingers to the warmth of her skin, and the crowds dropped away as if they did not exist. Niall said roughly, 'Let's go to your apartment. I won't jump on you, I swear.' His smile was crooked. 'I've always been known to have a strong will. But I would like to be alone with you.'

She wanted the same. Fifteen minutes later, after a journey during which neither of them said very much, she was ushering Niall in the door of her apartment. Nasturtium, curled up on the chair, opened her eyes, yawned, and went back to sleep.

'Some chaperon,' said Niall.

Joss knew, which Niall did not, that Nasturtium would be their only chaperon for at least two hours; Magda was always late on Friday nights. The apartment seemed very quiet. it was, she realised, the first time she and Niall had ever been truly alone. She took his coat and hung it in the closet. 'Sorry about the mess, my roommate isn't what you'd call tidy. All the furniture is hers, I'm just living here for the summer, she's getting married in the fall. She's the one who got me the job at the Red Lion, she's a singer, too——'

Niall put a hand on her shoulder as if he was soothing a frightened animal. 'Slow down,' he said.

'I'm acting as though you're my first date!' Joss wailed. 'You look so calm and collected.'

'Then I'm a good actor. Do you think I'm not aware that we're alone in this apartment and that behind those two doors there are undoubtedly beds and that I'd like to be in one of them with you? Of course I would. But we're not going to do that, Joss; it wouldn't be right. So why don't you put the kettle on and tell me what the cat's name is. I've always liked cats—such self-contained creatures.'

'Like you,' Joss said with a tiny smile. 'Regular coffee or decaffeinated?'

She busied herself in the kitchen, trying not to think about the beds, and put some of Magda's delicious almond cookies on a tray with the coffee. She and Niall sat decorously on the chesterfield and talked sensibly about the state of the world, while Naturtium purred away on Niall's lap. When they had finished Niall carried the tray back into the kitchen for her, Nasturtium following close behind; Nasturtium had taken a fancy to Niall.

The kitchen was very small, made more so by Magda's collection of cookbooks. Niall pulled out a book on Moroccan cooking, saying absently, 'I spent a summer in Rabat with the company several years ago.'

Joss rinsed out the mugs, reached behind her for the cookie tin and stepped on Nasturtium's tail. Nasturtium yowled. Joss leaped clear of the cat, stumbled against Niall and suddenly found herself locked in his arms. The cookie tin fell off the counter and clanged on the floor. Niall said roughly, 'Very appropriate sound effects.' Then he kissed her.

At some level Joss had known since the beginning of the evening that this would happen, and she welcomed it with all her heart. Trustingly she closed her eyes, put her arms around his neck and kissed him back.

The cookie tin rolled into a corner, fell on its side and was still. Nasturtium muttered away to herself in a disgruntled fashion. But for Joss there was nothing but the strength of Niall's embrace, the warmth of his lips, and the clean, masculine scent of his skin. Paradoxically she felt as though she had everything in the world to

learn, yet knew all there was to know. She moulded her
body to his and parted her lips to the dart of his tongue.
Nasturtium, looking affronted, jumped up on the counter
and butted her head hard into Niall's ribs.

Taken by surprise, Niall raised his head just as
Nasturtium dug her claws into his sweater and stretched
lazily. He glowered at the cat. 'Did I say you weren't much
good as a chaperon?' he growled. 'I take it all back.'

Joss gave a shaky laugh. 'I think we must have ruined
the rest of the almond cookies, as well.'

'To say nothing of my equanimity.'

Niall's eyes were pools of blue, fiercely alive. 'Who
jumped on who?' Joss asked.

He ran his fingers around his collar; she could see the
pulse pounding at the base of his throat and wondered if
hers was doing the same. 'We could debate it,' he said. 'Or
we could blame it on the cat. What time did you say your
roommate gets home?'

Joss wanted him to kiss her again. She would swear
Niall had been shaken by his passionate response to her,
and she did not know how else to attack his reticence or
weaken his defences. Sex was not a weapon she would
have chosen had there been unlimited time. But always, at
the back of her mind, hovered the thought of Sunday. She
said truthfully, 'Magda doesn't get home until two on
Fridays and Saturdays. She sings in a club, you see, so her
hours are different from mine.'

Niall was frowning. 'Did you say her name was Magda?
What's her last name?'

'Trevanian. She sings in the Coq d'Or.'

'Will you be seeing her tonight?' he rapped. 'Or
tomorrow?'

Puzzled, Joss said, 'I probably won't see her now until
Monday . . . we almost never connect at week-
ends because she spends the days with her fiancé.
Why?'

Niall gave his head a little shake. 'The name seems

familiar, that's all. Joss, I should be going.'

The man so officiously looking at his watch did not seem like the man who had kissed her so hungrily a few moments ago. Unable to disguise a crushing disappointment, Joss faltered, 'Already?'

'It's late.'

'Is there something wrong?'

He must have seen the distress in her face. 'There's nothing wrong. But I mustn't kiss you like that again or we'll end up making love on the floor among the almond cookies.'

Even though she knew he had not really answered her question, she valiantly tried to match his tone. 'With Nasturtium watching every move.'

'You know what they say—three's a crowd.'

Joss trailed after him into the living-room and watched him take his coat off the hanger. She felt tired and confused, not nearly as sure of her ability to alter the events of Sunday as she had been a few moments ago. 'So I haven't done anything to offend you?' she burst out.

He turned to face her. 'On the contrary,' he said slowly. 'Everything about you delights me. Which is, of course, part of the problem. What time will I pick you up tomorrow, Joss?'

'Any time after nine.'

'One minute past.'

'So you do want to spend the day with me?'

'Are you seriously doubting that?'

'I don't know what I think any more,' she said with unhappy truth.

'We'll have a good day, Joss—a day to remember.' He leaned forward and kissed her briefly on the lips. 'Sleep well.'

The door latched behind him. Joss turned the key in the lock then leaned her back against the door. The room looked very empty without him. Of what use were memories, she thought painfully, when what she wanted was the real man?

CHAPTER FOUR

JOSS woke early the next morning with all her optimism renewed. She still had Saturday and Sunday, two more days of Niall's company; remembering that explosive kiss by the kitchen counter, she could not believe he would simply get on a plane and disappear. She sang in the shower, dressed in her prettiest flowered skirt and her newest sandals, and purposely chose a low-necked knitted top to go with the skirt. She put her swimsuit, sweater and running sneakers into a canvas bag, and was down on the pavement waiting when Niall pulled up at two minutes to nine.

He reached across and opened the passenger door. 'You're early,' he said. She smiled at him, a smile as bright as the morning sunshine, and leaned over to throw her bag on the back seat. He added in a stifled voice, 'What are you trying to do to me, Joss?'

She glanced at him in surprise, realised that she had presented him with an unobstructed view of her cleavage, and turned scarlet. She sat down hurriedly. 'I've got a shirt that buttons to the collar with long sleeves,' she babbled. 'I could go and change.'

'Please don't,' he said. 'I like the view.'

That she had chosen the low neckline on purpose made matters worse. Joss did up her seat-belt and said, 'This is a nice car. Is it yours?'

'Rented. Aren't you going to kiss me good morning?'

She had recovered a little of her poise. 'Do you think we should? Nasturtium isn't here.'

'Let's risk it.'

His lips were warm and made demands Joss was only

too ready to respond to. She murmured against his mouth, 'At lunch time you could kiss me good afternoon. If you want to.'

'Seems a long time to wait. How about every hour on the hour?'

'Better and better.' The sunlight seemed to be coming from within her, enveloping her in its brilliance. Joss said impulsively, 'At this precise moment I am completely and absolutely happy.'

'Oh, God, Joss,' Niall said helplessly.

She had never seen such a combination of naked longing and frustration in a man's face before. 'Shouldn't I have said that?'

'You took me aback, that's all. I'm happy to be with you, too.'

But behind his smile, fleetingly, was a shadow that no smile could have erased, the shadow of an unhappiness deeper than words. Joss saw it and then it was gone, and she was left to wonder if she had imagined it. Feeling as though in a few short seconds she had run the gamut from joy to pain, she said prosaically, 'Where are we going?' and then wondered if he would see her question as a *double entendre*.

Apparently he did not. 'To the country.'

'I haven't been outside the city since I came here. Show me a cow and I'll probably embrace it.'

'Just as long as it isn't a bull.'

'I do know the difference,' Joss said, glancing at him through her lashes. 'I've known it ever since my brother Jake watched a movie about rodeos and tried to go for a ride on my dad's Holstein bull . . . I was about five at the time. The bull, needless to say, was not happy. Neither was Jake when my dad had finished with him.'

As they drove north on Yonge Street she chattered on about the farm. But when they pulled up at a traffic light by a fashionable dress shop, she exclaimed, 'Drive on quickly—that's exactly the raincoat I'd like to own. The only thing wrong with it is the price.'

Obligingly the light changed to green. 'That shiny blue one?' Niall asked.

'Mmm . . . two hundred and twenty dollars. I priced them downtown.'

'You'd look nice in it.'

'I know I would.' Joss sighed. 'You know, that's another reason against medical school. I'm awfully tired of scrimping and saving. I'd like to buy that raincoat with a jazzy umbrella to go with it and knee-high boots. I'd like to own six pairs of Italian shoes, all different colours, and at least two pairs of leather boots . . . if I go to med school I'll be lucky if I can afford a pair of socks.'

'But those are kind of transitory things, aren't they?'

'The first time I met you you were wearing a very expensive suit.'

'That's true—so I suppose it's easy for me to say clothes aren't important.' Niall glanced over at her. 'They're not, though, Joss. It's where they carry you that's far more important.'

'OK. But I'd also like to help my brother Gilbert with his new business and buy my mum and dad a VCR.'

'Perhaps by going to medical school you'll be giving them something they really want . . . money isn't always the most meaningful gift. Your parents sound like the kind of people who'd be proud to have a doctor in the family. And I know you're not interested in it for the money.'

Joss looked at him thoughtfully; everything he had said made sense. 'So did you work as hard as you did for the money?'

'Power, more likely. Ambition. Although money went along with it, of course. It's a rat race, Joss, believe me.'

'What will you do next?'

His hands tightened on the wheel. 'I don't know. I

haven't given it a lot of thought.'

'You have to get out of the city in order to think,' she said darkly.

He laughed. 'So you'll be brainstorming among the bulls, will you?'

'I haven't got long to make up my mind. A week at the most.'

Niall gave her a heart-warming smile. 'You'll do the right thing, Joss, I know you will. You're a good person.'

'You will, too,' she said slowly. 'It will be more difficult for you, somehow—although I don't know why I'm saying that.'

'My choices are much narrower,' he said with sudden savage emphasis. 'That's why. Let's not talk about it, Joss. I want to enjoy the day with you.'

The words were out before she had time to think. 'Are you in trouble with the law?'

'God, no!'

'That's one way of having your choices narrowed.'

'Joss, dear, I am neither a Hell's Angel nor a Mafioso—scout's honour. Tell me more about your brother Gilbert and your two sisters.'

As they drove north across the flat countryside she complied. An hour later they left the main road for a side road. The industrial sites had been left behind; the land was hilly, with groves of trees clustered in the valleys; the first farmhouse appeared. Niall said, 'There's a cow. Want to give it a hug?'

'It's a she and that's an electric fence . . . I think I can restrain myself. Oh, Niall, this is wonderful! It's the *country*—you don't know how much I've missed it.'

'We'll stop in a while and go for a walk.'

They meandered on, taking side roads at random until they came to a narrow dirt road that followed a river. Niall parked the car in the shade of an oak tree. 'Want to walk? We could take our swimsuits.'

The road was roofed by the spreading limbs of old elms, while the river whispered to itself, its brown waters overhung by willows. A kingfisher preened on a sunlit branch. The air smelled of river water and ferns and the damp carpet of leaves from many autumns. When Niall took Joss's hand she knew again the clarity of perfect happiness.

Round the first corner they came to the driveway of an old farm set well back from the road. Two little girls were riding their bicycles up and down the driveway; a third, younger, was wrestling red-faced with a yellow skipping rope that had entangled itself in the spokes of her tricycle. She was plainly on the verge of bursting into tears.

Niall said calmly, 'I can get that out for you if you like.'

She eyed him distrustfully, like a puppy about to bolt. 'It's stuck,' she said, and jammed her thumb in her mouth.

Niall knelt down beside the tricycle, which was battered enough to have belonged to each of the older girls. 'You did a job on it, didn't you?' he said, his long fingers setting to work on a knot. 'My name's Niall. What's yours?' With a grunt of satisfaction he loosened the first knot.

The child removed her thumb, said, 'Kimberley Dawn *Rut*ledge,' and replaced it. She had a mop of brown curls and pugnacious little features. Joss had the feeling that Kimberley Dawn had to fight for what she wanted; certainly her two sisters were paying no attention to her predicament.

Patiently Niall worked away, chatting to the child as he did so. She crept closer, until the two brown heads were very close together, both bent over the front wheel of the tricycle. Joss watched with a lump in her throat, for this was a side to Niall she had not seen before. He spoke to the child without condescension, yet with quiet

kindness; for a crazy moment she found herself
fantasising that Kimberley Dawn was their own child,
hers and Niall's. She would like to have Niall's child,
she thought blankly. That, too, felt right.

Niall pulled the last few inches of the skipping rope
free of the wheel. 'There you go,' he said.

'Lotsa knots in it,' said Kimberley Dawn.

'Want me to take them out?'

'Yup.'

It took him about five minutes. But finally he handed
the rope back to the child. 'That's better.'

She smiled for the first time, a smile that brought
radiance to her grubby face. Opening her palm, she
disclosed a small, black rock. 'I found this,' she said
solemnly. 'You can have it.'

'Thank you,' Niall said with equal solemnity, and
took the rock. 'Goodbye, Kimberley Dawn.'

'Bye.' She threw the rope on the ground, jumping on
the tricycle and pedalled furiously up the driveway after
her two sisters. For a moment Niall stood watching her,
something so forbidding in the set of his profile that
Joss looked away; his thoughts, whatever they were,
were intensely private. She picked up the skipping rope,
wound it in a neat coil, and put it back on the ground.
'You did a good job,' she said easily.

'Cute kid.' He suddenly hunched his shoulders. 'Let's
find somewhere to swim.'

Within ten minutes they came to a bend in the river
where a bank of shale edged a deep pool. A robin was
singing in the thicket; the sun bronzed the water.
'Perfect,' said Joss. 'I can get changed in those bushes.'

'You go first.'

She scrambled into the ditch, scratching her bare legs
on the alders. Once she was hidden from view she took
off her clothes, adding more scratches to her anatomy.
Her swimsuit was an abbreviated one-piece, brilliantly
flowered. As she looked down at herself she wished

there were a few more flowers, for what had seemed sophisticated in the store now seemed merely brazen. She draped the towel strategically, put her clothes in her bag and inched her way out of the bushes on to the shale. Niall was watching her from the roadside. After she waved at him he disappeared into the alders.

Joss spread her towel on the smoothest part of the bank and sat down. Her surroundings, with their myriad shades of green and ever-shifting patterns of sun and shadow, were very peaceful, yet she felt absurdly self-conscious. She had always taken her body for granted, considering privately that her legs were too long and her breasts rather too full, certainly when compared to the willowy models who were so fashionable; but she had never worried about it overmuch. Now she was wondering what Niall would think of her, discovering that his opinion mattered quite inordinately.

Branches rustled behin her, and she heard footsteps on the shale. She looked round. Niall's body was tanned and rangy, his chest a tangle of dark hair, his legs long and muscular. Very muscular for someone who claimed to be out of shape, she thought doubtfully. Then she saw the narrow red scar that curved around his ribs and forgot her suspicions. She said sharply, 'What happened there?'

He bent to spread out his towel and said, his back to her, 'I was involved in an accident. They had to operate.'

So was the accident a clue to all his silences? she wondered, and knew she lacked the courage to ask. Turning, Niall reached out a hand to her. Slowly she stood up. Their hands still linked, he let his eyes wander over her, and there was in them such a mingling of pleasure and desire that unconsciously Joss stood taller. He said huskily, 'I can't get over how beautiful you are. And yet I knew you would be.' He kissed the tip of her nose. 'Time for a swim—the water had better be cold.'

The water was wonderfully refreshing. They swam quietly, because the serenity of the woodland pool somehow precluded noisy horseplay, and then walked back up on the bank. Joss lay back on her towel. 'Wonderful,' she said lazily. 'Who needs shiny raincoats?'

'You look much nicer as you are.'

Niall had spread his towel next to hers and was leaning on one elbow, watching her. She said, 'Your eyes are the colour of the sky.'

'Yours are the same colour as the river. Mud-brown,' he teased. But then he added, 'Joss . . . beautiful Joss,' and leaned over to kiss her.

It was a kiss suffused with sunlight and the songs of birds, as gentle and deep as the river; it lasted for a long time. His chest was touching her wet swimsuit. She stroked the smooth, wet planes of his back and knew that in a place many miles from the orchard she had come home.

He covered her with his body and kissed her again, more intensely, almost with desperation. With one hand he cupped her breast; her legs were tangled with his so that she felt against her thigh the hardness that was the essence of his desire. She kissed him back, trying to tell him with her lips and the surrendering curve of her body that he was the only man in the world for her. But then, so suddenly that she was shocked, Niall lifted himself off, his face only inches from hers, his rapid breathing stirring her hair. 'We've got to stop,' he said hoarsely. 'I don't want to, but we must.'

She felt bereft. But more important than her own feelings was the torment in his eyes, a mixture of pain and terrible longing that caught at her throat. Wanting to make him smile, she moved that thigh very slightly and said, 'I know you don't want to stop.'

Some of the tension relaxed in his face. 'No secrets,

huh? Joss, I want to make love to you, I don't have to
tell you that. But I'm leaving tomorrow and I can't have
a one-day fling with you. Whatever it is that's between
us isn't casual—at least not for me.'

She answered his unspoken question. 'Nor is it for
me.'

She was not altogether unhappy that he had pulled
away. Never having met the right man before, she had
never made love before, either, and when she and Niall
did make love she wanted them both to feel right about
it. She was increasingly sure that they would make love,
for mingled with the hunger in his eyes there had been
tenderness. Their relationship, which had begun with so
much conflict, had become far more intimate today;
and she cherished Niall's honesty with her. By
tomorrow, she thought confidently, she would
understand the source of his reticence.

She said, smiling, 'I'm hungry. For food.'

'As well as . . .?'

'As well as. Sublimation, you call it.'

'I could do with a good dollop of sublimation right
now.' Niall traced her cheekbone with one finger. 'So
you figure a hamburger will be an adequate
distraction?'

'Along with a chocolate fudge sundae with whipped
cream and nuts.'

'You left out the french fries.'

Joss loved to see him laugh, for it always made him
look years younger. 'And the ketchup,' she said.

His fingertip had moved to the curve of her eyelid. He
peered suspiciously at her eyes. 'Those lashes weren't a
dollar forty-nine at the drugstore. They're the real
McCoy.'

She chuckled. 'They always were. I put mascara on to
make them longer.'

'The better to trip me with.'

She said soulfully, 'A million-dollar industry just so

I'll catch myself a man.'

'You'd have tripped me up without the mascara, Joss.' His smile faded. He hugged her to his chest with all his strength, his face buried in her damp hair, and muttered, 'I wish to God I'd met you five years ago.'

She would have been sixteen five years ago. But she did not remind him of this. Instead she held him as hard as she could, feeling anxiety drive away her confidence, knotting itself within her as tightly as the tangles in Kimberley Dawn's skipping rope. Something was wrong, horribly wrong; she had known that from the beginning. She had to find out what it was. 'Niall,' she said, her voice smothered against his chest, 'can't you tell me what's the trouble? No matter what it is, I'll do my best to understand.'

'I can't, Joss—it's too late. And it wouldn't be fair.'

'What you're doing now hardly seems fair.'

He raised his head. 'I warned you yesterday that this is the way it would be.'

'I didn't realise it would be so difficult.'

He levered himself off her and tweaked her hair; but his smile did not reach his eyes. 'It's as difficult as we make it,' he said dismissively, getting to his feet and pulling her up to face him. 'Let's go find that chocolate fudge sundae.'

She met his gaze. 'I'll never forget this place,' she said with total sincerity.

He flinched. *'Don't*, Joss.'

'Will you?' she persisted ruthlessly.

For a brief moment all his anger showed. 'You don't have to ask that question—you know the answer already.'

'I wanted to hear you say it.'

'No, I won't forget this place! No, I won't forget you. Are you satisfied?'

'This is a crazy game we're playing,' Joss said in a small voice. 'I keep breaking the rules because I don't understand why you won't make love to me.'

'I explained that to you.'

'I think you're afraid to!'

'I told you the truth, I swear.' His smile was wintry. 'You know as well as I do the times we live in . . . I am not carrying any unmentionable communicable diseases, and I've all the appetites of a normal man. Tomorrow I may well kick myself for being so goddamned noble . . . but that's the way I want to play it.'

His will was like a steel door, totally impenetrable. Again Joss wondered if she would be able to find the key in the short time she had, and felt a flicker of terror. She fought it down, for she was not one to admit defeat easily. 'I'll get changed,' she said. 'Then we'll go in search of that sundae.'

'Thanks, Joss,' Niall said, making no attempt to camouflage his relief.

They walked back along the river road almost in silence; the three little girls were nowhere to be seen. But when they were driving to the nearest town in search of a restaurant they passed a dairy farm where a mixed herd of Holsteins and Guernseys were grazing in a field that bordered on the road. Without being asked, Niall pulled over. Joss got out and walked over to the fence, a newly painted white-board fence that her father could not have afforded. Three or four cows ambled over to investigate, blowing at her shirt-front through grass-stained nostrils and suffering her to scratch their bony foreheads. 'This is a really good herd,' she said to Niall, and began explaining some of the technicalities of milk production. The shadow that had lain across her spirits since the embrace on the riverbank vanished, particularly when Niall asked some purposely dim-witted questions, and they were in perfect accord when they got back in the car. They ate in a country inn beside the river and afterwards wandered hand in hand through some ornamental gardens on the outskirts of the town. As they walked under an archway overhung with frothy, cream-coloured roses, Joss inhaled with delight. 'They must be an old-fashioned variety; the newer ones never seem to smell, do they?'

Niall cupped a blossom in his hand. 'I've always had a yen to grow roses,' he said absently.

'Why don't you, then? It would be one way to quit the rat race.'

'A surefire way, I should think.' He suddenly grasped her shoulder so tightly that she almost cried out with pain, and muttered, 'When I'm with you, I forget . . .'

Joss stood very still; the sunlight gleamed in his thick dark hair. 'Forget what, Niall?'

He dropped his forehead to her shoulder. In a muffled voice he said, 'Hold on, Joss . . . just hold on.'

She put her arms around him, feeling the tension in his shoulders, hearing his rapid, shallow breathing. A rose brushed her elbow; an ant was crawling up the pink-tinged, velvety petal. She watched it absorbedly until she had conquered the urge to cry out, 'What's wrong, Niall? Tell me what's wrong!' Instead she said softly, rocking him in her arms, 'It's all right, I'm here . . . I won't let go,' and prayed that no one would disturb them.

No one did. Her arms were cramped by the time Niall raised his head. He said almost inaudibly, 'You comfort me, Joss.'

'Niall, please——'

He shook his head. 'Don't ask. For God's sake, don't ask.'

She could not possibly have persisted, for something tight-held in his face forbade it. She said gently, 'Maybe you need to grow some roses, Niall—it would give you the time to sort out whatever's wrong.'

He straightened to his full height, rubbing at the back of his neck, his eyes avoiding hers. 'Time is exactly what I need,' he said in an emotionless voice. 'Talking of

time, shouldn't we head back to the city? You have to
be at work at five.'

She did not want to go back to work, thought Joss, as
they strolled across the grass towards the car, Niall's
arm looped around her shoulders. What she wanted to
do was book a room in the nearest inn, take Niall to bed
with her and hold him in her arms. Maybe they would
make love. But her motives would be a simple matter of
desire . . .

She said nothing of this, and sat quietly on the drive
home, her hand resting on his knee; the physical contact
was a link between them all the more powerful for being
unacknowledged. Niall dropped her off at the
apartment, promising to meet her at the Red Lion
midway through her performance. She showered,
changed and took the subway to the hotel.

The bar was packed, the noise level the usual dull roar
for a Saturday night, the smokers much in evidence.
Feeling horribly out of place, Joss began to sing. She
did not want to be in the Red Lion singing songs she had
sung a hundred times before. She wanted to be with
Niall. Even when he arrived about quarter past seven
her mood did not much improve. His face was only one
among many; and, according to him, it would be his last
visit to the pub.

Nine o'clock came. She ran to the staff room,
changed into her most stylish dress, a tangerine linen
belted at the waist and worn with a pristine white jacket,
and hurried to the side door. Niall was waiting for her;
impetuously she threw her arms around him, burrowing
into his chest and creasing the linen.

'I was afraid you might not be here . . . oh, Niall, I've
got lipstick on your shirt.'

'I said I'd be here.'

'I know you did. But I keep thinking I'm going to
wake up and find out this had all been a dream.' She
fished in her bag for a tissue and scrubbed at his shirt,

frowning in concentration, her tongue between her teeth. 'There,' she said finally, 'that's better.'

Glancing up, she caught him looking at her with such concentrated emotion that she totally forgot whatever she had been about to say. He said flatly, 'Despite everything, I'll never be sorry we met, Joss. Never. You've taught me such a lot.'

'I *have*?'

'You're so real. You're rooted in sanity, in the kind of values I'd almost forgotten—if indeed I ever knew them.' Briefly he squeezed her hand. 'Thank you.'

His words had a finality that frightened Joss. Burying her fear, for there was still tomorrow, she mumbled, 'I was only myself.'

'Never say only.' He tucked her arm in his. 'I made a reservation at Scarlatti's.'

Scarlatti's was one of the most chic places to eat in Toronto; being on a budget, Joss had never been there. Glad that she had worn her tangerine dress, she said fliply, 'I should have put on more mascara.'

'Or your dollar-forty-nine lashes.'

Niall was wearing a tailored summerweight suit that enhanced his dark good looks; his arm felt substantial under her palm, a reality of flesh and blood that could not possibly disappear. 'Let's go!' she said brightly.

The ceiling of Scarlatti's main dining-room was made of glass, while a fountain surrounded by orchids splashed into a pool in the middle of the tiled floor. Potted plants in a profusion of colours climbed a spiral staircase against one wall, their petals glowing in the candlelight; fig trees garlanded with tiny lights branched to the rooftop. 'You've brought me to the country again, Niall,' Joss exclaimed, clasping her hands in childlike wonder.

'I thought you'd like it here.'

Again they had a corner table, alongside some magnificent bird of paradise plants, the flowers like exotic orange and purple butterflies. Joss sat quietly, letting all the colours sink into her consciousness. 'My sister Blanche would like this restaurant,' she said eventually. 'She's the gardener of the family; she lives in Vancouver. It seems a little crude to think of actually eating here.'

'Don't let the waiter hear you say that—he'd be insulted.'

Joss managed to eat quite a lot, however, because the preparation of the food matched the care that had been taken with the décor. Throughout the meal she and Niall avoided personal subjects by unspoken consent, discussing everything from movies to music, and politics to plays. Again Joss was happy, and it showed in the light in her eyes and the lilt in her laughter; Niall watched her, playing with his wineglass, his own face unusually contented.

It was midnight when they left Scarlatti's. The street seemed very bare after the lush interior of the restaurant; they strolled along arm in arm in no particular direction until they came to University Avenue, Joss's favourite street in the city. Along the boulevard little white lights twinkled on the trees, with the imposing buildings of the university on either side. 'You can hardly see the stars in the city,' said Joss. 'Maybe that's why so many places use those lights. We should go the museum tomorrow, Niall, it's not far from here—I love the dinosaur exhibit.'

'I'm leaving tomorrow, Joss—I told you that.'

'Not first thing in the morning,' she teased. 'You said we had two days, so I've got all kinds of plans for tomorrow.'

Niall had stopped on the pavement. He said evenly, 'I meant yesterday and today, Joss. My plane leaves early tomorrow morning.'

She gazed at him in consternation. 'You mean tonight is it? I won't see you tomorrow at all?'

Trying to joke, he said, 'It's already tomorrow. But you won't see me in the morning, no.'

She unlinked her sleeve from his and crossed her arms her her breast; she felt very cold. 'You're going to give me your address and your phone number, though, aren't you?'

'No, Joss. Don't you remember what I said? No further contact after this weekend.'

'But that was before we spent so much time together! Didn't you enjoy yourself today?'

'Of course I did. But——'

'Deny that you're attracted to me.'

'I can't deny that and be honest with you. Anyway, there'd be no sense in denying it—I made it fairly obvious down by the river, didn't I?'

Her heart was beating in sick, heavy thuds, as if she was fighting for her very life. 'It's more than sexual attraction, Niall—I'd swear it is. We're right together, you and I, in all ways. Not just sex.'

He said tightly, 'We didn't make love today—so how can we know that we're even right together as far as sex is concerned?'

'You're playing with words!' Another couple was approaching them on the pavement. Joss waited until they were past, then resumed in a furious whisper, 'I've never made love, but I would have today with you——'

'You've *never* made love?' Niall interrupted.

'I'm a throwback to the Victorian age—twenty-one-year-old virgin. And do you know why? Because I'd never met the right man. Until last Wednesday, that is.'

A spasm crossed his face. 'Don't, Joss—please don't!'

'It's true, every word.' She suddenly clasped his sleeve. 'Niall, you can tell me I'm crazy if you like—but I'm convinced you and I could fall in love very easily. And I don't mean just for a week or a month or even a year. I mean for a lifetime.'

His laugh grated on her nerves. 'People don't fall in love for a lifetime any more, Joss. Look at the statistics on the divorce rate.'

'Yes, they do. People like me. And people like you.'

Her eyes searched his face for the slightest sign of relenting and found none. She dropped his arm and said in a voice she scarcely recognised as her own, 'I'm not asking much, Niall. Only that you keep in touch in some small way. But please don't just vanish from my life.' In spite of herself her voice broke. 'I don't think I could bear that.'

Niall had shoved his hands in his pockets. Deep lines scored his cheeks. Cutting off each word, he said, 'That was the agreement.'

'Don't talk to me about agreements!' Joss cried wildly. 'Was it in the agreement that you kiss me the way you did beside the river? Or laugh with me all day? Or look at me with love—yes, love, dammit!—when you met me at the hotel this evening? Agreements are for lawyers and business executives, Niall—not for living, breathing people like you and me that have blood in their veins and care about each other!'

'This had gone far enough, Joss,' he snarled. 'Come on, I'm going to take you home.'

She struck away his hand. 'You haven't answered my questions.'

'Nor do I intend to.'

She spread her hands in utter helplessness. 'What do I have to do to get through to you?'

'You can't.'

The two words fell like stones into the depths of her heart. 'You mean that, don't you?' Joss whispered.

'Yes.'

'You've never even told me your name.' She pressed her palms to her cheeks, terrified that she was going to wep. 'Can't you at least tell me why?'

He held her impaled in the bitter blue of his eyes and

said loudly, 'I lied when I told you I wasn't married. I am married, Joss—and I'll never leave my wife.'

For a split second Joss thought he was telling the truth. Then she said evenly, 'I don't believe you. I'd know if you had a wife.'

'Feminine intuition?' he sneered.

'I'd know.' She made one last attempt. 'Niall, please just give me your name and where you're from. I won't bother you or chase you, I promise—but at least I'll know.'

'No, Joss.'

'Just your name!' she begged.

'No!'

The cruellest word in the language. 'I can't believe you're doing this to me.'

'You knew all along that I would—you just chose to avoid the truth.'

Joss took a deep, shuddering breath. 'Then it's over, isn't it?' she said in a dead voice. 'Over before it's begun.' Briefly she closed her eyes, willing herself not to cry. When she opened them they were brilliant with unshed tears. 'I suppose all that's left is to thank you for the two happiest days of my life. And to wish you well, Niall.'

She could not force herself to say goodbye. With infinite relief she saw a cruising cab come along the boulevard towards them. She stepped off the pavement, waving her arm, and saw the cab veer her way. It pulled up beside her. She opened the door, then looked back over her shoulder. Niall was standing on the pavement in a pose she now recognised as characteristic of him: shoulders hunched, hands thrust in his pockets. She said in utter despair, 'We'll regret this for the rest of our lives, Niall,' and saw him take a step backwards, as though physically rejecting her words. She climbed in the cab, slammed the door, and gave her address in a choked voice. Then she leaned back in the seat and closed her eyes so she would not risk seeing him again. The blackness under her lids was the only refuge she had; she hugged her body with her arms and longed for the familiar surroundings of the apartment.

Magda was not home, would not be home for another hour. Nasturtium opened one eye, yawned, and shut it again. Joss kicked off her shoes at the door and prowled around the apartment, picking things up and putting them down again, all her movements as jerky and uncoordinated as a very small child's. Her throat was tight and her eyes burning, yet she was afraid to give in to tears for fear they might never stop. There was another reason. Niall knew her address. Perhaps, just perhaps, he would change his mind and follow her here and take her in his arms, and this unbearable, waking nightmare would be over.

But, although the minutes crept around the old-fashioned clock on the shelf, no one knocked on the door. One-twenty, one-thirty, one-forty . . . Magda would be home shortly after two. Joss knew she could not face Magda's bright-eyed curiosity at this time of the morning, so she went into her room, closed the door, undressed and got into bed. She was cold, her fingers as clammy as those of the dead. She lay very still, for if she moved too fast she might shatter into pieces, and stared up at the ceiling.

Some time later a key turned in the lock and Joss heard Magda speak to Nasturtium, who did not reply. For a few minutes Magda crept around the apartment, her exaggeratedly quiet movements striking on Joss's over-exposed nerves like hammer blows. Then the narrow line of light under Joss's door disappeared and Magda's bedroom door closed softly. The darkness was absolute.

Niall would not come now; it was too late. Joss clenched her teeth and felt the first tears seep from the corners of her eyes.

CHAPTER FIVE

THE digital clock on the dresser beside the bed said eleven minutes past ten. Joss rubbed her eyes, which were swollen from weeping, and looked again. The right-hand number had changed. Twelve minutes past ten. She had the feeling that a noise had woken her, dragging her upwards from a sodden sleep in which she had been dreaming. Or had the noise been part of her dream?

Twelve minutes past ten. Would Niall have left Toronto by now? She was quite sure that, for him, early in the morning would be before ten o'clock, and knew at the same time that she would not leave the apartment before noon, just in case he phoned. He knew Magda's last name; he could find the number in the book. She had meant to wake up early to be alert for the sound of the phone . . . she had no idea what time she had fallen asleep, although she remembered that the dawn light had been edging its way between the curtains.

She closed her eyes and tried to remember the beach near the farm, with the rock that was shaped like a charging buffalo, the curling lace of the waves, and the hissing of the eel grass in the onshore winds. But all she could see was the passionate hunger in Niall's blue eyes and all she could hear was his voice repudiating her, denying her the knowledge of even his name.

She could not bear her own thoughts. Pulling on her housecoat, Joss went out into the living-room. There was a note propped against the bowl of overripe bananas on the bamboo table, its gist that Magda had already left to spend the day with Charlie and would be home late tonight. So that was the noise that had awoken her.

Reading the note, Joss discovered that she now craved company, and company other than her own. She poured some of the very black coffee left in Magda's filter machine and looked at the clock on the shelf. Ten-seventeen. For the first Sunday that summer she wished it was a weekday so that she could go to work at the bookshop and then sing at the Red Lion. Even Mr Jodrey's company looked good today, she thought wretchedly. She picked up Saturday's newspaper and tried to read.

The telephone did not ring; not that Joss had really expected that it would. At noon she forced herself to eat something, then put on her jeans and went out. The sky had clouded over and there was a brisk wind, weather that she much preferred to the oppressive August heat. She began to walk and, whether consciously or unconsciously, her steps retraced all the places she had been with Niall: the newspaper stand where she had screamed his name in the rain; the crowded piers at the Harbourfront; the mellow brick facade of Scarlatti's; the wide boulevard of University Avenue. It was almost as thought she hoped to conjure him up. He would appear among the Sunday afternoon strollers and take her arm, smiling at her with his blue eyes, and her world would be back on its axis.

She ate a salad at one of the pavement cafés, down by the water, trudged home, and fell asleep on the chesterfield cocooned in the pages of Saturday's paper, Nasturtium curled in the crook of her knees. At eight-thirty the telephone rang.

Joss leaped off the chesterfield. Nasturtium tumbled to the floor, her tail lashing with indignation; two pages of the entertainment section drifted down on top of her. Joss grabbed the receiver and croaked, *'Niall?'*

'Oh, dear, have I got the wrong number? I was sure I

dialled correctly, the trouble is there are so many numbers to remember. I'm terribly sorry to have bothered you.'

'Mum? It's OK, it's me, Joss.'

'Darling! You sound dreadful. Have you got a cold?'

Joss raked her fingers through her hair. 'No. I was asleep.'

'Why don't I call back later?'

'No, that's all right. How are you? And how's Dad?'

'Just fine.' Ellie MacDougall liked to talk, and the fact that a computer was charging her so much per minute for the privilege never discouraged her. She rambled on with assorted family news, which gave Joss the time to collect her wits. In the middle of a story about Gilbert's latest girlfriend Ellie suddenly said, 'Are you sure you're all right, Joss? You sound funny. Not quite all there.'

It was a good description as any of Joss's emotional state. Wishing with all her heart that she could be transposed to the comfortable old couch in the kitchen of the farmhouse, she blurted, 'Mum, I met the right man—the one you always said I'd meet.'

Ellie prided herself on her liberated views. 'You mean he's there with you now—in bed? In that case, I *will* call back.'

'No, Mum, he's not!' Joss tried to steady her voice. 'I wish he were.'

'Begin at the beginning, dear. You're not making any sense.'

So Joss did, and found it a great relief to be able to speak about Niall openly. Ellie might talk a lot, but she also had the rarer capacity for being a good listener; putting in the occasional question, she heard her daughter's story from beginning to end. 'Very mysterious,' was her first comment. 'The most logical explanation is that he really is married.'

'If he is, then everything he said and did was a lie. I

can't believe that. I think he told me he was married just to get me off his back.'

'Maybe he's gay.'

'No, Mum.'

'Perhaps he's a famous politician who can't afford any romantic liaisons.'

'He told me he was a business executive. And if he was famous I'd have recognised him.'

'An undercover agent for narcotics or gunrunning. A spy. A member of the CIA. There could be all kinds of reasons why he didn't want to give you his name.'

'You've been reading too many of Gilbert's paperbacks.'

'Well, darling, if he was as truthful and as attracted to you as you say, there has to be a reason for his behaviour, doesn't there?'

Ellie's logic could never be disputed. 'Yes,' Joss said miserably. 'Maybe the simplest explanation is the real one. He really was married, and I was a fool to be taken in by him.'

'If he was unscrupulous enough to lie about his marital status, then he wouldn't have any trouble making up a false name. Besides which he would certainly have taken you to bed. Because you were, I gather, willing.'

'He felt so *right*,' Joss said in a whisper.

'Oh, dear. Then I really don't know what to say. Maybe he'll think it over and write to you.'

'Maybe the moon is made of green cheese.'

'*That* would please the dairy industry,' said Ellie. 'Darling, I wish you were nearer, I'm worried about you.'

'It's all so painful right now,' Joss gulped. 'It only happened yesterday. Surely in time I'll forget about him, or else decide he really wasn't the right man. Won't I?'

'The women in our family have a reputation for longevity in their love affairs,' Ellie said dishearteningly.

'Apart from my grandmother.'

'The exception who proves the rule. You'll be home in about three weeks, won't you, Joss?'

Home . . . Joss's throat closed in sudden loning. She swallowed hard and said, 'It depends what I do. I was offered a job at the research lab in Halifax, Mum, starting in October.'

'But what about medical school?' Ellie said in dismay.

'Medical school costs money.'

'But look how much you earn once you're finished. Why, Dr Hennigar just last week had a swimming pool and tennis courts built at his place. The pool was kidney-shaped. Rather bad taste, I thought.'

'I wouldn't earn a penny for six years, though.'

'Darling, you're only twenty-one. And medical school wouldn't give you much time to brood over this man.'

'Physician, heal thyself?' Joss said drily.

'You've got to admit that Dr Jocelyn MacDougall has a certain ring to it.'

Joss said curiously, 'You really want me to be a doctor, don't you?'

'You'd be underselling yourself to settle for a job in a lab. Both your father and I think you have a great deal to offer in a medical career.'

'Oh.' Joss swallowed again, touched. 'Well, I have about three days to decide, because I have to send my final deposit soon. Mum, this phone call is going to cost the entire month's milk bill.'

'Your father says the same thing every time I pick up the phone. Joss dear, take care of yourself. And call any time, you know I'm always here. We love you.'

'I love you, too. Thanks, Mum.' And Joss rang off.

Perhaps because she had been able to share her burden, she slept better that night. But Monday dragged by, for her whole psyche felt fractured. Either Niall was the man of integrity she had taken him for, in which case she was left with the riddle of his departure; or else he had deceived her from start to finish, which meant she could no longer trust her own judgement. Tired and heavy-eyed, Joss busied herself unpacking new shipments at the bookshop and arranging the books on the shelves; she had to force herself to enter the Red Lion at five o'clock, for a demon of hope had persuaded her that by some miracle Niall would be there waiting for her. He was not, of course. But the pub was full of memories, and she avoided every one of Cleo Laine's songs.

She got back to the apartment at nine-thirty, and stopped in the doorway in surprise. 'Magda! What are you doing home?'

Magda and Nasturtium were artistically arranged on the chesterfield, Madga in a long housecoat of unrelieved black that illuminated the creamy pallor of her skin. 'Stomach 'flu,' she said. 'Keep your distance.'

'Can I get you anything?'

'Nothing that bears any relationship to food.' Magda frowned at her friend. 'Looks to me as though you could be getting it too, Joss. You don't look so hot.'

Joss sat down heavily in the nearest chair, first removing Magda's knitting and a slithery pile of magazines. 'I wish all I had was stomach 'flu.'

Joss was not a complainer. Magda sat up a little straighter. 'I knew something was wrong.'

It seemed easier to talk about Niall the second time round. 'I met a man in the bar last Wednesday night,' Joss began.

'About time,' Magda announced. 'You've been living like a nun all summer.' She scratched Nasturtium between the ears. 'What did he look like?'

'Tall, dark hair, blue eyes,' said Joss, thinking even as she spoke what an inadequate description of Niall that was. Any number of men were tall and dark with

blue eyes. 'Very good-looking,' she added, and went on
with the story. But when she reached Thursday night,
the night Niall had drunk so much, Magda, who had
been listening intently, interrupted, 'Did he give his
name?'

'Only his first name. Niall. Without an e.'

'Not his last name?'

'He never did tell me that.'

'Was he thin and kind of intense with a sprinkling of
grey hair over his ears and an old-fashioned watch?'
Magda asked with growing excitement. 'It looked
expensive.'

'He was thin, yes. His watch was Swiss, with Roman
numerals and a leather strap, Joss said dazedly.

'Right on. And his eyes were the same colour as
Charlie's car.'

Charlie's car was a very old Ford painted a lurid
shade of azure. 'His eyes were a much nicer blue than
Charlie's car,' Joss protested. 'They seemed to see right
through you. But Magda, how do you know him?'

'He was at the club last Tuesday night. I was talking
to him in one of my breaks.' Magda was encouraged to
be friendly with the patrons, unlike Joss. Now Magda
widened her eyes. 'No wonder you're depressed.'

'What do you mean?' Joss said slowly. 'I haven't told
you what happened yet.'

'Goodness, Joss, it's terribly sad! He's so young.'

Wondering if perhaps Magda had a fever, Joss said,
'Are you delirious or something? I don't have any idea
what you're talking about!'

'You mean he didn't tell you?'

'Tell me *what?*'

'That he's dying,' Magda said.

The clock ticked on the shelf. Nasturtium whimpered
in her sleep, her whiskers twitching. *'Dying?'* Joss
repeated blankly.

'Yes. Cancer, he said. The doctors have given him less

than a year.'

Aghast, Joss stared at her roommate, and the pieces of evidence fell into place in her brain one by one. Niall's leanness. Her initial impression of exhaustion. The so-called stitch he had taken when they were dancing. The curving red scar round his ribs. Even his peculiar reaction when she had mentioned the name of her roommate.

Strangely enough, in the midst of encroaching horror her first reaction was one of relief. Niall was the man of intergrity she had thought him to be. She understood his reticence now, his refusal to give a last name that would allow her to trace him. She even understood his reaction to the story of Jake's dying wife. Nor had he lied to her: simply kept to himself an appalling secret. But then horror swamped that tiny pocket of reason and she pressed her hands to her face.

'Joss, don't look like that! You're scaring me.'

Though a pain that was actually physical, Joss managed to focus on Magda's distraught face. 'Why did he tell *you*?' she cried. 'He didn't tell me.'

'Because he knew he was never going to see me again,' Magda said forcefully. 'You look as though you're going to fall apart, Joss—go to the cupboard to the left of the sink right now and pour yourself a brandy. Go along.'

Lacking the will to resist, Joss did as she was told. Some of the brandy slopped on the counter because her hands were shaking so badly that the neck of the bottle rattled against the glass. She carried the glass back into the living-room and sat down again.

'Now drink it,' Magda ordered.

Obediently Joss swallowd a large mouthful of the brandy. It tasted as she had always imagined her father's paint stripper would taste, but it left a warm glow in the vicinity of her stomach. She said, and her voice was not overly friendly, 'Tell me exactly how you met him.'

'He came to the club late last Tuesday night. He was
stone-cold sober and he only ordered one drink the
whole time he was there. I couldn't figure out why he'd
come—he seemed scarcely aware of his surroundings
and he sure wasn't having a good time. But his eyes
reminded me of Charlie's car and he was very good-
looking, you've got to admit that—so in my break I sat
down at his table and asked him what was wrong. He
looked at me and said, "I'll never see you again in my
life, will I?" So I said, "Not unless you come back to
this club, you won't." "I won't do that," he said. "If I
don't tell someone soon, I'll go crazy." Then he went
on in the kind of voice you'd use to order another drink,
"I had the prognosis confirmed today. Less than a year
to live. A year from now the world will still be merrily
spinning on its axis, but I won't be here to see it." '

Magda paused, her head to one side. 'We get a lot of
weirdos in the club. But I knew right away this was for
real. This guy meant every word he'd said. So I asked
him if he had cancer and he said yes, and then I asked if
he had any family. "A father I don't get along with,"
he said. "That's all. Just as well I never took the time to
get married and have a couple of kids, isn't it? At least I
get to face this thing on my own, with no one hanging
on my coat-tails."

'I didn't like that attitude very much, so I said,
"Families help out when you're ill." He laughed—a
horrible laugh, like glass cracking—and said, "You
couldn't be more wrong. I learned as a kid that each of
us is alone. Separate. Disconnected. We live alone and
we die alone." Then he finished his drink and said, "If I
thought I'd ever see you again, I'd never have told you
this. Thanks for listening."

'By then my break was over, and he left before the
next one. On purpose, I'm sure—he didn't even look at
me when he went out.'

Joss said quietly, 'I met him the very next night.'

'You're acting as though you fell head over heels in love with him,' Magda said astringently.

'I did. And I'm almost sure it was mutual.'

'Oh, lord,' said Magda. 'What did you do that for?'

'I didn't know he was ill—not that it would have made any difference.'

'You'd better tell me the whole story.'

Madga interrupted rather more than Ellie had, and Joss was more loquacious, not being under the constraints of long-distance; but eventually she finished her story. 'Did you know what my very last remark was?' she said miserably. ' "We'll regret this for the rest of our lives" ' . . . how could I have said that, Magda?'

'You didn't know.'

'He should have told me!'

'I can understand why he didn't.'

Joss had been looking for an ally. She gave her friend a suspicious stare. 'So tell me, if you're so smart.'

'Let's assume he fell in love with you—it sure sounds as though he did. What's he got to offer you, Joss? Marriage? That's a laugh! He'd be ill the whole time you were married and then you'd be a widow in less than a year. I think he did the right thing by pulling a disappearing act. In fact, I don't think he should even have got involved to the extent he did. Look at you—you're a wreck!'

'You're both wrong,' Joss said aggressively. 'If he'd told me, at least we could have been together. That's what life's all about. Sharing. Helping each other out. Being there.' She glared at Magda. 'If you go around looking for guarantees, you'll be safe, sure—but you won't have much of a life.'

'So he was noble but screwed up?'

'He was wrong,' Joss repeated stubbornly.

Magda gave Joss a long, considering look. 'Is there any way you can trace him?'

Joss hadn't even considered looking for Niall, all her thought processes having been submerged in a welter of emotion. 'I have a description that could fit dozen of men, a first name, and I know he caught a flight out of Toronto early this morning, but I don't know where to . . . it's hopeless. Magda.'

Magda threw aside the afghan that was over her legs and eased free of Nasturtium. 'I've got to go to the bathroom. Put the kettle on, Joss, and make some tea. We've got to think.'

Joss went into the kitchen, filled the kettle and put it on the stove. Then, as if a bullet had slammed into her chest, she bent almost double, pain searing every nerve-ending in her body. Niall was dying . . . *dying*.

Madga's voice seemed to come from a long way away. 'Joss, what's wrong?'

Blindly Joss turned into her friend's embrace and began to weep, harsh, tearing sobs that she was helpless to stop. She cried for a long time and came back to reality to find her nose jammed against Magda's collarbone. She pulled back. 'I've probably soaked your housecoat,' she quavered.

'It's drip-dry.'

'Thanks, Magda. I've been needing to do that for the last two days.'

'As you so aptly remarked, that's what life's all about—sharing,' Magda said flippantly. 'OK, kid, blow your nose, make the tea, and let's go in the living-room. We've got to plan a strategy.'

Belatedly Joss said, 'If you're not feeling well, this is the last thing you need.'

'Nothing like a real-life tragedy to put stomach' flu in its place. The tea, Joss.'

Joss said, sounding more like herself than she had all evening, 'It's a good thing Charlie's got a strong personality— you'd tromp all over him, otherwise.'

'Charlie is untrompable. That's one of the reasons

I'm marrying him,' Magda said smugly. 'The tea-bags are in the canister.'

Joss produced an approximation of a laugh and made the tea. When she and Magda were settled in the living-room Magda said briskly, 'The first thing you have to decide is whether you do want to trace this man. He doesn't want to be traced. And after all, you only knew him for four days.'

Without hesitation Joss said, 'I have to try, Magda. He's the right man for me, and if we've only got a year there's no time to waste.'

Madga raised expressive brows and said, 'OK. You can check the ticket agents at the airport, and the hospitals. And that cab driver would probably remember him.'

'The two restaurants we went to—he made a reservation at each one.'

'Now you're talking. I'll check at the club—he might have paid his bil with a charge card.'

'I can do the same thing at the Red Lion.' Joss crinkled her brows. 'I can't think of anything else.'

'Out of all that we'll surely get his last name.' Magda raised her mug. 'To the search!'

Joss drank the toast in brandy, feeling it might be more efficacious, and shortly afterwards went to bed. She felt almost peaceful after her storm of crying, and full of hope. She would find Niall because he and she were meant to be together for whatever time he had left. She was clinging to this thought when she fell asleep, and it was still with her in the morning.

At the bookshop on Tuesday Joss arranged to have the next day off. She would lose a day's pay, but that couldn't be helped. At four she ran all the way to the little Italian restaurant where she and Niall had eaten last Friday, and asked the *maître d'* if she could see the reservation list for that day. He gave her sweat-streaked face a quizzical look, but produced his book obligingly enough. 'Nine-thirty on Friday, you say? Only three names, madam. Brooks, Diamond and Bernardi.'

'Diamond?' she repeated weakly.

'Yes. His second visit . . . although he didn't have a reservation the first time. A tall, dark-haired gentleman. In fact, you were with him, were you not, madam?'

Quailing at the thought of explanation, Joss gasped, 'Yes. Thank you for your help,' and left the restaurant with as much dignity as she could muster. Once outside she began running again, trying to rid herself of a crushing disappointment. She made it to her stool in the pub by one minute to five, and started with a couple of guitar solos so she could catch her breath.

In her break she phoned Scarlatti's. Although the list of names was considerably longer, among them was the name Diamond. Neither of the other names from the Italian restaurant was repeated. Joss hung up, biting her lip. She had had high hopes of the reservation list.

At nine o'clock Joss approached the cashier at the front desk of the Swansea. Her name was Helen, and she was from Nova Scotia. Cheerfully she went through all the credit card receipts from the Red Lion for the four nights Niall had been there. Although two men with the first name Neil had paid by credit card, both spelled their name with an e, and both had been guests at the hotel. Another dead end.

On Wednesday Joss spend a harrowing two hours at the Toronto hospital that was renowned for its cancer treatment. The number of departments and the proliferation of specialists were mind-boggling, and she spoke to at least a dozen receptionists, who ranged from pleasant to rude. The last was the worst. She was a sharp-nosed woman in her forties with thin lips, who used a minimum of words. After Joss had described Niall and given the probable dates, the woman said officiously, 'The patient's last name?'

'I don't know it—I explained that to you.'

'I cannot access the computer without a surname.'

'I'm not asking the computer,' Joss said as politely as
she could. 'I'm asking you if you remember him.'

'I see something like a hundred patients a day. I could
not possibly remember them all. Now if you'll excuse
me, I have work to do.' She turned away, giving Joss a
view of the back of her head, where her hair was scraped
into a stingy little bun. Joss left.

She took a bus to the airport. More line-ups, this time
blanked-face travellers surrounded by mounds of
luggage, old people in wheelchairs, children squalling.
By dint of making enquiries, Joss succeeded in leaving
notices posted in various staff rooms; she did not know
what else to do.

Her last stop was the dingy office of the cab
company. Two city maps interspersed with graffiti. Joss
gave the registration number of the cab to one of the
controllers, who told her the cabbie would be checking
in during the next hour. Joss sat down on a wooden
bench to wait.

One of the controllers had smoked eleven cigarettes,
and the other, six, before rescue came in the form of a
remembered voice speaking over the intercom. 'Herb?'
said the older woman, lighting her twelfth cigarette
from the butt of the eleventh. 'Lady at the office wants
to see you, c'n you drop by on your way?'

'Sure thing,' squawked Herb. 'Gimme five minutes.'

Joss smiled her thanks and went outdoors to wait. A
yellow cab pulled up by the kerb a couple of minutes
later and Herb got out. He saw Joss, clapped a hand
dramatically to his forehead and said, 'Don't tell me! I
bin readin' this book about developin' your memory.
Wait, now . . . I got it. The guy who nearly got run over
and then left you standin' in the rain. Boy, did I tell him
a thing or two. Listen, mister, I said to him, that gal
saved your life and you didn't even say thanks. Serve

you right if she didn't bother next time, just let you get run over deader 'n a doornail——'

Joss covered her ears. She was not convinced she had saved Niall's life, but if she had, her action must have seemed ironic, to say the least. 'Here's another test for your memory,' she said quickly. 'Did he tell you his name? And where did you take him?'

'Lady, you 're not still chasin' that guy He ain't worth it. Lots more where he came from.'

Joss clasped her hands, looked piteous and said with the utmost sincerity, 'It's *very* important that I find him.'

Herb shook his head. 'My old man always used to tell me it's a waste of time tryin' to figure out what goes on between a broad's ears. Blamed it on the moon, he did, all them——'

'Herb!' Joss said loudly. 'Where did you take him?'

'OK, OK, I was gettin' there. No, he didn't tell me his name. Didn't tell me anythin', come right down to it. Guess he didn't appreciate what I had to say.' Joss looked about ready to burst. 'I let him off at the corner of St Clair and Yonge,' Herb finished hurriedly.

'You mean he didn't ask for a particular place—a hotel or an apartment block?'

'Nope. Corner of St Clair and Yonge. Out he got and walked off into the rain. I sure didn't try to follow him . . . why should I?'

Yet another dead end. 'Did he tip you?' Joss asked.

'Paid his fare and split. Would you tip someone who read you a lecture?'

'I guess not.' She took a bill out of her purse. 'Thanks for talking to me, Herb.'

'Any time—sorry I couldn't help you. You take my advice and forget that guy.' Herb leaped back into his cab and took off down the street. Joss began walking in the direction of the Red Lion, and when she related her lack of results to Magda the next morning was given advice very similar to Herb's.

'He paid cash at the pub as well,' Magda said. 'So your only hope is that someone at the airport will remember him.' She went on earnestly, 'You've done all you can, Joss. Let sleeping dogs lie and get on with your life. Sure, it's painful right now, but you'll forget him in time, I know you will.'

Ellie used much the same words on her next phone call. 'Forget him, darling. It's not easy, but I think you must. After a while he'll seem like a dream you had, you'll see.'

Joss did not believe any of these well-meaning sentiments. Niall was still achingly real to her, his dreadful predicament weighing on her mind night and day, his absence as keenly felt as an amputation. However, because of him, the decision about her future was easily solved. She would become a doctor so she could help people like him; and she would go to the university that was only a hundred miles from Toronto on the off-chance that somehow she would meet him again. She sent off her deposit and on the first of September took the train home to Nova Scotia for a five-day break before classes began.

Her family and the old clapboard farmhouse enfolded her in their arms. The sweetbriar roses were still in bloom, and Bert the collie stirred himself to lick her hand. Ellie, after one look at her daughter's strained features, cooked all Joss's favourite meals, while George unlisted her help in bringing in the final hay crop of the season. Joss had always loved haying, and now the hard physical labour coupled with day-long doses of country air helped her to sleep.

On her last evening home she and Ellie walked to the orchard together. Joss looked up the slope between the straight rows of trees. No blossoms, no dandelions, no blue-eyed stranger stepping out into the clearing. 'This is where I always pictured myself meeting the man of my dreams, Mum,' she confessed. 'How's that for teenage fantasy? Me in a white dress, him bathed in sunlight, violins playing in the distance.' Her smile was twisted. 'Didn't quite work out that way, did it?'

'Real life can be very cruel,' Ellie said soberly.

'If he cared for me at all, I still can't understand why he didn't tell me,' Joss cried.

'He did what he felt was best. That's all any of us can do.'

In a low voice Joss said, 'Do you know what the worst part of al this is? I'll never know what happened to him.'

Ellie put her arm around her daughter's waist. 'Darling, anything I can say sounds like a cliché. But time does heal, and we do learn to love again. You have so much of life ahead of you—in time Niall will take his proper place in your memory and you'll find someone else to love.'

Joss bowed her head. Oh the branch brushing her sleeve hung half a dozen slowly ripening apples: the blossom had borne fruit. But in her case frost had touched the flowers and the tree was barren. Her mother was wrong, she thought dully. Niall had her heart. In a strange way he always had; and he always would.

CHAPTER SIX

DR JOCELYN ELEANOR MACDOUGALL, MD, Speciality in Family Medicine, regarded herself in the mirror with a certain satisfaction. Today she and her two partners had signed a one-year lease for the building on Queen Street West where they planned to open a clinic; renovations were to start at eight o'clock tomorrow morning. Three weeks, said the contractor. Joss was counting on at least a month. Either way, by June of this year she would be beginning the practice of medicine, the goal for which she had worked so hard the last six years. While her accumlated student loans were astronomical, and while she had reached the remarkable age of twenty-seven on her last birthday, she was well content with the path her life had taken. She loved medicine. She had thrown herself into her studies all those years ago, sparing nothing, and had been rewarded with the surety of a vocation.

She leaned forward and began swiftly applying her make-up; last year during her internship she had learned to do many things in the least possible time. Bryan was taking her out for dinner. Bryan in theory espoused punctuality, which meant in practice that if a problem arose in his research he would be late, but that if he were on time he throughly disliked having to wait for anyone else. Joss had threatened him with dire consequences were he to be late for their wedding, due to take place two weeks from Saturday. He had given his rare laugh, which she liked so much, and had told her Dr Michaud would be taking over the research progamme for a whole week; he, Bryan, would be waiting for her at the altar.

She smoothed green eye-shadow over her lids and out-

94

lined the lower edge with a pencil. Dr Bryan MacFarlane worked for the Hospital for Sick Children in Toronto; Joss had met him when he had given a number of lectures in paediatrics to the fouth-year medical students at Western. His courtship had beeen slow and deliberate, which had suited her fine, giving her time to appreciate the brilliance of his mind and his dedication to his job, as well as to be secretly amused by the conventionality of his morals. She had never made love with Bryan, for he had made it very clear that he wished to wait until the fourth finger on her left hand was encircled by the expensive platinum and diamond wedding band that he had chosen for her. Although she rarely admitted this to herself openly, she knew in the secret recesses of her mind that a large part of Bryan's attraction was the difference between him and Niall.

Joss uncapped her mascara and remembered, as she almost always did, the dollar-forty-nine lashes. She had never forgotten Niall, although now she could remember him without pain, as a brief, intensely meaningful espisode of her life that had changed her irrevocably. Because of Niall she had learned about helplessness in the hands of fate and about the pangs of grief, and she knew that these hard-won lessons had made her more understanding with her patients, more sympathetic and more tolerant.

The first year after she had met Niall had been the worst, for, with her during her lectures and labs and hours of study, she had carried the knowledge that his illness must be progressing. She had been sure she would know intuitively the moment of his death, and had discovered as the months passed that even that was denied her; she had never received any sense that Niall was no longer on this earth. She had kept very much to herself her first two years at medical school, but during her third year had tentatively started to date a little. Bryan had been good for her, never rushing her or applying undue pressure, apparently content with the warmth and steady affection she gave him. She could not give him passion or the fierce flame of a love that brooks no denial, for those had been Niall's and seemed to have been snuffed out over the slow, agonising months of that first year.

Joss recapped her mascara, applied a coral lipstick and inserted the gold filigree ear-rings that had been Bryan's graduation gift to her. Then she ran a brush through her hair; it was the same streaked, tawny blonde that it had been six years ago, although she had had it cut during her second year—the year in which there was the highest percentage of drop-outs from medical school—because there simply had not been the time to spend drying its long, thick waves. She now wore it feathered about her head with her ears bare, a style that gave more prominence to her gold-flecked eyes and to the new maturity of her features.

Quickly she stood up. Her green, Chanel-styled suit, a Christmas gift from her parents, was hanging in the wardrobe. She slipped it on, added elegant taupe pumps that she had bought with her first pay cheque, and checked her appearance in the mirror again.

The mirror reflected a beautiful and assured young woman, warm, approachable, yet with a sense of inner depths that would be accessible to very few. Joss did not see any of this. She adjusted a shoulder pad in her jacket and the neckline of her cream-coloured blouse and decided she would do.

The doorbell rang. Bryan was exactly on time. She opened the door and said, 'The tissue cultures must have behaved themselves today.'

'All very well for you to talk—you're a lady of leisure.'

She laughed; when she had finished interning two weeks ago, she had flown home and lazed on the farm for ten blissful days. 'Tomorrow I start bugging the contractors,' she said.

'And reading up on measles and mumps,' Bryan said drily.

She led him into the kitchen and poured him a drink.

4 Doctor Nurse Romances plus 2 gifts — Yours free!

The fascinating real-life drama of modern medical life provides the thrilling background to these gripping stories of desire, heartbreak, passion and true love. And to introduce you to this marvellous series, we'll send you 4 Doctor Nurse titles plus a digital quartz clock and surprise mystery gift absolutely FREE when you complete and return this card.

We'll also reserve a subscription for you to the Mills & Boon Reader Service, which means you'll enjoy:

☆ **SIX WONDERFUL NOVELS** — sent direct to you every **two** months.

☆ **FREE POSTAGE & PACKING** — we pay all the extras.

☆ **FREE REGULAR NEWSLETTER** — packed with competitions, author news and much more. . .

☆ **SPECIAL OFFERS** — selected exclusively for our subscribers.

There's no obligation or commitment — you can cancel your subscription at any time. Simply complete and return this card today to receive your free introductory gifts. No stamp is required.

FREE CLOCK &
SURPRISE
MYSTERY
GIFT

Mills & Boon — DOCTOR NURSE ROMANCE — The Doctor from Wales — SARAH FRANKLIN

Mills & Boon — DOCTOR NURSE ROMANCE — Surgeon in Portugal — ANNA RAMSAY

Mills & Boon — DOCTOR NURSE ROMANCE — Flying Doctor — BETTY NEELS

Mills & Boon — DOCTOR NURSE ROMANCE — No Cure for Love

Free Books Certificate

Dear Susan,

Please send me my 4 free Doctor Nurse Romances together with my free gifts.

Your FREE
Digital Quartz
Desk Clock

Please also reserve a special Reader Service subscription for me. If I decide to subscribe, I shall receive 6 superb new titles every two months for just £7.20, post and packing free. If I decide not to subscribe, I shall write to you within 10 days. The free books and gifts will be mine to keep in any case.

I understand that I am under no obligation whatsoever — I can cancel my subscription at any time simply by writing to you. I am over 18 years of age.

Name: _____
(BLOCK CAPITALS PLEASE)

Address:. _____

_____ Signature _____

_____ Postode _____

 10A8D

To Susan Welland
Mills & Boon Reader Service
FREEPOST
Croydon
Surrey
CR9 9EL

SEND NO MONEY NOW

NO
STAMP
NEEDED

'You don't really approve of the clinic, do you?'

'I'd rather see you specialise; it's the only way to get ahead. Paediatrics, for instance.'

'Practised out of an elegant suite in Rosedale.'

He raised his glass. 'You know I'm being honest with you, Joss, when I say I worry about the neighbourhood you've chosen. Pretty rough, and they won't all see you as an angel of mercy.'

'But you're taking me out to dinner to celebrate signing the lease,' she said provocatively.

'If I've learned one thing since I met you, it's that you're going to do what you're going to do. I want you to know my opinion—but I won't try to stop you.'

'Freedom,' Joss said thoughtfully.

'Very important.'

So it was. But she would have preferred Bryan to have endorsed her plans for a family clinic in a poor area of town. She said lightly, 'We could take our drinks in the living-room.'

'I've been sitting all day. I had to do statisical analyses on the last batch of reports.' He began describing the results, his voice as animated as it ever got. A lot of Bryan's research concerned burn victims, and in practical terms his long hours in the laboratory had resulted in less pain, less danger of infection and more comfort for the patients. Joss knew this, so her interest in and respect for his work were genuine.

They finished their drinks and Bryan checked his watch. 'We should leave.'

'Where are we going?'

'Scarlatti's . . . I know you like it there.'

The first time Bryan had taken her to Scarletti's, nearly two years ago, had been the first time Joss had been back since the evening she had spent there with Niall. She had found that second visit unexpectedly painful. The strong resurgence of memories had taken her aback; their clarity and immediacy had frightened her. She had said nothing of this to Bryan, for she had not known him particularly well then; and somehow the occasion had never arisen since then for her to talk about Niall. Those four days had been so brief and ephemeral an experience, so deeply felt yet ending so inconclusively, that she had shrunk from exposing them to a man as rational and pragmatic as Bryan. Anyway, Niall was gone. What was the use of talking about him?'

Now she joked, 'It's their chocolate decadence dessert that I like!'

'You don't have to worry about your figure, Joss.'

She said a touch tartly, 'I'm never sure that you even notice my figure.'

'Oh, I do. Don't you worry about that.'

'You're a dark horse, Bryan MacFarlane.'

'They're the ones who often win the race, Joss.'

She gave him a sudden gamine grin, because it was exchanges like this that convinced her their marriage would work out. She said, 'You look very smart this evening yourself, sir.'

Bryan, at six feet, looked taller because he held himself so straight. His brown hair had a military cut, while his grey eyes were his most expressive feature in a face that was conventionally good-looking. He rarely bought off-the-rack clothing and he disliked leisure pursuits that involved getting dirty. He had visited the farm with Joss and, while he had been polite, he had not fitted in; Joss had seen him surreptitiously removing Bert's hairs from hairs from his creased grey flannels and eyeing the manure pile with fastidious distaste. George had been puzzled by him, and Ellie a little over-friendly. Jake had said bluntly, 'He's the wrong man, sis,' and had walked away before she could argue. The wedding was to be held in St David's Church in Toronto, the reception at Bryan's mother's house. Of Joss's family, only her parents were attending.

As they left the apartment, Joss carrying her spring coat because she knew the air would be cold later on, she began chattering about wedding plans. Although originally she had wanted a small, intimate wedding, the list of guests Bryan had given her had precluded any notions of intimacy; she had, however, chosen a very beautiful white silk suit instead of a full-length gown, and had dissuaded Bryan from an engagement ring. 'I'd rather we spend the money on a trip.' she had said.

'Joss, I earn enough that we can do both. I'd like to buy you a diamond.'

'A great big diamond ring would look totally out of place at the clinic,' Joss had argued. 'Besides, someone might bop me over the head to steal it.'

'That's exactly what I dislike about that clinic,' Bryan had said touchily. But to Joss's relief the discussion about an engagement ring had never been reopened.

It was May now, and the city's trees were unfurling fresh green leaves. Bryan parked near the restarant. He locked his car, a black BMW, and he and Joss walked towards the brick steps of Scarlatti's. The restaurant's tiny walled garden had pollarded cherry trees in fragrant bloom, white as a bridal wreath. City version of an orchard, Joss thought wryly. The orchard at home would only be in bud now.

Restrained elegance was the keynote of Scarlatti's foyer. The carpet was plum-coloured and the lighting discreet; crimson roses glowed in an oak-panelled alcove. The *maître d'*, whose name was Rupert, recognised Bryan immediately, for Bryan and his colleagues were regular customers. 'Good evening, Dr MacFarlane. Madame, may I take your coat? The evenings are still cool, aren't they?'

Joss passed over her coat. 'Your trees are very pretty, Rupert,' she said politely.

'Thank you, madam. They are enjoying their brief moment of glory,' Rupert replied with a grandiloquence that Joss had come to expect from him; it went with his waxed moustache and the flourish with which he hung up her coat, rather as if he were a bullfighter and it the red cape.

Behind him the leaded-glass door of the restaurant opened again. 'Ah, good evening, sir,' Rupert said with something approaching genuine warmth. 'How nice to see you again.'

Joss half turned to see who the gentleman was who had elicited so much enthusiasm from Rupert. A couple had entered the door, the woman ahead of the man. She was a striking, patrican-faced blonde whose fur jacket would have paid off at least a year of Joss's student loan. Then the man stepped into the pool of light cast by the crystal chandelier and Joss dropped her bag. Her whole body went ice-cold with primitive terror. Her ears roared. I'm dreaming, she thought, panic-stricken. This isn't happening. It can't happen.

The man who was standing in the foyer was Niall.

She must have made a tiny, choked sound. His eyes, the blue eyes that she had never forgotten, swivelled round to look at her. She watched the colour drain from his face and from a distance that seemed immeasurable heard his shocked whisper, *'Joss . . .'*

'N-Niall?' she stammered.

'My God—Joss!'

He took a step towards, her; she could not have moved to have saved her soul. 'You died,' she croaked. 'Five years ago.'

Rupert said reprovingly, for this was a scene and Scarlatti's did not favour scenes, 'Mr Morgan is a regular customer, madam. May I please show you to your table?'

Bryan said impatiently, 'Come along, Joss,' and the patrician blonde looked down her elegant nose.

Joss wanted to scream at them all to go away, for this scene was between herself and Niall, and no one else mattered. Striving for some kind of normality, she faltered, 'Bryan, I'd like you to meet a—an acquaintance of mine. Niall——' She stopped in consternation. What name had Rupert given him?

Smoothly Niall filled the gap. 'Niall Morgan,' he said, stepping forwards and holding out his hand.

Short of outright rudeness, Bryan had to take the proffered hand. 'Bryan MacFarlane,' he said in a chilly voice.

Niall put a hand on the blonde's elbow. 'My friend, Trilby Henderson-Smythe.'

Joss was shot through by a red-hot jealousy from Niall's most casual of gestures. The blonde *would* have a name like that, she thought meanly, and tried to produce a smile from lips that seemed to have congealed on her face. 'I'm pleased to meet you,' she said mechanically.

With a great aplomb Bryan said, 'Good evening, Miss Henderson-Smythe.' The blonde favoured him with a smile that could have graced the pages of *Vanity Fair*. Joss and Niall said nothing. Joss was afraid to look at Niall for fear he might have disappeared again; the only way to convince herself that he was flesh and blood was to touch him, and that she could not bring herself to do. Then Bryan put a proprietorial arm around her shoulders and said heartily, 'Very nice to have met you both. I hope you'll enjoy your meal here as much as we always do—you have quite a reputation to live up to, Rupert.'

'Indeed, sir,' Rupert said suavely, and took two leather-bound menus and a wine list from the glossy mahogany buffet. 'Please come this way, Dr MacFarlane.'

Joss shot one last desperate glance over her shoulder. Niall was still standing by the blonde. He had not disappeared. In a sudden surge of emotion that filled her eyes with tears she said clearly, 'I'm so glad you're alive, Niall.' Then she automatically followed in Rupert's wake.

The spiral staircase was ablaze with scarlet and orange tulips, fringed and fluted. Daffodils nodded around the fountain. Rupert led them to their regular table, seated Joss with much ceremony and passed her the menu, which was as heavy as a book. He shook out her serviette and placed it on her lap. She had never realised before how much that gesture irriated her.

Bryan said politely, 'Your usual, Joss?' She nodded, and he ordered a Martini and a Manhattan. Then he opened the menu.

Joss's back was to the entrance. But by the prickling of hair on the back of her neck she knew when Niall came into the room. Fortunately the tables immediately surrounding them were all filled, for she did not think she could have borne to have had him sitting too near to her. She sneaked a surreptitious glance over her shoulder. He and the blonde were being escorted to a table near the fountain; by turning her head only slightly she had a perfect view of them. Niall was facing her.

Because she was still not convinced that this was not a dream, Joss put her hands in lap and pinched her wrist, hard. It hurt, nor did she wake up to find herself in bed in her apartment with its west-facing windows that never admitted the morning sun. She was awake. This was real. Niall was not dead.

He was very much alive, she thought with a constriction in her chest. Alive and something like sixty feet away from her, sitting with an extremely beautiful woman who also looked—Joss had to be fair—intelligent. The woman was not his wife, at least she had that much to be grateful for.

'You haven't even looked at the menu,' Bryan said.

She started nervously, looking at her companion with a puzzled frown, as if wondering who he was. 'Pardon me?'

He added grimly, 'Let's get dinner ordered and then we can talk.'

Everything in order and under control, Joss thought with a touch of hysteria. She did not feel the slightest bit hungry, and the mere thought of chocolate decadence made her feel ill. She opened the menu, quickly picked out a garden salad and sole *bonne femme* and closed it again. Niall was looking at the menu; even at this distance she could see that he was frowning. Then the waiter interposed his starched white shirt and green satin cummerbund between her and Niall. She gave her order. After asking for mussels *à la provencale* and prime rib of beef *au jus,* Bryan began to discuss the choice of wines with the waiter. Joss did not contribute to the discussion; she did not even feel capable of deciding between white and red.

When the waiter went away, Niall and Trilby Henderson-Smythe reappeared. Bryan said testily, 'I wish you'd stop starting at that chap. Who is he, anyway?'

She took a healthy swallow of her Martini, and its bite jolted her back to awareness. 'I knew him very briefly six years ago,' she said, looking straight into Bryan's level grey eyes. 'Then he simply . . . disappeared. I found out afterwards that he had terminal cancer. So naturally I'd presumed him dead. It—it was like seeing a ghost to meet him again.' She ran out of words and fished the olives out of her Martini, chewing them thoroughly.

'Did you have an affair with him?'

She looked up, surprised. Bryan was not normally intuitive; she must have looked ghastly at that first sight of Niall. 'I've never had an affair with anyone, Bryan, I told you that,' she said slowly.

'I thought you were going to faint when you saw him.'

She said carefully, 'Even though I only knew him for a short time, I was very attracted to him. So it was a shock to see him again.'

'Particularly as he had never done you the courtesy of letting you know he survived.' Bryan only used that clipped voice when he was angry.

'He wouldn't have known where to find me, I suppose.'

'So are any other skeletons going to emerge from your closet before we get married, Joss?'

His tone was joking, his eyes were not. 'Maybe I should have told you about Niall,' Joss said. 'But I was convinced the man was dead years before I met you, Bryan. The whole episode was over. Dead. Gone. Buried.'

'You sound very vehement.' Bryan stabbed at his drink with the cocktail stick.

Recklessly she took another large gulp of her Martini. 'Are we having a fight? You're the last man in the world I would have suspected of jealousy.'

'I wouldn't have suspected myself of it, either. But there was something about the way the two of you looked at each other . . .' He shrugged his shoulders irritably. 'I sure didn't like it.'

'Neither did Rupert,' Joss answered, trying to lighten the atmosphere between them.

'Rupert does not care for unbridled emotion. He thinks eating at Scarlatti's is the acme of civilised behaviour.'

She had to laugh. 'Don't ever tell him that it's not.'

Bryan suddenly reached across the table, took her hand in his and said, 'I love you, Joss. I want to marry you.'

Bryan only rarely verbalised his feelings. Feeling as farouche as if Niall was standing behind her chair listening to every word, Joss said weakly, 'We *are* getting married. In just over two weeks, in case you'd forgotten.'

'I wish it was tomorrow,' Bryan said forcefully.

She, Joss discovered with a sinking of her heart, was glad it was not. But how could she say that to Bryan? She discovered within herself a strong craving to be alone. All by herself in her apartment, so that she could sit quietly and assimilate the astounding knowledge that Niall was alive.

But she was not alone. Bryan was sitting across from her with an expectant look on his face: clearly he wanted an answer. She had no idea what to say. 'I'm sorry I'm behaving so peculiarly,' she managed. 'For a moment I really did think I was seeing a ghost. We all make light of ghost stories, don't we? We tell them around the campfire and then we creep off to bed looking back over our shoulders. Haunted houses and nervous giggles . . . it's not funny at all when you really are convinced you're seeing a ghost. I was terrified.'

'Will you see this Niall Morgan again?' Bryan demanded.

Joss looked at him blankly. She had scarcely taken in that Niall was alive; she had not even thought about seeing him again. 'I don't know where he lives, what he does . . . I don't know anything about him.'

'You're not answering the question, Joss.'

'It's not the right question!'

'I would have thought it a very pertinent question. All things considered.'

Dimly, she supposed he was right. She shot a hunted glance at the table near the fountain. Niall was staring at her. Her eyes skidded away.

With a timing for which she could feel nothing but gratitude, the waiter's cummerbund blocked her view of the fountain. A green salad was put in front of her. Bryan was given an array of mussels broiled on the half-shell, pungent with garlic. Quickly Joss picked up her knife and fork and began to eat. Bryan, she knew, was still waiting for an answer and was obstinate enough to be silent until she produced one. Two can play that game, she thought, and buttered a slice of Scarlatti's warm herb bread.

Bryan was the first to speak, although not until their appetisers had been removed and they were waiting for the main course. 'I can see you're not going to answer me,' he said coldly.

'I can't. I don't know what to say. Bryan, can't we talk about the deficit or the effects of viral hepatitis? Please.'

'It's unlike you to be anything but straightforward,' was his pompous reply.

'I'm sorry!' Joss cried in exasperation, looking anything but sorry. Then they sat in strained silence until the arrival of the sole and the beef *au jus*. Joss bolted her food, which would have further upset Rupert, her one desire to be gone from Scarlatti's and never to come back. She had cleaned her plate before Bryan was even half-way through his meal. She picked up her bag, said, 'Excuse me, please,' and headed for the cloakroom.

The anteroom of the ladies had the same plum-coloured

carpeting as the foyer, chairs vaguely reminiscent of the eighteenth-century French style, and two artistic floral arrangements. Joss liked her flowers natural, not with wires stuck in their stems. She sat down and found herself once more staring at her own reflection in a mirror. She repaired her lipstick, fluffed up her hair and adjusted the neckline of her blouse again; it had never lain quite straight. She should have returned the blouse right after she had worn it for the first time, but she had been interning in obstetrics then, running short on sleep, and returning a blouse had been low on her priority list . . . oh, God, what was she going to do?

Niall was alive. He had not died, after all.

She found herself repeating those two sentences over and over again, as if repeating them would somehow make sense of them. It did not seem to.

Another woman came in, gave Joss a curious look, and went through to the other room. Joss stood up. Much as she might like to, she could not hide in the woman's room for ever. She pushed open the door and stepped outside.

Niall was standing in the dimly lit corridor, a situation so reminiscent of the Red Lion that Joss felt a thrill of superstitious terror. 'What are you doing here?' she cried, and by 'here' could have meant here on earth or here outside the Ladies.

Niall grabbed her by the sleeve, as if he was afraid she might turn and run. 'I had to talk to you,' he said hoarsely.

She looked down. His hand was just as she remembered it, the long, lean fingers, the sprinkle of dark hair. Overcome by an emotion she could not have defined, she suddenly leaned her forehead on his shoulder, the nape of her neck a vulnerable curve. 'I can't believe you're alive,' she whispered helplessly, and felt his other arm go around her and hold her as if the past six years had never happened.

'How did you know I was ill?' he asked. 'I never told

you.'

'Magda.'

'One of life's little coincidences that you happened to be rooming with the one woman in Toronto to whom I'd told the truth,' he said caustically.

'Not really a coincidence. The club was near the hotel, and she's the one who got me the job at the Red Lion. Niall, why are we standing here talking about Magda?'

His arm tightened. 'I've got to see you again.'

'I don't know whether——'

'Joss, I've *got* to! To have found you after all these years . . .'

She raised her head, her eyes blazing. 'It was your choice to lose me in the first place.'

'I know, I know. I did what I thought was best.'

'I don't think it——'

'Look, we can't get into that now. Give me your phone number and I'll call you first thing tomorrow morning.' Niall's face changed. 'God, Joss, you're more beautiful than you ever were.'

The other woman emerged from the cloakroom just as he spoke, and gave Joss an even more curious look. Joss said inanely, 'I'm going out at ten o'clock.'

'Then I'll call at nine-thirty. Please, Joss.' He gave her a crooked smile, his eyes very blue. 'Don't take all evening to decide . . . when I left the restaurant the gentleman at your table was looking rather fussed.'

Niall had given her the perfect opportunity to say that the gentleman at her table was her fiancé. Joss said nothing. Opening her handbag with fingers that shook, she found a notepad and a pen, wrote her phone number on the pad and tore off the piece of paper. For a moment she held it in her hand, knowing that by giving it to him she was doing something momentous, the consequences of which could disrupt her life.

Perhaps Niall sensed this. He loosened her grip on the paper and took it from her, first folding it carefully then putting in in the inner pocket of his suit jacket. 'Nine-thirty,' he said. 'Now you'd better go back to your table—it would hardly do for your gentleman-friend to pursue us to the cloakroom.'

'How can you manage to joke about this?' she muttered.

'Joss, if I didn't keep this conversation on some kind of even keel I'd be throwing you on the floor and making love to you.'

'Oh,' she gulped. 'Oh, I see.' She added idiotically, 'Rupert would not approve.'

'Nor would Bryan MacFarlane or Trilby. Off you go, I'll follow in a minute.'

Joss made a groping gesture with one hand, dropped it to her side in frustration, and said with desperate honesty, 'You promise you'll phone? You won't just disappear again?'

'I promise.'

He was a man who kept his promises. She turned away, a simple physical movement that seemed to take a huge effort of will, and hurried down the corridor to the restaurant. Bryan was sitting exactly where she had left him. He looked thunderous. She slid into her seat; the dinner plates had been removed.

'Did you enjoy that little tête-à-tête?' Bryan said nastily. 'Which cloakroom did you choose—the men's or the women's?'

Joss felt anger flood her veins. 'Bryan, I did not plan that little tête-à-tête, as you call it. Niall and I only talked for a minute or two. But he's going to call me tomorrow morning.'

Bryan had obviously not expected such frankness. 'I trust you told him that you and I are engaged.'

Her eyes fell. 'I didn't, no. I will tomorrow.'

'I'd appreciate that,' he said sarcastically. Then with a complete change of voice he said to the waiter, 'Ah, thank you . . . yes, that one goes to the lady.'

The waiter put a dessert glass in front of Joss; it contained chocolate ice-cream, chocolate mousse and chocolate sauce. She looked at it with concealed loathing, and heard Bryan say, 'I knew you'd want chocolate decadence.'

'Thank you,' she said, knowing he had meant well and knowing she must make an effort to eat it. From the corner of her eye she saw Niall edge through the tables near the fountain, and forced herself not to stare. She took a large spoonful of the mousse, which was laced with rum, and said valiantly, 'Wonderful.'

The waiter brought coffee, cream and demerara sugar. While Joss plugged away at the chocolate decadence, Bryan began to discuss the common stocks he had sold the day before at an excellent profit margin. Joss tried to listen intelligently, recognising the conversation as an oblique attempt at reconciliation, wishing that chocolate had never been invented. When she finished the dessert Bryan lit a cigar, something he called his only vice. He smoked it with agonising slowness.

The waiter brought the bill, discreetly encased in a leather folder; Bryan inserted his credit card into the folder and the waiter bore them both away. Normally Joss would have split the bill with him, but tonight was Bryan's treat, to celebrate the lease on the clinic. Which had not, she realised, been mentioned since they had left the apartment. Her ten-thirty appointment the next day was with the contractor.

Finally they were ready to leave. Bryan stood up and pulled her chair out for her. She also stood up. For a split second she looked towards the fountain. Niall was watching her. She dropped her eyes and walked steadily out of the restaurant, remembering to nod at the waiter, then making polite small talk with Rupert in the foyer. Yes, the dinner had been excellent, as usual; yes, she would put on her coat. The air would be cold after being indoors; thank you so much, goodnight, goodnight.

Joss had never been so glad to leave a restaurant in her whole life. Once seated in the car, she leaned her head back and closed her eyes. Bryan accompanied her up to the apartment as he always did, and, although she would infinitely have preferred to be alone, she let him follow her inside without comment. He hung up her coat, then said punctiliously, 'I'm not going to stay long, Joss—early day at the lab tomorrow. But I do want to say that I'm sorry about tonight. I over-reacted, I know. I hope you'll forgive me.'

He was standing ramrod-straight and made no attempt to touch her. He also looked reassuringly real; Bryan would never disappear as Niall had. In swift compunction Joss said, 'Of course you're forgiven. *I* over-reacted, too. But to see someone walking around whom you'd believed dead is an awful shock, and one for which I had no preparation whatsoever.'

'I hope he will call tomorrow. It might be as well for the two of you to get together—for explanations, if nothing else.' Bryan cleared his throat and added awkwardly, but with great sincerity, 'I have every faith in you, Joss. I know you'll handle the situation well, and I know you'll never deceive me.'

She was touched by these sentiments. Very naturally she moved into his embrace, something she would not have thought possible five minutes ago. 'Thank you for being so understanding, Bryan.'

He kissed her firmly on the lips, then moved back. 'Something I neglected to do this evening was to wish your clinic every success, Joss. You're excited about it, aren't you? You'll do a great job, I'm sure.'

'I'm as excited about it as a kid at Christmas,' she confessed. 'I wish we could move into the building right away.'

'Put a bomb under the contractor tomorrow,' Bryan said in his staid voice.

Her eyes twinkled. 'I'll do my best. Thanks for dinner,

Bryan. I didn't thank you properly at the time.'

'My pleasure.' He kissed her once more. 'I'll see you tomorrow. We're having dinner with my mother at seven, remember?'

Joss locked the door behind him, still smiling. Somehow Bryan had made everything right between them again; and undoubtedly his advice was sound. She should see Niall and hear what he had to say. Once the mystery of his reappearance was explained he would assume his proper place in her life; a man whom she had cared for out of all proportion, and mourned sincerely, but not a man who had a place in her present or her future.

CHAPTER SEVEN

JOSS'S sensible attitude towards Niall lasted until about
nine o'clock the next morning. She had woken early,
bathed and dressed, and then carefully studied the plans
for the clinic, wanting to have as many facts as possible
at her fingertips before meeting the contractor. Her
parents would be there as well, Susan and Michael
Devon, a husband and wife team who had been in
practice for five years and who were as enthusiastic as
she about the new venture. The intricacies of plumbing,
wiring and partitions occupied Joss's attention until the
brass clock on the bookshelves struck nine. The clock
was the wedding gift of Bryan's boss, whose position
Bryan eventually hoped to fill, and was, Joss was sure,
horrendously expensive.

Nine strokes, each mellifluous and perfectly in pitch.
Niall should phone in half an hour, she thought. If he
was as little as one minute late she would immediately
suspect that he had vanished again. He wouldn't be late.
Of course he wouldn't.

Why should it matter, Joss? said a little voice in her
ear. You don't get upset when Bryan's calls are late.
Why should you for Niall's? Bryan is your fiancé, after
all. Not Niall.

She had to tell Niall about Bryan today. It was
entirely possible that Niall also was engaged, she
thought, frowning, for Trilby Henderson-Smythe had
not been exactly thrilled to meet Joss. She discovered
that she disliked that thought about as much as the
prospect of Niall not phoning, got up from the table
where she had all the blueprints spread out and began

112

pacing up and down the living-room. She would be moving out of this apartment soon after the wedding, because she and Bryan had signed for a condominium with a view of Lake Ontario. She did not want to think about condominiums. She did not want to think about the wedding. She wanted Niall to phone.

At twenty past nine the telephone rang. Joss ran for it, seized the receiver and gasped, 'Hello?'

'Hello, Joss. Are you free after your ten o'clock appointment?'

She would have known that voice in the middle of the Sahara. Or in the middle of Toronto. 'I'll be finished about two,' she said; she and her partners were having lunch together.

'I'll have the car—where can I meet you?'

'You're assuming that I want to meet you.'

'That's right.'

Although his confidence irked her, it was fully justified. 'I'll be at the corner of Queen and University at two-fifteen,' she said crisply.

'Wear a red rose.'

The receiver went dead. Joss put it down slowly and remembered walking along a sun-dappled dirt road beside a river. She had been happy then. She was happy now. Happy in a way she had not been for years.

Nursing that happiness, for it was too new to take for granted, she went into her bedroom to get dressed. She had planned to wear a severely cut navy blue dress, having the vague idea that contractors preferred to deal with men; instead she put on a red knit skirt, a long white top and a loose jacket splashed with huge red flowers that might or might not be roses. She was smiling irrepressibly when she left the apartment. The contractor, who reminded her strongly of her brother Harvey, was as anxious as she to get the work done quickly, and she and her partners talked non-stop throughout lunch. They dropped Joss near City Hall at ten past two, and she walked past the fountain and Nathan Phillips Square to the corner of Queen and University.

The sun was shining. A breeze blew her gored skirt about her legs and teased her hair, and she was somehow not surprised to hear a piercing wolf whistle emanate from a dark green sports car illegally parked by the corner. A dark-haired man was waving at her from the driver's seat. The tingling sense of anticipation that Joss had carried with her all morning burst into happiness again. She gave the man a wide, incautious smile and ran across the pavement towards him. 'You called, sir?' she said primly.

In a Humphrey Bogart drawl Niall said, 'Get in the car, baby. You wanna good time, I'll show it to you.'

She got in. 'Where's your fedora?'

'You dames are all alike . . . complain, complain.' He grinned at her. 'Hello, beautiful. How are you?'

He looked wonderful: young, vital, blazingly full of life, very different from the gaunt man with the haunted eyes whom she had known so long ago. She said inadequately, 'I'm fine. There's a policeman watching you from across the street.'

'He's just envious.' Niall pulled out into the traffic. 'We'll go somewhere by the water so we can talk . . . you're not trying to pass those flowers off as roses, Joss?'

She glanced down at her jacket. 'They're red.'

'A new hybrid, perhaps. You'll find the real article in the back seat—a present for you.'

A tissue-wrapped bundle was lying on the seat. Joss reached for it and began to unwrap it. It contained a huge spray of glorious red flowers that were indubitably roses. She buried her nose in them. 'They even smell like roses,' she marvelled. 'You didn't buy these in a shop, Niall.'

'I grew them. In a greenhouse.'

'They're beautiful, thank you.' She looked at him sideways. 'So you're not a harried executive any more, Niall? You take time to smell the roses?'

'I'm a harried market gardener instead. For the past four years I've owned three hundred acres north of Toronto in the Humber Valley. I'm into organic gardening—none of these damned chemicals that we're poisoning the earth with.'

Joss said faintly, 'For the past six years I've been at the University of Western Ontario—scarcely a hundred miles from you.'

'I looked for you,' he said violently. 'I remembered that you'd talked about medical school, so I got in touch with Western and Dalhousie, and when that failed, with every research lab in the Halifax area. Same answer at all of them. Sorry, sir, no one here by the name of Jocelyn Gayle.'

Joss looked at him, appalled. 'Jocelyn Gayle isn't my real name—it was the name I used at the Red Lion,' she said. 'I *must* have told you my real name.'

He braked sharply at a set of lights. 'You're kidding,' he said flatly.

'My real name is MacDougall. But Mr Jodrey at the Red Lion didn't like the sound of Joss MacDougall— not romantic enough. So I became Jocelyn Gayle.'

'No wonder I couldn't find you,' Niall said savagely. 'I even went to your apartment building. Sorry, sir, no forwarding address.'

'Magda got married that autumn. So we went our separate ways.'

'And all this time you've been less than a two-hour drive away from me . . . how the gods must have laughed.'

The traffic surged ahead. Niall changed lanes to get on the expressway heading west. Joss sat quietly; her instinct six years ago to remain in Ontario on the chance of meeting Niall again had been perfectly valid. 'What made you choose the Humber Valley?' she asked.

'I wanted to be as close to Toronto as possible . . . I thought by some miracle we might meet again. Why did you choose Western?'

'Same reason.'

'I even went through all the Nova Scotia phone books looking for the name Gayle—you'd never told me the name of your home town. Luckly it's a sparsely populated province.'

'When did you do all this?' she said in a low voice.

'About a year after we met.'

Although Joss knew there were many more questions to ask, she was crushed by the terrible waste of all the months and years that she and Niall had been apart. She said at random, 'I always wondered why I didn't have some sort of intuitive sense of your death. I was sure I would know . . . because of my gypsy grandmother, if nothing else. I understand now, of course, why I didn't.'

Niall was staring straight ahead of him. 'It went deep with you, Joss.'

There was no point in denial. 'Yes. With you as well, I presume. There must be quite a lot of phone books in Nova Scotia.'

His laugh was devoid of humour. 'Deep enough that I suppose subconsciously I've been looking for you ever since.' The traffic light at the intersection ahead of them turned amber, so he braked to a halt. 'This is a long light; I should have taken it,' he muttered.

I've been looking for you ever since . . . 'There's no hurry,' Joss answered absently.

He turned in his seat. 'I still can't believe you're sitting beside me, Joss,' he said. Almost tentatively, as though he was afraid she would disappear if he touched her, he reached out his hand and lifted one of hers from her lap, bringing it to his lips. Her fingers were warm; fleetingly he closed his eyes.

For Joss, the six years fell away as if they had never been: the man she had always been waiting for was here beside her. Her eyes filled with tears.

Niall looked up. With an inarticulate groan he seized her in his arms and kissed her, his mouth ravishing hers, his hands moulding her shoulders, finding the softness of her breast under the loose flowered jacket, straining her as close to his body as he could in the confines of the car.

Behind them a horn blared. Niall said an unprintable word, thrust Joss away from him and drove across the intersection. 'I suppose I should apologise for that,' he said roughly. 'But I'm not going to.'

Joss straightened her clothes with trembling fingers and said nothing. Her mind was blank, her body on fire. Clutching the edges of her jacket, she remembered the sureness of his hand on her breast and her own leaping, instinctive response, and was afraid.

Niall glanced over his shoulder before changing lanes; Joss's head was downbent. 'Say something, Joss, for God's sake,' he pleaded.

She made a small, helpless movement with her hands. 'I don't know what to say.'

'I shouldn't have kissed you like that,' he said violently. 'Maybe I had to prove that you were real . . . words can be so damned inadequate.'

'Yes,' she said faintly; she could not have agreed more.

To her relief he put on his signal light. 'We'll turn off here, there's a park down by the water.'

People were flying kites in the park, the bright squares of silk like a colourful parade in the sky. Joss got out of the car, thrusting her hands in her pockets of her jacket as she and Niall began to stroll across the grass. 'Why did you start looking for me a year after we met?' she said in a carefully emotionless voice.

He accepted her lead. 'To explain that, I'd better

begin at the beginning . . . I was given the original diagnosis in Vancouver, which is where I was living at the time. But I have a very good friend in the medical profession in Toronto, so I came east to get a second opinion. The day I talked to Magda was the day the prognosis was confirmed—less than a year. The next day, by one of those crazy strokes of fate, I met you. I knew the moment I laid eyes on you that you and I were meant for each other. What I should have done was walk out of the Red Lion and never to back. But I couldn't—the pull was too strong. So then I figured that if we spent some time together I'd find out that you were just an ordinary woman, no one to get excited about, and that love at first sight was a myth perpetuated by the pulp magazines. I found out differently, of course—I don't have to tell you that.' He stopped on the path, the wind ruffling his hair, his eyes like fragments of the sky. 'So I ran away, Joss. I didn't know what else to do.'

'You could have stayed,' she answered, all the bitterness of those wasted years in her voice. 'We could have gone through it together.'

As if he were explaining himself to a child, Niall said patiently, 'Joss, I thought I was going to *die*.'

'We all have to one day. Why couldn't I have been with you?'

'I couldn't do that to you,' he said implacably.

'Relationships aren't just built on good times, Niall—you share bad times as well,' she answered just as implacably.

'Look, I'd read every book I could lay my hands on about the type of cancer I had, so I knew what it could do to me—do you think I could expose you to that? What kind of person would that have made me?'

'A person capable of being real,' Joss said emphatically.

'A totally selfish person,' Niall retorted. He began

walking towards the water again. 'So I flew back to
Vancouver that Sunday morning, and a month later my
friend in Toronto called. A brand-new drug was being
tested in the States. He knew the director of the clinic in
Boston, and if I wanted to go I could be a guinea pig. So
I went—what did I have to lose? For six months I went
through hell, because some of the side-affects were
horrific. But at the end of a year the tumour had
disappeared—which is when I started looking for you.'

'If only I'd told you my right name!'

Niall turned to face her again. 'Maybe it's better that
we didn't meet then. You see, they said down in Boston
that if in five years there was no recurrence then I was
completely cured. The five years are up in three weeks,
Joss. I feel great, and I'm ninety-nine per cent sure
they'll give me a clean bill of health at my check-up.
Which means that in three weeks you and I could start
all over again.'

He was smiling at her, and she saw in his eyes a vast
upwelling of tenderness. Her face felt stiff and there was
a sinking sensation in the pit of her stomach. She said
tonelessly, 'I'm getting married two weeks from
Saturday.'

Behind them the kites snapped in the wind. Joss's
skirt flapped against her legs. The smile had faded from
Niall's face. 'You're serious, aren't you?' he said
finally.

'Yes. St David's Church in North York at two o'clock
in the afternoon. The invitations have all been sent.'

'But you're not wearing an engagement ring.'

'I didn't want one.'

'Are you marrying the man in the restaurant?'

'Yes. I met him two years ago. You see, I stopped
looking for you five years ago, Niall.'

He flinched. 'Yes—of course you would have . . . I'm
not blaming you, Joss. But, my God, I thought we'd
been given a second chance!'

Her hands were clenched in her pockets. 'I guess life doesn't work that way.'

For a few moments Niall stood still, staring at the ground, his face concentrated in thought. Then he said, 'You were in love with me six years ago, weren't you, Joss?'

As well to deny that the sun rose in the east. 'Yes, I was.'

'Do you feel the same way about this man?'

'His name is Bryan,' she said irritably. 'You know that. He's a doctor. And he's a very different person from you; how could I feel the same way?'

'Remember the riverbank? Did you go to bed with him the first time you were alone together?'

She paled. 'I was young and naïve then, Niall. I'm older now.'

He gripped her elbow; lines were etched in his face. 'We never went to bed, did we, Joss? But we'd have been good together, you know that as well as I do. Is he as good? Is he, Joss?'

She shook her arm free, her eyes glittering. 'That's none of your business!'

'So he's not.'

'I never said that! How dare you think you can reappear in my life and pick up where you left off and ask me all kinds of impertinent questions?' she cried incoherently. '*You're* the one who disappeared, Niall Morgan, remember that!'

'I take full responsibility for that,' he said heavily. 'And if you were engaged to someone who made you ecstatically happy, even though it would break my heart, I'd step back and be happy for you. But you don't look ecstatically happy. And I remember your honesty, Joss—if you and this guy were fantastic in bed, you'd tell me so.'

'I've never been to bed with him!'

There was a perceptible silence. 'Has he got iced

water in his veins?'

'He's old-fashioned enough to want to wait until we're married.'

Niall said silkily, 'You and I wouldn't have waited. And look how you responded to me in the car, Joss.'

She wanted to cover her ears and scream that he was crazy. 'Niall, you've got to stop this! I love Bryan and I'm going to marry him.'

'If it kills you,' Niall said grimly.

'I'm doing the right thing,' she retorted.

'Don't you see what a cruel joke this is? That you're getting married just a few days before I have my final check-up?'

It was Joss's turn to pause. Then she said with ominous quietness, 'Are you telling me that if Bryan didn't exist, you and I would not be getting involved again until *after* your check-up?'

'If we've waited six years, what's another three weeks?'

She said evenly, 'So you're still looking for guarantees.'

'I have to know that I'm cured!'

'People who love each other and live together don't vanish if one or the other of them gets ill. They hang in—that's what love's all about.'

'But we're not living together. I can't take that kind of risk, not when a mere three weeks would remove it.'

Joss said hopelessly, 'You haven't learned a damned thing from the past six years, Niall Morgan. You're still running.'

'Maybe you're doing the same,' Niall said in an ugly voice. 'Why else are you marrying an uptight professional who hasn't got the guts to take you to bed?'

'Let me tell you something,' she flared. 'I've never gone to bed with anyone! I told you why six years ago—because I hadn't met the right man. *You* were the right man. I knew that. Four hours, four days, four years, it wouldn't have made the slightest difference—you were *right*. But you took off, didn't you? You vanished. Once Magda told me what the problem was I turned Toronto upside-down trying to find you. But I couldn't find you. I couldn't find you anywhere. So I mourned you instead, and for the best part of three years I didn't even go out on a date. Then I met Bryan. I respect him, I like him, I'm going to marry him. *He'll* never disappear. Not like you.'

To her horror, her voice had broken and her eyes had filled with tears. She turned her back on Niall, trying to focus on the wavering horizon of the lake.

For several seconds Niall said nothing. Then he brought her round to face him. Putting his arms around her, he held her close in a way that was different from the way he had held her in the car.

He was wearing a sweater over a shirt. Joss could hear the rhythm of his heart and was encircled by the strength of his arms and knew she had never forgotten his embrace; it had been engraved on her, and nothing Bryan had ever done had erased it. She knew something else. This time, she was sure, Niall had only intended to comfort her. But along with a sense of utter security his closeness was arousing other feelings, feelings that until today had been buried for years. She wanted him just as fiercely now as she had at the river's edge, she thought with painful truth; just as fiercely as she had in the car. As she raised a face to him that was full of doubt and confusion, he bent his head and kissed her.

The sweetness of honey, the unfolding of apple blossoms, all the promise of spring was in his kiss. Joss clung to him, abandoning herself to the warmth of his lips and her own hunger, that eclipsed reason and restraint. She felt alive again, fully alive, a desirable woman whose body had been fashioned with needs that only Niall could meet.

Against her lips Niall muttered, 'We must observe some kind of decorum—this is a public park. Joss, you can't marry this guy. You still love me.'

She felt as if she had been dunked in the cold waters of Lake Ontario. She pulled back and said, not very sensibly, 'What have I *done*?'

'It's not what you've done, it's what we've done,' Niall said with aggravating logic. 'We've discovered that the old magic is still there. We're dynamic together, Joss. We were six years ago and we still are. So you can't marry your precious doctor.'

She threw caution to the winds as if it were a kite. 'So go to the city hall,' she said trenchantly,' and get a special licence. You and I could get married this weekend.'

His face hardened. 'You're playing games.'

'You mean the answer's no?'

'In three weeks I'll be in the clear, Joss!'

'In three weeks I'll be married to Bryan.'

'You'll be making a hell of a mistake.'

'As big a mistake as you made six years ago when you got on the plane to Vancouver?'

'I'll never see that as a mistake!'

'How can we possibly get married when we have such radically different views about the nature of love?' Joss said despairingly. 'Love isn't just dynamite sex, Niall. It's being together . . . for better, for worse, in sickness and in health.'

'Then we're at an impasse,' he said levelly.

A turquoise kite with a long pink tail suddenly lost its balance and did a spectacular nosedive. At the last moment the handler saved it from collision with the ground. It lurched upwards, then soared freely on the wind again. Joss had watched all this. She said thoughtfully, 'Niall, can you tell me why you feel the way you do? You mentioned once that your mother died many years ago—is it something to do with that?'

With a steel edge to his voice he said, 'Now who's asking impertinent questions?'

She raised her chin. 'I'm only trying to understand.'

He sighed. Then he said with a visible effort at control, 'We've been dealing with some pretty high-powered emotions here, Joss. Why don't we cool it for a while? Let's walk down to those birches by the water and you can tell me about medical school and I'll tell you about market gardening.'

So she was not to be given the reason. She managed a small smile. 'Sounds like a good idea to me.'

Milky waves were slopping against the stone abutment and a few lazy seagulls hovered over the picnic area as Joss and Niall began to talk. Two hours later they were still talking, with the ease and camaraderie of two people who are in tune. Joss had been describing the clinic to Niall, drawing a rough plan of the layout on her notepad, when she caught sight of her watch. 'Is that the time?' she squeaked.

He checked his own watch, the same one he had six years ago. 'You're two minutes slow.'

'I've got to go! I'm meeting Bryan for dinner at his mother's tonight.'

'So we're back to reality,' Niall said drily.

Joss still couldn't believe the time could have passed so quickly. 'Yes, I guess we are.'

'What are we going to do, Joss? Will we see each other again?'

'I don't know,' she said helplessly. 'I simply don't know.'

'I want to.' He took the notepad from her lax fingers. 'I'll give you my phone number—business and home. You can call me any time, Joss.'

With a flash of spirit she said, 'I won't interrupt you with Ms Trilby Henderson-Smythe?'

'You will not. A casual date, Joss. The only kind I've had the last five years.'

She got up from the bench, shoving the notepad back in her purse, knowing whatever happened she would cherish the piece of paper with Niall's handwriting on it. Avoiding his eyes she said, 'I really have to go, Niall. Could you drop me off near a subway stop?'

'I'll take you to your apartment.'

'I'd rather you didn't. Bryan might get there early to pick me up.'

'I see,' he said quietly. 'This is a difficult situation, isn't it?'

Understatement of the year, she thought unhappily. 'Look at that kite, it's got five separate sections,' she said.

They talked about kites, the poor conditions of the expressway and a recent warehouse fire until Niall pulled up by a subway station. Then he said abruptly, 'So is this it, Joss? You'll get married in two weeks and we'll never see each other again?'

'I can't deceive Bryan!' she cried. 'I won't go behind his back.'

'You always were honest, Joss.'

'If I'm honest, I feel as though I'm being torn apart,' she said in a ragged voice.

'Then tell him you're still in love with me.'

'I thought I loved him!'

Niall banged the flat of his hand against the steering wheel. 'I'll call you in the next couple of days. You'd better go, you'll be late.'

His profile was turned to her, his jaw set. She said breathlessly, 'Goodbye,' and scrambled out of the car. Not until she was on the subway platform did she realise that she had left the red roses in the back seat of the car.

CHAPTER EIGHT

To JOSS'S great relief, Bryan was not waiting for her at the apartment. She changed into tailored beige trousers with a crocheted sweater and tried consciously to relax, for her brain was whirling and her eyes overbright. When Bryan arrived she found herself turning her cheek to his kiss and hustling him out of the apartment right away. When they were headed north on Yonge Street Bryan said, 'I tried to call you this afternoon.'

'I met Niall after lunch.'

'That was probably a wise move, Joss. Get it out of your system.'

She remembered the kiss by the lake and winced inwardly at her duplicity. 'I suppose so.'

'You won't be seeing him again.'

Bryan had made it a statement, not a question. She felt a flicker of rebellion, squashed it, and said, 'I'll be busy with the clinic and with the wedding.'

'Mother says more gifts have arrived.'

Bryan's mother Leah, of whom Joss was very fond, was happily doing the lion's share of the wedding preparations. She was an attractive widow who had a sparkle that her son lacked. She greeted Joss with a kiss. 'Lovely to see you, dear. Bryan darling, pour some drinks, will you? Three huge boxes arrived today, Joss. I'm dying for you to open them.'

Wedding presents, thought Joss numbly. She had to unwrap them, write thank-you letters, store them in her apartment, then move them to the condominium after the wedding. After the wedding . . . *Niall*.

'Joss, are you all right?' Leah said sharply.

Joss gave her head a little shake. 'Must be pre-nuptial nerves,' she joked, heard the tension in her voice and knew Leah must have heard it, too.

The first box contained a very lovely hand-turned wooden salad set, the second a marble lamp whose base reminded Joss of a headstone, and the third a ceramic ornament, four feet tall, replete with fat bunches of grapes and smirking cupids. Joss looked at it in horror, for it seemed to express the debasement of passion to a simpering, mass-produced sweetness. I can't give Bryan passion, she thought frantically. I'll never be able to.

'Well,' said Leah, 'you could always hide it at the very back of the garden.'

'We won't have a garden,' Joss said. She, who had grown up on a farm, was going to be living on the tenth floor of a high-rise. She couldn't grow roses if she wanted to. She closed her eyes, feeling the wings of panic beat about her head.

Bryan put his hand on her shoulder. She jumped, splashing some of her drink on her trousers, fighting a ridiculous urge to burst into tears.

'I'll get a cloth,' Leah said briskly.

'I'm beginning to wonder what happened this afternoon,' Bryan said stiffly, his grey eyes very watchful.

'Nothing!'

'You're not yourself at all.'

'Of course I am—I'm fine. It's just . . . oh thank you, Leah.' Joss made a valiant effort to pull herself together, and the rest of the evening went more smoothly. After she and Bryan had lugged the boxes up to her apartment, she closed the spare room door on them and said with perfect truth, 'I'm really tired, Bryan. I think I'll go to bed.'

He put his arms around her. She stared at his immaculate shirt-front and old school tie and heard him say, 'Joss, you're not going to back out of the wedding, are you?'

The tie had a pattern of tiny gold unicorns. 'Seeing Niall today upset me,' she blurted.

'The invitations are out, the presents are arriving, all my colleagues are invited—it would be extremely awkward to call the whole thing off.'

'A wedding should be more than a social occasion,' she protested.

'I wish to God I'd taken you to any restaurant other than Scarlatti's last night!'

Bryan almost never swore. 'Better to have met Niall now than two weeks after the wedding.'

'Better never to have met him at all. He's part of your past, Joss.'

She had the beginnings of a headache. 'I thought he was,' she whispered.

'He is. You and I belong together. We have all kinds of interests in common, and you know how fond of you my mother is.'

But were those sufficient reasons to get married? Joss wondered, and felt again the flutterings of panic. Then Bryan raised her chin and kissed her and panic exploded into denial. She shoved him away. 'Please don't!' she gasped.

'Joss, I'm your fiancé!'

'I don't know what's wrong with me. I feel like I'm being torn apart.' She had used the same words with Niall, she remembered with a touch of desperation.

In a cold voice Bryan said, 'I don't want you to see that man again, Joss. Ever. He's bad for you. Everything was fine until he came along.'

Never to see Niall again? Impossible. 'You can't turn the clock back,' she said.

'You can avoid making the same mistake twice. He abandoned you six years ago; he could do the same thing again.'

In three weeks he could do the same thing again, she

thought wildly. The headache had become a pounding reality. 'Bryan, I'll do the best I can and I promise I won't deceive you. That's all I can say—except goodnight,' she added with a fractional smile.

'It's little enough,' he said huffily. 'Goodnight, Joss.'

She went to bed as soon as he had gone, and dreamed of ceramic grapes tossed with red rose petals in a wooden salad bowl.

Joss spent the morning at her apartment tidying up some correspondence and reading medical journals. The phone rang once during the entire morning, and it was neither Niall nor Bryan. It was Magda.

Magda's faith in Charlie had been fully justified. He had patented two inexpensive pollution control devices for the pulp and paper industry four years ago, and he and Magda now lived in an architecturally designed house on Crescent Road. They were expecting their first child any day and had become, to Joss's amusement, mini-encyclopaedias of obstetrical lore.

'Hi, Joss. Not a labour pain in sight,' Magda groaned.

Joss, the medical expert, said soothingly, 'You can't rush nature, Magda.'

Magda discussed various internal details at some length, then said more cheerfully, 'And how are you?'

'In a mess,' Joss replied succinctly, and proceeded to describe the events of the last two days. It was a great relief to talk about Niall to someone who knew the whole story.

Magda listened in a fascinated silence, then said, 'It's very simple. Tell Bryan the wedding's off and marry Niall.'

'Before or after the check-up?' Joss snorted.

'He can't disappear a second time, Joss, not if he's got a three-hundred-acre farm just outside the city.'

'He hasn't asked me to marry him.'

'Well, you are engaged to someone else.'

'Bryan is afraid I'm going to change my mind.'

'Bryan's not a bad guy,' Magda said judiciously. 'He loves his job, he's nice to his mother, he's an upright citizen who'll never get a speeding ticket in his life. But you don't light up when he comes in the room, Joss. After six years, when Charlie comes home after work I still feel as though someone's turned on every light bulb in the house.'

'You're no help,' Joss said crossly.

'You've been given a second chance—take it, that's all.'

'Easy for you to say—you don't have a spare room full of wedding presents.' Joss proceeded to describe the ceramic cherubs.

After Magda had rung off Joss went out to do some errands. Then, on impulse, she headed down to the clinic. The workmen were tearing down partitions and ripping out the old plumbing fixtures; dust motes fogged the air. Joss stepped over a pile of old lumber and went into the room that would eventually be her office. The grimy-paned window looked out on the peeling paint of the next-door tenement. She ran her finger along the sill. She'd put plants on it, she thought, and hang her credentials on the wall beside it. Here in this room she had no doubts as to who she was . . .

Behind her a familiar male voice said, 'Dr MacDougall?'

Somehow not at all surprised to hear that voice, Joss adopted a businesslike smile and turned around. 'Good afternoon, Mr Morgan.'

'I know I haven't got an appointment,' Niall said. 'But I'm suffering from the most disturbing symptoms.'

'Would you describe them for me, please?'

He said promptly, 'Palpitations of the heart, weakness in the knees, sweating palms . . . plus one other effect I'd be embarrassed to describe to you. But I only

THE RIGHT MAN

get these symptoms when I'm with a twenty-seven-year-old blonde who had gold flecks in her eyes.'

'You could stop seeing the blonde,' Joss suggested.

He put his head to one side. 'Lurid dreams,' he added. 'I forgot to mention those. The kind you wouldn't tell your mother . . . doctors are not supposed to blush.'

'*You're* not supposed to be here.' Nor was she supposed to feel so incredibly happy to see him—a symptom she kept to herself.

'I wanted to see your clinic. Will this be your office?'

A plank rasped free across the hall, followed by the thud of falling plaster. 'If you have faith in miracles,' said Joss, and began to describe the layout. She was soon carried away by her enthusiasm and by Niall's evident interest; his questions were intelligent, and one or two of his suggestions well worth investigating. They ended their tour at the front door, where two chipped porcelain basins lay drunkenly on the pavement.

Niall looked up and down the street, which looked depressingly tawdry. 'You might want to hire a male receptionist,' he remarked. 'Someone who's been a bouncer in a nightclub, for instance.'

'Not a bad idea,' she said drily.

'Is your fiancé involved in this?'

'No. He'd like to see me practising paediatrics in one of the snootier suburbs.'

Niall made a noise loosely translated as, 'Humph.' Then he said, 'This street is about as far from the farm as you can get, Joss.'

'I like Toronto a lot better than I used to,' she answered defensively. 'And of course Bryan works in the city. But I don't know that I'll ever feel at home here.'

'You can take the girl out of the country, but not the reverse.'

She did not want to talk about the farm or the

country. 'Niall, why are you here?'

He moved to one side to allow a workman to dump a load of old lathes on the pavement. 'I had to see you. When I called your apartment there was no answer, so I figured you might be down here.'

'I thought we'd agreed we wouldn't see each other again.'

'We didn't agree on anything.'

'I'm engaged to Bryan!'

'The symptoms are real, Joss.'

She said levelly. 'Take me with you when you go to Boston for your check-up.'

'No. But I'll call you as soon as I get back.'

'If the results are positive,' she retorted bitterly.

His gaze was unflinching. 'That's right,' he said.

'Niall, go away,' she said with the calmness of despair. 'This is lunacy. I can't bear to be hurt by you all over again, I just can't bear it. I love Bryan and I'm going to marry him. Go away and leave me alone!'

Another workman had lugged two buckets of broken plaster out of the building. ''Scuse me, miss,' he said.

Hurriedly Joss stepped aside. It was beginning to rain, and in a burst of ill-temper she cried, 'Of all the hundreds of restaurants in Toronto, why did Bryan have to pick Scarlatti's?'

'We'd have met sooner or later. Joss, don't marry him.'

'You've got a nerve!' she exploded. 'You want me to break my engagement and change my whole life, even though you're not prepared to change a damn thing. No, sir—you're going to play it safe and wait until you've got a nice little certificate of health in your hand before *you* make any commitments.'

'If you marry him we'll never have a chance.'

'I'll marry whom I please,' Joss said furiously.

Niall was white about the mouth. 'I'm begging you not to marry Bryan.'

Suddenly she could not bear the turmoil of emotion in her breast. 'I've had enough of this—go away, Niall,' she said breathlessly. 'I'm going inside to get my coat, and when I come back I want you to be gone.'

He said with icy precision, 'If I go I won't be back.'

She ignored a hot stab of pain that seemed to pierce her to the core. 'Good!' she snapped, pivoted and ran back in the building. Stumbling over the uneven boards, she went into her office. She did not have a coat there; she had known she would not have the courage to stand on the pavement and watch Niall drive away.

A wrecking bar clanged to the floor in the next room, and the steady whump of a mallet seemed to echo her heartbeat. Joss stared out of the window, counting slowly to one hundred. Then she went back outside. Niall's sports car was gone.

It was raining harder, spotting her beige trousers, dampening her hair, bouncing on the roof of her car. Niall had taken her at her word. He had gone. And she knew him well enough to be sure he would not be back.

She crossed the road very slowly, her heart still beating with the heavy strokes of the workman's mallet. A disagreeable symptom, Dr MacDougall, she thought wretchedly, and recalled her blind, unreasoning happiness when she had seen Niall standing in the doorway of her office.

He would never stand there again.

She drove home with exaggerated caution. When she opened the door of her apartment the telephone was ringing. She ran across the room and grabbed the receiver. But it was Leah on the line, not Niall. Trying to swallow a disappointment caustic as lye, Joss heard Leah say, 'I'm just down the road, dear. As you're home, can I drop off a brochure from the florists?'

'Sure. I'll put the kettle on,' Joss mumbled, and hung up, trembling in reaction. She had been a fool to think Niall would call. She had told him to stay away, hadn't she?

She was still standing by the phone when the doorbell rang. Leah's hair was freshly tinted and her raincoat the newest fashion. She kissed Joss and remarked, 'You must have got caught in the rain without a coat.'

'Yes,' Joss said vaguely. 'I guess I did.'

Leah put her head to one side. 'Joss, what's wrong? You weren't yourself last night, and Bryan nearly bit my head off when I phoned him at work today.'

Joss met Leah's gaze; Leah's eyes were the same grey as her son's, yet lit by a warmth Bryan showed only rarely. 'I forgot to put the kettle on,' she said.

'Go and change your clothes and dry your hair. I'll make the tea, and then we'll sit down and have a good talk.'

'Is this your bossy mother-in-law act?' Joss asked with something like a genuine smile.

'Someone's got to get bossy around here. Off you go.'

It was comforting to be told what to do; Joss missed her own mother rather more than she would admit. Within five minutes she had changed into a comfortable track suit and was curled up on the chesterfield with a cup of Earl Grey. Then, beginning with her first sight of Niall at the Red Lion six years ago, she told Leah the whole story. She was well into her second cup by the time she finished with the scene on the pavement at Queen Street.

Leah poured herself another cup of tea. 'What you've told me explains so much,' she said reflectively. 'Don't get me wrong, I dearly love my son. But he can be a bit of a stick-in-the-mud—rather like his father—and it's often puzzled me why you chose him. You're so full of warmth and spontaneity, Joss. And—let's use the word—passion. You'd be good for Bryan, I'm sure. But I'm not sure how good he'd be for you.'

'He has been good for me, Leah,' Joss argued. 'He

was really the first man I dated after Niall, and he's been so patient and understanding. I owe him a lot.'

'But do you owe him marriage?'

'I would hardly have expected you of all people to ask that question,' Joss countered in exasperation.

'I care for both of you. Too much to see you make a mistake.'

Leah's smile was singularly sweet. Joss said in a rush, 'I care about you, too. I want to do what's right, Leah. That's what I was trying to do this afternoon by sending Niall away.'

'Right for whom? For Bryan? For Niall? Or for you?'

'For everyone,' Joss said helplessly.

'If Bryan weren't a doctor, would you be as fond of him?'

'I'm not interested in the money he makes!'

'I wasn't suggesting that. But Bryan does excellent work, and because you threw yourself so wholeheartedly into medicine, I wonder if you've ever quite separated him from his job.' Stirring her tea Leah added delicately, 'One doesn't go to bed with a doctor. One goes to bed with a man.'

'I've never gone to bed with Bryan. Or with Niall,' Joss said clumsily.

'So which one would you choose?'

Joss's hesitation went on too long. Leah said gently, 'I see. Be awfully careful, Joss. When sex goes well, it takes its rightful place in marriage. But when it doesn't, it can be horrendous.'

Intuitively Joss knew Leah was speaking of her own marriage, to a man who had been very much like Bryan. 'But if there's any doubt about Niall's condition he'll push me away again.'

'There are two separate problems here, Joss. The first is whether you should marry Bryan—do you honestly believe your feelings for him are strong enough for a lifelong relationship? The second is Niall's inability to share the bad times along with the good. I'm not sure how one would cope with that. But they are two different issues. You're in danger of treating them as one.'

Was Leah right? Joss gave a heavy sigh. 'If I have any more tea I'll be water-logged,' she said. 'I know you're not going to tell me what to do, are you, Leah?'

'Definitely not,' Leah said crisply. 'Although I will say it's easier to break an engagement than to get a divorce.'

'You sound like my friend Magda.'

'You're getting advice from all sides, aren't you, dear? You'll do the right thing, I know.'

Joss wished she could be as sure.

The telephone rang once more that day, about four-thirty. 'Joss, it's Bryan. An emergency's come up at the hospital. A bad fire in Scarborough, a number of children involved, so it looks like it'll be an all-nighter. Can you get someone else to go to the theatre with you?'

She had forgotten that she and Bryan had tickets for *Cats* that evening. 'I'll see if Magda will go with me—it'll take her mind off motherhood. I hope everything will go all right, Bryan.'

'They're calling in extra staff. I'll probably sleep tomorrow morning, but maybe in the afternoon we could go out to the country and find somewhere to eat.'

Joss recognised this as a sacrifice on his part, for Bryan did not like the country. Then he added, 'I go away on Sunday afternoon. You'll take me to the airport, won't you, Joss?'

She had forgotten that, as well. Bryan was going to Switzerland for an international convention and would be away for a week. In a great flood of relief she thought of having a whole week to herself, with time to think and sort out all the emotional chaos of the past three days.

'Joss, are you still there?'

'Of course I'll take you to the airport. Good luck tonight, Bryan, I'll be thinking about you. And I'll see you tomorrow.'

'Thanks. 'Bye.'

His mind, she knew, was more on his upcoming patients than on herself, which did not bother her at all. Quickly she dialled Magda's number.

'Love to,' said Magda. 'I'm sick to death of being pregnant . . . who are you engaged to today?'

'Bryan, of course,' Joss answered haughtily.

'Your conscience is as scrupulous as an archbishop's,' Magda complained.

'I have to try and do what's right.'

'And how does Niall react to that?'

'Niall and I are not on speaking terms,' Joss replied even more haughtily. 'I'm not inviting you out tonight so we can talk about Niall, Magda.'

'Just remember there's a lot more to marriage than the wedding,' Magda said portentously.

'Oh, hush!' Joss said.

Cats, however, successfully distracted Magda from engagements and babies and Joss from weddings. Joss drove Magda home aferwards and slept soundly that night. The next day Bryan was not free until dinner time. He had had less than four hours' sleep since the day before and had to go back to the hospital that evening. He described a number of the cases to Joss, which she knew from experience was his way of rechecking that he had done everything he could. She listened intently, putting in the occasional question, realising what a bond this sort of conversation was. He looked very tired. She kissed him goodnight with genuine affection, almost glad she was not on speaking terms with Niall, for she could be fairer to Bryan this way. The next afternoon she drove Bryan to the airport.

'Don't come in,' he said as he unlocked the trunk and

took out his suitcase. 'I'm going to the first-class lounge to snatch a half-hour's sleep.'

'You've put in some long hours since Friday.'

'Mother regularly accuses me of being a workaholic.' He smiled at Joss. 'I've felt better about our relationship the last couple of days, though. I think we're over the hump.' Then he kissed her goodbye very thoroughly and disappeared through the sliding doors.

As Joss watched his upright figure vanish into the crowd the tight coil of tension that had been with her since the evening at Scarlatti's began to loosen. A week to herself. A week to relax. A week to decide.

This plan, however, lasted for only the first hour she was home. Then Michael Devon, one of her two prospective clinic partners, phoned her. His wife Susan was ill. Could Joss take over her practice for the week?

Joss sputtered a number of ifs and buts, agreed to do so, spent Sunday evening with Michael familiarising herself with the set-up, and then worked all week as hard as she had ever worked in her internship. The work was exhilarating and exhausting and she loved it; on Friday it was past midnight when she got to bed.

Nevertheless, Joss woke early on Saturday morning. Her first thought was that a week from today she was supposed to be marrying Bryan; her second was to wonder what Niall was doing; her third that she was to meet Bryan at the airport the following afternoon and she did not seem to have made any kind of decision. She buried her face in the pillow, cravenly trying to obliterate all thought. But she could not go back to sleep. She got up and prowled around the apartment, filled with a strange restlessness. The sun was shining. It was a beautiful May morning. What was she doing cooped up in an apartment in the city?

Not stopping to think, she dressed in shorts and a cotton top, grabbed a banana for breakfast and went down in the lift to the car park. Her aged Volkswagen started on the first try, which seemed a good omen to Joss, who then chugged out of the garage and headed north, out of the city. The tenth exit on the turnpike named the little town of Braxton. Niall's farm was on the outskirts of Braxton. She took the exit.

Braxton was ten kilometres to the west. The road meandered between low-lying hills covered with newly leafed birch trees that were loud with birdsong. Joss stopped by a brook and picked a bunch of violets, their little white faces veined with purple among heart-shaped green leaves. She felt suspended in time and space. If she was as intent upon doing the right thing as she kept telling everyone, she should not be anywhere in the vicinity of Niall's home. Yet a strange impulse had brought her here; and although she felt as shy and tentative as the violets poking up between the rocks, she knew she would not turn back.

She packed the violet stems in wet moss, got in her car and drove on. Five minutes later she came to a very attractive scrolled sign beside a narrow lane that disappeared into the trees. Morgan's Market Gardens, said the sign. Fruit Trees. Shrubs. Strawberries.

She turned into the lane, which was overhung with oak and beech trees; long ago Joss had decided that there was no green quite as fresh as a newly unfurled beech leaf. She discovered that she was singing to herself.

The lane climbed steadily up an incline, then widened in front of a small, grey-painted cabin. Two mongrels rushed up to meet her, barking enthusiastically. A cat that reminded her of Magda's Nasturtium—who now presided over the architecturally designed house— yawned at her from a sunlit bench in front of the cabin. The other occupant of the bench was a wizened old man in a pair of incredibly dirty dungarees. Joss got out of the car.

The cabin was flanked by forsythia bushes like miniature sunbursts. The air smelled clean and sweet. Joss smiled at the old man and said, 'Is Niall Morgan here, please?'

The old man screwed up his face. 'Yeah. He's here.'

'Where would I find him?'

'You want to buy trees, or shrubs?'

'Neither. I just want to see Niall.' Which was the simple truth, she thought in wonderment.

'You the dame he's mooning over?'

She looked straight into his rheumy old eyes. 'Who are you?' she responded.

'Name's Clem.' He spat in the dust. 'Known Niall since he stood no taller than a gooseberry bush.'

'He *told* you about me?'

'Him?' Clem gave a cackle of laughter. 'Not likely. Never known any one so close-mouthed. But I'm no fool, I saw him pick them roses. I c'n put two and two together and get three and a half any day of the week.'

Joss leaned against the side of her car. 'Did you say you knew him when he was a little boy?'

'Yep.' Clem fondled the ears of the brown and white mongrel, who was sniffing the cuffs of his disgraceful dungarees.

'Tell me how his mother died,' Joss demanded.

Clem leered at her. 'Now that's a funny question from a pretty little thing like you.'

'Don't be sexist. It will help me understand him.'

Clem gave another cackle of laughter. 'He's like one of them hedgehogs—touch 'em and they curl up in a ball. He ain't into being understood.'

'Did she have a long illness?' Joss persisted.

'Say, you're sure curious. You know what curiosity did to the cat?'

'*You're* exasperating!' Joss snapped. 'Why won't you tell me?'

'Ask him, not me. It was his mother.' Clem tipped the brim of his cap. 'You gonna marry him?'

Joss said sweetly, 'Ask him, not me.'

'So you got spunk.' Another leer. 'I'll tell you somethin'. Everythin' was kept very hush-hush those years his ma was ill. But he changed . . . yeah, he sure changed.' Abruptly Clem stood up, dislodging the mongrel. 'I got work to do. Drive past the house and you'll hear the tiller, he's workin' up a new bed.' Clem cackled again. 'Not the kind you're interested in,' he said. Then he whistled to the dogs and disappeared behind the cabin. Joss, red-faced, got in her car and drove down the hill.

The house, made of stone, nestled in the valley. Newly planted fields took up the flats, orchards striped the slopes, quince and rhododendrons and azaleas edged the road. Joss drove past the house, which had a blue front door flanked by trumpet honeysuckle, and parked the car. The growl of a roto-tiller came from her left. She walked up the slope.

Niall, stripped to the waist, his hands protected by heavy gloves, was throwing rocks into a wheelbarrow. Then he turned back to the tiller, engaged the gear, and began churning up the rich black earth. Beyond the garden a grove of cherry trees was in bloom.

It was not the orchard back home, thought Joss with a catch at her heart. But it was near enough. She stepped from between two forsythia bushes and waved at the blue-eyed man in the garden.

CHAPTER NINE

NIALL saw Joss immediately. He turned off the tiller and into the ringing silence said quietly, 'Joss . . . am I dreaming?'

'No, I'm real.'

He pulled off his gloves, draped them on the handle of the tiller and walked towards her, his boots sinking into the soil. 'Are you alone? No fiancé?'

'He's away,' she said. Bryan had no place in this beautiful valley.

Niall stopped a couple of feet away from her. 'But he's still your fiancé?'

'Yes.' Niall's chest was slicked with sweat; there was a daub of mud on his shoulder. She fought the urge to wipe it off and wondered dizzily what she was doing here.

As if he had read her thoughts, he asked, 'Why are you here?'

'I . . . don't know.'

The sun was full on her face. 'You look tired,' he said.

'I put in some long hours this week.' Quickly Joss explained about Susan's practice.

Niall said gravely, 'So you thought you'd go for a drive this morning, and when you saw my sign you decided to drop in.'

She smiled, knowing he was as glad to see her as she was to see him, knowing also he was not going to ask any more awkward questions. 'You need a coffee break.'

'You can stay for coffee, for lunch and for dinner. But I'm warning you, I'll probably put you to work.'

The scent of freshly turned earth teased her nostrils. 'There's nothing I'd like better.'

'What do you think of the place, Joss?'

She looked up at him and said softly, 'It's an enchanted place.'

Without laying a finger on her, Niall bent his head. Their lips met in a long, drugged kiss that left Joss weak with desire. She wanted to rest her cheek on his chest and inhale the mingling of sweat and soil on his skin; she wanted to hold the scarred ribs under her palm and keep him safe. He was real to her, real in a way Bryan had never been. How could she marry Bryan? she wondered; and wondered also if the decision was not making itself, if her visit here this morning was not in its own way a decision. Quite unable to share any of this, she said weakly, 'Coffee.'

Niall lifted one brow. 'Iced water?'

She laughed and suddenly everything was all right. As they wandered towards the house, Niall explained how he was developing the property, and his plans for the future. The house had beautifully proportioned rooms that were extremely clean but very bare; all Niall's energies had gone into the outdoors, thought Joss, her imagination stirred by so many blank walls and empty corridors. None of the blank walls in the condominium had stirred her at all.

After they had drunk cold orange juice on the patio, they worked together at the new garden for a couple of hours, Joss happily taking her turn at lugging rocks, her slender calves lost in a pair of Niall's work boots. Then Niall said, wiping his forehead, 'You know what we should do? Let's pack a picnic and take the canoe out on the lake.'

'You mean you own a lake as well?'

'On the other side of the hill. I bought up all the land around it last year.'

'Sounds like a great idea.'

Half an hour later they were launching the canoe from a rickety old wharf at the head of the lake. Bullrushes speared the water; lily pads floated in the shallows. The

lake itself basked under the noonday sun, the slow thrust
and drip of the paddles scarcely disturbing the silence.
They headed towards a small island cupped in a cove and
beached the canoe. Naill lifted out the hamper. 'Hungry?'

Joss looked longingly at the water, where the ripples
from their approach had already smoothed. 'I'm hot and
dirty and I'd love a swim.'

'We swam once before, Joss—remember?'

She looked up at him and said quietly, 'I've never
forgotten anything we did.'

His face was suddenly as naked to her as his sweat-
streaked chest. 'Neither have I. Nor will I. Ever.'

Her eyes fell. *You'll know the right man*, her mother
had always said. Niall felt as right to her now as he had six
years ago; but in all good faith she had promised to marry
someone else, and Niall would make no promises at all
until he had passed his check-up. 'And will you remember
today?' she cried with a bitterness that shocked her.

'Yes. You're part of my soul, Joss.'

She turned away in sudden anguish. She would hurt
Bryan if she broke their engagement; but would she not
hurt him more if she married him feeling the way she did
about Niall?

She kicked off her sandals, ran into the water in her
shorts and top, and plunged under the surface, trying to
drown out Niall's image in the surge and hiss of the lake
water. But as she surfaced and struck out from the shore,
she was beginning to understand what had brought her
here today; she had wanted to know if Niall was as real to
her now as he had been six years ago.

Her wet clothes dragged at her body, slowing her down.
The lake was cold. She trod water, watching Niall stroke
past her in an energetic overarm crawl, knowing she
already had her answer. Then she swam back to shore.

Her blouse was clammy against her back and her shorts
were dripping; the air that had seemed so warm only a few
minutes ago was cool now, making her shiver. Clambering

awkwardly over the rocks on the shore, Joss edged behind some bushes until she was screened from the lake. Then she took off her outer garments, wringing the water from them. It was an act of courage to put them on again. Cursing herself for her own stupidity, she made her way back to the little beach. Niall was just emerging from the lake, shaking the water from his hair like a puppy. He was only wearing shorts. It's an unfair world, thought Joss sourly, and heard him call, 'Feels great, eh?'

'I'm freezing,' she said irritably and inaccurately.

'Take off your shorts and blouse and spread them over the bushes. They'll be dry by the time we've eaten.'

'I can't do that with you here,' she retorted.

'Joss, I promise I won't lay a finger on you.'

'I shouldn't be here at all!' she cried, feeling tears bite at her eyes. 'I'm engaged to someone else. It was wrong of me to come.'

Niall took her by the shoulders. 'Stop wallowing in guilt!' he snapped. 'Are we doing anything wrong?'

Her chin dropped to her chest. 'I shouldn't *be* here,' she whispered.

'But you are here.' He gave her a little shake. 'For whatever the reason, we've been given a day together—let's enjoy it.'

His remark touched her on the raw. She could feel her temper rising and made no effort to check it. 'Enjoy the present and to hell with tomorrow?' she said waspishly.

'One thing I learned when I was ill was to take each day as it comes.'

'But you're not ill now, and no one can live solely in the present—what of tomorrow, and tomorrow, and tomorrow? One week from today I'm to marry Bryan!'

Niall's fingers tightened with unconscious cruelty. 'Do you think I don't know that? If my check-up had been last week I'd be making love to you right now, Joss, fighting for you with every weapon I possess. But I can't do that. So I have to stand back and let you make up your own mind, even it that half-kills me.'

'You don't have to stand back!' she blazed. 'You could ask me to go to Boston with you and share in the results of the check-up, whatever they might be.'

'We've been through all this before!'

'Why was your mother's illness so hush-hush, Niall? Why did it change you?'

His face stilled. He said flatly, 'You've been talking to Clem.'

'Oh, Clem's like you—he's not about to give away any family secrets. Tell me about your mother, Niall.'

'No.'

'So you don't care if I marry Bryan on Saturday?'

Niall's features were as unyielding as the granite rocks Joss had hauled out of the ground. 'You've got to make up your own mind, Joss,' he said.

Leah had said more or less the same thing. Joss looked down at her wet blouse and knew she would keep it on, for how could she flaunt her body in front of this man who wanted so desperately to make love to her? Then Niall said evenly, 'This is difficult for you, Joss, I know. It's difficult because you're loyal and honest and true, and your agreement to marry Bryan wasn't a casual one.' His smile was wry. 'By some kind of convoluted reasoning I'd have thought the less of you if you'd broken your engagement the night we met at Scarlatti's.'

She gazed up at him dumbly and into her mind the three small words *I love you* lay as clear and limpid as the lake water over the rocks. She did not say them. She said, with a huge effort at restoring normality, 'I don't suppose Bryan would mind if we ate the picnic.'

So they did, seated on rocks in the sun, and afterwards paddled back to the gardens. When they were walking to the house Niall looked up the hill. 'Customers,' he remarked. 'Up by Clem's cabin.'

'Why does Clem live with you, Niall?'

'My father sold the family property two years ago and

moved into an apartment, so Clem had nowhere to go—he'd been with us for years as a general handyman. Now he works when he feels like it and complains the rest of the time . . . excuse me for a few minutes, will you, Joss?' After passing her the empty picnic basket, Niall jogged along the driveway towards the customers.

Joss carried the basket to the house, leaving it in the shade by the front door; Niall and the two customers had disappeared among the trees. She knew exactly what she was going to do. She walked up the hill, found Clem seated on his bench and said bluntly, 'Will you tell me where Niall's father lives?'

Clem took a tobacco pouch from his pocket and began rolling a cigarette. 'I might. Then again, I might not.'

The brown and white mongrel was still at Clem's feet, gazing at him adoringly. Stupid dog, thought Joss, and said, 'Do you enjoy being hard to get along with, Clem?'

He peered at her through eyebrows like unpruned hedges. 'Could be. Or else I'd just like to know what kinda stuff you're made of.'

'You're a manipulative and cantankerous old man,' she said sweetly. 'I want to find out about Niall's mother. He won't tell me. You won't tell me. His father is the logical person to ask.'

The cigarette, shreds of tobacco dangling from one end, was apparently completed. Clem began searching his pockets for matches. 'You never told me if you were gonna marry Niall.'

'I'm engaged to someone else,' she said tartly.

'Yeah? Get unengaged.'

'Only if you'll tell me where Niall's father lives.'

Clem sniggered uncouthly, lit the cigarette and exhaled a cloud of noxious blue smoke. 'Think you're pretty smart, eh?'

'Smart enough to know you'd like me and Niall to get

married,' Joss said slowly.

Clem shot her a disconcertingly shrewd glance. 'Not many people'd let me live with 'em,' he said. 'Niall took me in right away. You willin' to fight for him?'

She grinned. 'I'm standing here talking to you, aren't I?'

Clem puffed out another cloud of smoke. 'His dad lives in Vancouver. Montpelier Apartments on Straughan Avenue.'

Joss had not expected to win quite so easily. 'Thank you,' she gulped.

'Doubt that he'll let you past the door. Tight-lipped fella—like his son, only worse.'

'If I go all the way to Vancouver, he'd better let me past the door,' Joss said with a scowl.

'You better get rid of the other guy first. Look a little strange, otherwise.'

Joss had temporarily forgotten about Bryan. 'You're very fond of telling people what to do.'

'You should get back to the house, too. Unless you want Niall to know we bin havin' a cosy little chat.'

'I'm beginning to think Niall deserves a medal for having taken you in,' she said vigorously. 'Goodbye, Clem. *You* should quit smoking.'

'Keeps the flies away.' He winked at her. 'See you around.'

Fortunately Niall was still busy with the customers when Joss arrived back at the house. She put on his work boots again and trudged over to the garden, where she started the tiller and began ploughing the soil. There were a great many rocks, which gave her even more respect for the beauty Niall had created in the little valley. A few minutes later Niall came through the gap in the forsythia bushes that formed the garden's eastern boundary. Joss smiled at him.

'You've got mud on your face,' he said. 'Also on your knees and your shirt.'

'Also under my fingernails. Did you sell anything?'

'Four apple trees and two hundred strawberry plants. I might break even this year, having been in the red for the last four.'

'You've put a lot of money into the place.'

'I made a lot in my executive days. The rat race pays—that's why people stay in it.' Without altering his voice Niall added, 'You look absolutely right standing in my garden, Joss. You don't know how many times in the past four years I've pictured you here.'

Because the sun was at her back, Joss's face was in shadow. Perhaps this gave her courage. She heard herself say, 'Niall, do you love me?'

The sun in its turn exposed every nuance of feeling on his features. 'I wouldn't have thought you needed to ask that question.'

'I'm asking it.'

'Yes, I love you. I fell in love with you six years ago, and finding you again has simply confirmed it. I'll always love you, Joss.'

She tried to quench a happiness as golden as the petals on the forsythia. 'So your fear of illness goes very deep.'

'It's something I can't change.'

'Not even if you risk losing me again?'

His jaw was rigid. 'Are you going to marry Bryan?'

She said slowly, 'I'm not sure you have the right to ask that question, Niall.'

His eyes held hers. 'Then we'd better talk about something else, hadn't we?'

Strangely enough, although she knew she had been defeated, Joss was exhilarated by the battle. Her spine very straight, she said, 'I guess we had.'

'I not only love you, I like you,' he smiled.

'I can't imagine why,' she said demurely. 'A nag like me.'

'With mud on her face.' Niall stepped closer and wiped her cheekbone with his fingertip.

She could see the laughter in his eyes and felt his chest brush her shirt. He was standing close to her purposely, she knew; the mud on her face was only a pretext. 'Sex is not a fair weapon,' she said.

He widened his eyes in mock innocence. 'Am I kissing you with unbridled passion? Am I enticing you into the forsythia brushes to make love? Or worse, into the gooseberry patch? I think I'm behaving admirably under the circumstances.'

Disarmed, she said, 'I've always loved to see you laugh.'

'You've always been able to make me laugh.' He gave her the crooked smile she knew so well. 'The gooseberry bushes are starting to look very inviting, thorns and all—I think we should get back to work.'

She put her head to one side. 'How can I make you change your mind about Boston?'

'You can't. I learned certain lessons as a kid, Joss, and I can't unlearn them.'

'Won't.'

'Can't. But as soon as I get back from Boston, I'll court you as assiduously as I know how.' He raised one brow sardonically. 'Providing, that is, that you're not a married woman.'

Joss glowered at him. 'I hate it when you have the last word.'

He laughed. 'Why don't you use the tiller while I dump these rocks?'

They worked side by side for nearly two hours, by which time three-quarters of the bed had been tilled with peat moss and compost. Then Niall struck two large rocks. 'Have to use the mattock for these,' he grunted. 'Do you want to go up to the house, Joss, and bring back a couple of cold beers?'

'Great idea. Don't you get those out on your own, though—too hard on the back.'

He gave her a mock salute. 'No, Doc.'

'Today has been really good for me,' Joss said spontaneously. 'Last week was my first experience of a regular practice, so I wanted to do everything right—with the result that I was exhausted last night. Hauling rocks is great therapy.'

'Not everyone would see it that way . . . try not to trip over your toes on the way up to the house, huh?'

'Are you insinuating I can't fill your boots?'

Joss was smiling while she walked up to the house, and still smiling on her way back with two cans of beer. She came round the forsythia hedge, then stopped dead in her tracks. Niall was hunched over the tiller, clutching his side, his face contracted with pain.

He's ill again, she thought, and felt agony rip through her own body. I'm going to lose him. Oh, God, I can't bear it. Not again.

Then she started to run, the boots flopping on her feet. She dropped the beer cans on the ground at the edge of the garden and gasped, 'Niall, what's wrong?'

He was ashen-faced, half leaning against the handles of the tiller. 'Caught my hand between the rocks,' he muttered.

Only then did Joss take in the blood dripping between his fingers on to the sharp-edged boulders at his feet. In an immensity of relief that left her weak-kneed, she realised Naill had had an accident: nothing to do with his illness, nothing to do with his check-up. Instantly she became the calm, level-headed professional. She straightened out his left hand and assessed the damage, then said decisively, 'I'll run you to the nearest hospital—you'll need stitches and an X-ray to check for broken bones. You stay here and I'll back my car down.'

'Clem will take me.'

'*I* will take you.'

Incredibly Niall managed a smile. 'Yes, Doc.'

Joss covered the distance to the house in record time,

thrust her feet into her sandals and found a clean cloth in one of the kitchen drawers. When she got back to the garden she carefully wrapped Niall's injured hand in the cloth, then eased him into the car seat; he was leaning on her so heavily that she knew he was in shock. At the top of the hill she told Clem what had happened before driving down the lane towards the highway. 'Which is the nearest hospital, Niall?'

'Turn right. Right again at the next intersection. Hospital's in Stirling.'

His voice was thin with pain. She drove as fast as she could, found the red brick hospital with no trouble and ushered him in the door of the emergency department. He was whisked away by a very pretty nurse, and Joss was left to fill in the necessary forms and to wait.

She waited for nearly an hour, which gave her far too much time to think about that moment of sheer terror when she had first seen Niall bent over the tiller. Her visit today had more than achieved its purpose, she thought grimly. Niall was as real to her as he had ever been, and as right for her.

A white-coated attendant ushered Niall back into the waiting-room. Joss stood up, her eyes searching his face. He said rapidly, 'No broken bones, five stitches and a tetanus shot.'

There was a little colour in his cheeks and the lines of pain had eased from around his mouth. 'And you're chock-full of pain-killers,' she said.

He grinned. 'We could go dancing.'

'Not tonight,' she said firmly. 'I'm taking you straight home.'

'You sound just like the doctor,' he complained. But when they were seated in the car and the attendant had disappeared into the building he added quietly, 'I'm sorry I scared you, Joss. There was a moment when you dropped the beer cans that I thought you were one one who was going to pass out.'

'You weren't supposed to see that.'

'It was only an accident.'

Unwisely she stated the truth. 'For a moment I thought you were ill again—that the clock had gone back six years. That's why I looked so scared.'

He was silent for several seconds. Then he said, 'That proves my point, doesn't it—the high risk of being involved with me. That's why I'm not screaming at you to break your engagement.'

'It doesn't prove anything!' she cried. 'When you love someone there's risk involved—that's a fact of life.'

He did not pursue her use of the word love. 'Just take me home, will you, Joss.?'

In swift compunction she said, 'We shouldn't be arguing, not now. I'll take you home and you're to go straight to bed.'

'Then I want you to leave,' he said inflexibly.

His words cut her to the quick. 'As Bryan's coming back tomorrow, I'd scarcely stay,' she said coldly, as she clashed the gears and drove out of the car park. They did not speak on the way home.

Clem was sitting on the front step of the house when they arrived; the two dogs circled the car, yapping at Joss's ankles, fawning around Niall's. Clem said acerbically, 'Caught your fingers between two rocks, eh? Dumb thing to do.'

Niall straightened, supporting his left wrist with his right hand. 'Not very bright,' he agreed.

'I ain't gonna be your nursemaid.'

'Good,' said Niall.

Clem pointed a dirty finger at Joss. 'She'll look after you—take you soup in bed.'

'Clem,' Niall said strongly, 'there are times when I can't stand the sight of you, and this is one of them. I'm going indoors to lie on the couch and Joss is going home.'

'To her fi-an-cey?' Clem sneered. 'You got blood in that hand, Niall Morgan, or apple juice?'

'Get lost!' Niall yelled.

'OK, OK, I c'n take a hint.' Clem whistled to the dogs. 'I'll be down later to check on the two of you,' he snickered, and shambled off up the hill.

'My father must have been a saint to have put up with him all those years,' Niall muttered. Then he turned to Joss. 'Thanks for your help, Joss. I'll be all right now.'

His blue eyes were as flat as his voice. She said clearly, 'I'm coming into the house to see you settled. I'll leave some food out for you and make a sling for your wrist. I shall then leave. I will not attempt to rape you.'

'Your eyes shoot little gold sparks when you're angry,' Niall remarked.

Her nostrils flared. 'Clem's got nothing on you! Get in the house, Niall Morgan, before you drop.'

The chesterfield, which was covered in old-fashioned chintz, was long enough to accommodate Niall. Joss stalked upstairs to his bedroom, a room that filled her with a confusion of emotions, grabbed a pillow and blanket from his bed and marched downstairs again. Scrupulously not touching him, she spread the blanket over his legs and put the pillow under his head. In the kitchen she mixed up some soup in a saucepan on the stove and made a couple of sandwiches, wrapping them in waxed paper and leaving them in the refrigerator. Then she went back into the living-room.

Niall was asleep. The drugs had done their work.

He had told her to leave; but she did not want to. Impulsively Joss knelt beside the chesterfield, resting her cheek on his chest, which was rising and falling with the slow rhythm of his breathing. She closed her eyes. She did not want to leave. She belonged here.

A hand was stroking her hair; her neck was cramped.

Joss opened her eyes. The room was almost dark, so dark that Niall's eyes were a smoky, mysterious grey. She nestled against his hand and said softly, 'I like that.'

'You were supposed to go home.'

'I didn't want to leave you.'

The darkness seemed to free him, for he said roughly, 'I'm glad you didn't . . . come here, Joss.'

She tried to get up, yelped from the pain in her knees, and sagged against the chesterfield again. 'Where's your sore hand?'

'Safely out of reach. Come closer, Joss.'

She eased herself beside him on the chesterfield, lying full-length, sliding an arm across his chest. The darkness enfolded them as he kissed her, his good arm pulling her almost on top of him with surprising strength, so that she was also enfolded in the warmth of his body. When he released her she said with a catch in her voice, 'I like that, too.'

'Amazing what one can accomplish with one arm.'

She giggled. 'How are you feeling?'

She could feel him smile in the darkness. 'Lousy,' he said succinctly. 'I think the needle's worn off.'

Joss was all doctor immediately. 'I'll get you a pill.'

'Lie still a minute—I'll survive,' he said lazily.

She relaxed, loving the tautness of his arm, the hard curve of his ribcage against her breast, the warmth of his throat by her cheek. She would be content to stay here for ever, she thought dreamily.

Then, with the crazy illogic of a dream, she heard Clem's cracked voice echo in her ear as if he was standing beside her in the room. 'You willin' to fight for him?' Clem had asked.

The dream collapsed; she could not stay for ever, not as things were, because Niall would not let her. To stay, she had to fight. And what better time than now? she realised in sudden excitement. Now, when Niall was holding her close and they were alone in the house. She would never be given a better one.

She said with the same lazy inflection as he, 'This is what it's all about, Niall. Being together—even though right now you're not feeling well. Holding on to each other in the dark.'

Along the length of her body she felt the tension gather in his. 'Joss, hush.'

'I can't.' She twisted, leaning her weight on one elbow so that she could discern his features. 'This is what love means to me . . . sharing the bad times as well as the good. There's nothing complicated or difficult about what we're doing, Niall—in fact, it's the most natural thing in the world.'

'Let it drop, Joss,' he said irritably. 'You know how I stand as far as the check-up's concerned—nothing's going to change my mind.'

She paused, marshalling her forces, which seemed pitifully inadequate against the iron wall of his will. 'What if your check-up went fine and we got married, and then a few years down the road you became ill again . . . would you abandon me?'

'That's a theoretical question—I can't answer that.'

'So you're a fair-weather lover.'

'Stop putting words into my mouth.'

'Niall, please let me go to Boston with you. Just so we can be together.'

'I have to go alone, Joss, I've told you that a dozen times.' He shifted on the chesterfield; she could feel his breath on her cheek. 'Look, my philosophy of life is very simple—we're born alone and we die alone. And you don't ask anyone else to share that dying.'

'I couldn't disagree more,' Joss cried. Her voice passionate with conviction, she made one last attempt. 'I told you about my brother Jake and his wife, didn't I? That's what love means to me, Niall—a sharing of the very worst life can throw at you . . . because two people are immeasurably stronger than one. That's the kind of marriage I want. I won't settle for less.'

Niall's voice was ice-cold. 'Then I have nothing to offer you.'

I've lost, Joss thought numbly. I tried, Clem. But he won't listen and I don't know what else to say . . . if only I can get out of here without bursting into tears. Please God, don't let me cry.

She swung her legs to the floor and stood up, desperately grateful for the darkness. 'I must go,' she said, her voice sounding as though it belonged to someone else. She added politely, 'Goodbye, Niall. I hope your hand will feel better tomorrow.'

He neither moved nor spoke. Searching for the doorway, Joss stumbled across the carpet. The hall was longer than she remembered. The front door opened smoothly and just as smoothly closed behind her, and her car was exactly where she had left it. She drove up the hill, past Clem's cabin, and down the tree-shrouded lane. At the bottom of the lane, where it widened, she stopped the car, leaned her arms on the steering wheel and wept.

She had been exiled from paradise.

CHAPTER TEN

WHEN Joss woke from a leaden sleep the next morning to the shrill of the telephone bell, she thought for a moment that she was an intern again, back at the hospital on thirty-six-hour duty. Then she remembered Niall, and with a thrill of fear picked up the receiver. 'Hello,' she croaked.

'It's Magda. I've had a baby!'

Gamely Joss rose to the occasion. 'Congratulations! A boy or a girl? Did everything go well?'

'A girl, seven pounds four and a half ounces, and, if you want the truth, a funny-looking little thing,' said Magda joyfully. 'Charlie thinks she's beautiful. When are you coming to see us?'

Joss peered at her clock. Six-thirty. 'Seven?' she ventured.

'I know it's awfully early, but I'm so excited I'm calling everyone I know. My mum and dad are flying up tomorrow. We made grandparents out of them—imagine that! As for Charlie,' Magda added complacently, 'he says nothing he could ever invent would approach the perfection of the baby. We've been arguing about names. He favours Greek mythology and I go for Hollywood stars—but we've both agreed on Jocelyn for her second name.'

'That's very sweet of you.'

'Hurry up and see your namesake!'

So Joss hurried, and at ten past seven was admitted into Magda's room. Charlie was holding the baby, his face a huge, seraphic smile, while Magda was propped up against the pillows. Magda talked for ten minutes without stopping, pointing out all the marvels of the baby's form, from her wrinkled little face to the minuteness of her toenails. Then she said generously, 'You can hold her if you like . . . OK, Charlie?'

Charlie's razor-keen mind seemed to have forgotten that Joss was a graduate in medicine who had delivered a number of babies. 'Be careful, Joss, she's very tiny,' he admonished. 'Have you got her head? It's very important to support her head . . . there you go.' With some reluctance he relinquished the baby.

The tiny head with its fuzz of brown hair fitted neatly under Joss's chin; the baby seemed almost weightless. Filled with tenderness and with an incredible wonder for new life, which no medical textbook could adequately explain, Joss sat very still. The baby gave a little snort, as of complete boredom. Joss chuckled with delight.

'You look just fine holding a baby,' Magda remarked. 'Doesn't she, Charlie? Time you had one of your own, Joss.'

Joss gaped at her friend. What if this were her child? The father could not possibly be Bryan. The only man to give her a child had to be Niall. She said over-loudly, 'I'm going to break my engagement, Magda.'

'Thank goodness,' said Magda.

'What do you mean, thank goodness?' Joss bristled. 'Don't you like Bryan?'

'Of course I do—he's a fine, upstanding citizen. But Niall's the man for you, not Bryan. You're so loyal, Joss, with all those old-fashioned virtues—I was terrified you'd marry Bryan just because you'd promised to.'

'Oh,' said Joss weakly. 'Well, I won't. I'll have to tell him this afternoon when he comes home from Switzerland. What on earth will I say?'

'You'll think of something,' Magda said heartlessly. 'Can I have the baby now? Charlie wants to call her Thea or Thalia or even Diantha, can you imagine that?'

'While you'd call her Sissy or Meryl,' Joss teased. 'Well, there's always Venus. Or Cher.'

She had the dim feeling she ought not to be joking on the day when she was going to break her engagement. But the open acknowledgement of a decision that had been brewing ever since the night at Scarlatti's had filled her with relief and a lightness of spirit. It was the right decision. The only decision. While Bryan would be hurt, he would be hurt a great deal more were she to marry him when she was in love with someone else.

I'm in love with Niall, she thought, carefully handing the baby over to Magda. I've loved him since the first moment I saw him at the Red Lion, and I always will love him. I don't know if we'll ever be together. But I do know I can't marry anyone else.

Which, for now, was enough.

When Bryan's plane arrived at three that afternoon, Joss was waiting at the barricade outside Customs. She had chosen to wear a plainly cut navy blue dress with a white collar and cuffs, for it seemed to suit her mood: relief had been usurped by panic.

Bryan was one of the first through Customs. He was wearing one of his innumerable pinstripe suits which gave him such an air of distinction, and his smile when he saw her was uncharacteristically wide. He was not a man to indulge in public displays of affection, but before she could turn her cheek he had kissed her firmly on the lips. 'Wonderful to see you, Joss. I missed you. You're looking very—er—regal.'

She managed a smile. 'Hello, Bryan.'

'One week from today you'll be my wife.'

A little girl tripped over Joss's foot, and the frantic mother pushed through the crowd to grab her. It did not seem an opportune time for Joss to explain that she was not going to marry him. Instead she gulped, 'Let's get out of here.'

'Good idea. The conference was marvellous, I've got so much to tell you.'

The conference, fortunately, lasted them all the way to Bryan's apartment; he lived in a luxury flat near the hospital. Joss carried in his briefcase. Bryan dumped his suitcase on the floor, closed the door and said, 'Come here, Joss.'

His words were an uncanny echo of Niall's. In a brittle voice Joss said, 'Bryan, I'm terribly sorry, but I can't marry you.'

He dropped his keys on the very beautiful ormolu table by the door; the noise seemed shockingly loud. 'Would you mind saying that again?'

'I can't marry you,' she repeated, and because she was so nervous she sounded unfeeling.

'Are you going to marry Niall?'

'No.' Bravely she met Bryan's eyes. 'But I still love him, Bryan. I guess in a way I never stopped, and then when I saw him again . . . I'm so *sorry*, but I can't marry you, it wouldn't be fair to either of us, and why does everything I say sound like a Victorian novel?'

Her hands were clasped in front of her, the knuckles as white as her cuffs. Bryan took her hands in his, saying evenly, 'Are you sure about this? I know it was a shock to meet him again—maybe we should delay the wedding until you're more used to the idea that he's still around.'

'I'm sure.'

He rubbed her wrists, which were as rigid as steel bars, and with a shock she realised that he was not completely surprised by her decision. She muttered, 'You were expecting this, weren't you?'

'I guess so. Perhaps it was one of the reasons I didn't call you from Switzerland—I wasn't sure what I'd hear.'

Although Bryan was doing a good job of hiding his emotions, she knew him well enough to discern the hurt beneath his reserve. 'I feel dreadful,' she whispered. 'I thought I loved you, Bryan. But this other . . . it's like a force of nature. I can't help it, it's bigger than me.'

'I only hope he'll make you happy,' Bryan said stiffly.

She did not want to talk about Niall's one-sided view of love. 'Will you tell your mother?' she asked.

'I'll go and see her. But I know she'll want to see you as well; she's very fond of you, Joss.'

So eight o'clock that evening found Joss opening the door of her apartment to Leah. Leah embraced her and said forthrightly, 'I know this hasn't been easy for you, but you've made absolutely the right decision, Joss. I'd have been very upset if you'd married my son when you were in love with someone else.'

'I hurt Bryan, though.'

'I don't want to belittle his emotions. But Bryan loves his work, and once the fuss about the wedding had died down he'll find great comfort in that. Now,' she went on briskly, 'we have a lot to do. I'd suggest you put a notice in the newspaper tomorrow announcing that the wedding has been cancelled. I brought a list of the out-of-town guests with me, we could split those between us and phone them. Then there's the minister, the organist, the florists, and the caterers at the hotel. You can probably return your dress. Bryan said he'd look after the condominium lease and cancel the arrangements for the honeymoon.'

Joss had paled under this onslaught. 'I've got a room full of gifts, too,' she said.

'They'll all have to be returned.'

'Do you think people sometimes get married because cancelling the wedding is too complicated?'

'I wouldn't be surprised.' Leah gave Joss a sideways smile. 'I'm glad you're not one of them.'

The next three days long remained in Joss's memory. After the first two or three phone calls she evolved a formula for announcing the cancellation of her wedding, and became more adept at fielding the inevitable awkward questions. The minister tried to turn her call into a counselling session, which she ended by announcing that she was in love with someone else; the organist was pleased because it meant he could go to his cottage for the weekend. She forfeited a huge deposit at the caterers and a lesser one at the florists. She returned her white silk suit. Only then did she turn her attention to the spare bedroom, where each gift would have to be rewrapped with a note enclosed. After buying quantities of brown paper, string and tape, Joss set to work.

On Wednesday morning, when the pile was considerably depleted, she came to the box containing the ceramic cherubs and the bunch of grapes; the cherubs were still smirking indefatigably. Quite suddenly Joss found herself with her hands pressed to her eyes and tears spurting from between her fingers. She was so glad to be getting rid of the cherubs and yet she felt so guilty about breaking her engagement.

Bryan had been weighing heavily on her mind. They had had to meet the day before to sign the condominium release form, a meeting which had excoriated Joss's spirits, for although Bryan had been very much on his dignity, he had let it be known that he was not sleeping well and had lost five pounds; she would have felt better had he thrown the release form at her and called her a heartless bitch. She herself was not sleeping well, either. She had not informed Niall of her broken engagement, for what was the use? He would not take her to Boston or allow her the intimacy she craved, and she knew from experience it was useless to beg for either one.

Wednesday afternoon she took the last box to the post office, spent an hour at the clinic and then visited Magda, who was home with the baby. The baby had been named Diana Jocelyn. 'Diana after the princess and the goddess of the hunt,' Madga said triumphantly.

'Charlie says Artemis is the proper Greek name, but I drew the line at that. Joss, you look awful.'

Joss picked up Nasturtium and buried her face in the cat's fur, trying to hide the fact that she was on the brink of tears again. 'I'm tired, that's all. People are funny when you break an engagement—some of them talk in a hushed voice as if you'd died, and others ask all kinds of rude questions. I'm not sure which is worse.'

'Why don't you go away for a few days?'

'Oh, I couldn't leave the clinic.'

'Joss, you've hired a very competent contractor to remodel the clinic, and you were going away on your honeymoon next week, anyway. Bermuda, wasn't it? So go away a bit earlier, that's all.'

'But——'

'You don't have to go to Bermuda!' Magda said, exasperated. 'Go home and see your parents, or go to New York and spend lots of money on Fifth Avenue. But get out of Toronto.'

'That's a good idea,' Joss said slowly. 'You see, I keep hoping Niall will call, even though I know he's not going to.'

'He's a damned fool.'

Joss looked up, more life in her face than she had shown all week. 'I could go to Vancouver,' she exclaimed. 'If I talked to his father, I might understand Niall better. Magda, you're a genius!'

'Charlie's the genius,' Magda grinned. 'I've just got common sense. One of your sisters lives in Vancouver, doesn't she?'

'Blanche—I could stay with her. I'll book my ticket as soon as I get home.'

'You can't go home until you've admired Diana.'

It was no hardship to admire Diana, who was sleeping very peacefully for a child who, according to her mother, had astoundingly active lungs. Joss went straight home afterwards, and after two phone calls had a flight out at six o'clock the next morning which would be met by Blanche. She threw some clothes in a suitcase that night, and with a feeling of genuine escape left her apartment at four-thirty the next morning.

One of her first actions in Vancouver was to look up Niall's father's telephone number. But although she tried at different hours each day, she did not get an answer until Monday. The weekend had been pleasant enough, shopping and chatting with Blanche, and lying in the sun in her sister's beautiful garden; the wedding that should have taken place on Saturday seemed very remote. But the thought of Niall nagged at Joss continually. Would he know by now that she had not married Bryan? Or would he even have checked? Was he worried about his trip to Boston? Even, on a more minor scale, had his hand healed? She did not know the answer to any of these questions, nor could she go home to ask them; until she reached Niall's father she was in limbo.

On Monday morning the telephone was lifted on the second ring. A very precise male voice said, 'Gerald Morgan speaking.'

Overwhelmed by relief, Joss was glad she had rehearsed her lines. She said pleasantly, 'Mr Morgan, my name is Jocelyn MacDougall. I'm a good friend of your son Niall; we first met six years ago.' She crossed her fingers behind her back, for she had decided to tell an untruth to strengthen her case. 'When Niall knew I was coming to Vancouver to visit my sister, he asked me to phone you and invite myself for tea.' She gave a charming little laugh. 'I hope you don't think that's too forward of me. Clem asked to be remembered to you, as well.'

'Ah, yes, Clem.' Gerald Morgan cleared his throat. 'When would be a convenient time for you, Miss MacDougall?'

'Would this afternoon be too soon?'

'Not at all. Shall we say four o'clock? You know the address?'

'Thank you, yes. I'll see you then.'

She rang off and uncrossed her fingers. One hurdle was cleared. Now all she had to do was persuade a man who sounded like no fool and who had a reputation for being close-mouthed to talk about the illness of his long-dead wife.

She wore the navy dress with the white collar and cuffs, minimal make-up, and carried a small bunch of freesias as a gift. The apartment building overlooked Stanley Park and the mountains, and reeked of opulence; a place more different than the Nova Scotia farm would be hard to imagine. With a sinking heart Joss gave her name to the uniformed security guard and was eventually permitted to tap across the marble-floored foyer to the brass-doored lifts. Mr Morgan's suite was on the tenth floor, where her shoes now sank into a plush pink carpet. Trying to take courage from the memory of Niall stripped to the waist in the garden, she pressed the bell and, because of the peephole, composed her face. The door swung open.

All her carefully prepared speeches were forgotten. Joss said naïvely, 'You're so like your son! I would have known you anywhere,' and gave Gerald Morgan the full benefit of her smile.

She was a very beautiful young woman. Gerald Morgan pressed her hand and said, 'Do come in, Miss MacDougall. It is Miss MacDougall? Or do you prefer Ms?' He made the latter abbreviation sound in questionable taste.

Joss had recovered a little. 'It's Dr MacDougall, actually,' she said smoothly. 'I'm starting up a medical practice in Toronto this summer.'

'Really?' He gave a dry laugh. 'In my day such a charming girl as yourself would not have been exposed to the unpleasant realities of a medical career.'

Her smile did not waver. 'I'm sure you see the changes as an improvement, Mr Morgan.' Holding out the tissue-wrapped freesias, she added, 'To thank you for your kind invitation.'

Very briefly a sly humour lurked in the blue eyes that once must have been the deep blue of Niall's. 'In my day the men gave the flowers to the women . . . another improvement. Please take a seat, Dr MacDougall, and I shall bring in the tea.'

The window had a breathtaking view of the harbour and the mountains and the chair was a highly uncomfortable antique. Joss sat very straight, crossing her ankles, and when Mr Morgan brought in a silver tea service, putting it on the hand-carved table between the two chairs, she took the opportunity to study him. Gerald Morgan's likeness to Niall was more a matter of height and bone-structure than personality, for whereas Niall crackled with vitality, Gerald Morgan seemed dessicated, his smile rarely used, his emotions well hidden. After he had poured the tea into equisite bone china cups, he offered her a choice of lemon or milk and passed her a plate of tiny cakes. Then he said politely, 'You mentioned that you've known Niall for six years. You're too young to have been one of his medical attendants, surely?'

Joss balanced the cake on her embroidered serviette, whose creases were knife-sharp, and decided to use shock tactics. 'I only completed my internship a couple of months ago,' she said. 'The summer I met Niall I was singing in a downtown pub in Toronto.'

'Indeed.'

Gerald Morgan could make one word express a great deal. 'Indeed,' she said agreeably. 'We knew each other for four days. We fell in love, Mr Morgan.'

He leaned back in his chair and crossed his legs. 'I do not believe I have ever heard my son mention your name.'

'I would be surprised if he had.' Joss discovered that she was enjoying herself, for in Gerald Morgan she had found a worthy oponent. 'Niall vanished after four days, having told me he had a wife.'

'A palpable lie,' Mr Morgan murmured.

'Quite inadvertently I discovered that instead of being married, Niall was, or so he believed, terminally ill. I tried to trace him but I was unsuccessful. The tragedy was that he had not seen fit to tell me the truth.'

The faded blue eyes did not respond to her challenge. 'Once cured, did he then trace you?'

'He tried—but he only knew my stage name. So for five years I believed him to be dead.'

'Dear me, said Mr Morgan.

Joss stifled a swift surge of anger and said calmly, 'I have a second confession to make—apart from being in love with your son, I mean. Niall has no idea I'm in Vancouver. I came here today entirely on my own accord.'

'Your character begins to intrigue me, Dr MacDougall.'

'Do my motives intrigue you, Mr Morgan?'

'I am sure you will reveal them in time.'

'Indeed,' she said drily. 'I met Niall quite by chance in a restaurant nearly three weeks ago, and it soon became obvious that our feelings for each other had not changed.'

'So am I to congratulate you?'

'No.' Letting the single word hang in the air, Joss took a sip of her tea.

'Perhaps you are mistaken in my son's feelings?'

'Your son refuses to commit himself to me until he has passed his final medical in Boston. His appointment is later this week.'

'A very sensible decision.'

'No, Mr Morgan—a very bad decision. Six years ago Niall vanished because he couldn't share the facts of his illness with me. He is, in effect, doing the same thing again. If his check-up is OK, sure, he'll marry me. But if it's not—forget it. You won't see Niall for dust.' Joss leaned forward, her gold-flecked eyes fierce with emotion. 'I came here today to find out why.'

'My son and I are not close, Dr MacDougall.'

'Niall's mother—your wife—died after a long illness. Clem would tell me very little, but he did say Niall changed during the course of that illness. Why, Mr Morgan?'

There were patches of colour in Gerald Morgan's lined cheeks. 'That is a question you have no right to ask.'

She gave him a disarming smile. 'I have every right to ask—I'm in love with your son, Mr Morgan.'

'You'd run him round in circles,' Gerald Morgan said pettishly.

Her laugh was a genuine, delightful cascade of sound. 'Niall? You don't know him very well!'

'No, I don't.'

Joss would have had to be deaf not to have heard the bitterness in the precise voice. 'You could, though—it's never too late,' she said with deep conviction. 'Mr Morgan, I'm quite sure you think that I'm a brash and horribly modern young woman with no inkling of her proper place . . . and I'm now going to make matters worse by giving you my theory. I think you kept your wife's illness—and I have no idea of its nature—hidden from Niall. Tucked away. Out of sight. Because of that, I believe it assumed far too much importance to him, while simultaneously he was taught no skills to deal with it. I believe that ever since then he has been afraid of illness, and that's why he won't marry me before his check-up.'

'Brash is too mild a word,' Gerald Morgan said sharply.

She refused to back down. 'Try honest.'

'So you would marry him, even knowing he was ill?'

'Yes. I love him, you see. For better, for worse.'

'Niall hated to discuss his illness with me. But being a doctor, you might know what the worst can entail.'

'I am not making the choice out of ignorance, but out of love,' said Joss.

Gerald Morgan turned his head to gaze out of the window; his profile reminded Joss so strongly of his son's that she was suddenly faint with longing for Niall. In an expressionless voice Niall's father said, 'You are quite correct in your assumptions. I did keep Sylvia's illness a secret from Niall.'

Joss sat very still. She said gently, 'What was wrong with her?'

He was still staring out of the window. 'Today it would be called Alzheimer's, I believe. She became forgetful and disorientated. She would wander the streets and be unable to tell anyone her name, and the police would have to bring her back. Twice she nearly set the house on fire by putting food to cook on the stove and then leaving it . . . how could I share all this with a young boy?' Not waiting for an answer, he went on, 'She got worse. At times she was paranoid, and you'd find her cowering in the wardrobe. Other days she became frighteningly aggressive—I hid all the knives and kept the tools locked up. Sometimes she'd even throw off her clothes and yell obscenities at me . . . my beautiful, gentle Sylvia.' He looked directly at Joss, dry-eyed. 'I kept her hidden from Niall as much as I could, yes. How could I share with him what I could not bear myself . . . the woman I loved changing into another woman who was a stranger to me'

His back was rigid; but his hands were trembling very lightly as he reached for his teacup. Her heart aching for him, Joss said, 'I understand—it must have been terrible for you.'

With more emotion that he had yet shown he said, 'I

was *glad* when she died. How could I tell Niall that?'

'I do understand,' Joss repeated helplessly.

'I believe you do.' Gerald Morgan inclined his head in a courtly gesture. 'My son is a fortunate man.'

Joss led him on to talk more about his marriage, until the vivid images of a crazed Sylvia were replaced by happier images of earlier times. She told him how she had broken her engagement to Bryan, and when she spoke of Niall she allowed all her love to shine in her face. Then she looked at her watch. 'I've overstayed my welcome,' she said. 'Thank you, Mr Morgan—you've been more than kind.'

He stood up and formally shook her hand. 'It has been my pleasure. I would like to think that you might be the catalyst to bring Niall and myself closer together . . . I trust this will be the first of many meetings.'

With all her heart Joss hoped the same. She left the apartment, went back to Blanche's, and was lucky enough to get a booking on the first flight east the next morning. Partly because of her training, partly instinctively, she had been able to fill in the details of Gerald Morgan's bleak little narrative. To a young boy, an only child, the change in his mother must have been terrifying, doubly so because they were shrouded in secrecy. No wonder illness loomed so large in Niall's imagination; no wonder he felt he could not expose Joss to the kind of suffering he himself had gone through.

Somehow, and she had no idea how, she had to change this view.

CHAPTER ELEVEN

AT FOUR-THIRTY the next afternoon, Toronto time, Joss was walking up the front steps of her apartment building. She felt stale and tired, and not nearly as sanguine that anything she could do would change Niall's mind.

The superintendent, who was middle-aged, overweight and unfailingly glum, was vacuuming the entrance hall. Joss summoned up a smile and said brightly, 'Good afternoon, Mr Garner.'

He did not smile back. 'Do you know someone called Niall Morgan?' he said suspiciously.

Her hand tensed on her suitcase. 'Yes.'

'He said you did. But I knew you were engaged to that doctor with the black car.'

Panic-stricken, Joss asked, 'Is anything wrong?'

He smiled sourly. 'You've got an apartment full of dead flowers, that's all that's wrong.'

She plunked her suitcase on the floor. 'What are you talking about?'

'He came here on Friday looking for you, that Niall Morgan. Said he'd been phoning your apartment and you weren't answering, maybe you were ill. I finally had to tell him you were away, only way to get him off my back.' Mr Garner made a couple of unenthusiastic passes with the vacuum cleaner.

'What's that got to do with dead flowers?' Joss said blankly, wondering if jet travel had affected her mind.

'He came back that afternoon with all these flowers. He wanted to put them in your apartment, but I told him that was against the rules.' Mr Garner leaned on the

172

handle of the vacuum cleaner, his brow furrowing in unaccustomed thought. 'Hard guy to say no to. First thing you know, I'd let him into your apartment. I stayed with him the whole time, mind you, I didn't let him out of my sight,' he added righteously. 'But that was Friday and here it is Tuesday. You're kind of late as far as those flowers are concerned.' he sniffed. 'Left you a letter, too, he did. Funny way for a guy to behave when you're going to marry someone else.'

'I'm not,' said Joss with an incandescent smile. 'Maybe I'm going to marry him instead.' She suddenly grabbed the superintendent and waltzed him around in a circle. 'You've made my day, Mr Garner!'

'That's nice,' Mr Garner said dourly, detaching himself as fast as he could. 'You better get the flowers in the garbage before the truck comes—and don't forget your suitcase.'

Joss had been rushing for the lift. She ran back, picked up her case, gave him another dazzling smile and hurried back to the lift, which then seemed to take forever to reach her floor. She was so excited she had trouble fitting the key in the lock of her door. But finally she pushed it open and walked in.

The apartment smelled of dead flowers. The living-room table was a veritable forest of wilting apple blossoms, tarnished forsythia, and drooping roses. A large white envelope bearing her name was prominently displayed in front of the foremost bouquet of roses. They had been, in their prime, red roses. Joss kicked the door shut behind her and tore open the envelope.

Across the single sheet of paper in an untidy but very masculine sprawl was written, 'Darling Joss, will you marry me? Niall.'

Joss sat down hard on the nearest chair and burst into tears.

Although they were tears of happiness, it took her two or three minutes to stop their flow, and not until then did she turned the paper over and check the inside of the envelope. Nothing else. Not a word of explanation, not even the date that the letter had been written. Just that one, simple quetion to which she already knew the answer.

Pushing back the chair, Joss hurried to the telephone and dialled Niall's number. After eight rings she broke the connection, then dialled again. No answer. He was out in the garden, she thought in frustration. She had to see him. She couldn't wait.

Taking the letter with her, because otherwise she was afraid she might think she had dreamed the whole episode, she took the lift to the basement and started her car. The traffic was heavy heading out of the city, so it was after six when she turned into the leafy lane and drove past Clem's cabin. Clem was not in sight. But the gardens were spread out before her in their order and beauty, and she knew she had come home.

She checked the house first. Both the front and back doors were locked and no one answered either bell. Biting her lip, Joss walked around the front of the house again. Bees hummed among the rock plants and the wind sighed drowsily in the birches. But that was all. She could not hear the tiller or the tractor, or even the sound of voices.

She drove around the rest of the property, searching for Niall's tall figure in the fields and orchards. She even checked the wharf, where the canoe was tipped, keel up. Slowly she drove back up the hill towards Clem's cabin. Niall's check-up, she was almost sure, was the day after tomorrow. She had not expected that he would already have left.

Clem was at the crest of the hill, slouched over a wheelbarrow, a dog at each heel. Joss barked and called out of the window, 'Where's Niall, Clem?'

'Boston.'

'Oh, damn,' she said unhappily. 'When did he leave?'

'Yesterday. His appointment got put forward.'

'When will he be back?'

Clem shrugged. 'Dunno. He said he'd call.'

'You didn't answer the phone this afternoon,' she said snappishly.

'I don't answer nuthin' after five o'clock,' Clem announced.

He shoulders sagged. 'I don't even know where he is in Boston,' she said, and with a chill of superstitious fear remembered her hopeless search in Toronto six years ago.

'You bin away?' Clem asked.

'Yes,' she said absently, drumming on the wheel with her fingers, wondering how long it would take her to contact every hospital in Boston. She wanted to be with Niall. Now. He needed her, she was sure of it.

'You see his dad?'

'Niall's father? Yes, I did. I found out everything I wanted to know.'

'You did?'

There was a new note in Clem's voice, one she had not heard before: respect. Even in her distress Joss felt a quiver of inner amusement. 'Yes,' she said artlessly. 'He told me all about his wife's illness.'

'Didja hold a gun to his head?'

She ticked off her fingers. 'I lied to him on the telephone and then confessed that I'd lied. I told him I used to sing in a pub. And I told him that I love his son.'

Clem gave one of his uncouth cackles of laughter. The brown and white mongrel wagged its tail. Then Clem fished in one of the deep pockets of his dungarees, which Joss would swear had not been washed since the last time she saw him, and produced a ring of keys. 'The gold key'll unlock the front door. Maybe he left the name of the hotel lyin' around. Or else you could call his local doctor. Edward Stairs. He likely could tell you where Niall is.'

She seized the keys in case Clem changed his mind and said pertly, 'You must approve of me, Clem.'

'You'll do. You get unengaged yet?'

'Yes.' Her mouth quirked. 'I might even be re-engaged. I'll let you know what I'm doing about Boston on my way out.'

The house was cool and tidy and felt very empty. The downstairs yielded no clues. But when Joss went upstairs and walked into Niall's bedroom, she immediately saw a typed official letter beside the telephone on the bedside table. The letter was from a Boston physician and named the times and places of Niall's various appointments. The final one was at one o'clock the next afternoon.

Joss sat down on the bed, her hand smoothing the covers with a peculiar sense of intimacy. She wanted to be with Niall when he went for that appointment. Whatever the result, her place was at his side.

There was a telephone book in the drawer of the bedside table. She booked a seat on the only available flight to Boston the next morning, that would get her in at quarter to twelve, put down the phone wondering how she was going to pay for all this junketing around the country, and discovered that she did not care. Taking off her shoes she lay down on the bed. The pillow smelled elusively of Niall's aftershave. A little smile on her lips, she closed her eyes.

A bell was ringing and a hoarse voice calling her name. Joss sat up, realising the voice was Clem's. This was the second time she had fallen asleep in Niall's house, she thought in confusion, trying to smooth the indentation of her head from his pillow. 'I'll be right down!' she called.

In the hallway Clem peered at her from beneath his bushy brows. 'Figured you'd fallen down the cellar steps,' he said bellicosely.

'What's the time?'

'Nigh on eight-thirty.'

'I—I fell asleep,' she said lamely.

'And you weren't using the guest room,' Clem sniggered. 'Time you two got hitched.'

Joss said loftily, 'You have a dirty mind, Clem. I'm flying to Boston tomorrow morning.'

He grinned at her; his teeth would have been an impecunious dentist's dream. 'Smart move.'

'I'm glad you approve,' she said and added incautiously, 'I'd better go home and unpack one suitcase before I pack the next.'

'You figurin' on stayin' over, eh?'

She blushed, said loudly, 'Will you lock up the house again, please?' and passed him the keys. The dogs were sitting patiently on the front step; they paid her no attention whatsoever as she got in her car and drove away.

The flight to Boston was fifteen minutes late because of head winds; there was a queue at the taxi stand, and the air was hot and humid. In the tall plate-glass windows Joss could see her own reflection, that of a composed young woman in a red skirt and a loose jacket splashed with big red flowers. She did not feel composed. She was a mass of nerves. Which was not a medically accurate term, she reproved herself.

The taxis came and went, the queue grew shorter and the hands of the clock crept around its circumference. She had not brought a suitcase after all, for to prepare for an overnight stay seemed to be tempting fate. Superstition was not medically acceptable either, she thought glumly. Finally the taxi that drew up was her own. She gave the driver the doctor's address and said she was in a hurry.

He took her at her word, racing yellow lights and swearing at unwary pedestrians. But he delivered her by quarter to one at a brick and glass tower that housed several medical clinics; Joss tipped him generously, pushed through the swing doors and was enveloped in the artificial chill of air-conditioning.

'I'm looking for Dr Mappin's office,' she said to the girl at the information desk.

'Eleventh floor, turn right, suite sixteen.'

The lift was computerised, and so quiet that Joss was afraid the other occupants would hear the pounding of her heart. She got off on the eleventh floor and turned right. The door to suite sixteen was closed. For a long moment she stood outside, trying to calm herself. Then she opened the door.

The doctor's office was painted a soothing shade of rose pink with an attractive display of plants and a seemingly casual arrangement of chairs and magazine tables; the doctor in Joss was taking mental notes for her own clinic, even while the woman in her was seeking out Niall. There were three people waiting in the office. Of the three, only Niall had his back to her.

The receptionist at the brightly lit counter said, 'Kindly shut the door, madam. May I help you?' She reminded Joss very strongly of Mr Garner.

Joss swallowed. 'I'm here with Mr Morgan,' she said, and hoped she was telling the truth.

Niall turned his head, dropped his magazine and stood up, looking thunderstruck. '*Joss* . . . how did you get here?'

'A plane,' she said intelligently.

'The superintendent didn't know when you'd be back—I never expected to see you here.'

In sudden panic she said, 'Maybe I shouldn't have come.'

He closed the space between them and took her in his arms. 'Don't be ridiculous,' he said, and kissed her at some length.

She kissed him back, briefly forgetting all her other

concerns in the joy of his embrace. Her body seemed to fit the circle of his arms; he was kissing her like a man in love. When he released her, they spoke simultaneously.

'Did you——' he said.

'How have——' she began.

He laughed. 'You first.'

'How have your tests gone?'

'OK. But I'll be glad when this is over.'

She was close enough to see the lines of strain in his face, and reached up a hand to smooth his cheek. 'I'm glad I'm here,' she said simply.

His hug was bone-cracking. 'Oh, God, so am I—I was an idiot, Joss, to try and keep you away. Did you get my letter?'

'Dr Mappin will see you now, Mr Morgan,' said the receptionist.

Joss turned in the circle of Niall's arms; the woman looked as disapproving as if Joss and Niall had been making love on the rose-pink carpet. Ignoring the receptionist, all his attention on the woman in his arms, Niall said, 'Joss, will you come in with me?'

She, of all people, knew the significance of that question. She took his hand and said gravely, 'Thank you.' The receptionist sniffed.

Dr Mappin rose to his feet when they entered his office, which was adorned with two very fine paintings and an antique mahogany desk; not, thought Joss, quite the right ambience for Queen Street West. The doctor was older than she had expected, with immensely kind brown eyes. He raised his brows a little when he saw her.

Niall said, 'Dr Mappin, I'd like you to meet my——' He stopped in mid-sentence. 'Joss, you didn't answer my question. *Did* you get my letter? Will you marry me?'

'Yes and yes,' she said, her heart in her eyes. 'Although I shall insist on some fresh roses.'

'Sweetheart, you shall have acres of them,' Niall said exultantly. He then completed the introduction more moderately. 'Dr Mappin, I'd like you to meet my fiancée, Dr Jocelyn MacDougall, from Toronto.'

'Delighted, Dr MacDougall.' Transferring his attention to Niall, Dr Mappin said, 'I have a wedding gift for you —you're in perfect health, Mr Morgan. Congratulations.'

Joss was standing close enough to Niall to sense an infinitesimal release of tension. 'I don't have to come back?' Niall said quietly.

Dr Mappin gave him a broad smile. 'I never want to see you again,' he joked. 'You did a very brave thing five years ago, and I'm extremely happy with the results.'

Niall gave his head a little shake. 'I can't quite take it in,' he said.

'I've left copies of all the reports with the receptionist; you might want to take them with you.' Dr Mappin talked briefly of a few technical matters, then smiled at both of them. 'May I wish you every happiness in your married life.'

The appointment was over. Joss ushered Niall out of the office, picked up the file at the desk and walked with him to the elevator. It was crowded, as was the pavement outside the medical building. The heat struck at them and the snarl of traffic assaulted their ears. Niall looked around him as if he was not quite sure where he was. 'This is crazy—I figured I'd be dancing for joy if all the reports were OK,' he said. 'Instead I just feel kind of numb inside.'

Joss took his hand. 'You've lived with fear for six years,' she said. 'You can't expect to do a complete turnabout in five minutes.'

He was looking around him like an animal trapped in a cage. 'I was going to paint the town red. Or at least a shade of pink. Now all I want to do is get the hell out of here.' He squeezed her fingers, looking into her eyes with desperate intensity. 'Don't get me wrong, Joss—I've never been so happy to see anyone in my life as I was to see you when you walked into the doctor's office. I'd marry you five minutes from now if it were legally possible, and I want to make love to you so badly it hurts. But . . . not here. Not in this city.'

She understood completely. Six years ago when Niall had submitted himself to all the risks of an experimental drug he had suffered here; and all his check-ups, those times of uncertainty and dread, had taken place here as well. Boston was not a city of happy memories for Niall; and she too wanted to break free of the past's tyrannical hold. She said calmly, 'We'll go to the airport and get on a plane. We can go anywhere we like.'

Niall put his arms around her waist, almost lifting her off her feet. 'Joss, you're a marvel,' he said.

He hailed a cab and they drove first to his hotel to get his luggage, and then to the airport. They held hands the whole way and talked very little. Inside the terminal Niall stopped twenty feet from the Air Canada ticket counter. 'I don't want to go home—not yet,' he said. 'Although I will give Clem a call. Do you know where I'd like to go, Joss?'

She smiled at him, love shining from her eyes. 'The North Pole is very popular these days.'

'I've never particularly wanted to make live on an ice floe . . . although when you smile at me like that I'd make love anywhere at all.' He grinned at her boyishly. 'You've made me forget my train of thought.'

'Our destination,' she prompted.

'As long as we're together it doesn't really matter, does it? I love you so much, Joss.' He put down his suitcase, took her in his arms and kissed her, and the ever-moving crowds of travellers, used to meetings and farewells, eddied casually around them.

'We're free, aren't we?' Joss whispered dazedly.

'Free of the past, free to be together. Niall, I'm so happy, it almost frightens me.'

'You don't have to be frightened—because no matter what happens we'll go through it together.' He gave her a quick squeeze. 'Let's see if we can get a flight to Nova Scotia so I can meet your parents.'

Her whole face lit up. 'Niall, that's a wonderful idea! There's nothing I'd like better.'

But the only available bookings would not get them into Halifax until nine that night. Joss said dubiously, 'It's a two-and-a-half-hour drive from the airport to the farm.'

'We could stay in Halifax overnight,' Niall said steadily.

Her lashes dropped to hide her eyes. She would like that, too. But, remember the presence of the ticket agent, Joss restricted herself to a sedate, 'That's a good idea.'

Niall paid for the tickets, then placed a call to Clem. Joss waited a short distance from the row of telephone, deciding privately that she adored the way Niall's hair curled on the nape of his neck. He talked for a while, made a second call, then came back to Joss.

'I got hold of Clem. When I told him the doctors figured I'd be around another fifty years or so, he said that would just about give him time to ship me into shape. I also told him I would be back for a couple of days. He wanted to know if you were with me, and sent his regards.' Niall gave her his crooked smile. 'The final barrier to our marriage is removed—Clem approves of you.'

Joss laughed. 'I can't believe he only sent his regards.'

'I wouldn't dream of exposing your maidenly ears to what he actually did say.' Niall's eyes were very blue. 'I reserved a suite in Halifax's most expensive hotel, as well . . . after all those years of medical training you can still blush, Joss.'

She scowled at him. 'A suite sounds very extravagant.'

'We've waited six years.' Niall looked at his watch. 'At the moment, six hours sounds like an impossibly long wait.'

'We could go to the observation lounge and watch the planes,' she suggested limpidly.

'Or we could play video games.'

She winced. 'Or toast our future at the bar.'

'Best idea yet,' he said promptly.

They wandered around the airport until flight-time, trying on silly hats in the souvenir shops, chuckling at the books of cartoons and generally, thought Joss, behaving like a couple of children. She had seen little of Niall's playful side. As they munched on gooey doughnuts in a café she said, 'I'm seeing a whole new side to you.'

He said simply, 'It's because I'm happy, Joss.'

'We've waited a long time for that, too, haven't we?'

'We'll make up for lost time,' Niall said confidently. 'Starting tonight.'

She could feel herself blushing again. 'I haven't even got a suitcase.'

'You don't need one. All I want is you.'

Joss hesitated, for the first time feeling afraid. 'But I've never——'

He covered her sticky fingers with his palm. 'Darling, I know you haven't. Don't be frightened. I'll be as good to you as I know how.'

She was very finely tuned to Niall. She said vigorously, although her cheeks were still red, 'I want you, don't have any doubts about that.'

He threw back his head and laughed. 'That's one of the things I love about you—you always speak your mind. Everything will be fine, you'll see.'

Joss was reassured by his words. But at ten-thirty that night, when she followed the bellboy into the suite in Halifax's most expensive hotel, she was filled with an unsettling mixture of excitement and panic. While the

bellboy showed Niall the various amenities of the three
rooms, she wandered over to the window, which
overlooked the calm black waters of the harbour on
which were reflected the golden lights of Dartmouth,
Halifax's twin city. There was an oil rig moored near the
other shore. She studied it with intense interest.

After a discreet rustle of bills, the door to the suite
closed and Niall slipped the chain into place. He said,
'Would you like me to order room service, Joss? Are
you hungry?'

They had had an indifferent meal on the plane. 'No,
thanks,' she replied, turning round to face him, wishing
she did not feel quite so much at bay.

'Why don't you have a hot bath? There's compli-
mentary shampoo and bubble bath.'

'I haven't even got a housecoat!'

'You can borrow mine,' he said with ineffable
patience.

He was very carefully keeping his distance from her,
and suddenly she was furious with herself for worrying
about housecoats when she and Niall were finally alone
together. She walked over to him, locked her arms
around his waist and said in a rush, 'Niall, take me to
bed.'

His answer was to switch out the overhead light so
that the room was lit only indirectly by the glow from
the city, and then to take her by the hand and lead her to
the bed. He pulled back the covers. 'Sit down and I'll
take off your shoes,' he said matter-of-factly.

As he knelt in front of her, easing her feet from her
pumps, his bent head filled Joss with tenderness. Then
he kicked off his own shoes and shrugged out of his
jacket before drawing her down on the bed beside him
and saying softly, 'We've waited a long time for this, as
well.'

'Too long.' Her smile was radiant and very trusting.
'I love you more than any one else in the world, Niall.'

'You are my heart's delight,' he said huskily.

He made love to her with gentleness and passion, with infinite care for her pleasure and yet with a fierce hunger. And she, who had waited so long, was glad she had waited, so that she could learn with Niall the intricate and beautiful dance of love. When it was over she was lying across his chest, her cheek resting on his breastbone where his heartbeat echoed in her ear, her arm curving round his scarred ribs to hold him close. 'I never want to let you go,' she murmured. 'Niall, that was wonderful. I'm glad you were the first one.' Realising the implications of what she had said, she gave a throaty chuckle. 'You'll also be the second and the third, I trust.'

'Give me five minutes.'

'According to what I learn in class about male sexuality——' she broke off as he began tickling her ribs. 'Stop that!'

'I bet your textbooks never described some of the things we just did,' he said complacently.

'Fourth Year Eroticism? It wasn't part of the curriculum.'

'One should always be open to new learning.'

'Indeed,' she replied. Then she suddenly sat up, forgetful of her nakedness, her face agitated. 'Niall, I have a confession to make!'

He clasped his hands behind his head in a way that emphasised, to her secret pleasure, the taut concavity of his belly, and said lazily, 'You had triplets at the age of fourteen.'

'I was madly in love with the Enwright boys at the age of fourteen,' she admitted. 'But they were only interested in playing baseball. Niall, while I was away I went to see your father.'

'In Vancouver?' he said incredulously.

'I have a sister there, so I stayed with her. He told me about your mother's illness.'

Even more incredulously Niall said, 'He actually talked to you about her?'

'Yes . . . I think he'd like to talk to you about her, too.'

'Her illness was always a barrier . . . Joss, I've got a hell of a lot of explaining to do.'

'You don't have to explain anything,' she assured him, curling up against his side and running her fingers through the tangle of his body hair.

'I owe you something for the past six years.' He brought her hadn to his lips. 'Do you know what made me change my mind last week? The thought that because I was too stubborn or too afraid to claim you, you'd marry Bryan. The Thursday before the wedding I couldn't stand it any longer. I called St David's and was informed by the secretary that the wedding had been cancelled. Not postponed. Cancelled.' He kissed her fingers one by one. 'I knew then I'd been given a third chance. I'd muffed the first two, but I sure wasn't going to mess up the third. So I started phoning you.'

'I left Thursday morning.'

'I finally extracted that piece of information from your superintendent when I turned up on Friday loaded with flowers and a proposal of marriage. He didn't approve of me at all. Kept telling me you were engaged to a doctor with a BMW.'

She said shrewdly, 'How much did it cost you to get into my apartment?'

'You're not supposed to ask. Anyway, I left the flowers and went home, and answered the phone on the first ring for the next three days.' He smiled at her. 'I have no doubt the delay was character-building. But, my God, I missed you.'

'When I got back from Vancouver yesterday, the first thing I did was go to your place. Which you'd already left. We should both have strong characters, Niall.'

He smoothed a strand of hair from her forehead. 'I

can tell you about my mother's illness now. I never could before.'

'Your father told me quite a bit about it. You see, once I'd broken my engagement and sent back all the presents, I couldn't stand being in Toronto. I'd managed to winkle your father's address out of Clem. So I went to Vancouver and on Monday had tea with him . . . I so badly needed to understand you!'

'I was running scared,' Niall said grimly. 'You have no idea what it was like growing up in that huge old house with the servants and my father all behaving as if everything was normal and my poor mother wandering around like a lost soul . . . sometimes she didn't even know who I was. One day I saw her turn on my father with a vegetable knife.' His smile was wry. 'A vegetable knife. Doesn't sound like much, does it? But his hands were bleeding by the time he got it from her, and then she collapsed on the floor sobbing hysterically . . . I've never forgotten that.'

'And no one ever told you what was going on?'

'No. I understand now, of course. But I was left with a terror of illness, not so much for myself as for the ones around me. Since I was a kid I've known what it's like to watch someone you love suffer. I decided a long time ago I'd never put anyone through that. I couldn't have told you the truth six years ago, Joss, not for anything—and even when I met you again, I wanted the check-up out of the way before I made any kind of commitment.'

She rested her head on one hand looking down at him. 'You'd never disappear again, would you, Niall?'

'Never—I swear. I did a lot of thinking over the week-end, remembering that boy in the old house and realising that it was past time to let go, that he'd been running my life for too long. I thought a lot about love too, Joss—love for better or for worse. You and I will love each other always, no matter what happens . . . I'd swear to that, too.'

'Then we're safe,' Joss whispered.

'Would you be content living in Braxton? We could keep an apartment in Toronto while you're working at the clinic.'

'Maybe I could eventually set up a practice in Braxton.'

'You always were a country girl at heart . . . I've wondered if that's why I bought the place, because I knew we were destined to meet again.'

'How terrible if we hadn't,' Joss said shakily, pressing close to his naked body.

'We had to. We were meant for each other. And we have a whole lifetime ahead of us to prove it.' With a spark of fire in his blue eyes, Niall began stroking the swell of her breast. 'Starting right now.'

'So the five minutes are over?' she asked innocently.

He slid his lips along the white skin that his fingers had been caressing. 'There's a great deal more that the textbooks omitted.'

'Teach me, Niall,' Joss said huskily. 'Teach me.'

Early the next afternoon Joss led Niall into the kitchen of the farmhouse in Alderney and said, 'Mum, I've brought the right man home.'

The Christmas present you won't want to part with.

Four great new titles in a seasonal gift pack for only £5.00. Long dark evenings of reading by a blazing fire. Will you keep it or will you give it away?

TRUE PARADISE_____Catherine George
TAKEOVER MAN_____Vanessa Grant
TUSCAN ENCOUNTER_____Madeleine Ker
DRIVING FORCE_____Sally Wentworth

Published October 1988   Price £5.00

Available from Boots, Martins, John Menzies, W.H. Smith, Woolworths and other paperback stockists.

TEACH
TO SWIM

TEACH YOUR CHILD TO SWIM

by

Geoffrey Budworth

M.Inst. BRM. Dip

PAPERFRONTS

ELLIOT RIGHT WAY BOOKS,
KINGSWOOD, SURREY, U.K.

Typeset in 10 pt Times by County Typesetters, Margate, Kent. Made and Printed in Great Britain by Cox & Wyman Ltd., Reading.

CONTENTS

Dedicated to the memory of
the late JESSE POULTON,
"Professor" of Swimming.

1
INTRODUCTION

Follow the advice and guidance in this book and, even if you are no great performer in the water yourself, you can teach someone else to swim.

GOLDEN RULE No. 1
Everyone can swim: those who cannot simply have not yet discovered that they can.

You can show them how, and, by giving the ability to swim properly, you will give them the means to secure health and happiness with a better chance of a long and active life.

As the teacher, you too will learn. Making it easy for your pupil will improve your own water skills.

Everybody should swim for personal survival. Later they may learn life-saving techniques so as to rescue others. A lot of enjoyable and exciting activities are open to the competent swimmer:- competitive swimming and diving; boating and canoeing; water skiing; board sailing (wind surfing); s.c.u.b.a. diving; triathlon (swim – bike – run); and more fun on a seaside holiday. Even anglers who only sit beside the water should be able to swim for safety's sake.

There is no right age at which to start to learn. Babies only a few weeks old can be taken into water, while every year many elderly people discover they can swim. True, to become an international or Olympic swimmer, an early start is recommended so that your great potential begins to show in your early teens. Many swimming teachers consider that 4–6 years is a good time to start but some specialise in parent-and-baby lessons and produce toddlers who can swim lengths of the pool.

Why do it yourself?
Thousands of children learn to swim every year through

school swimming lessons organised by local education authorities. A lot of adults, too, take to the water under the expert tuition of professional swimming teachers employed by municipal pool managers. Others have private lessons or join clubs. So, why should you try your hand at what experts already do? Well, children gain more from school swimming periods when they can already cope with water. Then again, even if they do have a weekly lesson, they should practise and reinforce what they have learnt at other times. Perhaps there is a lengthy waiting list for lessons in your area, or they are too costly. You may live a long way from a public pool but be fortunate and have the use of private water close at hand. Some beginners are timid and do not thrive in classes, needing instead patient and unhurried personal attention. Other individuals may have had an off-putting experience in water (or even with a particular teacher) and need quiet coaxing to recover confidence. For all these reasons and others, teaching swimming can be a do-it-yourself job.

You do not need to be a good swimmer to teach swimming. You must, however, be able to enter the water with confidence and obvious enjoyment. Any sign of apprehension or dislike will be sensed by your pupil who may be put off by it. Remember, everyone can swim; they just have to be shown that they can . . . and YOU can show them.

Benefits of swimming
Recently I underwent a complete physical check-up, the kind advertised by a well-known private medical organisation as vital for middle-aged men like me if unsuspected ailments are to be spotted in good time to remedy them. I was prodded and probed, scanned and monitored by a succession of thorough tests, and finally introduced to the doctor who would make the assessment in my case. He read my papers, looked at me curiously for several seconds, then asked; "Why did you come here?" It turned out I was wasting the time of the medical staff. Despite being a very ordinary and unathletic 50-year-old, I remain so fit through swimming that he could find nothing to tell me.

Swimming has many varied benefits:-
   * It is a lifelong activity which may be practised from a few
     weeks old until one's last day on earth.

* It can be a family outing, with grandparents and grand-children comparing skills, competing and playing together in the water.
* The generation gap disappears. (My younger daughter was a club swimmer who could out-sprint me every time, but I could swim miles further in cold water which did not suit her.)
* The trappings of society do not show when you wear a swimming costume, so rich and poor of every class and creed mix easily.
* It is a cheap sport needing only a costume and towel plus the price of admission to a pool.
* If you can treat yourself, however, there is merchandise to buy. It is mass-produced and so reasonably priced. Designed by leading sport and leisure manufacturers, such items as hats, goggles, floats, armbands, fins (flippers) and hand-paddles, along with the swim-bag to put them in, make good presents for swimmers and rewards for achievements.
* It is a clean and invigorating exercise performed in the pleasant and hygienic environment of a swimming pool. For many who dislike robust and sweaty sports it is an ideal way to combat soft modern life.
* Poise, confidence and self-esteem result from mastery of the strange medium of water with its healthy element of challenge and risk.
* It is, in fact, one of the safest physical activities. There is no deliberate bodily contact and a low risk of accidents or wear-and-tear injuries. 7 million people swim regulary in the United Kingdom. True, 650 drown each year, but many of those deaths were from needless foolishness by people who were not frequent swimmers.
* The sociable team member, and the loner too, can enjoy swimming.
* For those who seek more than simply a leisure pastime, swimming has a range of specialist pursuits:- sprint, distance and marathon racing; individual feats of speed or endurance; synchronised swimming (water ballet); water polo, etc., which can be practised to the highest standards.
* Badges, certificates and medals are awarded as parts of graded and progressive incentive schemes to encourage

and reward achievement in the art of swimming.

* There is a nationwide scattering of over 1,700 clubs (each with hundreds of members), grouped into counties and regions, also numerous Summer and Winter training squads and centres of excellence for swimmers.

* The welfare of young swimmers, including their amateur status, is conscientiously safeguarded by the sport's governing body.

* Youngsters who become absorbed into swimming are noticeably good at coping with success and failure, mixing with their own and the opposite sex, the demands of training and travel. They can work for long and short-term goals and manage their time so well that it is even claimed school and other studies benefit.

* Swimming is an Olympic sport with perhaps the most comprehensive structure of any sport. Teachers, coaches, tutors and officials are all trained and qualified by examination. They are supported by knowledgeable amateur governing bodies and committees who select and approve team managers, chaperones, medicos, etc. The professional teachers and coaches also have their own organisations.

* It is an ideal exercise that stimulates and improves every bodily function. Muscle and joint action, the workings of vital organs, blood circulation, breathing, digestion and elimination of waste, all are enhanced.

* The adaptations the body makes to cope with the exercise of swimming increases general fitness.

* Immersing the body in water gives it a gentle overall massage, while vigorous towelling down afterwards maintains good skin condition.

* With strokes swum horizontally, the load upon working parts is eased.

* Resistance is built up to certain minor infections.

* The overweight can exercise with their weight water-borne which is impossible for them on land.

* It is an effective way to recover following illness, injury or surgery, and is useful before and after childbirth.

* It can, with adaptations, be practised and enjoyed by even the most mentally and physically handicapped; for some, it is their only escape from gravity and their wheelchairs.

* It opens the way to other water sports.
* Worries cannot survive for long in the water as they are almost literally washed away by the altered body chemistry as you swim. Swimming always feels good and it can be sheer joy.

Disadvantages of swimming
They are few:-
- Long hair and fashionable hair-dos are impractical.
- Away from a suitable expanse of water you cannot do it.
- For the tens of thousands of youngsters (and their parents) caught up in the regimen of competitive training, hours are mortgaged every day for years; yet few will succeed and those who do will have only the satisfaction of a briefly held title or record.
- Sprint competition is for the very young, with world records made by teenagers who later retire still only in their twenties.
- It is an amateur sport with little scope for professionals and no big money to be made.

Those of us under swimming's spell readily agree these are small snags when compared with the overwhelming benefits.

Swimming the best exercise of all
"How can I get fit?" adults often ask me, yearning for their lost youth and vigour. "Fit for what?" I reply, because fitness – you should understand – is specific. The massively strong weightlifter could not run uphill for long; the wiry fell-runner with a heart like a greyhound could not handle the weight-lifter's barbell. The gymnast may not be as graceful as a ballet dancer but is perhaps more agile.

I suggest we need to be fit to carry our own bodyweight around all day, coping with work and chores, and still have enough energy and enthusiasm for healthy leisure pursuits. A number of physical activities would do the trick to an extent... but swimming scores highest with fitness factors.

6 fitness factors
S – trength ... overcoming resistance by muscle action.

S – peed... strength applied with speed is powerful.

S - tamina ... resistance to fatigue
        (a) heart/lung endurance ("good puff")
        (b) tireless muscles.

S – uppleness ... flexibility in each joint.

S – kill ... technique.

S – triving ... Motivation or drive, coming from unsatisfied
        hungers or unrealised goals.

Scientific research has shown how different physical activities can develop the fitness factors.

In tests done on a variety of physical activities, from aerobics to yoga, gardening to golf, with housework and walking included, hard swimming scored best at developing all the fitness factors.

History

Cavemen swam, I guess. Some primitive chap sat astride a log and paddled after an out-of-reach prize, then fell off ... and gasped and scrambled his way to dry land: or some selfless mum retrieved a reckless toddler from the water. Perhaps a few souls drowned before humankind had its first successful swimmer. From archaeological evidence the Assyrians were swimming in 880 B.C. So were other ancient civilisations from the Greeks to the Japanese. There are references to swimming in the Holy Bible.

The earliest written record of swimming in Britain concerns the Romans in 55 B.C. Julius Caesar was reputedly a fine swimmer who once swam 300 yards in the sea to escape capture, holding – so the story goes – important papers above his head with one hand and towing his cloak in his teeth. Geoffrey Chaucer, writing in the 1300s, mentions swimming. The first written treatise on swimming in Britain was done, however, in Latin in the days of Good Queen Bess by a controversial cleric and scholar, an M.A. and Fellow of Cambridge, named Everard Digby.

There is a classic myth of a youth named Leander who each night swam The Hellespont (ancient name for The Dardanelles) to meet secretly with his lover, the priestess Hero, and then he swam back again. As it is 1¼ miles across at the narrowest, but a fast tide race would carry you as much as 4 miles off course in the time it took to cross, that would be a fine feat if true. Hence a number of swimming clubs have been called "Leander S.C." In 1810, the romantic poet Lord Byron did swim across The Dardanelles with a Royal Navy lieutenant named Ekenhead to show it could be done.

The first public swimming bath in England was a sea-water establishment built and opened by the Liverpool Corporation in 1818. London followed suit with fresh water baths (The Thames being unspeakably filthy then) and they spread throughout the country. By the 1860s there was renewed interest in swimming and clubs were formed. The public schools and universities led the way. Then, in 1875, wide public interest was aroused when a dare-devil 27-year-old sea captain, Matthew Webb, breast-stroked his way across The English Channel from England to France in 21¾ hours. It was thought a superhuman achievement but it gave ordinary swimming a great boost. Today, some young swimmers have completed 2-way non-stop Channel crossings in less time than that; while on 18 Aug 87, 23-year-old New Zealander Philip Rush did a 3-way non-stop Channel swim in 28 hours 31 minutes.

On the international speed scene, male freestylers regard 60 seconds and less for 100 metres crawl as commonplace and they can reel off metric miles (1,500 metres, 30 lengths of a full-size pool) in around 16 minutes. The best men will always swim faster than women, although a world-class female can quickly leave a club or county-class man behind; and women are unequalled in synchro. (water ballet) and when it comes to durability in cold rough marathons.

'Master swimmers' are men and women who compete in age groups and they set high standards. I read in a swimming journal recently of a 50 metres sprint in 35 seconds (just you try it!) by a man of over 70 years of age. I know a woman in her late 60s who flies the Atlantic to compete in top-class American masters events and comes home with Gold and Silver medals; and a man friend who is now past 70 regularly swims the 9–13 miles (it depends on the tides and shifting sandbanks) across Morecambe Bay in Lancashire.

Swimming, once learnt, is never forgotten. It can be a life-long pleasure and preoccupation, or merely a Summer recreation to be taken up again for a few fine weeks each year.

When Benjamin Franklin, one of America's great sons,

first came to London in 1724, he was then 18 years old. He swam the Thames from Blackfriars upstream to Chelsea "performing" (the records says) "sundry feats in the water as he went along." I wonder what he did?

From an account of a Victorian swimming family comes this priceless gem:- "Mrs. Samuda's sister was also a magnificent swimmer, and on one occasion, when she was sixteen years of age, swam ashore a quarter of a mile completely dressed, not only wearing all the ordinary garments of a lady, including corsets, but also attired in a heavy fishwife serge dress, boots, hats and gloves, carrying in one hand a huge scarlet Turkey twill umbrella opened, and in the other a large bouquet of somewhat gaudy flowers, presented to her for the occasion."

The greatest swimmer of all time was named Johnny and he was born in Pennsylvania, U.S.A. His parents were German-Austrian from Vienna and their name was Weiss-muller. Johnny Weissmuller was the first man through the 50 second barrier for 100 yards (the swimmer's 4-minute mile) and he broke between 50 and 75 world records, depending upon whether or not you count those he already held. He represented his country at 2 Olympic Games – Paris in 1924 and Amsterdam in 1928 – winning his events in new Olympic times. He never lost a race and retired undefeated at the age of 24, having dominated the world swim scene for 8 years. Yet Johnny Weissmuller became famous for something quite different . . . he was Tarzan! The fourth actor to play the role in Hollywood's versions of the Edgar Rice Burroughs' stories, his films are still shown on T.V. today. In them he can be seen swimming jungle rivers or fighting to the death with crocodiles. He was in his 30s when he made those films and his world-beating crawl stroke was changed to look better to the cameras; still, we are seeing someone very special when Tarzan, in a flurry of spray, powers through the water to do battle with another crocodile.

Read on to learn how we go about the art of swimming. I have written as if your swimmer is male. As an enthusiastic coach of female swimmers I can assure you that the text applies equally to girls and women.

2
GETTING STARTED

The first visit to a public swimming pool can unnerve small children. There is some formality with money and tickets which they do not fully understand. They are taken to a changing room (many of which now mix the sexes) along corridors that echo and smell strange. They are not sure they could find their way out again. Their clothes are taken off them and stuffed into one of hundreds of identical lockers. More corridors (pool buildings generally isolate the "wet" from the "dry" side) ensure they really do lose all sense of direction. Then they emerge into a big hall brilliant with light reflected from lots of shiny water. If it is crowded, it will be noisy and splashy too.

At this stage do not expect devoted attention to swimming lessons. They are probably wondering if they will ever see their clothes again, or where they go to the toilet.

Take them to the pool a couple of times to see friends or family swim and eliminate a lot of vague fears before they are asked to appear on the bathside stripped for action.

Choose your pool – if there is a choice – to suit your purpose. One of the latest generation of leisure pool complexes, with an extra-warm shallow-water teaching pool, slides, palm trees, islands, fountains disguised as spouting whales, wave-making machines, and the like, is preferable to the traditional plain rectangular tank of colder and deeper water.

Allay anxieties from the moment you enter the building. Explain every step of the way, the ticket and locker routines. Find and use the toilets. Remove any make-up. Blow your noses and use the footbath, sprays or other pre-cleanse facilities.

Pool managers go to college for years to study pool water

chemistry and learn how to combat pollution and germs. Creating safe and attractive water is a clever and costly business. Do not make it more difficult. I once managed a pool to which each evening a roof tiler came, grimy and sweaty from a day's hard work. He enjoyed his daily dip but treated my pool like a bath, coming out a good deal cleaner than he went in. He threatened to hit an attendant who mildly suggested he should use the soap and showers provided before having a swim. He would not accept that you should be clean to swim. Unremoved dirt or cosmetics will wash off in the water and be inflicted on other bathers. Please acquire the habit of using pre-cleanse amenities.

On the poolside, show your beginner how to recognise the shallow end. Look for a sign 'Shallow End'; other beginners clearly standing on the bottom; steps or ladders with only a few rungs; warning lines or tiles of a different colour to the remainder of the pool; depth markings (at the most around 3 feet deep (1 metre), probably less). Keep away – for now – from the deep end. If in doubt, ask the pool attendant/lifeguard who should be nearby in uniform. If your pupil is tall enough to stand in that depth, show him where on his body the water will reach.

The latest generation of irregularly shaped leisure pools have a sloping "beach" going gently from no depth at all out into shallow water.

Walk, do not run. Poolsides covered with water are slippery. The soles of your feet can lose all adhesion and aquaplane if you do not take it steadily. A fall on tiles always jars and it might break bones.

Buoyancy aids

A pair of inflatable armbands is indispensable for little learners. They can be bought at most sports shops and departmental stores or at the cashier's office in some pools. They are not expensive. Buy ones with safety valves which keep the air in even if the plugs come out accidentally, yet can still be deflated when you know the trick. Choose a make which has a flat section under the arms, allowing each arm to hang naturally at the side. It is also an advantage to have armbands with twin compartments so that, as your pupil becomes proficient, they need have only one half of each armband inflated.

Alternatively, a 'Polyotter' swimsuit is made with polystyrene buoyancy blocks inserted around the body of the costume in panels. These float segments can be removed one at a time as the learner improves until finally he or she swims unaided.

Another aid you will need almost from the outset is a swim float, a rectangular plastic board for your learner to hold on to while practising leg kicking. They can be had in various sizes – small children only need a little one – and a nervous beginner might find it helpful to hang on to two at once (one under each arm). For tiny tots, my wife just cuts one big one in half. Children take absent-minded bites out of floats, so avoid brittle (polystyrene) ones and get the tougher (polyethylene/polythene) kind.

Rings and belts are not a good idea as they do not always support the learner in the right position and have a tendency to slip. There are, however, swim rings and collars specially designed for the support and extra security of disabled swimmers.

Wearing inflated armbands or a buoyant swim suit, the smallest beginner can experience from day 1 in the pool how water supports him as he bobs about. He does not need to put his feet on the pool bottom and is free to try kicking and pulling to go in roughly the right direction.

In time, improvers become less dependent upon buoyancy aids. Inflate armbands less; remove some flotation segments from swim suits. Soon or late, they must swim without them. Most pupils can be weaned off buoyancy aids. A few cling (literally) to them. Teachers must be patient. My wife Barbara recently met a new pupil, a 4-year-old boy, and the first question she heard him ask his mum was; "Will she make me take my armbands off?" So it can be a big worry for a little person. Just 4 sessions later that boy swam a few yards without aids. She gained his confidence and worked at his basic swim skills until one day he just did not need armbands anymore. I know of one child who kept them on when they were completely deflated . . . he felt incomplete without them. His enterprising teacher cut a pair of wide circular bands from a motor cycle inner tube and let him change to those. Eventually, even he saw the pointlessness of wearing them.

Entry and warm-up

Your first task is to give your beginner some way to get into the water quickly, without dithering about, and an activity

which starts him moving about. Edging down steps and
standing shivering are to be avoided.

You enter the water first. Then hold your beginner firmly
beneath the armpits with both your hands and lift him down,
immersing him shoulders under. Encourage him to kick or
"run". My daughters Susan and Julie, when they were 5 and 3
respectively, enjoyed the following warm-up activity. Having
dunked them in the water, one at a time I would tow them
here and there about the shallow end with the following
commentary; "Kick your legs – let's get warm – look, there's a
polar bear – let's catch him and take him home with us – come
on, kick or we won't get near him – harder, he's getting away –
ah, got him – tie a piece of string to him – come with us, polar
bear – hey, there's an elephant – quickly, after him – that
elephant's swimming fast... etc., etc." We covered quite a
distance that way and found the most improbable animals in
the pool.

Very young children may like to take a favourite toy, one
that floats, into the water with them. Please make sure before
you allow this that the pool manager agrees. You can buy
small inflatable plastic ducks, fish and dolphins, frogs and
penguins, boats and the like, for pool use.

Learners can soon enter the water unaided by sitting on the
bathside, reaching down to grasp the handrail or overflow
channel with one hand, then slipping into the water and
turning to grasp the rail or channel with both hands. They can
jump up and down to get wet and warm, finishing with
shoulders under water.

They may progress to jumping in (at first holding your
hands, later unaided) if they can stand within the depth of
water or are wearing buoyancy aids.

Where you can walk down a gradual slope into a warm and
shallow teaching pool at a comfortable temperature of 86° F/
30° C, children can paddle, sit, lie and roll in the water. The
main pool is deeper and cooler. If it is below 80° F/27° C, that
is nearly 20° F below body temperature, healthy and
invigorating for an adult but enough to make your pupil gasp
with surprise. Add to this the solid weight of the water on
chest and tummy, and breathing is actually a trifle harder
than on land. They may sense this even if they do not
understand it. Distract them. Keep them busy and they will
forget the sensation. After a couple of visits they will not even
notice it.

GOLDEN RULE No. 2
Shoulders under water.

In the water always keep your shoulders submerged and rest your chin on the surface when not swimming. Let your pupil see experienced swimmers standing in a crouched posture, shoulders under water and bodyweight almost wholly water-borne. That way they are in a good position to push off in any direction... and they are out of any draughts.

Safe walking
Learners big enough to stand on the bottom of a pool must be taught to walk without slipping or overbalancing. Because they do not weigh so much in water, feet have less grip. They cannot move fast because the water slows them down, and, if impatiently they stand up to walk, their top halves go on ahead of their slower bottom halves. They should slide their feet at first, using their arms like oars (shoulders underwater) to pull themselves forward. Later they can try picking up their knees and leaning against the water, like a slow-motion deep sea diver on the ocean bed. Once they have the feel of that, try a walking race across the width to put fun and effort into learning to move around.

Submerging
The prone swim strokes can only be swum properly with the face immersed in the water most of the time. Beginners must become accustomed to submerging. Even swimming on the back (supine) they will not avoid water on their faces.

Start by luring them into games where splashing and the occasional ducking come almost by chance. Give them enjoyable distractions:- blow bubbles into the water; blow ping-pong balls along the surface (have races, or compete for the same ball); play the old game of apple-bobbing, trying to bite half-inflated balloons given weight with a little water inside them; improvise a version of "This is the way we wash our hair".

Complete submersion of the head for the first time is a lot to ask of any beginner. There is no way to disguise it totally but you can still dress it up. Ducking quickly underneath a floating object as part of a make-belief escape adventure is much more likely to be attempted than; 'Now I want you to be brave, hold your breath, and go under the nasty water when I say 'Go'." Let them shut their eyes for now.

Encourage them to spend more time beneath the surface. Having the external ear canals full of water does no harm to healthy and intact ear drums. Play "Ring-a-ring-o'-roses", submerging after "... We all fall down," and "Humpty Dumpty had a great fall." Have your pupil discover that sounds travel much further underwater. Tap some hard object beneath the surface across the width (or even down the length) of the pool while they submerge to listen for it. Try to understand one another conversing in "bubble talk" under water. Think how noisy the ocean must be to whales and other sea creatures.

Swimmers have to open their eyes under water to swim straight along the black lines provided down the centre of each racing lane. They need to sneak sideways glances at competitors alongside who might be edging into a lead, and to spot the point ahead to go into a fast tumble turn. Then again, lifesavers must be able to search river or lake bed for sunken victims. Synchro. swimmers must keep exact formation in a chorus line and not lose their sense of direction during tricky somersaulting and twisting movements.

Start your learner off with quick peeps, gradually prolonging the time they can keep their eyes open. Give them things to look at. Count tiles on the pool bottom; examine steps and other underwater fittings; look at makers' labels and badges on swim suits. Check whether or not they are truly looking by means of an underwater quiz; "How many fingers am I holding out?" "What coloured object do I have now?"

Some teachers pretend submerging is not at all strange or unpleasant. I say; "Yes, it feels funny at first; but it won't harm you and you'll soon get used to it." Eyes opened under water feel cold and sting just a tiny bit. This may actually do them good; when do we otherwise give them such a thorough antiseptic bath? You do not have to keep them open all the time. Swimmers do not. Take a good look now and again, closing them between times to reduce exposure if that makes you feel better. Most swimmers also shut their eyes as they pass up or down through the surface (the blink reflex takes care of it).

Do stop your beginner rubbing his eyes when he surfaces or that will make them sore. Let him blink a lot instead. Eye lashes, tell him, are like paint brushes; they hold big drops of

water which blur vision when the eyes are first opened. Clear
the view by blinking.

(Do NOT let them start wearing swim-goggles at this early
stage.)

Water creeps up your nose when you submerge. It is not
enough just to hold your breath. You have to put a little air
pressure into your nostrils to keep the water back. When
completely upside-down (in a handstand, surface dive or
somersault) you may have to leak a little air out of your nose
in bubbles to stay watertight, as all that weight of water above
you has a straight run down (that is, UP) your nose when it is
inverted.

Teach your pupil nose-blowing without a handkerchief.
Press one nostril closed with finger or thumb and snort out
through the other. Do each in turn. Do it whenever necessary.
The pool's filtration and disinfection systems can easily cope
with the contents of all our noses, so do not worry about
hygiene. A runny nose, on child or adult, is not a pretty sight
and so we swimmers habitually wipe off our upper lip at
frequent intervals (to be confident we always look our best).

The odd sniff or squirt of water will now and again force its
way up into nasal passages and make your cheeks ache
slightly. This also brings a tear to the eye and causes a sneeze
or two, but it drains away itself. Carry on swimming and
disregard it. Do not let your pupil adopt a nose-clip – unless
one is advised for some medical condition – or they will never
acquire the water skill and awareness needed to remain
watertight and comfortable without it. Only when swimmers
undertake concentrated practice of advanced activities such
as racing tumble turns or synchro. movements may nose-clips
be a useful protection. (I suffer from hay fever for just 6 weeks
of every year and I wear a nose-clip during those miserable 40
days or so to avoid aggravating the poor old nose.)

Nose-clips and goggles are nuisances. It takes practice to
wear them without trouble; meantime you have to fiddle
around a lot with them. This distracts learners from their
lessons. Leave them for later ... much later.

Other submerging games include:- diving through teacher's
legs (move to one side occasionally to discover if they really
do open their eyes); treasure hunts for objects on the pool

bottom; handstands, cartwheels and somersaults.

Horizontal position
Little beginners launched afloat in buoyancy aids will be
vertical, running on the spot and making ineffective hand
motions in the water, to start with. They must lean forward in
the direction they want to go, letting their legs come up to
kick behind them. Hands must pull back towards their legs if
they are to go along.

GOLDEN RULE No. 3
Swimming is getting flat, then moving along.

In very shallow teaching or leisure pools, your pupil can
easily lie down in just a foot (30cm) or so of water, supporting
himself on his hands, and mimic real swimming by kicking
while walking his hands along the pool bottom. This can turn
into swimming. Try it prone, then supine. Make sure he
travels across the shelving bottom and not out into deep
water.

Feet off the bottom
Pupils big enough to stand in the water, even wearing armbands or other aids, have to be persuaded to lift their feet off
the pool bottom and this can take time. Keep them away
from the handrail lest they become dependent upon it and
nervous about straying far from it. With their shoulders
under water, and some submerging practices mastered, point
out how much lighter they are in water. They can extend their
arms sideways beneath the water, and, with supportive
backward and forward sweeping movements, lift their feet off
the bottom momentarily. If they are able enough to remain in
the water with you when a wave-making machine is
operating, simply crouching (shoulders under) on the balls of
their feet, each passing wave will lift them up and plonk them
back down again. Caution – it will also carry them along with
it for a short distance. Be there to prevent them falling down.
Indulge them in towing, swirling and whooshing games. Let
them hold your hands and perform somersaults through your
arms if they can do them.

Regaining the standing position
Beginners will only adopt the horizontal position when held

securely by someone they trust not to let go of them because
THEY CANNOT REGAIN THE STANDING POSITION.
Grasp this vital fact. Unaided they cannot stand up again. Do
not ever be tempted to let go of them to swim or sink. Many
older non-swimmers will tell you that is just what was done to
them, and most of them never went near water again. If you
say you will hold them, do so. Before they can be expected to
make more progress you must teach them how to stand up
from both a prone and a supine glide.

GOLDEN RULE No. 4
Regaining the standing position comes before swimming flat.

In water of standing depth have your pupil lie out flat on his
front supporting himself with his hands, arms extended
forward straight, on your hands. To stand, he lifts his head,
tucks up his knees beneath his body, and presses down on
your hands. This rotates him until his feet are beneath him
once more, when he stands up. This is shown in fig. 1.

Fig. 1   Standing up from prone

A = direction of pull
B = direction of rotation

Caution – A common failing is not tucking sufficiently and then trying to stand before the feet are directly underneath them. They slip. A ducking results. Another imperfect (and rather more frantic) try is made, water is swallowed, and it becomes rather frightening. Drill into them; "Head up – tuck up tight – press down (wait for it!) – and stand up."

Progress to having the learner hold a float in both hands, arms straight, and you hold the other end of the same float. To stand up they press down on their end of the float. Then let them try with the float under their own control (be there to help if needed). In the end they must discard the float and master this essential stage pulling down on the water with the palms of their hands only.

Regaining the standing position from the back glide needs to be learnt before back stroke is tried. Supine, supported by teacher's hands beneath his shoulder-blades, the learner lifts his head (forward, chin on chest), tucks up the knees tightly, and you roll him around and forward until he can put his feet

Fig. 2 Standing up from supine

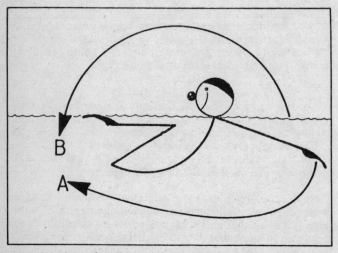

A = direction of pull
B = direction of rotation

down and stand up. Legs and feet have further to travel around before they can be placed firmly on the pool bottom from a supine layout. They must tuck tightly and allow time to rotate. If they open out too soon they will flounder and sink. Drill in; "Head up – tuck up (extending arms sideways and back) – scoop strongly from behind down and forwards." It is a bit like wielding a skipping-rope backwards, and shown in fig. 2.

Standing up is possibly the single most important lesson in this essential early training. Beginners may play happily in water, ducking under the surface, and giving every impression of poise and confidence. They will refuse to try to swim, however (or hop half-heartedly along with one foot on the bottom), if they have not been taught this vital step. Once they have it, they are already to go on.

Floating

Improvers who can put their faces in the water and also regain the standing position can try a couple of motionless floating skills.

1. *Star (or "dead man's") float*
   Shoulders underwater, take a deep breath and hold it. Lie gently face down in the water to float in a star (or 'X') shape. See how long they can comfortably hold it. They must stand up to breathe again.

2. *Tucked (or "mushroom") float* (fig. 3)
   Starting – as always – with the shoulders under water, take a deep breath and hold it. Gently lower the face forward into the water and at the same time tuck up the legs and hold them snugly to the chest with the arms. Allow the bobbing to settle down and float with just the back breaking the surface. Stand up to breathe.

Most people can do these two floats. Early difficulties occur only if they fail to take a deep enough breath (it is the lungs full of air that make floating possible), or they bob up and down so much that they think that they are sinking when they are not. Take a deep breath and go into the floats very gently to avoid bobbing.

A few skinny or heavy-boned and muscular individuals do

Fig. 3   Mushroom float

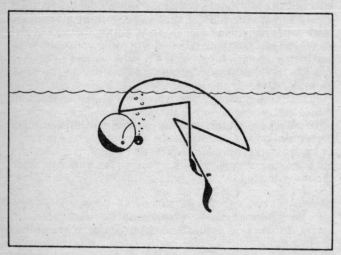

sink to the bottom in a mushroom float despite all coaching. These true "sinkers" lack the buoyancy of the average person. It does not matter much – some of the world's best swimmers have been sinkers – except that you, the teacher, will have to make sure they reduce gliding in strokes to a minimum and see they use their arms and legs to compensate for a low body position in the water.

Pushing-and-gliding

Whether a swimmer dives out into the water, pushes off from the side, or merely switches from one stroke to another mid-way along the length, he takes up a stretched and streamlined glide position (either prone or supine) prior to taking the first stroke. It is a basic swimming position.

GOLDEN RULE No. 5
Everything comes from the push-and-glide.

Learn to push-and-glide from the side. Standing, back to the side of the pool, and reach back to take hold of the rail or overflow channel with both hands. Walk the feet up the wall so as to hang suspended in a tucked position. The bodyweight is waterborne, head facing forward, chin resting on the surface. The feet should be flat on the wall, hip-width apart, on a level with one another, toes pointing down. To push and glide prone, let go and quickly bring both arms around over the surface to an extended position in front: at the same time straighten the legs and push off strongly, taking a breath and putting the head down between the arms. Glide as far as possible, stretched and streamlined, like a diver entering the water . . . only horizontal. As speed dies away, the legs sink. Stand up.

In a leisure pool with the wave-making machine operating, try surfing into the beach on the waves.

Pushing-and-gliding requires an effort. Entwine the thumbs, to prevent the hands coming apart, and lock the elbows straight. "Hold the head on" by squeezing it between the upper arms which cover the ears. Hands must be flat, alongside one another, with palms downwards. Fingers are straight and together. The natural curves of the backbone are retained. The legs are extended out straight behind and pressed together at knees and ankles. Feet are pointed backwards, toes curled neatly. Tightening or tensing the bottom muscles helps to keep the legs up, to glide flat, heels breaking the surface.

A push-and-glide along the surface pushes up a big bow wave which can be fun but it puts the brakes on. It is smoother and faster (and the swimmer travels further) to push off *beneath* and then glide up to the surface. All practised swimmers do this. Show your swimmer how to pause, having let go of the side, and deliberately sink down beneath the surface, before lowering the head and extending the arms to push off under water. Aim to come off the wall about 2 feet (0.6 metre) deep and glide upward to reach the surface in a swimming position.

After the initial push-off, you travel faster under water than you could swim. So, hold the glide. Do not swim. As the glide speed slows to your intended surface swimming speed (and just before you surface), start kicking to arrive back on top of the water ready to pick up with the arm action.

Try pushing-and-gliding supine with the arms at the sides. Face the wall, hold the rail or channel with both hands (closer together this time, shoulder-width apart), and walk the feet up the wall. Feet once again hip-width apart, toes upwards.

Simply let go of the side with both hands at once, lie back with the head pillowed in the water, and push off strongly. Have fun making as big a bow wave as possible. Make sure there is no-one behind you first!

To eliminate most of the bow wave, for an efficient push-and-glide, the arms must be extended beyond the head as in the prone position (but hand palms upwards). This demands flexibility and some muscular effort in the shoulders. It is a somewhat advanced movement and not every learner will want to persevere with it. The glide is a little unstable ("tippy") as the speed comes off it. Kicking the legs helps steady the body. Supine pushing-and-gliding submerged is awkward and uncomfortable at this stage in a swimmer's development. Try it... but do not labour it.

Front ("dog") paddle

Swimming doggy fashion can be tried almost straightaway in buoyancy aids. The legs kick up and down alternately and continuously at the back (similar to a crawl swimmer's kick) and the swimmer leans forward flat to pull back alternately with the hands out in front of the face. The head is raised to look forward, with the chin in the water, and the mouth too if they can time a breath without swallowing water. Dog paddle is slow and quite tiring. Practice makes it easier and beginners often do their first width of 10 metres (nearly 11 yards) this way, with lots of encouragement from teacher.

Without buoyancy aids, and having learnt to stand up, learners must first hold either the teacher's hands or a float and practise kicking. Then they can try pulling with just one hand while the other still holds on to its support. Once they have the idea, push-and-glide, add kicking, and then have a go at a few arm pulls before standing up. Gradually extend the distance covered and the number of strokes.

To polish their dog-paddle, work on the following teaching points. The legs should kick to a maximum depth of 12" (30cm), making a small splash at the surface of the water. Count "1, 2, 3; 1, 2, 3," as they kick to establish a steady rhythm. One arm pulls to the first count of 3 beats, the other arm to the other 3 kicks (the beginnings of the classic 6-beat crawl stroke you will teach them later). They breathe *IN through the mouth* and *OUT through mouth and nose.* Hands must be flat or slightly shaped (palms concave) to pull

backwards – rather than downwards – against the water.
Fingers are held together, thumbs in line with the fingers. The
legs are mostly straight, the water resistance bending the
knees a little on each downbeat before they straighten again.
The feet are turned inwards just a bit, big toes brushing past
one another, to drive the water backwards off the top of each
foot in turn.

Big faults at first are:- legs bicycling, bending much too
much at hips and knees so that the kicking is all wrong; arms
pawing downwards on the water. Aim to flatten your
swimmer out and send him travelling *along* through the
water.

Back paddle

With support from armbands, a float held firmly under each
arm, or supported just enough by teacher's hands, the learner
lies back supine and kicks rhythmically up and down from
the hips. He need make no attempt to bend the knees, the
water will do that, so that the effect is a flexible whip-like
effect travelling from the hips down to the toes. He must
thrust the water away from them off the top of each foot in
turn.

In a shallow water teaching pool learners can walk on their
hands in the back position.

Once free from artificial supports like floats, they can use
their hands in helpful scooping actions. This hand action will
later turn into figure-of-eight sculling. Instruct them in how
to look up and follow lines on the ceiling (as good swimmers
do) so as to swim straight although they cannot see where
they are going.

Anytime now your beginner will complete his first width,
swimming without aids. When he does, reward him with an "I
Can Swim" badge; there is one with those words on it.

All the essential early confidence training we have gone
through is ... precisely that; it is confidence training which
must be introduced early because it is essential. You cannot
truly swim until you can cheerfully cope with an unintended
ducking and stand up again without help. The progressive
steps I have listed and described are not conveniently
mastered in that order. Children (and adult learners) can
often swim a fair distance but still dislike water on their faces.
But they are not yet fully competent swimmers and you

should return to submerging practices at intervals.

Not all beginners are timid souls. It is possible with some, who are not strangers to water, simply to point to a nearby swimmer and say; "Try what they're doing." With armbands you can certainly have little learners mobile on the first visit to a pool. Remember, though, that submerging and regaining the standing position are vital skills for all swimmers. They must be done.

Now is the time to think ahead. Sooner rather than later you will equip your improving pupil with an efficient stroke to replace the slow and clumsy front and back paddle. Shortly after that he will swim his first length.

GOLDEN RULE No. 6
We learn to swim across widths but become swimmers over lengths.

This first length should always start *at the DEEP end* so that, by the time stamina and determination are flagging, the swimmer is back in familiar surrounds at the shallow end where he did his early work. The snag is how to start off from vertical step ladders, or hanging onto the side channel, when swimmers are not in a flat swimming position. A good push-and-glide solves that; but what if they stop part way along while still out of their depth? I have seen new swimmers nearly drown and need rescuing when brought to a standstill upright and unable to get going again. It can happen after an accidental collision or even if someone passes close in front of them. A nervous grown man once grabbed me round the neck and dragged me underwater with him when I unknowingly swam too close for his peace of mind. Another time I saw a mature woman – who had swum lengths of the pool before – rescued by a friend after she had stopped for some reason and then, to save her life, could not start off again. It is a link in the swimming chain of progression (often overlooked by teachers), yet fundamental to survival, that you are not a swimmer until you can regain the swimming position unaided.

GOLDEN RULE No. 7
Regaining the swimming position from vertical comes before swimming in deep water.

There is not much to it. Lean forward and commence pulling by means of whatever arm stroke you are best at; at the same time push your bottom up towards the surface and start climbing imaginary stairs behind with the tops of your feet. Practise holding on to a float or teacher's hands, replacing this support with your own hands in the water when you feel able to do so.

3

INFANTS & TODDLERS

Teaching babies to swim was the speciality of a few teachers working around the poolsides of film stars in sunny California, U.S.A. over 20 years ago. Crooner Bing Crosby's young daughter Mary Frances hit the headlines when, aged 2, she became the youngest child in history to receive the American National Red Cross Beginner's Certificate for swimming. His sons Harry and Gary also swam very young.

Swim-baby classes reached the U.K. years ago but people still question if it is worthwhile or even safe to teach swimming to the very young. Infants during the first 6 months after birth mostly feed and sleep. Swim-babies feed, SWIM and sleep, a harmless enough extension of their daily routines. There is convincing medical opinion that infants who undergo a swim programme show greater alertness, eat and sleep better, and may actually be less susceptible to cot deaths.

The claim sometimes heard that swim-babies will be more intelligent is probably nonsense; nor are they more likely than any other child to become an Olympic swim star. Indeed, too much swimming too early could put them off it. That has happened. They may not even turn out to be very polished performers in the water.

Still, it is nice and natural for infants and toddlers to enjoy water. After all, the foetus grew for 9 months in a sac of water and the best time to reintroduce baby to water once again is as soon as possible after birth.

It might take between 50 and 100 hours of baby's time and yours before he is reasonably able in water, can tumble in and regain the surface to breathe, turn around and propel himself in the direction of safety. Even then swim-babies' immature minds cannot cope with complications. Climbing out may be beyond them. So they can NEVER be left alone.

Lessons may last only 5 minutes for babes new to the world and to swimming. They lose heat fast. Later, as acclimatised veterans of 1–2 years of age, they will be able to manage 30 minutes (and the occasional 45 minute session when everyone is feeling particularly good). They need a minimum of 3 lessons a week to progress but would do twice as well with daily sessions.

Start at home. Use a small baby bath for serious washing but take him into the big bath with you, naked, for a daily playtime. Do not have soap or other stinging substances or liquids in the water. Babies have no fear of water. Make sure yours does not acquire it. Hold him reassuringly, cuddle and kiss him gently. Move him to and fro in the water with slow and deliberate movements. Hold baby at arm's length in the water and draw him to you BENEATH the water. Infants do not breathe under water and will cope better than you may imagine. Lift him up and give him a cuddle and quiet praise. Float him on his back, ears submerged, carefully supporting his head to compensate for weak neck muscles (and avoid water going up his nostrils). Sing nursery rhymes. Have a cute toy in the water with you both. Splash about a bit. Wet your own face and pretend to wash your hair. Say: "That's fun ... what a good game." Do it to him. Smile away any uncertainty he might have about it.

Babies may have no instinctive fear of water but they are born with a fear of loud noises. Be as sure as you can that they have no nasty noisy shocks while playing in the bath, or they may link the two and grow fearful of bathtime. I would even remove them from the bathroom before I pulled out the plug to let the water gurgle down the waste pipe. You canot be too careful.

When you decide the time is right, transfer baby's dips to a small and shallow teaching pool (sometimes called a "baby pool"). This will generally be a public pool. It must be very warm, around 85°F (29°C). Do not use the main pool which will be too cold. A municipal swimming pool complex can be crowded and noisy, so enquire beforehand when quiet times occur and visit then if you can. Perhaps go once or twice with your baby and just watch and grow used to the strange new atmosphere. Your first visit will generally be when baby is 2–3 months old, after he has had his first immunisations and is fit to go out into public places.

You must always be in the water with baby. If you cannot swim, at least show you are enjoying yourself. If you are not relaxed, your infant will be uneasy too. Be sure you can regain your feet if you slip over.

Do not swim baby immediately after a meal. Full feeds should take place 2 hours beforehand, giving him time to bring some of it back up and to fill his nappy. Thus "topped and tailed", there is only a slight risk of embarrassment in the pool. Alternatively, you might give him a light feed an hour before going into the water, followed by a full feed and a sleep afterwards. (Mums can enjoy a sleep too!)

Baby should wear a small and snug-fitting lightweight pair of pants, just like a real little swimming costume. Little girls who are old enough to have a swimsuit should wear one-piece outfits with no frilly extras. There is no need for bulky nappies or other protection. Hats do not suit little ones. Braid a toddler's hair if it needs to be kept out of the eyes and mouth.

Grown-ups should wear a bright and distinctive costume. Babies keep their eyes open underwater and will look for you when they submerge. Always wear the same costume so that they have no trouble locating you.

It is a curious fact that babies instinctively hold their breath when submerged in water. Once mouth and nose are immersed, they simply do not breathe, nor do they close their eyes, making possible some remarkable photographs of babies apparently "swimming" underwater, relaxed and alert. These pictures are misleading. It may be that, as soon as the snapshots were taken, someone had to pluck the little mites up out of the water before they drowned. Experienced teachers of infant swimmers have used this odd congenital reflex, however, to school them into surfacing, breathing, and swimming unaided. Many apt pupils then go on to be real water babies who can dive happily for objects on the pool bottom, bob up again, swim about, and generally enjoy themselves.

The big difference with an infant swim programme is that, whereas old beginners are invited to duck beneath the surface voluntarily, the babies have no say in the matter but are submerged by parent or teacher. Forcing infants under water is controversial. The Royal Society for the Prevention of

Accidents is opposed to it. Some swimming teachers who
were once keen to practise it have now recanted. They still
take baby swim classes, and do not object to a bit of splashing
about, but they omit forcible immersions of infants. Pushing
babies underwater looks alarming – and it could be overdone
– but I worked for a year with one of this country's leading
practitioners of baby swim programmes and saw nothing to
make me think it was harmful. Be aware that it does excite
strong feelings. Seek the views of parents who have taken part
in baby swim programmes and medicos who have experience
of infant swimming. Make up your own mind whether or not
submerging practices, done sensibly, should be part of your
baby's watertime activities.

Take baby into the water with you, bouncing gently up and
down and moving around. Hold the child securely (but not
too firmly) with both hands, one either side of the chest
beneath the armpits, thumbs forward and fingers to the rear.
If you are going to include submerging, now is as good a time
as any. Use some little warning phrase which, with repetition,
he will quickly learn is the signal for going under, like; "Let's
swim," or "Here we go," or some-such, and immerse him
completely in the water. Do not hesitate as you submerge him
or he might mis-time taking a breath. Do not let go of him.
Bring him slowly to the surface, give him a kiss and a cuddle,
and move around the pool occupying his attention with other
things. Treat it as normal. Be sure of yourself. Do not worry if
he cries or swallows a bit of water. It happens to most
swimmers occasionally. Repeat bobbing and submerging 2 or
3 times in this first visit.

Adopt a predictable routine each time you and your baby
or toddler go to the pool so that he knows what to expect.
Undress at the same spot (if possible); enter the water the
same way; let each swim session develop a familiar pattern;
even round it off with the same game, signalling time to leave
soon. If baby cries or grizzles persistently in the water, it
could well be for some reason other than dislike for
swimming . . . discomfort, boredom, a pain, cold, hunger, or
inactivity.

Hold your tiny pupil so that he can see you all the time. Get
him to kick his legs whatever way comes naturally to him.
One lady teacher I know says that tickling his feet usually
does it. When he does it (NOT before), say; "Kick, kick,

kick." Praise only purposeful movements. Do not praise inaction. When he does kick and makes vigorous arm movements in the water, you say; "Good baby... baby swim." Link their involuntary actions with the right words. Later, you will be able to say; "Kick," and have them respond.

Play simple games, like "Peek-a-boo!" Blow tickly bubbles against his skin. Press a floating toy down into the water and watch it pop up again.

The next step is for baby to float face down in the water for just a few seconds. Start him kicking, use your customary warning phrase, and lay him prone in the water. Let go. Count to '3' and pick him up again. Have a little cuddle and involve him in other things.

(Young babies may need "burping" from time to time when a hard and swollen tummy tells you. Practised swim babies do it themselves with a complete lack of self-consciousness, often loudly enough to make everyone else in the pool turn their heads and smile.)

Progress to bouncing baby up and down, submerging him to about 18″ (nearly ½ metre) deep, slowly guiding him back up to the surface. This is how he will learn, with kicking and arm movements, to regain the surface himself.

Babies who surface too quickly, popping up like corks, have to be caught before they drop back and go under again. Continue with guiding them up at the proper speed. Surfacing slowly is less of a problem; but, if too slow, you might give them a little boost upwards with hand or foot.

Occasionally a baby sinks, rolling off his prone position. Scoop him back up towards the surface. He does not usually lack buoyancy. More likely he just did not have a full pair of lungs that one time. Stand by at all times to ensure he arrives back at the surface at the right speed to breathe; then praise him.

When they have the knack of it, join them. Go down and come up together.

Holding baby securely, perhaps also contriving to support a relatively heavy head on inadequate neck muscles, limits you and baby. He can experience more freedom of movement if you make a harness which you hold in one hand only. A soft material, folded several times lengthwise, goes around the chest under armpits and is secured at the back to a short rope or other handhold. Do not let it slip down around his waist or he might up-end.

Baby's first distance swim will be a metre or two (3–6 feet). Float him face down, legs kicking, and gently push him away to a partner. If you are alone, pull him towards you. To do this, crouch (shoulders underwater) and walk slowly backwards. Draw him towards you and then let go. He will be pulled towards you by the low pressure area of swirling water in front of your chest. Do not get too far ahead of him or contact will be broken. Stay close and you will suck him along. Pick him up again.

Distance will increase as kicking and pulling improves to become dog paddle or a rough-and-ready breast stroke. The day the little swimmer can lift his head to take another breath is a big break-through. All of this does not happen in a few lessons. It comes from weeks and months of patience and kindly encouragement coupled with regular sessions and purposeful activity.

Babies over 6 months old brought to the pool for the first time need a longer introduction to water. By 9 months they are losing their underwater ease. They shut their eyes and may come up gasping and dismayed. Submerging practices must not be forced. One year after birth, the new-born baby's post-natal amphibious nature has gone. You must go through the usual essential early confidence training we all needed when we learnt to swim.

Practised water babies can go on to more advanced water skills. Float them on their backs. Stand by their heads, looking down over them so that they know where you are. Support them with your hands while their arms and hands try out the necessary counterbalancing movements in this new position. Small infants can only manage this back float for up to half a minute before their neck muscles tire. 2–3 year-olds can be turned over from front to back to front again.

Children as young as 6 months can be sat on the poolside and then, holding their hands in yours, gently pulled down into the water in a sort of half-jump/half-dive. Soon they will wriggle themselves to the point where they overbalance and fall in. Let them go right under and be sure (help if necessary) they can recover the surface to breathe. When they can walk, they can stand up and jump in.

Just as some children walk early, others late, so some soon swim while others do not. Do not fret and do not try to speed their progress. As long as they enjoy their dips, that is fine. After crossing their first width of a small teaching pool (5 metres), some toddlers can by 1 year of age swim 25 metres (1 length of the main pool). The National Savlon Water Baby Scheme, jointly with the Amateur Swimming Association, aims to reduce infant drownings (a quarter of the drownings in England and Wales are under 15 years of age, and many of them are toddlers) and grants awards for all children up to the age of 5. These, however, must be gained through recognised parent-and-baby classes held under the direction of an A.S.A. approved teacher.

Award 1 is for babies who swim a width or 10 metres *with* swimming aids;
Award 2 is for babies who swim half a width or 5 metres *without* aids.

Then what? I recommend... nothing. Stop there. Do not try to instruct them in formal strokes. That would be boring and, anyway, children who have undergone an infant swim programme can be such little tadpoles that they are hard to interest in doing things properly. That can come later. Meanwhile, let them have lots of fun and games in the water. Keep them company; they are still not safe alone.

A little boy named Adam, who had been a star pupil in his own mother's parent-and-baby classes was watching her teach older children to swim. He was puzzled. "Mum," he said, "I could always swim, couldn't I?" Is that not a good goal to aim for... a child who cannot recall NOT being able to swim?

4

YOU, THE TEACHER

A famous sculptor was asked to explain his methods; how did he go about creating, say, an elephant from a lump of rock. "Well," said the great man, "I half-close my eyes and I gaze at the rock and I picture an elephant; and any bit that doesn't look like an elephant, I knock it off!"

Teaching someone to swim is much the same. Knowing what an effective stroke looks like, anything your learner does within that outline you leave alone. Drastic differences must be corrected or eliminated.

You do not need to be a good swimmer yourself. Your job is to involve your pupil in activities which lead inevitably to them swimming the right way, then polishing their efforts.

Beginners find water thin, insubstantial stuff. When at first they pull and kick, their hands and feet have no noticeable effect. They can neither go along nor support themselves and they sink. Until they acquire a feel for it, swimming is a mystery beyond them. You must enable them to discover the water is thicker than they suppose; that when they kick and press down upon it, it will support them; that when they pull and push, they will go along.

GOLDEN RULE No. 8
Swimming is handling water.

The moment that water does not feel thin any more is when swimming starts. Floundering and going down turns into going along. Just a stroke or two, maybe, but there is no mistaking when it happens. Before the great day arrives, you have some teaching to do.

I assume you will be in the water with your pupil. So, when you have a minute to yourself, try this. Swim a width of your favourite stroke, but swim it badly. Open the fingers of one

hand so that the water escapes through them. Close the other
hand into a fist. Dorsi-flex your feet to swim "with clown's
boots on" (or, if you swim breast stroke, point your toes
instead). Lift your head up out of the water so that your legs
sink. Hold your breath until you go red in the face. Hard
work, is it not? You rev faster, go slower, and quickly tire.
Well, that is what learners do. That is what you will be putting
them through. Do not let them suffer for long. Flatten them
out and streamline them. Teach them to pull back with closed
hands and to kick with the right shaped foot to go along
easily. Until they have the knack, vary stroke work with less
strenuous activities such as pushing-and-gliding, floating,
submerging, diving and games.

Progress will be quicker with frequent lessons. Visit the
pool 3 times a week for 3 weeks, rather than 1 session a week
over 9 weeks. Your timetable will, of course, be disrupted
now and again when you catch a cold or have to work
unsocial hours. Never mind. Make the best of it.

Trial and error is not a good way to learn anything,
especially a physical skill like swimming. Read this book, and
keep one chapter ahead of your pupil to remove much of the
aimless experimentation. There is nothing wrong with
learning quickly.

Do not use land-drills, going through swim strokes "by
numbers" out of the water. This method – beloved by old-
time P.T. instructors – is just about useless and a waste of
everyone's time. Doing it that way does not help with doing it
in the water at all. It awakens the wrong muscle groups,
sometimes the very opposite of the ones you want them to use
in real swimming.

1. *Explanation/demonstration*

Tell your pupil what you want him to do. Use simple words.
Be understood. A vague expression like; "Try hard" could
mean "Go fast," or "Copy exactly," or "Keep going longer".
Say what you mean. Keep talk short. Teacher's chat
sometimes totals over half the lesson time. Let us go for more
swimming and less talk.

Merely telling is not teaching. Give him a demonstration to
watch. If you cannot do what is required yourself – and even
if you can – point out some other swimmer who happens to be
doing what you want to show them. If the display has some

fault or flaw, point it out and tell your learner that you do not want that bit. Any demonstration you do must be exactly right. Practise in a mirror beforehand. Children copy faithfully the smallest detail, so a rough exhibition is not good enough. If you show a movement in slow motion, errors can creep in; so also demonstrate it at the correct speed.

Make yourself a "little teacher" (Fig. 4) or prevail upon someone else to make one for you. Use stiff plastic of some kind which can be cut with shears and rivet the joints tightly enough to stay where they are set. It is a handy device to show what you mean and save words. You can also use it to mirror a swimmer's faults to himself.

Fig. 4   A "little teacher"

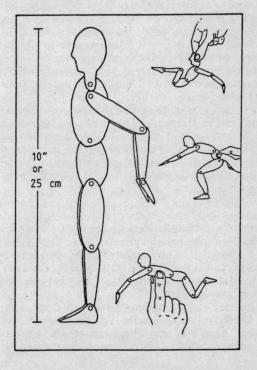

10"
or
25 cm

2. *Action/observation*

Swimming is a physical skill acquired by DOING it. Keep explanations and demonstrations brief, then let him have a go while you watch. It is your task to teach and his job to perform, but activity must have an obvious point. Give him a teaching point (a tip to polish the stroke or water skill being practised), for example "Keep your fingers closed when you pull." As a general rule, give only one teaching point at a time. Two teaching points can sometimes be mentioned when they link naturally together, like "Don't bend your knees so much; make less splash with your feet." Three teaching points together would be rare indeed, perhaps a reminder of a sequence of events already understood and now to be revised, such as for regaining the standing position from prone; "Head up – tuck up – pull down and back with your hands."

Sometimes you may take hold of one of your pupil's limbs and place it in the position you require of him, or move it through the limb track he needs to trace in the water. This beats all words and demonstrations, but be sure before you do it (especially if the child is not yours) that touching and holding are all right with him and will not be misunderstood by him or others.

Your viewing point should vary according to what you want to observe. Look side-on at your swimmer to assess his flat body position, depth of leg kick, length of arm entry, and so on. Have him swim head-on towards you to check stroke symmetry, narrow or wide hand entry, and the like. View breast stroke leg drive from behind as he swims away from you. You need to be looking down to see any snaking or wriggling that may be going on.

Take refraction into account. When you look down through air into water, everything underwater is fore-shortened and seems very much shallower. A badly over-deep leg kick may look reasonable from above. To gain an accurate idea of how arms and legs are doing below the surface, don swim-goggles or a full face mask and submerge. You will see your swimmer in a new light. It is the only way to learn how strokes are actually swum. Watching a televised swimming race is not much use unless there are underwater camera shots.

Swimming teachers must concentrate on what their pupils do underwater. They are like swans or ugly ducklings. What

they do above water is largely misleading; below is where the
energetic and skilful stroke-work goes on.

GOLDEN RULE No. 9
Underwater actions make the stroke:
Movements above water merely modify it.

3. *Comment/correction*
Comment immediately they stop what they were doing. If
they did it right, say so; "Good, keep it like that." If they are
getting the hang of it but it is still not quite right, praise and
encourage; "That was a good try; all you need to do now
is..." Knowledge of how they did is vital to learning
swimming, at the time, not much later. Do not let your
attention wander. Never have to say; "Do that again. I wasn't
watching."

GOLDEN RULE No. 10
Practice does not make perfect:
Practice makes permanent.

Right or wrong, do something often enough and it becomes
habitual. When that occurs, a fault is hard to eradicate
because it feels right. Stop big faults in swim strokes the
moment you spot them. Say; "No, that's wrong. Don't do it."
Do not let them continue out of misplaced kindness.

Adult learners like to know how and why an activity works
and where it is leading. We want to reason out movements in
our minds and know the goal. This can slow learning down
but we must be humoured or we may not do it at all.
Fortunately, youngsters can be put through a series of
practices without always needing to know the end. So do not
burden them with explanations. Guide their bodies, rather
than their minds, into good swimming.

A newly-tried stroke will be full of faults. Beginners cannot
concentrate on legs and arms, head movements and
breathing, and fit them all together properly. Then again,
some important skill may be missing (perhaps they still do
not like water on their face). Good swimming depends upon
polished techniques. You, teacher, must bit-by-bit rub the
rough parts away. Pick the most basic fault first. Cure that
and some of the others will disappear as well. A child who
"sits up and begs" in the water to avoid water on the face will
have a poor leg kick, faulty arms and breathing. Resolve the

submerging difficulty and he can flatten out, removing the limb track faults.

To correct a really grooved-in fault, you may have to ask the pupil to swim "so that it feels wrong" (persisting until the new and strange modification itself begins to feel right at last). It is easier to stop faults before they become ingrained.

Exaggerated corrections are occasionally useful. Say your pupil, swimming crawl, enters each hand into the water in such a way as to cross an imaginary centreline drawn through the body lengthwise. This results in a wriggling stroke. You would like the hands to go into the water ahead (and in front) of the respective eyes. The swimmer believes that is what he is doing, so telling him will not change anything. Apply an exaggerated correction. Ask them to put each hand in turn into the water WIDE of the shoulder. The adjustment they make might still be inaccurate and insufficient but turn out to be just what you wanted really.

4. Repetition

The teaching cycle continues when you send him off once again to try the stroke or skill, armed this time with some correction (by way of a fresh teaching point). You observe again, then comment and, if necessary, analyse faults and correct them. Praise and sometimes reward stages well done. Let him do what he does best and build on it. Return continually to weaker aspects and work on them too. Do not stress failure; rather, have him rehearse being successful.

Breathing – 2 kinds

The nose and mouth are submerged most of the time in modern strokes and only come up for a moment in the stroke cycle. That is when inhaling must be done. There is no time, however, for more than a quick in-breath. Breathing out has to be completed beforehand, the last bit blowing away loose surface water as the mouth emerges into the air.

Learners tend to hold their breath. They have so many things to think about that breathing is forgotten, no time allowed for it. The co-ordination is not easy. Even when they do lift or turn their heads and correctly go through the motions of breathing, often they are just gasping in, and in, and in (but *not* out). Fatigue soon brings them, red-faced, to a stop. I once heard a teacher I admire comment quietly to a youngster; 'If you don't breathe out you'll inflate like a balloon. Then someday you'll be found floating high up against the ceiling, crying piteously for food, and a kindly pool attendant will have to shoot you down.'

(If you tell that story to an imaginative child, be sure he knows it is only a joke!)

You must teach your pupil the habit of breathing *out*. Breathing *in* comes naturally, a survival reflex.

GOLDEN RULE No. 11
Breathe out regularly.

1. *Trickle breathing*
The swimmer blows a stream of bubbles out steadily through the mouth into the water until the point in the stroke cycle where an in-breath can be taken.

2. *Explosive breathing*
Practised swimmers, especially when they are sprinting, do not trickle breathe. They suck in a quick breath and then hold it until they are in a position to inhale again. Then they blow it all out forcibly through their mouth. There are advantages to this method; buoyancy is increased and it makes a firmer midriff for pulling muscles to work against. Perhaps the most powerful argument for it is that it is what accomplished swimmers (including those brought up on trickle breathing) instinctively adopt under pressure. In fact, versatile performers switch from trickle to explosive breathing and back again as the feeling takes them.

Teach trickle breathing to beginners. Once regular breathing is instilled, allow them to discover explosive breathing. (The only way you will know for certain what they do is by underwater observation).

Swimmers must breathe in through open mouths; nostrils are not big enough, and sniffed-up water droplets are uncomfortable. Well-mannered children and adults have to be shown that it is all right to gape wide open in this way, so always demonstrate a big open mouth and pantomime drawing in huge amounts of air. Breathing out is done through mouth and nose (mostly mouth).

Whole-part-whole

It is sometimes possible to demonstrate a skill and say to your pupil; "Try it yourself." Do not over-teach.

To improve the first rough-and-ready attempt, break the skill down into parts that can be explained, demonstrated, practised and corrected separately. Leg kicks, for example, can be done holding onto a float. This removes the need to think about arms and breathing.

Isolated practices are never quite the same. You can kick neatly up-and-down holding a float, whereas in crawl stroke the body rolls and the leg action follows suit. So always end up by putting the whole stroke together again ... whole-part-whole.

Goggles

Beginners do not need goggles. When a swimmer undertakes lengthy swims, face immersed, goggles become necessary to avoid sore eyes. Swimming bare-eyed in heated, treated pool water (or in the sea) will after a time result in miserable discomfort. The eyelids feel like sandpaper and the tears stream. You feel hot and your nose runs; and, whether you keep your eyes open or close them, there is no escaping it. This chemical reaction takes hours to go away. It does no harm but it is not worth the suffering. Buy a good pair of goggles.

It takes a while to master wearing them so that they remain watertight. Embedding the goggles into your eye hollows; adjusting the tension of the strap and the angle of its pull; it is a fiddly business. You have only to frown or twitch a cheek muscle for a crease in your skin to make a tunnel up which water squirts. When you finally manage to keep all water out, the goggles mist up. You must let a few drops in, and retain them, so that each time you turn your head you wash them clear.

Now you see why you should ban them from learners' short lessons. They are a nuisance and a distraction, wasting precious lesson time. Let them have a pair, later, as a reward for some success. Confine their use to free play and encourage them to go underwater and watch what more competent swimmers do with their hands and feet.

Do not wear contact lenses in water. You will never find one if you lose it. Anyone so visually handicapped that they must have corrected vision to swim may have swim-goggles made up to a prescription from a qualified optician.

Other gear
Costumes – Buy the brand names used by club swimmers. These have been designed to meet the needs of swimmers training miles and hours every day and they are light, hardwearing, and exactly right for swimming. They come in a tempting range of colours and patterns. Avoid the ones made as smart beachwear which are often quite impractical.

Footwear – Flip-flops are ideal for padding between changing rooms and poolside while keeping free from foot infections which might otherwise be a risk in damp and warm communal areas.

Anti-verrucca socks – These may be insisted on by some authorities if you are thought to have the virus.

Ear plugs – Do not let a pupil wear them without medical advice.

Fins (flippers) – They increase purchase on the water so that a novice, with very little guidance, can swim crawl strokes like a budding champion. They also shape the legs and feet to make correct movements. Take care your swimmer does not collide head-on with the poolside or another swimmer. Expert swimmers train in fins to maintain their ankle mobility and strengthen leg muscles. Let your learner try a pair but – forewarn him – it is an anticlimax when they are removed. Always swim some more without them to regain your feel for the water.

Hand paddles – These do for the hands what fins do for the feet, and may be used in small doses for the same reasons.

Hats – They are worn to keep hair out of eyes and mouth and for no other reason (unless you swim outdoors in cold water when they also retain warmth). Choose a lightweight, stretchy one.

Pull buoy – This is a float specially shaped to make it easy to hold between the thighs while practising pulling (arms only). An ordinary float will do but it does pop out and escape occasionally.

Pool lengths
Swimmers like to know the length of the pool in which they
swim to work out how many lengths make 100 yards (or
metres) or a mile.

Old pools are measured in Imperial yards. A common
length is 33⅓ yards, not as odd as it seems because 3 go to
make up 100 yards. Shorter pools are 25 yards long
(4 × 25 = 100), with regional 50 yard amenities (the so-called
"Olympic-sized" pool) for top-class galas. Then there are
unusual ones; my local pool is 30 yards and I have trained in a
16 yard one.

Nowadays pools are built to metric scale, commonly 25
metres, with 50 metre competition pools.

Between past and present, as architects realised the need to
align with the Continent, a curious generation of pool lengths
appeared which were nearly (but not quite) metric: for
example, 36⅔ yards (3 × 110 yards, the nearest thing to 100
metres) and 55 yards (2 × 55 = 110). A table of pool lengths
and distances follows.

LENGTH OF POOL		LENGTHS MAKING	
		100 yards or metres	1 mile
20 yards	18.3m	5	88
22	20.1	4.5	80
25	22.8	4	70.4
27	24.7	3.7	65.1
30	27.4	3.3	58.7
33⅓	30.5	3	52.8
36⅔	33.5	2.7	48
40	36.6	2.5	44
44	40.2	2.3	40
50	45.7	2	35.2
55	50.3	1.8	32
100	91.4	1	17.6
110	100.5	0.9	16

LENGTH OF POOL		LENGTHS MAKING	
		100 yards or metres	1 mile
25 metres	27.3yds	4	64.3
33⅓	36.4	3	48.3
50	54.7	2	32.2
100	109.4	1	16.1

NOTE
1 yard = 0.914 metre
1 metre = 1.094 yards

The basic principles of all swimming
Imagine you face a brick wall. It is a trifle more than head high and you must climb over. Think how you would do it. First you reach up with both arms extended and place your hands flat atop the bricks, a little more than shoulder-width apart. After 2 or 3 experimental knee bends you spring upwards, at the same time pulling strongly downwards to bring the top of the wall to chest level. You bend your elbows to keep close to the wall and, as soon as you can, you also lift them upwards above your hands. From this stronger "elbows high" position you turn the pull into a push which accelerates downwards until you can lock your elbows straight. You can hold your bodyweight in this position while you bring a leg up to scramble over the wall. Most of us were once young and vigorous enough to do that.

This is the way swimmers heave themselves out over the poolside. It is – remarkably – also the way their hands and arms work (laid horizontally) to swim. Teach your learner to climb out of the water this way, then discourage use of the steps, and each time they get out of the water they will be strengthening their pulling muscles. How the wrists bend, first flexed then extended, keeping the palms of the hands facing the way they travel is just what happens in crawl (one arm at a time) and dolphin-butterfly and breast stroke (arms simultaneously). It even occurs, less obviously, in back crawl. We will come across the relationship between climbing a wall and swimming strokes again and again.

GOLDEN RULE No. 12
Elbows high.

Catch – Just as the initial pull with the hands on the top of a
wall is needed to start the body moving upwards, so the
swimmer's hands do not begin to propel until they press
against solid water. As the swimmer is already moving
forward through the water, pulling hands must gather the
same speed backwards until they catch up with the water. The
sooner this "catch point" is reached, the longer and stronger
will be the pull. If the hand is lazy, half the stroke will be over
without its contributing anything to forward movement. The
pupil may go through the motions but the stroke will be
weak.

GOLDEN RULE No. 13
Catch the water quickly.

'*S*' *pulls* – From catch point, whatever the stroke, the pulling
hand draws a snaking line through the water. It is like a
flattened 'S', so we call it an 'S' pull. Only one hand actually
draws an 'S' shape; the other hand does the reverse (a mirror-
image). 'S' pulls are better than pulling straight through. All
accomplished swimmers use them.

GOLDEN RULE No. 14
'S' pulls are best.

Always demonstrate an 'S' pull when you show your learner
an arm stroke, and be pleased when you see him reproduce it.
Why 'S' pulls work is rather technical. Do not bother pupils
with it. Just let them do it.
"*Bernie...who?*" – To the casual observer, swimmers "row"
themselves along in accordance with the physical laws stated
by Isaac Newton. With their arms (and legs to an extent) as
oars, and their hips and shoulders the rowlocks, they lever
themselves through the water. Indeed, it will not mislead
learners if you say to them; "Press on the water and move past
your hand." Or; "Hold an armful of water and push it away
from you."

Swimming is actually much subtler than that. While you
handle the water, hauling yourself along horizontally
through it with your hands and arms, beating it off at the

back end with feeling feet, *the water is at work ON YOU!*
Because an 'S' pull limb track has movement sideways, the
hand in water acts like the wing of an aeroplane as it scythes
through air. The high pressure underneath (on the palm of
the hand) is supplemented by low pressure above (on the back
of the hand). Engineers know the effect as the Bernoulli
Principle. The plane is in fact held up as long as adequate
forward speed is maintained. Similarly, the swimmer's hand –
as it travels sideways, thumb or little finger first – is anchored
in the water. As you grip water with your hand, the water
grips your hand and provides a firm base over which to pull.
The Bernoulli effect is an invisible extra force which,
harnessed, turns mere strugglers into adept performers.

GOLDEN RULE No. 15
Dextrous swimmers go further, faster, with fewer strokes.

The strokes of polished swimmers generally appear leisurely
and effortless. It is an illusion. Swimming is a vigorous
activity which, while you must pace yourself to last the
distance, should take it out of you one way or another.

GOLDEN RULE No. 16
Sprinting is breathlessness without exhaustion:
Marathon swimming is exhaustion without breathlessness.

5
CRAWL

Crawl (there is no need to call it "front crawl") is also sometimes referred to as "freestyle". This is because – being the fastest known stroke – it is the only one swum in top class freestyle races, where almost anything is allowed but only crawl is used. An international male swimmer can sprint 100 metres in 50 seconds and females are only 5 seconds slower.

They can also cover a mile in under 20 minutes because it is the least energetic of strokes. Until you can do it, that is hard to believe. Beginners find it exhausting and stop, breathless, after half a width or so. Taught how to time turning the head to suck a quick breath in at the right moment in the stroke cycle, they discover the stroke is no more energetic than going for a brisk walk ... and the widths soon become lengths.

GOLDEN RULE No. 17
Swimming is breathing as you go along.

Crawl is the choice of Channel swimmers who must maintain 50 strokes a minute for at least 8 hours, and perhaps as long as 20, in water rarely above 60°F (16°C) as they cross 30 miles of busy commercial tideway. Crawl is smooth and steady. Like driving a car along the motorway in top gear, it is gentle on the mechanism and easy on the fuel.

Body position
Crawl is swum very flat and face down in the water. The surface of the water meets the forehead where the hair starts (but do not look at me ... I'm bald). There is a slight slope down the back from nape of neck to hips which must be submerged a few inches to enable the legs to work in water. Feet which thrash the air are no help.

Swimmers are not rigidly prone. Their shoulders roll or tilt

as much as 45° away from the horizontal when they turn their
heads to breathe. This permits a better elbow-high arm
recovery through the air. There is also a shoulder roll to the
non-breathing side, but much less (only 10° or so). The
rolling shoulders merely fit in with the needs of the head and
arms – no more, no less – and the body and hips go with them.
As a result, the legs are rarely kicking straight up and down.

Legs

The leg action is a rhythmic, alternate and continuous up-
and-down movement of both legs from the hips. There is
some flexibility at the knees. Ankles are extended (plantar-
flexed), feet stretched out with toes curled under to drive
water backwards off the top of each foot in turn on its
downbeat. An element of downward and (as the body rolls)
sideways pressure from the feet serves to hold the swimmer
flat and straight.

Flexing the hip pulls the leg into its downbeat. Water
resistance bends the knee a little, then the thigh muscles
contract to straighten the leg once more. In consequence a
whiplike wave pattern travels down the leg and out through
the pointed foot, a bit like kicking a ball or flicking off a loose
slipper. The buttock muscles then tighten to haul the leg back
up and the knee relaxes until the heel just breaks the surface
of the water.

Legs contribute a little propulsion on the downbeat, less on
the upbeat, and once the swimmer develops an effective arm
action will be mainly concerned with balance.

Arms

The arms take turns to pull through the water and recover
over it in a forward circling motion. The pulling arm takes
longer through the water than the recovering arm takes
through the air, so there is a noticeable "catch-up" (nothing
to do with "catch-point") whereby the entry of the forward
hand into the water occurs as the underwater hand is just
halfway through its phase. As this happens to each arm, they
never overtake one another... or it would be a very odd
stroke!

Each hand recovered forward through the air is slid neatly
into the water, palm down, fingers straight and closed
together, thumb in line with the fingers. The elbow is held

higher and there is a gentle slope down the forearm which
follows the fingertips into the water through the hole they
have made. The elbow-high shape of the entering arm
dictates the length of entry, preventing the swimmer over-
reaching. Each hand enters on its own side of the swimmer's
centre-line and within shoulder width.

Without a pause the hand is pulled back, palm slightly
cupped, until it catches up with the water ("catch") and comes
to grips with it. The wrist is flexed and the fingers begin to aim
downwards so that the palm of the hand is directed
backwards. The elbow bends and is kept higher than the hand
to steer it backwards as it pulls. Pulling downwards is a waste
of effort.

As the pulling hand and arm reach the halfway point
beneath the swimmer's shoulder he is working at his strongest
and the limb must not be allowed to falter or drift off course
at this stage. The pull becomes a powerful push, directed
backwards still, and the wrist extends to keep the palm of the
hand facing backwards as long as possible. This pull/push
phase ends with the elbow (still high) lifted from the water
first, bringing with it the forearm and finally releasing the
hand from its load of water.

The hand is carried forward and around, elbow as high as
the swimmer's flexibility will permit and aided by the roll of
the shoulders, one dipping, the other lifting, to be slipped
neatly into the water once again.

Each arm performs a mirror-image action, creating the
familiar overarm crawl stroke.

Seen from the front as the swimmer approaches, the hand
pulling from catch-point starts to travel outwards away from
the centreline. This occurs naturally and is the start of the 'S'
pull. Before it strays too far, however, the swimmer must
draw it back in towards the midline, bending the elbow to do
so. As the hand is being pulled strongly backwards at the
same time, bending the elbow has the effect of flattening out
the pull/push phase and making it longer. By the time the
hand has swung in on its curving limb track towards the
midline it must move outwards once more to brush past the
hip prior to leaving the water for recovery. If you lie on your
back on the bottom of the pool and look up as your swimmer
passes over the top of you, each of his hands should draw an
'S' pull (or its mirror-image).

Seen head-on, the elbow bends from being fairly straight at

catch to as much as a right angle at the changeover from pull to push, then straightens once more. The bent-arm 'S' pull should be instilled into swimmers. It is the best possible means of propulsion.

Each arm is propelling from the moment of catch until the hand is released from the water at hip level (by the costume hem). There should be no lull or pause in the arm cycle which is continuous. The pulling muscles obtain their rest while other muscles recover each arm in turn through the air, and vice-versa. Recovery should therefore become relaxed with repetition; it should also be fast, to minimise any sinking effect it might otherwise have on the swimmer due to all that unsupported weight in the air.

Breathing
Beginners may pick a favourite side to breathe. If later they become club swimmers, they will be drilled into breathing to either side as required. Anyway, the head is turned like a door-knob (teaching point; "Put your mouth where your ear was") and, as the mouth comes clear of the water, a quick breath is inhaled (fig. 5). There is no time to breathe out first.

Fig. 5   Crawl – breathing in

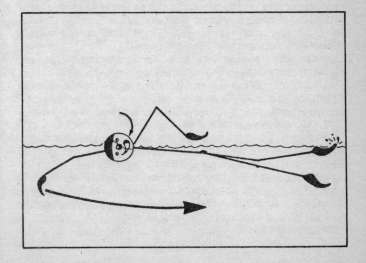

That must be done by trickle breathing or explosive breathing beneath the surface. The head is re-centred quickly and then is allowed to go somewhat past the midline along with a shoulder roll to permit a high elbow recovery of the arm on the non-breathing side.

Co-ordination

Fitting regular breathing into the arm cycle is what makes for mastery of crawl. The knack is to "see" (you do not actually have to open your eyes and look every time; it is sufficient to know that you could) the recovering hand on the non-breathing side into the water to arrive at catch point *before* smoothly rotating the head away to breathe on the opposite side. The pulling hand will support the swimmer, who – exhaling – now "blows away" (a good teaching point) the hand on the breathing side as it completes its push phase. Inhalation takes place as the arm starts to recover. The momentum of a good stroke builds a bow-wave in advance of the swimmer's head so that he can actually use the trough behind it for breathing in (fig. 6). This trough is below the normal surface level of the water so the head movement needed is less and the swimmer's body position is least disturbed. Learners will not be that good yet. The head must be re-centred, inhalation completed, in time to "see" the recovering arm on the breathing side in to catch point. It is a skilful bit of timing: see one hand in . . . turn the head . . . and back for the other hand's entry. Try it in front of a mirror before you demonstrate it to your pupil. It is like the game of patting the top of your head with one hand while describing a circular movement over your stomach with the other.

The classic crawl co-ordination is 6 leg beats to one complete arm cycle and beginners should acquire this. It means counting "1, 2, 3," with one arm pull and then again "1, 2, 3," with the other arm pull. Better still, say; "Kick, kick, kick; kick, kick, kick," which perhaps gives the idea of an even tempo and strength to each beat. It is a natural counterbalance to the arm action. As (say) the left arm starts to pull/push, the right leg goes down, up and down. The left leg is then uppermost and goes down, up, down, as the right arm pulls and pushes. Crawl is a rhythmic and continuous action with no real pause anywhere in the limb cycles.

Rest is gained from relaxation within the stroke. It is the

Fig. 6   Crawl (head on)

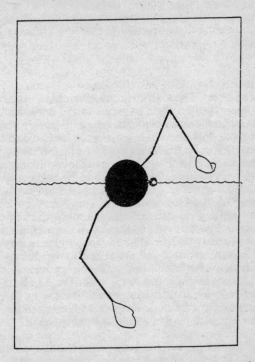

the same for all strokes. You cannot TRY to relax. In time it just comes.

GOLDEN RULE No. 18
Repetition brings relaxation.

An oddity in crawl which you – teacher – must correct is a tendency for the legs to travel sideways. Like a skidding car, the swimmer's back end (legs) will swing or drift off to one side. Checked, they come back to the centreline only to swing out to the other side. You cannot swim fast or easily like that. What causes this lateral leg swing is a low arm recovery. Fling one hand and arm around to the front in a low semi-circular movement and off will go the legs out to the opposite side.

Recover the other arm the same way and back will go the legs to the other side. The solution, already described, is a high elbow recovery on each side made possible by an adequate shoulder roll. As the remainder of the body follows the shoulder roll, the legs and feet can also beat somewhat sideways to counteract any sideways tendency.

Teaching

Crawl can be developed from dog-paddle. Make your pupil swim it faster, pulling right back under the body with each hand in turn, close to the centreline, as if "you're hauling yourself hand-over-hand along a rope stretched across the pool underwater." This racing dog-paddle is hard work because each recovering arm has to push forward underwater against the direction of travel. That puts the brakes on. Point this out and suggest how much better it would be to bring each arm back *over* the water.

Try racing dog-paddle again, this time with each elbow coming up out of the water at the end of the push phase and continuing to stick up above the surface as the arm is brought forward. Some of the resistance will have disappeared. Repeat, with the surface of the water cutting halfway on the forearm, then at the wrist with only the hands trailing through the water on recovery. Finally do it with fingertips just brushing the surface, elbows still high in the air. That way, they are swimming a rough-and-ready crawl.

(You can always point to a crawl swimmer and say; "Have a go at that." It might work. Never needlessly prolong the time it takes to learn anything by slavishly following a preset routine.)

Use whole-part-whole teaching. Have your learner hold a float (or two) and kick, legs only. Children with flexible ankles and big feet, plus a feel for the water, can go along quite fast. Aim for a very flat position, feet covered with water and heels just breaking the surface on the upbeat to make a series of small splashes. Some of us, our ankles stiffer and feet smaller, almost stand still when we kick on a float. No matter. The exercise strengthens the leg muscles and gives them endurance. In the full stroke the arms will pull us along.

Rehearse the arm action briefly standing (bent over from

the waist) or lying supported in the water, thinking about a high elbow throughout. Push and glide with a float, kicking, and release one hand to go through the arm pull and recovery back to hold the float once more. Work each arm in turn. Ignore breathing for the time being.

The swimmer now pushes-and-glides, picks up with the legs, then adds the full arm stroke (head down, breath-holding). Stress an early catch and a long 'S'-pull ending at the costume hem-line as shown in fig 7. Legs keep the swimmer flat and straight.

Stand, leaning forward in shallow water, and go through turning and re-centring the head between one hand entering the water and the other hand doing so. Try it with toes

Fig. 7   Crawl – "S" pull

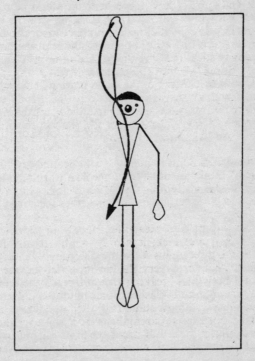

hooked onto the rail or overflow channel, and then swimming (arms only) with a float or pull-buoy between the thighs.

To fit it all together, push-and-glide adding the leg kick. Pick up with the arms and try one breath, re-centring the head to continue with a few strokes head down. Stop. Stand up. Do it again, sneaking more breaths until a regular pattern is established.

BIG FAULTS	CORRECTIONS
Legs Shallow, ineffective "flutter" kick; Thumping big splashes with feet coming out of the water; Bicycling legs.	Turn the pupil onto the back and practise the leg action supine, stressing drive off the top of the feet on the UP-beats. Scull with the hands for extra support and lift the head to see what is going on. Keep the knees underwater. Face down, do it with a float. Revert to full stroke, push-and-glide adding legs . . . and then arms for short spells, once the legs are going well.
Arms Entry – too far ahead or too close to face; too wide of centre-line, or crossing it.	Exaggerate the correction.
Pull/push – late catch, early release; wandering ("feathering") limb track with no power behind it.	Go back to dog-paddle, head up, with early catch essential for support. Turn it into racing dog-paddle, fewest strokes across width, stressing 'S'-pull.

BIG FAULTS	CORRECTIONS
Co-ordination Breathing to front with head raised.	Return to rail or channel and practise breathing (keeping ear wet on non-breathing side); Kick on a float, one arm crawl with breathing.

(Children with long hair habitually toss their heads to flick it out of the way. They must get a haircut or a hat.)

Irregular kick.	A perfectly good leg kick may go to pieces when the full stroke is first tried. It is too much to think about all at once. Return often to kicking practices (prone, supine, with a float, underwater).
Turning the head to breathe before the blind side hand reaches catch point.	Separate head and arm movements; practise them independently. Try "blind side hand entry... turn head" repeatedly; then do "re-centre head... other hand enters." Finally, put the two together again.

6

BACK CRAWL

Swimmers in trouble turn onto their backs. Back crawl com-
bines this reassuring survival position with speed through the
water. It is a graceful stroke, smooth and economical,
and trained back crawl swimmers can cover 100 metres in
around 1 minute. Every young swimmer should add it to his
repertoire.

It is not swum a great deal and is a Cinderella stroke,
neglected and underestimated. Indeed, I heard one eminent
older swimmer suggest – perhaps mischievously to start an
argument – that it was as pointless as running backwards. I
think that is nonsense.

When my most successful club swimmer Carol Pines was
16 years old in 1972, she broke the woman's all-comers record
across the Solent from Southsea in Hampshire to Ryde, Isle
of Wight, and back again non-stop to Southsea (total
distance 9 miles). Approaching halfway back she had a bad
spell and faltered, lapsing into breast stroke and then turning
over to swim back crawl. She did not feel good but she never
stopped travelling. Regaining composure, she turned onto
her front and did a short sprint dolphin-butterfly (at sea
amidst all those yachts and ships!). Then she settled down
into her powerful crawl and raced the last couple of miles to
cross the entrance to Portsmouth Harbour and land on
Southsea's shingle beach, smashing the 6-year-old record by
20 minutes, in a time of 3 hours, 52 minutes and 48 seconds ...
a record which remained intact for a further 8 years. Every
stroke is handy sometime.

GOLDEN RULE No. 19
A swimmer is a 4-stroke machine.

Body position
The swimmer lies supine, in a slightly saucer-shaped position

viewed from the side (fig. 8). The head is cushioned
comfortably in the water with the ears submerged. Eyes look
upwards. There is a gentle slope down from the neck to the
hips which must be sunk a few inches so that the leg action
can take place without the feet coming out of the water. It is
still a very flat stroke, with a slouching or round-shouldered
posture of the upper body.

Fig. 8   Back crawl

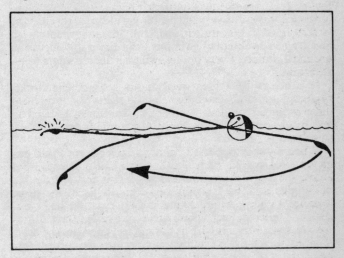

Seen coming head-on towards you, as in fig. 9, the
swimmer's head remains perfectly still, while the shoulders
may dip or roll somewhat to accommodate the arm action.
This roll may be – in a powerful racer – as much as 45° but the
swimmer remains strictly on the back throughout. The hips
do not follow the shoulder roll and the kick is firmly up-and-
down.

Legs
The leg action is similar to crawl but with emphasis on the
UP-beat. Kicking legs only to go along is easier supine. From
the lowest position the top of the pointed foot presses

Fig. 9   Back crawl (head on)

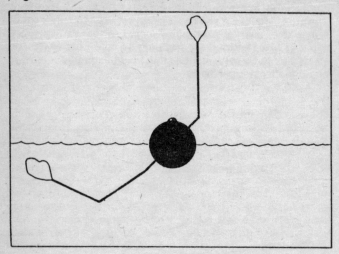

upwards to drive water backwards off the top of it. The action
starts off at the hip joint, knees straightening afterwards to
create a whiplike movement akin to kicking a ball in slow
motion. Toes just break the surface in a small splash. The leg
is pulled back down again by tensing the bottom muscles on
that side and relaxing the knee to let the lower leg drop
further down. The legs work alternately and continously.

As each leg hangs down momentarily at the end of the
downbeat it is a lot lower than the swimmer's streamlined
body position and has a retarding effect. The leg action must
not, therefore, be excessively deep. The powerful upbeat
provides most propulsion, while the rest of the thrashing of
the legs serves to keep the swimmer flat and straight. It is an
energetic action and it takes a while before the muscles gain
stamina for the job. Muscle groups rest alternately on up and
down beats.

Arms
The arms circle backwards alternately and continuously to
insert each hand in turn into the water, little finger first. Each
arm brushes past the ear on its own side prior to entry. The

flat hand, fingers straight and together, thumb in line with the fingers, quickly moves to catch the water. The wrist flexes to angle the palm of the hand so that it drives water towards the feet, and the swimmer pulls and pushes in a long stroke from catch to hips. As the pull develops so the elbow bends to shorten the arm, bringing the hand in closer to the body (just as a jet plane's engines are close to its fuselage) making it stronger. Halfway through, as the pull becomes a push, the elbow may bend as much as a right angle.

The pulling shoulder dips so that the arm can work without the hand breaking the surface of the water. The elbow is also held back so that the hand leads the way, pressing on the water while the elbow follows behind for added strength. (This is the supine equivalent of the crawl swimmer's high elbow.)

The elbow is extended to complete the push phase of the arm stroke, at the very end of which the hand turns palm downwards and gives a brief parting push to the water. It is lifted, relaxed, into the air and carried on a straight and vertical arm to brush past the ear and enters once again to move to catch. The shoulder of the recovering arm is lifted as the opposite one dips for the pull.

Seen from the side, each hand – as it starts to pull – moves downwards in the water. This dive is checked and, as the body of the swimmer moves past it, it moves up again until halfway through the pull/push it almost surfaces... but is pushed down once more. So, as in crawl, there is a bent arm pull AND an 'S'-shaped limb track acting together, the best possible combination.

The arms propel from catch to release in a long pulling and pushing stroke. Whereas crawl feels like a pulling stroke, back crawl feels more like a pushing stroke. The unsupported weight of the recovering arm in the air must be counteracted by the action of the pulling arm to minimise any sinking effect. The hand entering the water momentarily retards progress and must be slipped in with the least possible disturbance. Arms take their rest during the recovery phase which must be relaxed.

Breathing
Breathing can, surprisingly, be a problem in back crawl. Water collects in the eye hollows and also finds its way up

(down) the nostrils. Back crawl swimmers may look sedate and comfortable but they need to snort and spit and blink a lot.

Back crawl swimmers in the early stages also tend to hold their breath, going red in the face, and quickly getting puffed out. Ensure regular breathing by this simple rule; "Pick an arm, either arm. Breathe IN every time it *recovers*, and blow OUT as it *pulls*."

The recovering arm does not catch up and overlap the pulling arm in back crawl. The recovery speed must be controlled so that, as one hand enters and moves to catch, the other is completing its push phase and is lifting from the water. They are directly opposite one another.

Legs and arms fit together in a regular 6-beat co-ordination. The left arm pulls and the right leg goes down, up and down; the right arm pulls and the left leg goes down, up, down. Legs contribute more in back crawl than in crawl and can kick the swimmer through any weak sections of the pulling.

Teaching

Revise regaining the standing position from the supine back layout before tackling back crawl. Learners should also be able to swim back paddle, kicking and sculling with hands at hips, across the width. The strangeness of back strokes is largely not being able to see where you are headed. Make sure beginners have clear water ahead when they first try it. Later advise them to look at features (lines, girders, pipes, etc.) on the ceiling and steer a straight course by them.

Hold a float on the chest, or two (one under each arm) and practise kicking.

Replace the floats with sculling and develop this back paddle into legs only, with arms at sides.

Kick with arms extended beyond the head in a stretched and streamlined glide position on the back. Try a couple of arm cycles, then stop, stand up, and recover. Repeat, increasing the distance and the number of strokes without stopping.

Hold a float (or pull buoy) between the thighs and try one arm only. Learners often turn in a circle, so do ensure – if they start off across the width – that they use the arm which turns them towards SHALLOW water and not towards the deep end where they might get into difficulties.

Push-and-glide supine, arms extended, adding kicking. Pull one arm down to the side and then continue backward circling with both arms alternately.

BIG FAULTS	CORRECTIONS
Sitting in the water.	Show them their ungainly and impractical position with your "little teacher". Stress "tummy up" practices. Be sure they can regain the standing position easily. Go back to back paddle with sculling.
Legs Cycling; Legs apart, frog kicking; Ineffective "flutter" kick.	Return to legs only practices aided by floats or sculling with hands. Exaggerated corrections (e.g. straight legs "like a marching soldier") can be used to combat excessive knee bending.
Arms Hands entering wide; Hands leaving the water early.	Use an old-fashioned straight arm pull throughout. Stress "brushing the ears" on entry. Pull in a wide semi-circular sweep out and around to side. Reintroduce a bent arm pull at a later stage.

BIG FAULTS

CORRECTIONS

Co-ordination
A gross catch-up, with both arms ending up at the hips together.

On dry land or standing in shallow water, practise being a puppet with string over a pulley connecting the arms. As one arm pulls down, it draws the other one up. They are linked; one moves the other.

Try this notion while swimming; the pulling arm lifts the recovering arm because the two are joined by a piece of string.

7

BREAST STROKE

Breast stroke is an Olympic stroke. It is vital for life-saving and personal survival and is useful whenever you need to size up a situation or see where you are going. It is the slowest of strokes although a fit breast stroke specialist can complete 100 metres in around 65 seconds. It is a tiring stroke for long distances. Strange but true. Unlike crawl (cruising a motorway in top gear) breast stroke is like being caught in High Street traffic, up and down through the gears, using up fuel and increasing wear and tear on the mechanism.

Breast stroke today is an unnatural stroke. Top coaches and the world's best swimmers have between them evolved over many years a cleverly co-ordinated pattern of arm, leg and head movements which smooths out some of the jerkiness inherent in the stroke, while applying quick-revving power from both arms and legs. It is not something you can pick up left alone to teach yourself. The judges' rule book requires the stroke to be symmetrical, so each limb movement must be a precise mirror-image of its opposite partner's. That does not come easily to beginners, but they must still do it correctly because they might one day become club swimmers. An imperfect breast stroke would disqualify them from competing in that stroke, and, if they had swum it badly for some time, it might be impossible to cure.

The biggest bugbear in breast stroke is a "screw kick". This is actually a general label for every sort of incorrect leg action from a slight asymmetry to the most ugly slicing scissor kick. It is the bane of a swimming teacher's working life since most beginners have one and it must be eliminated as soon as possible. A few children – bless them – can do a symmetrical breast stroke leg kick naturally. Professional swimming teachers can often spot them in advance; they are the ones

with large feet that turn out when they walk or stand about.
They pick up breast stroke quicker than most... but then
spoil crawl and back crawl by kicking with feet dorsi-flexed
and everted (turned out)! Ah well, you cannot have
everything. Some of the time saved teaching them breast
stroke is spent pointing their toes for the other strokes.

Teachers lament; "Breast strokers are born, not made."
That is not quite true. You can teach them and must teach
them, but it may not be easy. I once coached, and my wife
taught, in a very successful club where all the young hopefuls
had to swim 3 technically sound strokes before they were
promoted from a teaching class (learning to swim properly)
to a training squad (to be conditioned for racing). Since few
had mastered dolphin-butterfly, they ALL had to acquire a
correct breast stroke to go with their crawl and back crawl.
This compelled the teachers to overcome the problems and all
those youngsters did learn the stroke. It can be done.

Body position
There is a glide phase after each breast stroke pull/kick which
can be extended for leisurely swimming or reduced until it
scarcely exists in the racing stroke. This is the familiar push-

Fig. 10   Breast stroke

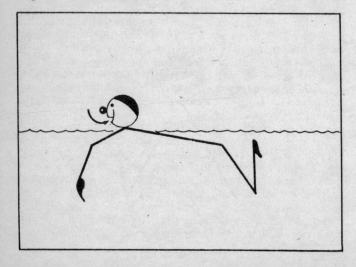

and-glide layout. The position then varies during the stroke
cycle. As the arms pull, the shoulders rise; as the legs are bent
and drawn up prior to the kick back together, the hips sink
and the angle of the body in the water steepens. (See fig. 10.)
With the powerful leg drive, arms extending forward, it
flattens again. Seen head-on, the shoulders remain perfectly
square to the surface of the water, body on the breast, as they
are raised and lowered by the arm action.

Legs

The leg action makes breast stroke. Forget any notion you
may have of a wide "frog kick" in which bringing the legs
smartly together somehow drives the swimmer forward.
Frogs do not swim like us and copying them does not work.
We use a narrow whip-kick which goes bend-and-drive,
bend-and-drive. For this the hips flex, the knees bend, and
the heels are drawn up as close as individual mobility will
allow to the buttocks. Feet are drawn up, big toes towards
knees (dorsi-flexed). The angle between body and thighs
must remain more than a right angle (obtuse).

The knees spread a trifle more than hip-width apart and the
feet are everted (turned outwards). Viewed from the rear, the

Fig. 11   Breast stroke (rear view)

swimmer momentarily creates a capital letter 'W' with his legs (Fig. 11.) The feet are then driven back, around and together, following – as seen from above – a narrow elliptical limb track, ending in the glide position. Strong propulsion comes from the feet catching the water early and driving back until they come together and glide. Just how propulsion works in this stroke was guesswork for ages. In fact each foot does a sort of sculling, like blades on a boat's propellor, and the two feet acting in concert really come to grips with the water; the swimmer, strongly extending hips and knees, is able to surge forward off his feet. Following on from the glide (if any), legs recover to the 'W' position, heels at buttocks, feet everted, ready to drive once more. Drawing the thighs forward against the direction of travel is a big retarding effect, so it is important to keep the body/thigh angle obtuse. It will vary between swimmers depending upon the flexibility of their joints. The driving muscle groups rest during the recovery phase, and vice-versa. The leg action rhythm is bend-and-drive... pause, bend-and-drive... pause.

Arms

From the extended glide position, the hands turn slightly outward and begin to pull down and out and around. The fingertips are pointed towards the pool bottom as soon as possible to direct the palm of each hand back against the water. Elbows are cocked up to help this "over a barrel" pull. While the hands are still ahead of the face – and the swimmer, looking straight ahead, can still see them at the edge of his vision – the elbows bend and the hands swing inwards to come together, still pressing backwards on the water. (Fig. 12.) The arm action rounds off with the elbows tucking into the sides of the body and the hands pushing carefully forward to the glide position. This neat and compact tucked position from which the hands reach forward with minimum resistance to forward progress is known as "swimming through a keyhole" and must be cultivated at the swimmer's front end so as to make the most of the powerful leg drive at the back.

Viewed from beneath looking up, the hands draw a heart-shaped limb track. (Fig. 13.) The arms propel from catch point by means of a pull which turns into a strong one-way scull inwards by each hand to the centreline where they finally

Fig. 12 Breast stroke (head on)

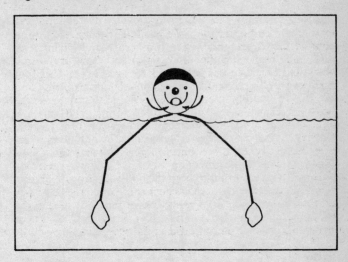

release their hold on the water. Pulling muscles rest during the recovery, and vice-versa.

Breathing

As the arm pull takes effect and the shoulders rise in the water, the head is lifted to look ahead on an extended neck. A quick breath is taken in through the mouth and this must be completed as the hands end their inward scull and release the water, when the head is lowered. Explosive or trickle breathing occurs during the remainder of the arm cycle.

Timing

The arms pull simultaneously, then the legs kick together, and the phases alternate – pull, kick... glide (if any); pull, kick... glide. In the early stages most of the driving power comes from the legs. Later the arms can do more, but, in contrast to the other three strokes (which are arm dominated) the balance is never more than 50/50.

As the arm pull starts, the knees relax and, during the later part of the arm pull and the first part of the recovery, the legs are drawn up into the 'W' position. The feet evert ready for

Fig. 13   Breast stroke (heart shaped pull)

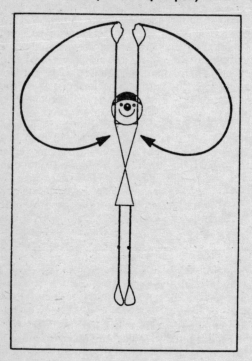

the whip-kick. The arms go narrowly forward (swimming "through a keyhole") before the legs drive strongly backwards. The swimmer aims to be like a paper dart, pointed at the front and broad at the back. The arms propel, counteracting the retardation of the leg recovery and they provide support to breathe. The legs are left to propel the dart-shaped swimmer surging forward.

Teaching
If your little learner is an apt and natural breast stroke swimmer – lucky old you. Having introduced him to legs, arms and breathing, fit them all together and polish the result.

Most beginners, however, will find mastery of the leg action a struggle and it is your job as teacher to make it as easy as possible. Direct their attention to their feet from the outset. Have them stand on flat feet, toes turned out ("like Charlie Chaplin"), then squat down. They should be aware of heels near bottoms. It is not an exact breast stroke position (because the thigh/torso angle is acute), so do not labour it, but squatting like this with the heels kept flat on the floor helps ankle mobility. Squat jumps reinforce the idea of driving with the legs while the feet are turned out.

Imitate Siamese dancers, balanced on one leg, lifting the other foot, dorsi-flexing and everting it. Do each in turn.

Sit your pupil on the pool edge, legs dangling over, leaning back with bodyweight supported on hands. Extend the legs straight and together, toes pointed. The knees relax and the lower legs drop to hang vertical. The feet are dorsi-flexed and everted. The knees part slightly. Now the feet, insteps leading the way, drive up, round and together on straight legs once more. This is breast stroke leg action (inverted). Repeat several times to achieve a rhythmic bend-and-drive.

The learner standing in the water faces the rail or channel and holds it for support. Draw one foot up close to the bottom, dorsi-flexed and evert, then extend that raised leg directly backwards straight without lowering it. Repeat several times to awaken the muscle groups involved in the movement. This is one time when there is some similarity between a drill and what will happen when the stroke is swum. Do it with the other leg.

(When you demonstrate or have swimmers practise any leg action balancing on one foot this way, always make a big joke about it. Explain that the reason you – or they – are only working one leg at a time is because, if you used the other one as well, you would fall down! Believe me, unless you point this out, many children will actually go off across the width faithfully kicking with one leg only.)

Get them holding the rail and assuming a horizontal swimming position. Stand behind them and place the palms of your hands one against each of their feet. Have them drive back simultaneously and let your hands yield as they push them away. Try the same idea with the swimmer supported on 2 floats, one under each arm to ensure they remain strictly on the breast. This time, as they kick back on your hands, do not yield and they will go forward. Both methods give the swimmer a good idea of using the sides of their feet to propel themselves.

A screw kick can be a strong means of propulsion; for example, a scissors kick is most effective in side strokes for personal survival and lifesaving. The point is that it is simply not allowed by strict racing laws for breast stroke and would disqualify the swimmer in any competition, whether it was world-class or the humblest scout, guide or school gala. So teach breast stroke first and only let your learner indulge in side stroke when the legal breast stroke kick has been permanently impressed.

Rehearse the arm action briefly on dry land, then standing in shallow water leaning forward with the water to pull against. Once the pupil has a half decent leg action, push-and-glide, kick a couple of times and then try pull/kick . . . glide, pull/kick . . . glide. Stop and stand up. Do not be concerned with breathing just yet. Repeat, increasing the number of stroke cycles and the distance covered.

When the swimmer needs to take a breath to carry on swimming, let him try breathing just once every 2 or 3 cycles. Do NOT use the arm pull to raise the head up to breathe; rather, raise the head to bring the mouth clear of the water at that point in the stroke (towards the *end* of the arm pull) when the body position happens to be at its highest. Lower the head and let the heels come up towards the surface before pulling again.

BIG FAULTS	CORRECTIONS
Legs	
Screw kick.	Go back to "legs only" practices and do all possible to make sure the swimmer stays perfectly on the breast (e.g. holding the rail with a wide grip; using 2 floats, or 1 float held sideways; human support at the hips).

BIG FAULTS	CORRECTIONS
	Supine, stressing "tummy up", swim leg action (inverted) keeping knees below the surface.
	Have heels recover to buttocks while touching one another, so that they both arrive at the same time.
	Do not drive until the 'W' position has been displayed.
	Revert to having the swimmer press the feet against your hands, so that you control the drive back.
	Check that the arms pull back together; if one precedes the other, then the shoulders can turn off the horizontal and create a side stroke which will ruin the leg action.

(This is one aspect of learning to swim when you must be relentless. Symmetry is the be-all-and-end-all of breast stroke.)

Arms

Pulling back asymmetrically;	"Draw a heart shape." Work on any screw kick.
Pulling back too far.	Go through the motions of the arm action on dry land or standing, bent over, in the water. The swimmer should look straight ahead but concentrate on never losing sight of the hands from peripheral vision.

BIG FAULTS   CORRECTIONS

Exaggerate the correction
and require a small circular
sculling action from each
hand way out in front of the
face. Enlarge it gradually.

Breathing
Rearing up too high.   "Legs only" kicking on a
                                float held out on straight
                                arms, chin "ploughing a
                                groove in the water".

                                Revise submerging practices.

                                Adopt an exaggeratedly
                                small arm action. Enlarge it
                                gradually, keeping the chin
                                near the water, stressing a
                                pull **BACK** *not down*.

Co-ordination
Pulling catches up with   "Legs only" kicking practices.
kicking, until arms are at
sides during glide.   Kick with arms extended
                                (thumbs locked together) in
                                glide position.

                                Full stroke, locking thumbs
                                together in the glide;
                                teaching point "Do not let
                                hands part until legs are
                                together."

                                Push-and-glide, kick, kick,
                                pull/kick... stop. Repeat
                                sequence, increasing strokes
                                and distance covered.

8
'FLY

Dolphin-butterfly ("fly") is the stroke in which both arms heave the swimmer through the water in a succession of powerful surges or leaps, then recover together forward over the surface (the "butterfly" part of the stroke). The legs balance the swimmer and drive him or her by a rhythmic fishtail up-and-down, both feet together (the "dolphin" part).

I know a man who swam 10 miles non-stop 'fly down the Spanish River Ebro and he completed many other swims of 5 miles or so in English lakes. I have seen it taught as a first stroke to beginners. So do not wrongly assume it is too strenuous for your pupils to try across the width. Let them have a go at it early on. When I was a professional coach I insisted that every one of the teenaged girls in my top squad swam 1 mile 'fly at some time (no matter what their best stroke was) just to say they had done it. We found that, when they returned to their other strokes after a spell of concentrating on 'fly for the mile effort, those strokes had improved too. Perhaps the power and co-ordination needed made the other strokes seem easy. Whatever the reason, it does a swimmer good to swim 'fly.

'Fly is also the first stroke to be swum in Individual Medley races (equal distance of 'fly, back crawl, breast stroke and crawl, swum non-stop in that order) which many of us consider to be the real test of an accomplished swimmer. Your water skills are incomplete without it.

Position
The body must be as strictly square to the water and as symmetrical in action as in breast stroke.

Seen from the side during the glide phase, with the heels close to the surface and the hands not yet at catch-point, the swimmer is very flat (Fig. 14). The head is almost submerged at the lowest point in the stroke cycle. This does not last. During the "flying" phase the head and shoulders come clear of the water altogether (Fig. 15). In addition, the heaving action of both arms supplemented by the double downward thumping of twinned feet raises and lowers the body in relation to the water surface. The swimmer also pivots about an axis through the sides of the lower chest as the hips rise and fall. All this lifting and dropping, rearing up and flattening out again, is not graceful when first attempted. Later, when the swimmer has forward momentum, it becomes a flatter undulating stroke of power and grace.

Fig. 14   'fly (gliding to catch)

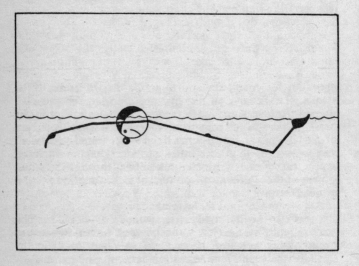

Arms
Despite sharing with breast stroke the disadvantages imposed by symmetry and spasmodic stop/go movements, 'fly has much more in common with the efficient limb tracks of crawl. So it is fast (around 55 seconds 100 metres by men, and 62 seconds for women). The hands and arms perform a double crawl stroke with slightly wider (shoulder-width)

Fig. 15 'fly (breathing)

entry. High, bent elbows and 'S'-pulls are also features of the stroke. As the 'S'-pull and its mirror-image are executed together, you can talk of "drawing an hour-glass" with the hands (although you may have to show youngsters a picture of an hour-glass or egg-timer before they understand what you mean). The pull accelerates into a very fast push phase. As the hands are at their strongest halfway through their limb tracks, underneath the shoulders, that is the time and place to pile on the power.

Recovery must be fast and relaxed to gain some rest before the next effort without retarding the body by sinking it. The arms completely clear the water on their way back to entry but recovery height (elbows high) will depend upon the flexibility of each swimmer's shoulders.

Legs
The legs fishtail up-and-down together, big toes touching at all times, a small spread allowed at heels, ankles and knees. The ankles are extended, toes curled under, driving water backwards off the tops of the feet. It is the crawl action, big toes glued together. Rest and recovery of the legs occurs after

each downbeat as they are brought back up to the surface and
pause for a fraction of a second before the next kick.

As skill and strength are gained 'fly becomes an arm-
dominated stroke. The leg action is concerned more with
holding the swimmer flat against the disturbing influence of
the arms and so should be no deeper than is necessary for that
purpose.

Breathing

The head is tilted to look forward and a quick inhalation
taken when the body is at its highest point. This is at the
completion of the push phase, as the hands release the water
and clear it on recovery. The head must be lowered again by
the time the arms – swinging forward – come level with the
shoulders (at right angles with the body) or they cannot
continue. Breathing in must be kept brief. Explosive
exhalations go well with 'fly.

Co-ordination

A badly-timed 'fly just does not work. It is ballistic; like dis-
charging a stone from a catapult, you cannot slow it down
much for demonstration purposes. Learning the stroke, and
swimming long distances with it, is done by stretching out the
glide phase and inserting a pause at that point... but you
must pull again before you slow down too much.

During the arm pull, from catch to release, the legs beat
down-up-down (thump, thump). This is the same action-and-
reaction counterbalancing action as in crawl, but doubly
done, rather than single and alternate.

Breathing-in comes from a parting push as the hands
disengage the water in combination with the second
downbeat of the feet.

Teaching

Push-and-glide prone with a float held in front on straight
arms, dolphin kick ("big toes touching"). Try it supine with
the float held on the chest, with emphasis on the UPbeat.
Push-and-glide underwater, prone, kicking with arms
extended ahead. Accentuate the up-and-down hip movement
to get the feel of undulating through the water. Have a go
lying on one side, then the other, even supine.

Swim breast stroke arms with dolphin leg kick ("beat down
with the feet as the arms pull"), breathing every other arm

pull.

Push-and-glide, kick, kick, pull/throw the arms... then stop and stand up. Repeat the sequence, increasing the number of stroke cycles and the distance covered (breath-holding; stop to breathe).

Push-and-glide with a float held in the hands with arms straight out in front; swim single arm 'fly, concentrating on 1 leg beat at catch-point and 1 leg beat during the push to release phase. Turn the head to breathe, as in crawl, on the pulling side. Repeat, pulling with the other arm. Now swim this one-armed 'fly with the following sequence:- 3 left, 3 right; 2 left, 2 right; 1 left, 1 right, 1 left, 1 right (turning the head to breathe to the pulling side).

Push-and-glide, dolphin kicking, pull/throw with both arms together (breath-holding, head down). Repeat, increasing the stroke cycles and the distance covered. When not breathing limits the distance, lift the head to the front and breathe in every other stroke.

BIG FAULTS	CORRECTIONS
Head up all the time with legs low and faulty arm action.	Return to swimming face down, breath-holding. ("Imagine you have eyes painted on the top of your head; it is those eyes that look forward as you swim along: your other eyes see only the bottom of the pool.")
Arms pulling DOWN, instead of back, from catch.	Practise heaving up out of the water onto the poolside. Stop with elbows locked straight and lower legs still in the water. Drop back down and repeat the process several times. Feel how the hands and arms work. Push-and-glide, pulling yourself along horizontally past imaginary walls built underwater. Do not breathe.

BIG FAULTS	CORRECTIONS
Only 1 leg beat (beginners tend to omit the second beat, or make it only weakly).	Revert to push-and-glide, with sequence kick, kick, pull/throw. Revise single arm 'fly, gearing the second downbeat with the breathing ("Blow the hand away and at the same time kick.")

Look around at the bathers in a public swim session. Most can swim after a fashion – some much better than others – but polished performers will be unusual. The majority are mediocre. Swimming makes demands upon all the fitness factors but especially technique. Only by working at the fine detail, grooving in precise limb tracks, rhythm and timing, can anyone progress beyond second-rate swimming to become skilled.

GOLDEN RULE No. 20
Swimmers are skilful.

9
EXTRA WATER SKILLS

Treading water
Staying vertical in one place, head above water to breathe, is a very necessary part of swimming. Swimmers should be able to do it for hours if needs be.

The best method is a half-hearted breast stroke in which the hands make wide-apart circular movements pressing down on the water to support you, while the feet are only half drawn up and then kick gently down again. Avoid bobbing up-and-down. Keep the chin near the surface. Experiment to discover the hand and foot movements needed to turn and face in any given direction or completely around.

Arm actions can be varied, backward and forward sweeping movements or quick little figure-of-eight sculling patterns.

Crawl leg kick works for a while (but is tiring); so does a slicing big scissors kick. Breast stroke whip kicks, done with one leg at a time alternately can lift you waist-high out of the water. It is known as "egg beater". All can be useful at times but the one first described is best for survival.

Drownproofing
Improvers able to swim several lengths of the pool can still get into difficulties and should not be left alone. An unexpected mouthful of water or an accidental collision with another swimmer could bring them to a standstill, vertical, out of reach of safety and unable to stand. Many teachers do not foresee the danger.

Once they can tread water, teach them how – by leaning forward just a little – they will make slow progress forward. Leaning sideways, they go sideways. Lean back to go backwards. Their safety is in their own hands (and feet) if they keep calm and use their limbs the right way.

Floaters & sinkers

Most people will be able to do a mushroom float. The portion of their back above the water, once bobbing and rocking about subsides, is approximately 1/50th of their body mass. Fat folk do it easily; so do mature women and teenage girls. Only body fat and lungs full of air make floating possible. Nothing else in the human body floats. Lacking fat, even a deep breath may not make up the lack of buoyancy. Sinkers who put on fat or increase their lung capacity may become floaters later. Meanwhile, they must compensate by using hands and feet a bit to stay afloat.

Vertical float (Fig. 16)
Floaters can arrange themselves so that the 1/50th of them

Fig. 16   Vertical float

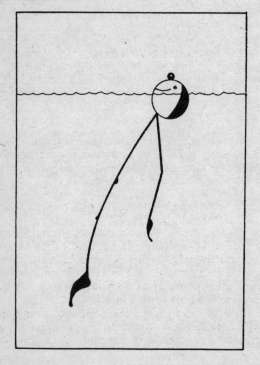

which is above the water is their faces. That way they can breathe.

Tread water, reducing the support until your ears are lowered into the water. Lay your head back and look upwards at the ceiling or sky with just your face above the water and ringed by it. Take a deep breath and hold it. Gently cease all leg and arm movements.

You will hang suspended. The legs will drift upwards until they are from 10° to as much as 30° from the vertical and remain there. Lift the head slightly and fold your arms on your chest if you wish to be more vertical.

To obtain another breath, blow out and suck in very quickly indeed (explosive breathing), so that you are buoyed up by full lungs before you can sink. If you breathe out slowly you will go down (try it . . . but be prepared to swim back up). This sequence of puff out/suck in – hold your breath; puff out/suck in – hold your breath, can be kept up for a long time. It is a handy survival skill.

Water is the same density wherever it happens to be in the pool, no matter the quantity or depth. It is NOT easier to float in the deep end (an ignorant myth you might hear around the poolside offered as advice). It IS easier to float in seawater than in fresh water, because seawater is much denser making the human body immersed in it more buoyant.

Surface ("duck") dives
Submerging can be vital for personal survival when you need to avoid floating hazards or find your way in or out of a confined space. Lifesavers have to descend and search sea, river or lake beds for people and objects.

Feet first – Tread water. Combine a pull or scull with both hands and a strong leg kick to lift you up as far out of the water as possible (bring the surface down around your lower chest or waist). Do nothing else but take a deep breath and your unsupported weight will sink you. Keep your legs neatly together and your arms at your sides to minimise resistance. If, at the highest point, you fling your arms up into the air, you will go down even further and faster.

Once underwater, arms at your sides, take a long upward scoop with both hands at once to drive you yet further down. With practice you can easily descend 10–12 feet (over 3 metres). To go deeper it would be easier to lower your head, lift your feet, and swim down head-first.

Head first – Swim breast stroke along the surface. Take a breath, pull your arms right around to your sides, pike (flex or bend) at the hips, and thrust your head and shoulders downwards deep into the water. Tighten your bottom muscles and lift both legs together into the air (bending the knees will at first make this big movement easier) while the arms scoop from behind forward. The unsupported weight of the legs will drive you down beneath the surface where you can then swim to greater depth or along as required.

Underwater swimming
Every swimmer should be capable of swimming a few yards or metres underwater. In clear water with good visibility (assuming you can open your eyes to see) the fastest and easiest stroke is breast stroke. You have to angle downwards to counteract the tendency to float upwards. Modify the stroke by pulling the arms right around to the sides of the body each time, to glide headfirst.

  In nil or poor visibility, with the likelihood of hazards, at least one arm must be extended forward in front of you to protect your head and face. In this case, crawl leg action is better but not so effective (unless fins are worn).

CAUTION: Never do deep breathing before an underwater swim. It can cancel out the warning signals telling you when to take another breath and you may go unconscious in the water without warning. Do not try staying underwater longer than anyone or compete to swim further underwater.

Sculling
Swimmers are adept at casual flipper-like hand movements to balance, stop, steer, turn, etc. Small pulling, pushing and scooping motions like this are generally labelled "sculling". Proper sculling is something more skilful. Synchro. swimmers get tremendous power and control from it, their hands like twin propellers on a motor boat.

  To work out how it is done, have your pupil stand, shoulders underwater, with arms extended straight out in front like an old-fashioned highboard diver, palms of the hands downwards. Instruct him to move the hands (in unison) out-and-in, out-and-in, horizontally about 6″(15cm) in each direction. The movements should flow smoothly. Now, as they move outwards, have him angle the hands (little fingers upwards). As they move inwards, reverse the angle (thumbs uppermost). "Imagine you are smoothing out and piling up sand; then smoothing it out and piling it up again." Change direction so as to describe figures-of-eight with the fingertips of each hand.

Any drive so far generated will have been downwards. Now have him extend the wrists by bending the hands backwards so that the palms face away from him. The drive should now begin to push him gently backwards off balance, so that he needs to take a small step or two. Bend the elbows somewhat to increase the power of the hands. Speed up the action, then slow it down, to discover the most effective drive speed of the hands.

Try it supine in the water, arms at sides, hands sculling at the hips to drive the performer along head first. Maybe start with the help of leg kicking but let the hands take over. Sculling can be either a deft, wristy little action or a strenuous muscular co-ordination of wrists, elbows and shoulders. All swimmers need to scull.

Lifesaving back stroke
This is swimming supine, breast stroke leg action (inverted), leaving the hands free for sculling, carrying essentials, or towing a person in distress.

Other leisure and survival strokes
Many old swimming strokes have been superseded by modern methods and are no longer taught in clubs because they do not feature in competition and might spoil the pure strokes of trained swimmers. Two of these strokes are, however, valuable survival and lifesaving skills and so are recommended.

1. *Old English back stroke*
This is a hybrid stroke, the leg action of lifesaving back stroke combined with back crawl arms (recovering through the air and pulling simultaneously). Each has been described already. Only the co-ordination is new.

From the extended glide position, supine, arms beyond the head, the hands are pulled around to the sides using bent-arm 'S'-pulls. A short glide ensues. The legs bend and drive and – as the legs drive, the arms are both recovered vertically through the air back to an extended glide position. A long glide follows. Note the critical timing of leg drive with arm recoveries to counteract the considerable unsupported weight of both arms in the air together.

With powerful forward impulsions from arms and legs alternately, and the insertion of two glide phases at appropriate points in the stroke cycle, this is a fast yet restful stroke. Breathe in as the arms recover.

CAUTION: Swimmers must take care not to bump their heads on the poolside or end as they swim into it. This is a real hazard with Old English Back Stroke as both arms pull strongly together and the head leads the way for much of the stroke cycle.

2. *Side stroke*
Do not introduce this stroke to young swimmers before they have been imprinted with correct breast stroke, for side stroke is a corrupting influence. Nevertheless, it is a valuable working stroke.

Approach it by swimming breast stroke and gradually turning onto one side (whichever you choose). With the head resting one cheek and ear in the water, the mouth is clear to breathe at all times and the eyes have a view of passing scenery. The leading arm plays a supporting role with a short pull and a flat-palm glide forward. The rearward arm executes a long pull/push, with high elbow, beside the body. Although they still come together and move apart simultaneously, as in breast stroke, the timing is totally altered as now each one pulls while its opposite partner recovers. This is an efficient arrangement.

The legs slice in a repeated scissors action. They are spread sideways, but, since the swimmer's hips are twisted vertical, the legs in fact extend forward and back in relation to the swimmer's body. The upper leg is straight but the lower leg bends at the knee, heel drawn up as far as mobility allows towards the seat. The two legs drive by vigorously coming together. Minor drive is gained from the back surfaces of the uppermost limb, with the major force off the top of the lower foot as the leg is straightened.

The various movements fit together so that as the forward arm pulls, so the legs recover (open and bend); as the rearward arm pulls, the other extends forward and the legs drive. A short glide is then possible before the next stroke.

This is another restful yet speedy stroke. Turn and raise the head to look forward every 2 or 3 strokes.

To go still faster for no more effort, try recovering the rear arm OVER the surface of the water: this is "overarm sidestroke".

Breathe regularly. Inhale as the head is supported by the leading arm pull.

Games
Children and even adults can often be lured by play into activities which might otherwise be unnerving or over-whelming. It takes their minds off things. Games may be very simple indeed yet still fascinate visit after visit.

. . . for infants and toddlers
  peek-a-boo;
  pressing a ball or other buoyant plaything down into the water, then releasing it to pop up again;
  plooshing a hand down into the water to watch the air thus entrapped bubble to the surface (do it close to the body and feel them);
  lifting children up high and plonking them back in the water;
  nursery rhymes, with actions suited to the words;
  towing, pushing or whirling beginners around in the water.

. . . for youngsters
  blowing table tennis balls along the surface (particularly in competition with others);
  walking or hopping races;
  ball games (if permitted by the pool staff);
  "tag", "touch" or "he" in the water (NOT on the poolside);
  follow-the-leader ("do as I do");
  Simon says (by calling out numbers or colours which are

linked to the required activities, you make this game into a memory-and-recall test too);

submerging to pick up objects from the bottom (treasure hunting), to look at underwater sights or to identify things.

... for confident improvers

swim-an-animal (grunting, snorting, barking, squealing, etc.);

leap frog, porpoising, diving through partner's legs astride;

jump-and-sink, moving along by pushing off bottom at an angle;

chains (sea serpent or crocodile), following the leader;

floating, various ways;

pushing-and-gliding, various ways;

treading water and floating (wounded survivor), pretending one leg is immobile, both legs are out of action, one arm is gone, one arm and one leg lost, etc;

two swimmers in a back layout (feet locked together), each trying to roll the other over by sculling;

underwater swimming but NO endurance tests;

handstands in shallow water;

somersaults and cartwheels;

sculling, with one leg in the air (then both legs);

sculling head first, feet first, prone and supine;

swim breast stroke, modified to travel *feet* first;

funny – but NOT reckless – jumps and dives (only those allowed by the pool staff);

act out a ship-wreck scenario:-

   (i) jump safely into deep water,

  (ii) surface and sprint a short distance to escape the suction as it sinks,

 (iii) tread water, treat injuries, take stock,

 (iv) start off on a long slow swim to safety (submerging head first and feet first at intervals to avoid such hazards as floating debris, oily water, etc.),

  (v) climb out at the end;

make a vortex (whirlpool) by sculling:-

stand in shallow water and scull strongly with one hand, palm downwards, the back of the hand only 4–6"

(100–150cm) below the surface. As the surface of the
water is stirred into circular motion, scull even harder
and the surface will be drawn down into a miniature
whirlpool. The silvery twist of water and air which
extends down to the back of your hand (like a sub-
mersible tornado) can be stretched by lowering the hand
a little more, widening the vortex. How large can you
make it? Try it with your other hand. Perhaps you can
make two whirlpools at once. It is certainly good sculling
practice;

swim widths, each one a different method of propulsion:-
  'fly,
  back crawl,
  breast stroke,
  crawl,
  side stroke,
  overarm sidestroke,
  old English back stroke,
  lifesaving back stroke,
  dog paddle,
  breast arm stroke + crawl leg action,
  'fly arms + crawl legs,
  back crawl legs + old English arms,
  breast stroke legs + crawl arms,
  breast stroke arms + 'fly legs,
  sculling, head and feet first (with and without kicking),
  'fly legs supine,
  'fly legs supine with old English arms,
  'fly legs supine with back crawl arms,
  etc., etc., etc. (invent others yourself).

For a joke, suggest your swimmer tries crawl arm action with
back crawl kicking... that IS impossible!

10
Diving

Diving can be dangerous. Health & Safety experts are so worried about the risks of diving into shallow water (a broken neck can leave you paralysed for life) that they recommend at least 8 feet (2.5m) of water for even the simplest dives from the poolside. As many modern pools are not that deep they have no diving boards and pool managers either ban diving from the side altogether or permit it only under the strict supervision of qualified teachers and coaches.

If the circumstances are right, and you have the opportunity, you may decide to teach your swimmer two basic dives. First they should learn the Plain Header, with a vertical (or near vertical) entry which pierces the water to take the diver quickly and safely down to the bottom without swimming. It is used from a height and for lifesaving. Then they can modify this into a racing plunge with a shallow entry to launch themselves into a swimming position on the surface from a low take-off point.

DIVING GOLDEN RULE No. 1
Eight feet (two and a half metres) is barely enough.

Most swimmers will never go beyond this diving ability. Springboard and highboard acrobatic divers are a different breed. The two arts are dissimilar. It is only their common need for a lot of water which brings them together in the same pool. The swimmer performs in the water, using it more or less skilfully: the diver is a gymnast performing feats of ability and grace in the air. For him or her, water is just a landing net. They aim to keep out of it for as long as possible. The two activities do not go together easily, so don't swim near diving boards nor dive when swimmers are below in the water.

Children showing an aptitude for gym at school may make good divers.

DIVING GOLDEN RULE No. 2
Swimming and diving do not mix.

Safety considerations compel us to do much basic diving tuition in deeper water, which will be beyond the pupil's standing depth. It follows that they must have the swimming ability to regain the surface, turn around and get their bearings, and return to the poolside. They must be able to swim a width and should perhaps be able to swim a length.

DIVING GOLDEN RULE No. 3
Divers must be swimmers.

The 4 stages of a dive

1.	STANCE	This is the ready position before any movement takes place.
2.	TAKE—OFF	The diver bends and straightens his legs to spring upwards, starting rotation by means of the hips, knees and ankles, with associated arm movements.
3.	FLIGHT	Movements are confined to controlling rotation and looking neat.
4.	ENTRY	Piercing the water with fingertips and following through until the toes finally submerge.

The SECRET of teaching diving

Teach stages 1, 2, 3 and 4 *in reverse order!* Take my advice. Accustom your trainee diver first to being upside-down under water. Next do some plunging down through the surface to end upside-down as before. Then progress to doing the previous activities from a sitting position on the poolside. Finally, stand them up to learn the take-off and they have only to launch themselves into a familiar situation. This turns learning – 'literally – on its head by steering learners from the unknown into the known, the opposite of how most teaching is done. This way we eliminate the biggest snag in learning to dive, loss of nerve, which results in learners (at the last second) jumping or falling flat to "belly flop".

In the water
Much essential early confidence training for learning to swim
will also equip your pupil for diving. Revise appropriate
practices, including:-

   submerging face and blowing bubbles

   opening eyes underwater

   jumping in

   then

   upward springing (arms in a 'Y' shape overhead) to
   submerge and sit on the pool bottom

   as above, turning to kneel briefly on the pool bottom with
   both hands on the tiles, stand up and (if the water is deep
   enough) push off to the surface

   mushroom floats.

NOTE – No child or adult will dive unless he can stand having
water on his face.

The swimmer's usual push-and-glide position is now used to
rehearse a diver's flight position.

   Push-and-glide along the surface, stretched and streamlined.

   Push-and-glide angled downwards to place both hands on
   the bottom of the pool, tuck up and stand up.

   As above in deeper water, tuck up and push off to the
   surface.

   Push-and-glide downwards, turning the hands slightly
   upwards (like horizontal steering vanes) to return to the
   surface.

   As above, aiming to go through partner's legs astride.

   Push-and-glide along the surface, pull the hands around
   to the sides in big semi-circular sweeps for added speed,
   then pike at the hips, scooping forward with the hands, to
   roll bottom over head in a forward piked somersault.

   As above, but tucked.

Through all this waterwork the budding diver is being
familiarised with being upside-down and arriving on the
bottom in the flight position. It can be taken further.

Push-and-glide into a handstand with the legs tucked.

As above, legs straight and together.

Standing in water chest-high, jumping over into a handstand (tucked, at first, then straight).

Less strength and determination are needed to perform a handstand in water than on land and so most of us can manage it.

Free "Porpoising", diving repeatedly over and into the water, standing up and pushing off from the pool bottom in a different direction each time.

Diving over partner's back (a sort of leap-frog but head-first entries with no body contact).

Seated on the rung of a vertical pool ladder nearest the surface of the water, feet firmly planted on a lower rung, to make a big porpoise dive down through the surface to place both hands on the bottom of the pool, tuck up and stand up.

For safety's sake be sure the water is deep enough to absorb the momentum of the diver's entry before he touches the bottom. Before he starts, check his hands are together and will stay together (entwine the thumbs). Arms must be straight, with the head down and squeezed between the arms for protection.

How a feet-first jump turns into a head-first dive

It is impossible to turn head-down, feet-up, while in the air. That is an illusion. What divers actually do is start the rotation which will end in an upside-down (head-first) entry as they push off from the poolside or board with their legs and feet.

DIVING GOLDEN RULE No. 4
Rotation comes from the take-off.

As they bend and straighten their legs, and then extend their ankles for a parting thrust with their toes, they angle their bodies forward and pike slightly at the hips. The effect of this is to send the divers' backsides up and over their heads and they rotate or somersault. They continue to rotate until they drop into the water and – timed right – achieve a nice neat head-first entry.

If we could remove the water (magic it away unexpectedly) the diver would continue to rotate, somersaulting down and down, until we put it back again. This is what you see when a diver misjudges the take-off and flight to "go over" and land painfully on the back. He was rotating too fast and the water did not intervene soon enough.

DIVING GOLDEN RULE No. 5
All dives are somersaults: a plain header is just half a somersault.

Be clear about it. Rotation is created at take-off. If it is wrong, the diver goes over or belly-flops. Divers do NOT merely jump up, turn over, and dive down.

From the poolside

(a) *Sitting dive* (Fig. 17): Move along the poolside to about 6 feet of water (at least 1.9m). The diver sits on the edge, heels securely lodged in the overflow channel or on the handrail. Arms are extended in the push-and-glide position, head down between the arms, back bent forward to point the arms at the entry spot on the surface of the water. The diver rolls forward to plunge down through the surface, aiming to place the hands on the bottom of the pool as usual. As balance is lost, straighten the legs and push the bottom upwards. Angle steeply downwards, piercing the water with the hands, all of the body and legs following neatly through the same hole to disappear toes last. On the bottom, tuck up and push back up to the surface. (The diver must be prepared for the fact that the poolside will be behind him and so must turn around to regain it.)

(b) *Crouch dive*: Move further along the poolside to a minimum depth of 8 feet (2.5m) of water. The diver stands on the edge, toes actually beyond the edge and curled downwards to grip it. This is a precaution against the feet slipping on take-off, which could result in a bad fall. Adopting the 'sitting dive' posture, there is a little more distance to travel to the water... but the momentum (body weight x speed) on impact will now be greater, so entry must be at a steep angle and tightly streamlined. Once again, stress

Fig. 17 Sitting dive

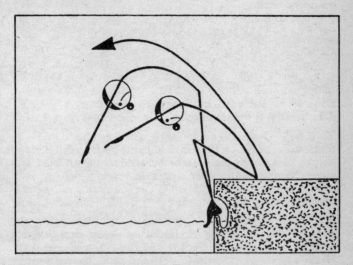

pushing up through the hips at take-off to go head down into
the water. Take the dive right down to the bottom, tuck up
and push to the surface.

DIVING GOLDEN RULE No. 6
Hips must go up for the head to go down.

Let your diver practise the crouch dive until he is happy with
it. Do NOT open it out, standing up more and more, moving
towards a proper standing dive. That is not the way to
progress. Retain the crouched posture and emphasize, rather,
a confident upward spring (through the hips) to give a slightly
longer flight time. Begin to stress neatness. The head stays
tucked between straight arms; the hands (thumbs locked
together) are flat with fingers closed. The legs are stretched
straight and together at knees and ankles with toes pointed.
Continue the dive right down to the pool bottom every time
and do not let the hands come apart until they have touched
the tiles.

(c)   *The 'Y' dive*: This is the last stage in the progression from
water confidence exercises carried out in shallow water to the

Plain Header, another easy step using all that has been
mastered already.

Stance – The diver stands on the edge of the pool, facing the
water, feet and legs together with toes gripping over the edge.
He stands erect (just to start with) while the arms are raised
above the head in a 'Y' shape with the palms of the hands
facing forward (fingers straight and closed neatly together,
thumbs in line with the fingers). The diver then pikes at the
hips so that the body leans forward at an angle of 10–15°.
This posture is held motionless.

Take-off – The bodyweight is moved forward fractionally. A
quick knees bend is followed by a strong push up through the
hips to start the forward rotation needed to make a head first
entry. The upthrust also produces the height which gives the
diver time to rotate head down. There is no other movement.
The diver is propelled into the air, hips still piked at the same
angle, arms holding their 'Y' shape, head still.

Flight – No movement should be necessary after take-off
except for slight adjustments to ensure a safe and neat entry
by controlling the speed of rotation. The longer a diver can
stretch out in the air, the slower he will rotate. So the 'Y' dive
offers a measure of control for the diver who is rotating too
fast (and may go over on entry). He can extend his hips and
bring his arms together. Shortening the diver speeds up
rotation. To avoid landing flat a diver can pike acutely at the
hips (or tuck up completely) and so contrive to get round
enough to enter comfortably. These controlling modifica-
tions are undesirable; the aim is to get the take-off right at the
start of each dive.

DIVING GOLDEN RULE No. 7
Shorten to speed rotation: lengthen to slow it down.

Entry – If the take-off was well judged, the diver has only to
bring the hands together (locking the thumbs to make sure
they do not part on impact with the water) and grip the head
between the arms, straightening out the piked hips and
stretching the legs, toes neatly pointed, as they go through the
surface at an angle of 80–90°.

The Plain Header (Fig. 18)
If a diver fully extended on entry measures 6' (nearly 2m)

from toes to fingertips, then his hands will touch the pool
bottom when his toes are barely submerged beneath the
surface. He needs at least 8' (2.5m) depth for this dive.

Stance – As for the 'Y' dive except that the diver now stands
erect. The natural curves of the spine are preserved in (viewed
from the side) a balanced posture. Correct the childish
tendency to stick out tummy and behind like a bantam bird.
Tuck the tail in and draw in the tummy too. ("Pretend you are
wearing grandmother's old-fashioned corsets.") The head is
held erect, eyes looking their own height or somewhat higher.

Fig. 18   Plain header

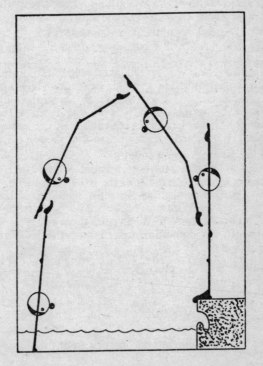

Take-off – The diver shifts his or her bodyweight slightly forward onto the balls of the feet, a hardly noticeable movement (look hard and at just the right moment you will spot the big toes point upwards for a second by a funny muscular action-and-reaction). Then the legs bend and straighten as before, the diver piking for necessary rotation. In the 'Y' dive it was already there. In the Plain Header, divers must insert the hip movement themselves and so the habit must have been impressed during previous practices.

Flight – No further movement, other than slight (mostly instinctive) controlling adjustments, until entry.

Entry – As for the 'Y' dive.

The Racing Plunge

Learn this dive in 6' (1.9m), although practised performers can execute it in 3' (0.9m) or even less.

Stance – On the edge of the pool, facing forward, feet planted parallel and a few inches (the diver's own hip-width) apart. (Fig. 19.1) Toes must be well over the edge and curled to grip it as, in this dive, the diver will overbalance and push BACK against the poolside. The knees are bent and so is the back in a comfortable crouch. The arms reach forward and a little outward. The head is down, eyes looking down but forward to spot the point of entry on the surface of the water. It is a balanced position from which instant action can flow, triggered by the starting signal.

Take-off – The diver starts to overbalance forward (pulling up the big toes momentarily as the front of ankles and shins tense). At the same time he pulls back with the arms, accelerating them into a backward circling (roughly resembling breast stroke) which brings them swinging forward fast. As the arms come forward past the body the legs straighten and push *back* against the poolside. (Fig. 19.2) The ankles extend and the toes give a parting push. The diver is propelled out over the surface of the water in a low trajectory. As he flies off, his arms are checked abruptly (Fig. 19.3) and the momentum they have developed is transferred to the diver's whole body in flight (the arms are not extended fully until later).

Flight – No movement takes place except the slow rotation

Fig. 19 Racing plunge

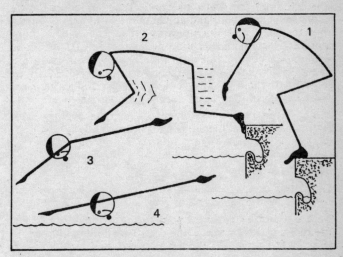

which lifts the diver's legs and lowers his head. The buttock muscles should be tensed to prevent the legs dropping. Little or no other control should be required.

Entry – The arms extend in line with the body just prior to entry, so as to cover the ears and protect the head, and must not be left in the prematurely stopped flight position. (Fig. 19.4) The angle of entry is shallow (20–30°) but distinct. Any flatter entry would "put the brakes on" abruptly; steeper would lead to needless depth and a prolonged return to the surface. The diver should flatten out beneath the surface to glide tightly stretched between 18″ and 2′ (0.5–0.8m) down.

At first, the diver is travelling faster underwater than he could swim. So instruct him not to swim . . . hold that glide. When the speed dies away to the intended surface swimming speed, he should kick the legs, take one arm stroke and surface to begin swimming.

CAUTION
Never dive into unclear and unknown water.
Always descend to a lower level if you can. Do not dive from a

height needlessly. If – in an emergency – you must enter from a height, jump feet first with legs slackened to reduce the risk of injury should you hit something.

11
SAFE . . . NOT SORRY

"One day I met with a serious accident whilst cycling, and fractured my leg. When I recovered, my leg was very stiff. My doctor said to me; 'Try swimming, old chap; it may benefit the limb.'" Thus Montague A. Holbein, a professional cyclist, took to swimming. In 1902 he almost became Capt. Webb's successor as the only man to match his feat and swim the English Channel when he was taken from the sea only 2 miles from land – having swum for 22½ hours – but defeated by an adverse tide.

Many since Mr. Holbein have started swimming on doctor's orders and, like him, found that water fitness overcomes or at least compensates for all sorts of ailments. Mind you, there are also a few hazards to health and safety around and in water, if you do not take sufficient care.

I am not medically qualified to advise you about illness and injury. You should seek the opinion of your own doctor if you are in doubt about any such matter. I can, however, discuss in general terms common problems which my swimmers and I have experienced over many years.

Accidents
Common sources of accidental injury in pools are reckless diving, jumping and running about. The manager's rules, strictly enforced by the pool lifeguards, are made to protect us from harm. No running is permitted on poolsides; no games of "tag"; no pushing one another into the water; no pick-a-back fights or acrobatics (not even in the water); no holding someone underwater. Special codes of conduct apply to the use of flumes (water chutes), etc. Much of what is forbidden may seem to you and me just good robust fun, but health and safety legislation grows daily more rigorous and

pool managers ignore it at their peril. If someone died or was crippled in their establishment their career would be blighted and so the poor man or woman has to be ultra-cautious. Do co-operate with them. Teach your pupil to play within the rules.

Children soon discover that inflated armbands will also fit on their ankles. Stop them! They might cope with being forcibly upended ... but some unaccompanied beginner (not even with you) could copy them and come to grief. Anyway, it unnerves the pool staff and you want to keep on their right side.

Every year, somewhere in the world, a child drowns in grisly circumstances caught up and pinned onto an outlet grating or drain cover in deep water by suction. It is a freak accident. Normally it is safe to approach them. Still keep clear at all times.

Acquired Immune Deficiency Syndrome (A.I.D.S.)

There is no evidence whatever that A.I.D.S. can be transmitted through casual contacts in swimming pools. The virus is fragile and outside the human body in chlorinated or otherwise disinfected pool water it would die.

There is a risk anywhere of infection through blood-to-blood contact, so even minor cuts and other open wounds should be adequately covered. Persons engaged in first aid need to take general hygiene precautions. Pool managers are fully aware of the threat posed by this infectious hazard and take all possible precautions on our behalf.

Allergies, asthma (and other respiratory disorders)

Australian Dawn Fraser was possibly the world's greatest female swimmer despite suffering asthma attacks early on in her career. She was also anaemic, had suspect lung shadows from teenage smoking, and was laid low by 'flu, bronchitis and pneumonia more than once. She was allergic to many things (even the paint used around the pool) and was out of the water almost every season with muscle problems or tendonitis. She had hepatitis once and another time chipped a vertebra in a car accident. Yet Dawn dominated the swim scene for six years and represented her country at three Olympic Games. Weaknesses and handicaps of this kind need not keep you from swimming.

Athlete's foot
Treat it early, this itchy cracking of the skin between the toes
(which may or may not be a fungal infection) and you can
check it in days. Left to gain a hold, it might take months to
clear up. Your doctor will prescribe treatment. Avoid
walking barefoot in pool buildings (wear flip-flops).

Bullying
Public swim sessions are often dominated by unaccompanied
youngsters and this makes pools like school playgrounds.
The children interact, the pecking order of school and street
persisting in the water. This may lead to a bit of bullying now
and then. The pool staff know they are temporarily in place of
parents and do what they can to ensure good behaviour.
Nevertheless, a child could (for example) "lose" a pair of
swim-goggles if they were borrowed by another, then passed
from hand to hand, and finally just not given back. Be as sure
as you can be that your child can cope before you let him visit
a pool alone.

Choking
Do not let your swimmer eat or chew in the water. Do not
swim until at least an hour has elapsed after a meal (even
swimming after a cup of tea or other drink can be
uncomfortable). The big danger is that the swimmer might
regurgitate a chunk of food, or be sick, and choke on it.

If anything blocks a person's windpipe, so they cannot
breathe, they will lose consciousness and soon die. Waste no
time. Forget about thumping them between the shoulder
blades or fishing down their throat to remove the obstruction
with your fingers.

Instead, get behind your patient and hold tight around
their waist with both your arms. Make the free hand into a
fist, thumb towards the patient's belly. Locate that fist just
above their navel – but below their ribs – in the soft area there.
Suddenly give a hug or squeeze (this is Dr. Henry Heimlich's
"Hug of Life"), pushing your clenched fist hard inwards and
upwards on their soft upper abdomen. The foreign object
blocking breathing will shoot or pop out. If the first go fails,
try again, but the Hug of Life mostly works first time.

Cold
When you have swum only in warm and cosy indoor pools,
you are totally unfit to survive in cold open water. It can kill
you quickly (and with no warning) by rendering you
unconscious so that you drown. Even fit club swimmers
become distressed if they take their skills outdoors into icy
rough water without preparation first. The British sea can be
a killer in Summer (averaging 56°F/13.3°C) which is over
40°F below body temperature. You must acclimatise to it
gradually and then only those of us with a good layer of fat
beneath our skin can hope to be comfortable. Skinny folk will
not enjoy it. Always end an outdoor swim before you start to
shiver and do NOT then go back in again.

(Badges and certificates issued by many swimming bodies
now carry a printed warning to parents and others if the test
was taken indoors in warm water, that the holder is not
necessarily fit to survive cold immersion outdoors.)

Colds and catarrh
Give swimming a rest until it clears up. It is unhygienic for
others. Also your nose and ears are connected by tubes and
infection might be washed back into the middle ear (inside
your ear drum) to produce nasty complications.

Cramp
Practised swimmers are rarely disabled by cramp, and, in
over 40 years around swimming and swimmers, I have never
seen or heard of anyone with the dreaded "stomach cramp"
which is said to drown us. Could it perhaps be a bogey made
up by our old-fashioned ancestors to keep children away
from water?
Most cramp in swimmers is a painful spasm of the double-
headed calf muscle contracting out of control. Sometimes it
affects just the instep of the foot (an odd thing, this, which
simply pulls the big toe away from the others). Neither will
drag you down and drown you. On land they would cause
you to hobble a bit. Swim to the side and climb out. Just
standing up and putting your weight on the foot concerned
can resolve it. Experienced swimmers pull the toes and foot
up (dorsi-flexing them) as they swim along. This can control
the muscle before cramp gets a tight hold ... it also ruins your
crawl stroke! Young swimmers should be taught to

counteract it this way. Treat it matter-of-factly. Do not make a fuss.

Cramp is caused by an impaired blood supply which fails to flush the muscles. This may be due to a tight costume, cold water, sudden muscular exertion, a blow to a muscle (such as being kicked by a passing swimmer). Excessive sweating, a common cause on land, is unlikely with swimmers. Swimming soon after consuming a heavy meal could lead to cramp as nobody has enough blood both to cope with digestion and fuelling the big muscles of movement.

Treatment is firm (but careful) extension of the affected part, to stop further contraction and then relieve the tightness altogether. Loosen and warm the muscle with gentle massage and dry it with a towel to loosen it and encourage the circulation.

Cuts (and other wounds)
Cuts and other open wounds should be adequately covered if you swim. Do not swim if it is likely to delay healing. Heated, treated poolwater is excellent stuff to immerse yourself in, the mildest of disinfectants yet it has a quick killing time for germs. Trainee managers go to college for years to learn how to get it right and public health inspectors make surprise checks to ensure they keep it so.

Swimmers rarely cut their feet; they do not put their weight on them very much. Bathers playing around in the shallow end sometimes do. It takes only the slightest sharp edge on a tile, or a minute bit of grit sculling around on the bottom, and wet soft feet can be sliced. It is often painless so that only seeping blood brings it to notice. Pool attendants have First Aid Kits. Tell the pool manager. He wants to know so that he can try to locate and rectify the fault. Do not grumble at him. It can happen with the most conscientious manager in the best run pool.

Disabilities
Physical or mental handicaps are not necessarily a bar to swimming. The Association of Swimming Therapy regards swimming as an important pleasure and exercise for the disabled (whether their handicap is from birth or acquired), provided the right help is at hand. A medical certificate is generally required prior to joining an A.S.T. club and it is

helpful if, in addition, the doctor includes details of secondary conditions (e.g. fits, diabetes, heart condition, etc.) to ensure the swimmer's safety in the water. Tell your pool manager if it would help to have staff alerted to your swimmer's special needs.

Drowning

About 650 people drown in the U.K. in one year. 75% of these tragedies occur in rivers, lakes, gravel pits and other inland waters, with the remaining 25% at the seaside. As 7 million swim regularly, and water sports are pursued extensively, swimming is still a very safe activity.

Drownings in municipal swimming pools are rare events due to high professional standards of safety. Still, you should be prepared to take prompt action if your pupil, or anyone else, goes unconscious underwater and stops breathing. Do not waste a second. He must have air. Bring him to the surface and – there and then, still in the water – turn him onto his back and blow up his nose with your mouth. Tilt his head back as far as it will go and pull his jaw forward so that it juts out. This straightens and unblocks his windpipe to make sure the air you supply actually reaches his lungs. Hold his mouth shut to prevent air escaping that way. You could blow into his mouth instead (in which case pinch his nostrils shut). It takes two hands to do all this. Blow in for a count of 3 seconds and then remove your mouth for 3 seconds. Repeat for as long as may be necessary to start him breathing on his own again. Mouth-to-mouth (or nose) resuscitation, the "kiss of life", is unseemly and messy if you think about it. Just let your human compassion take charge... and do it!

Ears

Healthy ears come to no harm at all from being immersed in water. Lengthy swim sessions done often – as club swimmers do – may lead to minor disorders requiring treatment in a few susceptible individuals. Some serious conditions, not actually caused by swimming, can make it essential to give up swimming completely for a time. Do not neglect even minor signs and symptoms of ear problems. Seek medical advice promptly and abide by it.

Epilepsy

Whether or not anyone suffering with epilepsy should be

allowed to swim is a vexed question, even for the medical profession. The National Co-Ordinating Committee on Swimming for the Disabled, in conjunction with the British Epilepsy Association, has produced a special leaflet called 'Swimming & Epilepsy'. Any epileptic who does swim must be watched and prompt action taken to safeguard him should he have an attack. The nearest to a fatality that I ever had while managing pools was a young man who, on his way to the dressing room having completed his swimming, was overcome and passed out face down in the footbath. His breathing and pulse stopped and only prompt resuscitation by an alert attendant revived him. Epileptics may, understandably, not wish to broadcast their disability to every stranger: pool managers would prefer to know so that staff can keep a friendly eye on them.

Infectious conditions
Keep away from the pool while you have any medical condition which you could pass on to others.

In natural open water there are risks to health. These can be less than we imagine and, understanding that slight chance of infection, it is still possible to enjoy a bathe in rivers, the sea, and other outdoor places.

A number of viruses are found in rivers, none in very great numbers. Poliomyelitis is an important one. The risk is minimal but ensure your swimmer is protected against this disease by first seeing his own doctor for the necessary inoculation. Despite gory stories of poor souls being stomach-pumped after falling into polluted rivers, this is not often done. Typhoid fever is not generally caught this way. Again, your doctor could arrange necessary inoculations. The main hazard is probably Weil's disease caused by contact with the infected urine of rats. Cases occur infrequently and after lengthy immersion. No protective inoculation is recommended but report any fever (particularly if associated with jaundice) occurring within a few weeks of a river swim.

Inhaled water
Water in the windpipe ("going down the wrong way") can be distressing. It occurs especially with front-breathing strokes, breast stroke and 'fly. At worst, you find yourself suddenly unable to breathe in or out. Stay quiet. Do not panic. It will sort itself out in a few seconds and you do not need to breathe

in that time. The inhaled water is actually much less than it seems and it will soon drain away, unplugging your breathing tubes once more. No swimmer can avoid this frightening experience altogether, although our throat's reflexes become quick at avoiding all but the most unexpected mouthfuls. A sore feeling will remain for a while, until the offending stuff can be coughed-up. Carry on swimming and forget about it.

Legionnaire's disease

First identified in the U.S.A. in 1976, there have been several outbreaks in Britain, including a major one in 1985. The disease is caused by inhaling fine water droplets containing the bacterium, which is common in nature and in the water systems of buildings, and may be spread by air conditioning. About 10% of cases are fatal, susceptible folk being smokers, the over 40s, and those with certain chronic illnesses. Good maintenance and operation of water treatment plant will minimise the risks but they may never be completely eradicated. Pool managers are trained and qualified in water treatment, aware of the Health & Safety Executive's guidelines, and practise all possible preventative measures.

Menstruation

Young girls new to the monthly routine who may be embarrassed or feel below par may be allowed some sympathy and understanding; but young females who are going to swim often can be taught that it need not interfere with their recreation. Dedicated club swimmers rarely miss a training session. They do not even wear an internal tampon. It is quite hygienic to be in the water without any protection. Many Olympic gold medals have been won at all sorts of sports by women and girls who were menstruating.

Nose bleeds

Common in children, rarer in adults, they look worse than usual in a pool because the blood is diluted and goes further. It is a nuisance, little more, embarrassing and unsightly. Whisk your swimmer out of the water and away from curious stares. Incline the patient's head forward and have him pinch his nostrils until the bleeding stops. The chill factor, as the wet swimmer quickly cools in air, hastens clotting.

    There is no reason why he should not go back into the

water again except that the first good snort down the nose can start it off again. If it does, hard luck, give up and come back another day. If a nose bleed does not stop, seek medical advice.

Sore throats

Stay out of the water, unless it is very trivial. You may be sickening for something.

Suspicious behaviour

The occasional odd character may be found in pools, especially when children are there. If you are concerned as to their motives, alert a supervisor who will take appropriate action.

Verruccae

A verrucca (plural "verruccae") is a wart which takes root in the underside of the foot and, because of the pressure on the sole from walking, grows inwards. At an early stage you may not know you have one but, unchecked, they can grow to be painful. It is a viral infection which can quickly spread, one child acquiring several or giving them to others, via warm and damp conditions such as those found in changing rooms and on poolsides.

Wear flip-flops in an effort to avoid verruccae. A few years ago the strict rule was not to allow anyone known to have a verrucca onto the poolside or into the pool. A few local authorities may stick to this precaution. Today some medical opinion says it is merely a childish ailment, so let them all mix together, catch one or two, and get it over and done with. Most cautious pool managers, school teachers, and others coping with verruccae advise foot checks and prompt attention from a doctor or chiropodist if one is discovered. To swim with a verrucca, buy a pair of skintight rubber 'anti-verruccae' ankle socks, and so avoid spreading the infection. The risk of picking up a verrucca in a pool building is low (I have had only one in over 40 years of almost daily swimming) and many of those which are spotted by conscientious swimming teachers checking children's feet were probably acquired elsewhere.

12
USEFUL WORDS TO KNOW

CATCH-POINT
(or "catch")

A variable point in the water where the swimmer's hand comes to grips with it and so propels or supports. The term is not generally used with reference to the feet, but could be.

CATCH-UP

When the hand moving through the water travels slower than the one going through the air, the faster arm catches up so that they are no longer exactly opposite one another.

CO-ORDINATION

The timing of various elements, the leg action, arms, head movements and breathing, to create a whole swimming stroke.

CYCLE

One complete movement or set of movements from start to end, ready to start again, of some part of a stroke or the whole stroke.

DORSI-FLEXION

Flexing the ankles to pull the feet upwards, big toes towards knees (like Charlie Chaplin or a Siamese dancer), an essential feature of breast stroke.

EVERSION

Turning the feet out sideways.

EXPLOSIVE BREATHING

Holding the breath throughout a stroke cycle, expelling it forcibly into the water just prior to the next inhalation.

EXTENSION | Straightening a joint like the elbow, knee or hip, through its normal hinge movement.

FLEXION | Bending a joint (the opposite of extension).

LIMB TRACK | The path taken through the water by arms and legs, particularly the imaginary line "drawn" in the water by the hand during propulsion.

PAUSE | Inaction at some point in the stroke cycle. Often it is a fault to be eliminated but a pause may be cultivated, e.g. a glide in breast stroke.

PIKING | Bending (flexing) the hips but not the knees, as in touching the toes.

POSITION | The standard body position in a streamlined and effective swimming stroke, together with acceptable changes which occur regularly within the stroke cycle.

PRONE | Face downwards in the water: 'fly, breast stroke and crawl are prone strokes.

PROPULSION | From catch-point to where the hand (or foot) releases the water, that part of the arm or leg cycle which propels the swimmer along.

RECOVERY | From where the hand (or foot) releases the water back to catch-point, bringing the arms and legs back – either over or under the water – ready to propel once more.

REFRACTION | The optical illusion apparent when looking down through the air into water, whereby the water appears shallower and all within it is fore-shortened and distorted.

REST   Within the stroke cycle rest is a
                             matter of unconscious ease result-
                             ing from practice. The swimmmer
                             puts effort into only what is
                             required. This enables the blood to
                             remove fatigue products from
                             muscles not in use.

RETARDATION   Elements in a stroke which oppose
                             propulsion, generally poor stream-
                             lining and underwater recovery
                             movements of the limbs.

RHYTHM   The subtle acceleration and slow-
                             ing down of various parts of a
                             co-ordinated stroke at its most
                             effective. A well-timed stroke
                             would still be robot-like, "swum
                             by numbers", without rhythm
                             which is a hallmark of the accom-
                             plished swimmer.

SUPINE   On the back, face upwards: back
                             crawl is a supine stroke.

TRICKLE BREATHING   Breathing bubbles out steadily
                             through the nose and mouth into
                             the water between inhalations
                             during the stroke cycle.

TUCK   To flex (bend) hips and knees and
                             spine so as to curl up into a ball,
                             e.g. the mushroom float is a tucked
                             position.

13
A summary of the
GOLDEN RULES
of swimming

1. Everyone can swim; those who cannot simply have not yet discovered that they can.

2. Shoulders under water.

3. Swimming is getting flat, then moving along.

4. Regaining the standing position comes before swimming flat.

5. Everything comes from the push-and-glide.

6. We learn to swim across widths but become swimmers over lengths.

7. Regaining the swimming position from vertical comes before swimming in deep water.

8. Swimming is handling water.

9. Underwater actions *make* the stroke: movements above water merely modify it.

10. Practice does not make perfect: practice makes *permanent*.

11. Breathe *out* regularly.

12. Elbows high.

13. Catch the water quickly.

14. 'S'-pulls are best.

15. Dextrous swimmers go further, faster, with fewer strokes.

16. Sprinting is breathlessness without exhaustion: marathon swimming is exhaustion without breathlessness.

17. Swimming is breathing as you go along.

18. Repetition brings relaxation.

19. A swimmer is a 4-stroke machine.

20. Swimmers are skilful.

A summary of the GOLDEN RULES of diving

1. Eight feet (two and a half metres) is barely enough.

2. Swimming and diving do not mix.

3. Divers must be swimmers.

4. Rotation comes from the take-off.

5. All dives are somersaults: a plain header is just half a somersault.

6. Hips must go up for the head to go down.

7. Shorten to speed rotation: lengthen to slow it down.

14
WHAT NEXT?

When your swimmer can competently handle two or three strokes, dive a bit, and is fairly safe in water (nobody is ever totally drown-proof), he might decide to pursue swimming further. In that case he should join a club where teachers will improve his strokes and coaches will condition him.

Some clubs have no competitive aspirations, merely teaching and providing pleasant leisure swimming. Most aim to introduce their members to racing and most racing is short to middle distance (25m to 400m). This is swum in age groups at first; then the better swimmers compete in Junior or Senior categories. Adult age group swimming flourishes under the title "Masters" swimming.

Long distance swimming (1 mile up to 10 miles) and marathon swimming (over 10 miles) is an open air activity to suit robust individuals, particularly if you live near to lakes, reservoirs or the sea where you can train.

Personal survival and lifesaving skills are fun to learn, useful to have, and form a sound basis for better swimming.

Synchro. (water ballet) is hard work and very skilful and exciting for those keen on performing arts.

Water-polo is a tough ball game requiring both sprint speed and stamina as well as ball-handling skills.

Adults wondering what to do with their newly-found swimming capacity can become active club supporters, study swim manuals, and graduate to duties as an official, team manager, chaperone, teacher or coach. There is even a career to be made in sport and leisure management.

The Amateur Swimming Association
The A.S.A. is the governing body in England (other A.S.A.s

exist elsewhere in the U.K. and the Republic of Ireland).
Founded in 1886, its principal objects are to (a) promote the
teaching and practice of Swimming, Diving, Synchronised
Swimming and Water-Polo, and stimulate public opinion in
favour of providing proper accommodation and facilities for
them; and (b) draw up, publish and enforce uniform Laws for
the control and regulation of amateur championships and
competitions in these aspects of the sport, and deal with any
infringements.

With approximately 1,760 affiliated clubs, a large awards
(certificate and badges) structure, a variety of technical
publications including their monthly magazine 'Swimming
Times' with a circulation of 15,500, and a teacher/coach
examinations department, they are pre-eminent as a sporting
body. The A.S.A. is involved in all levels of swimming from
the sponsorship of child and adult 'learn-to-swim' classes to
the Olympic Games.

Youngsters joining a typical A.S.A. club will be taught in
classes to swim properly and well, progressing to squads
where race training is practised. All aspects of fitness are
worked on: at the highest levels swimmers may be swimming
hard for several hours daily, and also working out with
weights and circuits in the gym. Swimmers are taught and
coached by qualified and experienced individuals in a highly
structured and disciplined regimen.

A.S.A. clubs are a source of good at a vulnerable time in
the lives of young people. They develop splendid physiques
and characters to match. I must try to scotch one persistent
myth. "Won't they put on weight when all that muscle turns
to fat?' Now that is ignorant and unscientific nonsense.
Muscle CANNOT turn to fat. They are different things: no
more could a lung turn into a kidney, or hair into fingernails.
Unused muscle fibres simply atrophy, shrinking back to their
previous condition. Retired athletes who do grow fat are
probably eating too much for their less energetic lifestyle.
Parents need not be anxious about exercise harming their off-
spring. The world's best coaches and swim doctors have
devoted years to working out what happens to the swimmers
in their charge. It is all good. Why not enrol your child in one
of this country's many excellent swimming clubs?

The British Long Distance Swimming Association
The B.L.D.S.A. was founded in 1956 to promote the art and
sport of swimming and particularly long distance swimming
in open water. They organise annual championships ranging
from sheltered races of 1 mile or less for new young swimmers
to rough and rugged senior competitions of 10 miles and
more. They also recognise individual marathon achievements, like the 3-lake (Windermere + Ullswater + Coniston,
within 24 hours) of 22 miles total; the Isle of Wight circum-
navigation of 55 miles; Eddystone Lighthouse to Plymouth,
14 miles; Loch Ness, 22½ miles; Ireland to Scotland (North
Channel), 22 miles; and many, many more. Some B.L.D.S.A.
members go on to swim the English Channel.

Long distance swimming can be a real family affair,
involving as it does travelling to distant venues, overnight
accommodation (many choosing to camp or caravan),
picnics at the water's edge, and accompanying the swimmer
as a pilot, lifeguard, boatman or official. Unlike the sprint
scene, where star performers are on the wane in their 20s,
mature swimmers of 30+ can still get placed... while
achievements by swimming grandfathers and mothers are
commonplace. Consequently, not only do parents act as
back-up teams for their children, some children find
themselves cheering on their parents!

The B.L.D.S.A. is affiliated to F.I.N.A. (Federation
Internationale de Natation Amateur), the world governing
body. The first World Long Distance Championships will be
held in Australia in 1991, while the Association's founders
dream that a long distance race (say 10 miles) will eventually
be included in the Olympics.

Long distance races are hotly contested, with no quarter
conceded, but these open water events are also contests of
men and women (even the youngsters are treated as such)
against the elements. Amazingly fast times are clocked by
winning swimmers, yet the slow one who plods in last and
several hours behind has – oddly – shown greater staying
power. Each can admire the other. Everyone who completes a
B.L.D.S.A. swim is deemed to be a winner.

The Royal Life Saving Society
The R.L.S.S. was formed in 1891 in an attempt to reduce the
annual toll of 2,000 lives lost in drowning accidents in the

U.K. Despite a massive increase in the use of water for sporting and recreative activity in the intervening period, the annual toll is now down to around 650. The aims of the Society, as laid down in its 1924 Charter, are (a) to promote technical education in life-saving and resuscitation of the apparently drowned; (b) stimulate public opinion in favour of the general adoption of swimming and lifesaving as a branch of instruction in schools, colleges, etc; (c) encourage floating, diving, plunging and such other swimming arts as would be of assistance to a person endeavouring to save life; (d) to arrange and promote public lectures, demonstrations and competitions, and to form classes of instruction, so as to bring about a widespread and thorough knowledge of the principles which underlie the art of natation.

R.L.S.S. clubs and classes are another excellent source of swimming tuition. Many swimmers and teachers owe their progress in the world of swimming to them, where they learnt water safety, rescue skills including resuscitation, and took part in voluntary lifeguard teams. The Society also has its own awards scheme, qualifies its own instructors, and organises lifesaving competitions.

The Institute of Baths & Recreation Managers

The I.B.R.M. (Incorporated by Royal Charter) was founded in 1921. It is a professional body, all full members being required to qualify by examination, which aims to improve the management of indoor recreation facilities. Members may be found managing "wet" and "dry" sports or leisure centres, halls, etc. The Institute emphasizes training in swimming pool management because swimming pools are the most used of all recreational amenities and they contain costly and complicated engineering services, requiring special attention to such aspects as hygiene, safety, energy conservation, maintenance and economy of operation.

Sport and leisure is a growing industry offering excellent career prospects to male and female alike. From sports assistants and pool lifeguards, they can progess through being charge hands or shift leaders, to become supervisors and trainee managers who will be sponsored on college study courses leading to Institute examinations.

Sports amenities are costly provisions which tend therefore to be municipal enterprises. So I.B.R.M. members are commonly also principal and senior local government officers. Institute members have the letters M.Inst.BRM. or M.Inst.BRM.Dip. after their names.

INDEX

THE KNOT BOOK

Learn how to apply the right knot to any given job. Such skill can be essential to the safety and enjoyment of leisure pursuits such as climbing, sailing and fishing; in rescue, life can depend on it.

Geoffrey Budworth has selected more than 100 best knots spanning over 30 years' practical knotting – from young Sea Scout to knotting consultant: he advises the National Maritime Museum, Greenwich, is a founder member of the International Guild of Knot-Tyers and created the knot identification method adopted by police forensic scientists.

Snippets of knot lore enhance the clear instruction and stage-by-stage drawings, making learning with Budworth a delight for youngster or adult. To everyone who wants to learn (or teach) knotting he brings, with THE KNOT BOOK, a new and inexpensive "bible" superbly organised for fast reference.

Uniform with this book

ELLIOT RIGHT WAY BOOKS
KINGSWOOD, SURREY, U.K.

OUR PUBLISHING POLICY

HOW WE CHOOSE

Our policy is to consider every deserving manuscript and we can give special editorial help where an author is an authority on his subject but an inexperienced writer. We are rigorously selective in the choice of books we publish. We set the highest standards of editorial quality and accuracy. This means that a *Paperfront* is easy to understand and delightful to read. Where illustrations are necessary to convey points of detail, these are drawn up by a subject specialist artist from our panel.

HOW WE KEEP PRICES LOW

We aim for the big seller. This enables us to order enormous print runs and achieve the lowest price for you. Unfortunately, this means that you will not find in the *Paperfront* list any titles on obscure subjects of minority interest only. These could not be printed in large enough quantities to be sold for the low price at which we offer this series. We sell almost all our *Paperfronts* at the same unit price. This saves a lot of fiddling about in our clerical departments and helps us to give you world-beating value. Under this system, the longer titles are offered at a price which we believe to be unmatched by any publisher in the world.

OUR DISTRIBUTION SYSTEM

Because of the competitive price, and the rapid turnover, *Paperfronts* are possibly the most profitable line a bookseller can handle. They are stocked by the best bookshops all over the world. It may be that your bookseller has run out of stock of a particular title. If so, he can order more from us at any time—we have a fine reputation for "same day" despatch, and we supply any order, however small (even a single copy), to any bookseller who has an account with us. We prefer you to buy from your bookseller, as this reminds him of the strong underlying public demand for *Paperfronts.* Members of the public who live in remote places, or who are housebound, or whose local bookseller is unco-operative, can order direct from us by post.

FREE

If you would like an up-to-date list of all *Paperfront* titles currently available, send a stamped self-addressed envelope to
ELLIOT RIGHT WAY BOOKS, BRIGHTON RD.,
LOWER KINGSWOOD, SURREY, U.K.